STAR FIRE

"Trust me," Gallant said, holding her tightly against him.

Cherry tipped her head back and frowned at him. "How could I trust you? You're a liar and a cheat and—" Before she could utter another insult, he silenced her with his lips.

Suddenly Cherry felt as though she had been thrown into a blazing inferno where the only escape was to become one with the source of the fire. Tangling her fingers into his thick hair to hold him still, she deepened the kiss.

His fingers curled beneath the neckline of her jumpsuit, and she stopped stroking his arms and chest to help him eliminate one more obstacle between them. He paused now, to give her one last chance to pull back as she had before.

But her eyes were filled with the size and the strength of him, her blood blazed with her hunger for him, as she gasped, "No, not this time, Gallant. You want me. I want you. Right now, nothing else matters. . . ."

STARDUST DREAMS

Dear Reader:

I hope you enjoyed Cherry and Gallant's story as much as it pleased me to write it. Topaz Dreamspun will continue the Innerworld series in June, 1994 with *STOLEN DREAMS*, my fourth futuristic tale of romantic adventure, featuring Romulus and Aster's daughter, Shara, a deceptively angelic-looking historian named Gabriel, and the lost continent of Atlantis.

I love to hear from readers (s.a.s.e for reply please): P.O. Box 840002, Pembroke Pines, Florida 33084.

DREAM ON!

Marilyn Campbell

STARDUST DREAMS

by

Marilyn Campbell

A TOPAZ BOOK

TOPAZ
Published by the Penguin Group
Penguin Books USA Inc., 375 Hudson Street,
New York, New York 10014, U.S.A.
Penguin Books Ltd, 27 Wrights Lane,
London W8 5TZ, England
Penguin Books Australia Ltd, Ringwood,
Victoria, Australia
Penguin Books Canada Ltd, 10 Alcorn Avenue,
Toronto, Ontario, Canada M4V 3B2
Penguin Books (N.Z.) Ltd, 182–190 Wairau Road,
Auckland 10, New Zealand

Penguin Books Ltd, Registered Offices:
Harmondsworth, Middlesex, England

First published by Topaz, an imprint of Dutton Signet,
a division of Penguin Books USA Inc.

First Printing, December, 1993
10 9 8 7 6 5 4 3 2 1

Printed in the United States of America

For Janice Dykes, a true friend through good times and bad, successes and failures, eccentric husbands and demon children—a toast to us for surviving it all so far.

Prologue

"Do not be frightened my children. I bring peace and goodwill to all mankind."

The group of twenty tourists paying their respects at the Our Lady of Lourdes Shrine gaped in stunned silence at the ethereal figure speaking the gentle words. Standing on a fluffy white cloud that hovered just above the Shrine, was a female angel, complete with golden halo and white feathered wings. With her light blond hair and flowing white dress, she could have stepped out of the pages of a children's Bible.

"You have been chosen as the first on Earth to receive the message, but you will not be the last. Judgment Day is near. Soon, the Messiah will take human form and walk among you. Behold the image of the Messiah." In the air beside her, a face appeared. "Remember, the meek shall inherit the Earth, and the nonbelievers will perish. Prepare yourselves to meet your maker."

As suddenly as the angel and the image had materialized before the people, they vanished. An Italian woman fell to her knees before the Shrine and crossed herself. An American family walked away smiling, satisfied that the special effects were up to what they would expect from such a famous attraction. One opportunist ran for the nearest telephone, while others shook their heads in bewilderment, uncertain about what they'd seen or heard.

And the one among them, who was not what she appeared to be, noted each of their reactions for the report to her superior.

Chapter 1

Innerworld—Planet Terra (Earth)

Cherry Cochran screamed at the top of her lungs as the man-eating, two-headed lizard caught sight of her. Tied to a tree as she was, there was very little else the petite brunette could do. She took a deep breath and let out another blood-curdling cry for help.

That scream, along with a lengthy list of other impressive talents, had propelled her to stardom. This particular performance—playing a damsel in distress—was one she had done so many times, it could no longer be called improvisation. She and most of the other actors and actresses who worked in the Innerworld Indulgence Center's Fantasy World tended to groan when this reenactment was requested. There was simply no challenge to playing out a fantasy where they all knew precisely what the others were going to say and do at any given moment.

But the dwarflike man who had purchased this fantasy had no way of knowing that, as he ran onto the set brandishing a sword that had been scaled down to his size.

Cherry stifled a yawn as the customer valiantly battled the robotic lizard. She had been told he was a Weebort—a humanoid specimen of small stature and grayish flesh, whose most peculiar feature was a forked tongue, and whose occupation was that of an intergalactic trader. His people often acted as middlemen in many deals, both legitimate and unsavory. Cherry guessed that he must have just closed a big one since his treat to himself was a holiday here in Innerworld, the Noronian colony in the center of the Earth.

Reminding herself of how much he was paying for this fantasy, she let out another hysterical shriek and struggled to get free of her bonds.

In two weeks the boredom might be ended. She had always wanted to make it into the big time and now it looked like she had the chance to make it into the biggest time of all.

Ten years ago, before a freak accident landed her in Innerworld, Cherry never expected her dream of becoming a star to come true. Abruptly, she had found herself in a place where dreams became reality, although the event that led up to her relocation was a trip into hell.

She and her best friend, Aster Mackenzie, had been invited on a fishing trip to the Bahamas, but no sooner had they reached the islands than the chartered yacht was hijacked by vicious drug smugglers. An elderly friend of Cherry's and a crew member were killed by one of the criminals before they reached their rendezvous point in the heart of the area known as the Bermuda Triangle.

Cherry's emotional outburst after her friend's murder resulted in a machine pistol being turned on her. The spray of bullets hit her right arm, partially severing it from her body. At the end of the frightening episode, the ship's captain was also shot, but with deadly accuracy. To the astonishment of the entire party, Cherry's and the captain's lives were restored once they reached Innerworld. A robotic right arm was her souvenir of the nightmare, and an artificial heart was his.

After their bodies were repaired, all aboard were told an incredible tale about where they were and how they had gotten there. Under the circumstances, the castaways had no choice but to accept the explanations given.

The smugglers' rendezvous point had been within one of the twelve magnetic fields located around the Earth. Cherry and the others learned that these sites served as doorways to a technologically advanced civilization in the center of the planet. Innerworld had been established by Norona ten thousand years ago when volterrin, a rare but vital energy source, was discovered in abundance in the Earth's core. The tunnels and doorways were constructed for travel to and from the colony.

Occasionally, as was the case that fateful day, a small vessel went undetected in the area when a doorway was opened, and the ship was subsequently sucked into the tunnel.

During their orientation, the group of new arrivals

were also informed that none of the transplanted Terrans, as the earthlings on the surface were called, were ever permitted to return to Outerworld.

Cherry noted that the Weebort had slain the first monster and was heading toward her. On cue, a second creature lumbered out from behind a rock. "Behind you!" Cherry yelled, automatically assuming a horrified expression. As the Weebort spun around to face his new adversary, Cherry had to conceal another yawn of boredom. One more monster and a giant to slay before she could be rescued.

According to this client's request, after he saved the maiden, she was to prostrate herself at his feet and swear to be his devoted slave forever. The thin gold choker around her neck housed the universal translator that would allow him to hear her words in his own strange language. Had he requested a more intimate reward, another actress would have been given the part.

Participating in sexual fantasies was an option Cherry had always declined. When she first arrived in Innerworld, she was intrigued by the sexually uninhibited attitudes of its inhabitants, even though her own strict upbringing prevented her from comfortably enjoying such freedom to its fullest extent. After living there for ten years, she didn't blink an eye at what the natives considered acceptable behavior, but she preferred to limit her intimate encounters with men to those she knew longer than the time it took to sign over the required number of credits.

Having fun with them was something else entirely.

Her friend Aster had given up hoping that Cherry would find the "man of her dreams" as she had. Cherry adored men in general and thoroughly enjoyed the way they all seemed to adore her, but none ever held her interest long enough to establish any kind of lasting relationship.

Fortunately, her refusal to share her body with strangers hadn't affected her rocketing career. Employees of Fantasy World were free to work in the types of performances they were comfortable with, and those of a sexual nature did not warrant more or less recompense or prestige than those that were not.

She had always considered herself rather ordinary-looking, with her brown hair and eyes, and smattering of freckles on her nose; and she was far too short and thin to be imposing. It was her talent that had made her a star in demand at the age of thirty-six, which, by Innerworld standards, was practically a youngster. Her pixie haircut reinforced that youthful appearance and was imitated by her admirers throughout the colony.

At the moment, however, few of her natural characteristics were visible. She was costumed in what she called early Viking—a heavy blond wig with long, thick bangs and two side braids, and a neck to floor sackcloth which was gathered at her waist by a rough rope.

Now she had a chance to become a star of the universe. Theodophilus, the director of the prestigious Noronian Performing Company, was making an unprecedented visit to Innerworld in two weeks.

Cherry had seen the announcement regarding his plans to audition players from Innerworld for his next intergalactic traveling show, but everyone had heard the rumor that he had already decided to hire Cherry. The audition was a mere formality where she was concerned.

Thoughts of heading off on an adventure into space, after not being permitted to leave Innerworld all these years, made this performance seem even more tedious than usual.

The Weebort had now done away with the third monster and was close to finishing off the eight-foot-tall ogre. Suddenly another, slightly shorter, giant burst onto the set. This one's head resembled that of a wild boar. His huge body was completely covered with coarse brown hair, and only a neck to thigh tunic of body armor shielded his beastly form.

Cherry had barely adjusted to the surprise of seeing a fifth enemy when that creature raised his arm and pointed a metal-encased finger at the Weebort. Letting out one of her best screams, she alerted him to the new danger. When he turned, the look of genuine terror on his face warned Cherry that something was wrong.

A split second later, a beam of blue light shot out of the boar beast's finger, but the Weebort bolted in time for his opponent to be hit instead. As the giant robot crashed to the floor in a deafening explosion of circuitry, the beast aimed his deadly finger at the Weebort's fleeing back.

The force of the blast catapulted the Weebort forward, slamming him into Cherry at the same moment the beast took off in the opposite direction. She saw his forked tongue snake in and out of his mouth as he slid to her feet, and could see he was trying to tell her something, but the pandemonium around them prevented her from hearing his words. Before her disbelieving gaze, his skin began to wither and turn black. Within seconds, the Weebort's body turned to ash, then disappeared completely.

"Calm down everyone!" a man ordered from behind Cherry. "That was only a test."

As she twisted her head from side to side to determine who the speaker was, he quickly untied her bonds and continued to try to calm the small group of frantic actors and actresses.

"Management felt you were all getting a little too complacent with that fantasy and decided to throw in a surprise. You all did very well. Congratulations. Cherry, I'd like a word with you privately."

She angled her head at the man who spoke with such authority. He had been assigned as a bit player right before this performance began. "Are you with the management?" she asked without making any move to follow him.

Over his left eye was a black leather patch, but his other dark brown eye hurriedly scanned the area before answering, "More or less." He grasped her elbow and tried to pull her along, but that action made her dig in her heels.

The man would have been incredibly striking even without the eye patch. A snow white streak began at each of his temples and ran to the ends of his wavy black hair, which fell just below his shoulders. A muscular physique was enhanced by a rather piratical costume of tight, black leather pants and a matching short vest, which revealed a bare, well-developed chest.

Hooked to his waistband was a small black box that Cherry thought looked like a weapon, but she was certain only security personnel were permitted to carry them. He looked like the devil's own spawn, and there was no way Cherry could have met him before and forgotten who he was. "Why don't I know you?"

He let out an exasperated sigh. "Look, we don't have time for an in-depth interview. Now, come with me."

Cherry's chin came up a notch as her self-protective instincts came into play. "I don't believe you're with the management, I don't believe that was a test, and I'm certainly not going anywhere with you until I get some answers."

Before she could say another word, his arm wrapped around her small waist and he lifted her off the ground. As she opened her mouth to protest, he covered it with his free hand. With a suggestive laugh, he told her coworkers, "We've only been lovers a few days, and there's still a few rough spots, as you can see. I'm sure you'll excuse us for a few minutes."

Cherry squirmed in his grip and tried to bite his hand, but that only caused him to tighten both holds on her as he carried her off the set. Her public reputation, as a fun-seeking, free-spirited woman who tended to "love 'em and leave 'em," worked against her. Her coworkers laughed and wished her captor good luck.

As soon as he found an unoccupied room, he put her down, but didn't release her. "I apologize for hauling you off like that, but I couldn't risk arousing suspicions. You have an incredibly powerful scream, Cherry. If you'll promise not to use it, I'll take my hand away from your mouth. I mean you no harm."

Cherry glared at him for a few seconds, then decided to give him a chance to explain what was going on. If he didn't satisfy her curiosity, she could always scream later. She nodded, and he slowly removed his hand from her face. When she remained quiet, he let go of the rest of her as well.

Immediately, she backed away from him and massaged her jaw. "So much for the Noronian code of nonviolence." She raised one eyebrow at him. "Perhaps you're not a Noronian."

Frowning, he said, "I don't have time to explain. I'm sorry if I hurt you, but my mission is extremely important. In a few minutes, Frezlo will be out of my tracking range. What did the Weebort say to you?"

"Frezlo? The Weebort? Something tells me you're guilty of breaking another Noronian code—the one about honesty. That wasn't any test back there, was it?"

"No, it wasn't. And more lives could be lost if I don't catch up with Frezlo. Now—"

"Frezlo's the one that looked like a wild boar, right?"

"Yes," he ground out, clearly frustrated with her questions.

The realization that she had been in the midst of a real-life adventure had her bubbling with energy, and she began pacing around him. "What is he, some kind of an assassin? Are you a tracker? And was the Weebort—"

"Enough!" he exclaimed, grasping her shoulders to make her stand still. "Just tell me what the Weebort said to you before he burned up."

Suddenly Cherry sensed that the dangerous look about this man wasn't created by a costume. It was inbred. "I don't know."

He gave her an urgent shake. "What do you mean, you don't know? You're wearing a translator."

She pushed him away from her, more angry than frightened by his macho behavior. He was acting like some American men she had known; not at all like a Noronian. "I *mean,* I don't know. I couldn't hear what he said. There was too much noise."

The man frowned at her again, but he appeared to believe her. "All right. I'll have to get someone to touch your mind. Even if you think you didn't hear him, your subconscious would have picked it up. If you'll accompany me to my ship—"

Cherry sidestepped the hand that reached out to her. "No way, mister. If someone's going to crawl around inside my head, it'll be somebody I trust. Governor Romulus is my friend. I'd let him do it."

"Romulus is my friend as well, but I don't have time to go looking for him. You'll have to come with me." He reached for her again, and this time she barely avoided his touch as she headed toward the door.

"Last chance, Cherry," he warned.

She glanced back to issue a smart retort, and saw the small black box in his hand. As her mouth opened to scream, he fired.

Gallant Voyager's chest tightened with near-panic as he saw her collapse on the floor. *Drek!* His paralyzer had been set to stop Frezlo, not a pint-sized female. Going to her quickly, he checked the pulse at her neck and was relieved to discover a faint assurance that he hadn't killed her.

He hadn't even meant to stun her—only convince her of the seriousness of the situation. But something about the way she defied, no *dared* him to stop her, had made him react with force rather than thought. He could hardly remember the last time he had allowed that to happen.

Yanking off his eye patch, he scanned Cherry Cochran from head to toe, as if the explanation for his error would make itself clear if he used both eyes. Her costume kept him from judging her perfectly, but there was nothing about what he *could* see that might have made him forget himself.

Even as he picked her up in his arms to take her to his ship, his instincts were sending warning notices that he should leave her there. He couldn't afford to be around someone who was capable of triggering a spontaneous *emotional* response from him so easily. Not only his mission, but his life depended on his keeping secret the fact that his ice-cold demeanor went no further than the image.

For the countless time, he cursed the fates that forced him to live a lie.

Despite the uneasiness he felt, he decided she could do him no harm in the short time it would take to discover what the Weebort had said to her.

Out of habit, he was about to replace the eye patch when he realized he would need both eyes to do what had to be done. In order to carry an unconscious female aboard his ship without answering any questions, he was going to have to perform a little "magic." Because it was another of his necessary secrets, he only used his special ability in extreme circumstances, and this was turning out to be one of those times.

The solid kick in the ribs jolted Romulus out of a deep sleep. "*Drek*! That one hurt." He rolled toward Aster and massaged the spot on her taut, swollen abdomen where their baby had called attention to itself. Whether it was his large, warm hand or the calming thoughts he was sending, the fetus soon settled back down.

Aster placed her hand over her mate's. "I'm sorry, darling. That one was a surprise. I didn't have a chance to block it from you."

"And I told you to stop trying to spare me. You've got enough to do just dealing with your own discomfort. Roll onto your other side and let me rub your back." As she happily obliged, he chuckled to himself. When they had joined ten years ago, they were not only bound physically, but spiritually and mentally as well. Aster's pregnancy was the first time since then that he was less than pleased by the results.

Although Innerworld's medical achievements were far beyond anything she had known in Outerworld, carrying a child for nine months wasn't much easier. The first bouts of morning sickness before Aster was treated for it left Rom weak as a baby himself. Later in her pregnancy, Aster prevented him from feeling most of her aches and pains and did her best not to relay her cravings and mood swings, but even the little she had not blocked was enough to let him know how uncomfortable she was. However, it would all be worth it in the end.

Attempts had once been made to develop the fetus outside the mother's womb, but the babies' minds and bodies were never quite as healthy as when it grew inside its mother. As Rom kneaded away the tension in her lower back, he felt his own muscles relax. At least they would not have to tolerate the kind of pain a woman in her world would during their daughter's birth.

Their daughter. The first child born of a mixed joining between a Noronian and a Terran. She wasn't even born yet and her responsibilities were already overwhelming. He stopped himself from thinking along those lines. There would be time enough for that later.

Though her gender was known, her physical characteristics were not. Genetic control had been limited to defects several centuries ago after a series of experiments went awry. He couldn't help but wonder what she would look like.

She'll be beautiful, of course, Aster thought back to him. Rom was six foot three, she was five foot ten, and they both had imposing physiques. Their child would undoubtedly grow to be a statuesque woman. She would probably inherit dark hair as well, but there was no way to tell if hers would prematurely gray in her twenties as Aster's hair had.

The baby's eye color was the only real unknown. Aster's eyes were an unusual midnight blue and Rom's were a green-brown shade of hazel . . . most of the time. Like many Noronians, his eye color changed with his emotions—a characteristic Aster had learned to use to her advantage shortly after they'd met.

It had been years since she gave more than a passing thought to the circumstances that brought her to Innerworld and Romulus. They were of two different worlds, and a joining between their races was forbidden by law. Yet the Noronian mating fever struck them both, proving they were soulmates, destined to be together for eternity.

Unfortunately, the same prejudice that had existed when Aster first arrived in Innerworld still simmered in some corners of the colony. Only the support of the Ruling Tribunal of Norona prevented the bigots from speaking out too loudly.

Aster prayed that their daughter would be strong enough to withstand whatever trials lay ahead for her.

Rom stopped rubbing her back and snuggled up behind her. With a soft kiss on her cheek he assured her everything would be fine. "In another month the worst will be over."

Aster laughed. "Ha! That shows how little you know about babies. But then I don't have much more experience than you. Being an only child didn't exactly prepare me for this role. Thank heavens we'll have Cherry to help. She never talks much about her childhood, but I know she had nine brothers and sisters, so she had to have picked up some practical knowledge about raising children."

Rom blocked his next thoughts from Aster. He liked Cherry and was glad Aster had been with her best friend when they arrived in Innerworld, but Cherry's high energy level and unleashed spontaneity always made him feel like he was caught up in a tornado. Whoever said "opposites attract" must have had her and Aster in mind. Imagining Cherry under his roof for extended periods of time did not fill him with the same sense of gratitude Aster felt.

Just before Aster fell asleep, she reminded Rom that Cherry promised to come by for lunch tomorrow. As always, she looked forward to hearing what her friend had done for excitement this week. Rom was her soulmate, but Cherry held an equally important position in her life.

Long before the disaster landed them in Innerworld, Cherry had appointed herself Aster's savior from workaholism. Cherry was her alter ego, surrogate sister, and the closest friend she'd ever had. Cherry had not only shared the most traumatic events in Aster's life, but she always forced Aster to see the bright side of everything.

If anything, her bond with Cherry had strengthened over the years because of their being removed from their world. Despite the fact that Aster and Rom shared thoughts, Cherry was the only person in Innerworld who could truly understand her feeling of alienness that never went away.

And the fears she harbored for her unborn child's future in a society where prejudice against Terrans still fermented.

Thankfully, Cherry was around to keep her fears from overriding the joy.

Cherry felt the softness beneath her and tried to orient herself before opening her eyes. A sense of danger swept through her, instantly followed by the memory of a wicked-looking stranger. At least she hadn't been incinerated as the Weebort had been.

Cautiously, she opened her eyes and surveyed her dimly lit surroundings. She was in a gray-walled room on a large bunk that took up most of the limited space. That devil must have brought her here . . . wherever *here* was. After a moment, she recalled his insisting she accompany him to his ship.

Panic assailed her as she leapt off the bed and pressed her palm to a square metal panel on the wall beside the door. The door slid open with a soft *whoosh,* and relief that she had not been locked in quickly replaced the momentary fear. Years of improvising on stage had conditioned her to instantly adjust to whatever situation she found herself in. She usually relished an unexpected turn of events, but this one made her furious.

Stepping into a narrow corridor, she noted it ended a few feet to her right at one door and two more doors were across from her. About fifteen feet to her left, light streamed into the corridor. She headed toward that light fully prepared for heated confrontation.

The angry words on the tip of her tongue were suspended by shock as Cherry reached the doorway and her worst suspicions were confirmed. Although she had never traveled out of Innerworld, she had no doubt she was on a ship. Her gaze quickly scanned what had to be a bridge, with no visible walls, ceiling, or floor. She would have examined the unusually clear glass beneath her feet, but the darkness beyond, accented by distant dots of light, brought the panic back in a surge. She was in space!

Two people were in the center of the bridge behind a control panel. Long black hair with two white stripes identified the man seated in the only chair. At his side, a tall woman stood facing Cherry, wearing a body-hugging, olive green jumpsuit and a very amused smile. Tight coils of chartreuse hair sprung out from her head, making Cherry think of the Statue of Liberty's crown, and she seemed to be patiently waiting for her to stop gawking.

"Greetings," the woman finally said in a deep contralto voice. "Are you well?"

The instant the woman spoke, the man started to swivel his chair around, but stopped abruptly and donned the black eye patch before turning the rest of the way to face her. That seemed odd to Cherry, but she had too many other concerns to question that. As he rose, she thought his expression looked somewhat contrite . . . until he opened his mouth.

"It's about time," he said abruptly, then turned to the woman at his side. "Well? What are you waiting for?"

"An introduction," she answered calmly in her husky voice. "I believe two people who are about to become intimately acquainted should at least know one another's name."

"Now hold it right there!" Cherry exclaimed, taking a step backward. "I draw the line at—"

"Calm down," the man interrupted with a wave of his hand. "No one's—"

"Calm down?" Cherry asked with disbelief. "I haven't *begun* to get upset. I had better hear some satisfactory explanations in the next ten seconds or . . . or I won't be responsible for my actions."

"She sounds dangerous, Captain. Should I restrain her?" the woman asked in a serious tone, but the sparkle in her emerald eyes let Cherry know she probably wouldn't do such a thing even if he ordered her to.

"Eight seconds, *Captain,*" Cherry warned, planting her fists on her hips.

He scowled back at her and crossed his arms. "I don't respond well to threats, particularly from someone half my size."

Cherry marched forward, poked him in his chest with the index finger of her robotic right hand, and sent him sprawling backward into his chair. "And *I* don't respond well to being abducted. Now you have three seconds left before you find out what all five of my fingers can do."

Rubbing his chest, he rose with a grimace. "I suppose an explanation is in order. I am Gallant Voyager—"

Cherry snorted. "Come on, you can do better than that. How about Luke Skywalker? I've always been kind of partial to that one."

Gallant straightened himself to his full height, which was actually only a foot taller than Cherry's. His tone of voice revealed that he was a bit touchy on the subject. "I assure you, that is my name. Gallant Voyager is a direct translation of my birthname, which is extremely difficult to pronounce."

"Okay, so you have a name. How about the explanation?"

"First, allow me to introduce you to my navigator. Cherry Cochran, this is Mar-Dot."

"Actually," the woman said with a grin, "I am Dot." She turned around, as if to present her back, but what Cherry saw was another front.

"And I am Mar."

Cherry gaped at the man in front of her. The hair, eyes, nose, and voice were the same as the woman's, but his lower face was covered by a kinky, close-trimmed, chartreuse beard. The snug bodysuit that had clearly displayed a woman's figure a moment ago, now showed that of a man, and a very well-endowed man at that.

Never one to let her curiosity go unsatisfied, Cherry circled Mar-Dot, her eyes filled with fascination. The creature had one body with two legs, but the booted feet extended in both directions, like pedestals. The male half and the female half each had its own pair of arms and hands, and Cherry thought she could have identified the gender of each pair even if Dot's fingernails weren't an inch long and painted lime green.

"Pardon me for staring," Cherry said as she came back around to Mar. "But I've never seen anything, or rather anyone, like you."

"Not many people have," he told her with a smile. "For all we know, we may be the only he-she in existence."

In the blink of an eye, the he-she turned and Cherry was facing Dot. "I tell this story better than he does. We were sold to a traveling circus as a baby. Unfortunately, no questions were asked at the time, so no one was ever able to tell us where we had come from. If it was not for the captain—"

"I believe you asked me for an explanation, Cherry," Gallant said, effectively cutting off Dot's story.

The fact that he didn't want her to hear whatever Dot was going to say automatically made Cherry more curious. But first there was the matter of her abduction. "I'm all ears. Why don't you start by telling me what the hell gives you the right to knock me out and kidnap me? Then work your way up to how you got me on this ship and out of Innerworld without a travel visa."

"I'm an agent for hire, currently on assignment for the Consociation of Planets, of which Norona is a primary member. My mission grants me . . . certain privileges."

Cherry narrowed her eyes at him. She still couldn't decide if he was the good or the bad guy in this scenario, and she was determined not to let his rakish appearance influence her one way or the other. "I've lived among Noronians for ten years, and there is no way they would condone what you've done to me for any reason. When Aster and Romulus hear about this, they'll cart you off for reprogramming so fast, you won't know what hit you."

"I've already sent them a message. Romulus knew of my presence in Innerworld, and by now he knows I've taken you into my protective custody."

Chapter 2

"Your *what*?" Cherry demanded, taking a threatening step toward him again.

Gallant stood his ground, but looked prepared to move out of her way in a heartbeat. "Protective custody. That's when—"

"I *know* what it means. I also know the only thing I've needed protection from lately is you."

"Wrong," he answered. "The moment the Weebort spoke to you, he put your life in danger."

"That's ridiculous. I don't even know what he said."

Gallant shook his head. "Irrelevant. If Frezlo got wind of it, he'd be back for you. And believe me, he wouldn't settle for tuning into your subconscious—which is all I asked of you—he'd simply incinerate you on sight."

Cherry frowned, trying to come up with a way to debate what he was telling her. "But you were the only one who saw the Weebort say anything to me."

Raising an eyebrow, he asked, "Would you be willing to risk your life on that?"

"All right, let's say there's a slim possibility my life

could be in danger. There are plenty of ways I could have been *protected* in Innerworld. I could have hired a tracker to watch over me." Immediately Cherry thought of her friend, Falcon, the empathic man whose unusual psychic abilities had helped Aster and Romulus out of several crises in the past. Although Falcon now lived in Outerworld, she was certain another similarly talented detective could be found in Innerworld to help her.

Before Gallant could refute her logic, she pushed further. "And another thing, if you were so anxious to tap into my subconscious, why didn't you just do it yourself, then take off?"

"I don't have any telepathic ability. Mar-Dot does. I told you I couldn't afford to waste the time. It was imperative I pick up Frezlo's trail before it dissipated. If you had cooperated with me to begin with, none of this would have been necessary. I would have left you in Innerworld after I found out what the Weebort said, if that had been your wish, but Mar-Dot had a problem with your untrained Terran mind." He shot them a glance that suggested he held them accountable.

Dot raised her chin defensively. "If you had not stunned the poor woman into oblivion, there would not have been a problem."

The he-she revolved a quick half-circle and Mar countered, "Your action was entirely justified, Captain."

"At any rate," Gallant continued, without responding to either comment. "Mar-Dot couldn't find out what I needed to know without your conscious participation. There was no way of telling how long it would take for you to come around, so we had to take off with you still on board."

"And just how long ago was that?" Cherry asked warily.

When Gallant didn't answer right away, Dot did. "About twenty-four hours. The paralyzer was set—"

"A *whole day*? Holy stars!" Cherry walked quickly back and forth in the confined area, her hands gesturing wildly as she spoke. "This is even worse than I thought. You've got to understand. Aster's having her first baby, and she'll be frantic with worry about me. A message from you about protective custody is only going to make her more nervous."

She stopped her pacing and took a deep breath. Nothing she'd been told so far changed the fact that she had been kidnapped and couldn't get home without Captain Voyager's assistance. "Let me see if I've got this straight. You need my conscious participation to get the information you want, which I assume means I have to agree to let Mar-Dot touch my mind. Right?"

Gallant nodded slowly.

"Fine. You take me back to Innerworld and I'll let them have a free tour through my feeble Terran brain."

"Not good enough. You could refuse again once I got you there and, in the meantime, I would have lost Frezlo also. He's the only lead I have left now. I'm not at liberty to give you details of my mission, but it is of universal importance. I had been on the Weebort's trail for months before I found him in

Innerworld. The information he had was vital. Unfortunately, Frezlo was on to him also, and *his* mission was to prevent the Weebort from passing on anything he might know."

Cherry had more or less figured that much out. "You and that Frezlo creature are both *agents for hire*?"

Gallant nodded slowly. "Working on opposite sides at the moment, however. And, I might add, with distinctly different methods of operation."

"So why didn't you stop Frezlo before he escaped?"

"Any attempt I might have made to intervene would have increased the chances of others being hurt. Frezlo has no conscience when it comes to eliminating anything or anyone in his way. Besides, I knew I could pick up his ion trail if I just got off-planet fast enough."

"His what?"

"Ion trail—charged particles emitted by the drive unit of his ship."

"Oh. Like a car's exhaust system. But I'd still like to know how you got me on board without anyone stopping you." Gallant hesitated long enough for her to grow suspicious.

"I hid you in a trunk," he said with a warning glance at Mar-Dot.

Cherry had a strong feeling that he was lying, but since she knew Noronians lived by a code of honesty, she let it pass. She also came to the conclusion that they were at a standoff, and he was not going to budge an inch. However, she was more or less convinced that, between him and Frezlo, Voyager was the lesser of the two evils. "Okay. If you'll promise to take me right back to Innerworld afterward, I'll cooperate with Mar-Dot."

"Granted," he said, then nodding at his navigator, stepped out of the way.

Dot held a manicured hand out to Cherry and led her to the Captain's chair. "Please try to relax," she said after Cherry was seated. "I will try not to invade your privacy any more than absolutely necessary. I need you to help me by concentrating on the moment when the Weebort spoke to you." Gently she pressed the first two fingers of each of her hands against Cherry's temples. "Now, close your eyes and picture the Weebort in front of you. His mouth opens and he says . . ."

Cherry recalled the narrow forked tongue flicking in and out like that of a snake, but she was still quite certain she had heard no words.

Without removing her fingers, Dot said, "Computer, record and translate the following sounds from the Weebort language." Dot did her best to imitate the garbled noises stored in Cherry's memory, but without a forked tongue, the pronunciation could not be duplicated precisely. After she analyzed the problem, Dot said, "Apparently, there was too much external noise for her universal translator to pick up the Weebort's speech, so she was never given a translation. Thus, she has no memory of such."

She tried again and this time the computer offered an interpretation for one of the sounds: counterfeit.

"Counterfeit?" Gallant asked, to be certain he'd heard correctly. "What the *drek* is counterfeit?" When neither the computer nor Mar-Dot answered him, he ordered, "Try it again. There has to be more than one word out of all that babble."

Mar-Dot made two more attempts to obtain a further translation, to no avail. "Sorry, Captain," Mar said with a grimace. "That is the best we can do. Perhaps he was referring to—"

A slight movement of Gallant's hand instantly silenced Mar. "Why don't you show Cherry the facilities? I'm sure she'd like to freshen up."

"It would be my pleasure," Mar said, offering his arm to escort her.

Cherry thought she noted a decided male gleam in his eyes a second before he whipped around. Dot's eyes held an entirely different message. "*I* will take her." She waved Cherry back into the narrow corridor. "This is a small craft, built for speed and maneuverability, rather than luxury or carrying large shipments of cargo."

As they passed the first door on the left, Dot noted, "The exterior door operates only when we are on the ground. There are three rooms—Gallant's"—she pointed to the door on the right where Cherry had awakened. "Ours"—she motioned to the left—"and the facility chamber."

She touched the door at the end of the hallway, and it slid open to reveal a gray-carpeted lounge about twice the size of Gallant's, furnished with a royal blue sofa, two stuffed chairs, and a low table.

On one wall of the room were two square metal panels and a computer monitor, which Cherry recognized as a supply station, but it was much smaller than the one she had in her residence.

Dot explained, "The computer will supply your verbal requests for food or clothing if at all possible, but I must warn you, this compact version undoubtedly has a more limited capacity than the supply station you are accustomed to. I would suggest you keep your orders fairly simple."

Cherry shrugged. "Since I'm only going to be on board for another twenty-four hours, it really doesn't matter. However, I have one need that isn't going to wait that long."

Dot smiled and directed her to the partition in the corner. "The commode functions in the normal way, but, because of the minimal storage space on board, there is no water for showers." Cherry investigated the cubicle as Dot continued. "The red button on the wall activates the sanitizing beam in the ceiling. You just remove your clothes and stand beneath it for one minute. You will be as clean afterward as if you had taken a hot shower; you just will not feel as refreshed."

"Nonsense," Mar countered, turning toward Cherry. "It is only a matter of getting used to it. Perhaps you would like to try it now. I will be glad to assist you."

Though the words were spoken sincerely, the look

on his face was downright lecherous. Before Cherry could tell if he was kidding, Dot was back in control.

"Pay no attention to him, Cherry. He is only a man and therefore cannot stop himself from behaving foolishly. We will give you your privacy now."

Cherry laughed out loud as Mar-Dot exited the chamber in a series of rotations, during which Dot waved good-bye and Mar blew her a kiss. Now that she knew she was on her way home, she could start enjoying her unexpected adventure. She might have liked getting better acquainted with Voyager, too, if he wasn't such a prig. His superior attitude and general unfriendliness completely negated how wickedly attractive he was.

A few minutes later she discovered just how limited her selection of fresh clothing really was. The choice of styles was between a pair of slacks and a vest, both black leather, in a large man's size; or a one-size-fits-all jumpsuit like Mar-Dot's, with or without an extra pair of sleeves. No shoes or underclothing were available. At least the second selection was offered in either olive green or white.

Since she wouldn't be caught dead in either black leather or olive green, she opted for a white jumpsuit and got ready to try out the sanitizing beam. Even if it wasn't a real shower, she felt certain freshening up would greatly improve her present condition and disposition.

"Shall I plot a return to Earth, Captain?" Mar asked after he returned to his place behind the control panel.

"No. Keep following Frezlo's trail," Gallant replied without looking up from what he was reading on the monitor before him.

"But, Captain," Dot said, "you promised Cherry you would return her to Innerworld."

"And I will, right after I deal with Frezlo."

Dot started to say something else, but Mar took over. "My guess is he will head for Zoenid."

"That's better than a guess. He's going to have to lay low for quite a while after pulling two incinerations so close together."

On Zoenid, the only law was that there was no law, including no extradition treaties. Frezlo undoubtedly intended to seek shelter in that planet's southwestern quartersphere, where he could blend right in with the transient inhabitants—not because they looked like him, but because there was such a variety of species residing in that inhospitable zone. The rest of the planet was a totally barren desert, where not even the most desperate criminal attempted to carve out a hiding place.

Tracking Frezlo at a distance the way they were, it was a simple matter to confirm whether or not he landed on Zoenid. After that, however, Gallant knew it would take a considerable amount of ingenuity to find the assassin and even more to get him to talk.

Oh, he had his ways, like any agent worth his credits. His ways just weren't like anyone else's. Gallant was certain he would be able to learn everything Frezlo knew, if he could find him. Although, as he had told Cherry, he possessed no telepathic capability, his special talent was worth a lot more. Only a handful of people knew the secret, and revealing it would result in dire consequences for everyone involved, primarily himself.

"Have you got a plan to draw Frezlo out?" Mar asked, knowing from experience how his captain's mind worked. "I doubt he will allow himself to be found once he reaches Zoenid."

"Right. I've been sitting here reviewing his profile. There's only one thing he fears enough for me to manipulate him with it. He likes to gamble, but how do I get him to my table? A rumor of a high-stakes game might attract him, but it would also dredge up every other animal in the area."

"Excuse me, Captain. This is not right."

Gallant looked up to face Dot. "What?"

"The trip to Zoenid will take another five days. Then there is no telling how long it will take to lure Frezlo to you. You clearly implied that you would return Cherry to Innerworld immediately after we touched her mind. How do you intend to explain that it took twenty-four hours to get here, but as much as two weeks to get back?"

Gallant frowned at her. He was doing his utmost to keep thoughts of Cherry out of his head. It was vital that he think of her as an inanimate object, rather than a living, breathing person. He could not afford to let his decisions concerning her be influenced by one of the troublesome emotional responses that perpetually simmered just beneath his image. "You know how important this mission is. I'll take her back as soon as it's convenient."

"What will you tell her?"

"I'll stick to my first excuse—that I'm trying to keep her safe from any possible repercussion from Frezlo. That should hold her for a while."

Mar asked, "Do you think there is any chance he is aware that the Weebort spoke to her?"

"Not one. If he had seen what I saw, her ashes would have landed on top of the Weebort's." Gallant leaned back in his chair and stroked his chin, as he often did when an idea was hatching. "But what if he found out about it . . . after the fact. Wouldn't he come looking for her . . . to verify the rumor?"

"No," Dot said firmly. "You must not do what you are thinking. Frezlo would come looking for her all right. To incinerate her."

"I'd protect her," Gallant countered confidently, already fleshing out his idea. "I'd only use her as bait to draw him out, then I'd put her safely out of the way." He slowly swiveled his chair around a full circle as he formulated a plan that would allow him to use Cherry and protect her at the same time. He knew Dot wasn't going to like it, but he counted on her loyalty and Mar's persuasiveness to keep her from objecting too loudly. "Tell me, Mar, do you still have that slave collar we used on you during the Orvanian uprising?"

Cherry felt so much better after taking off her costume and getting cleaned up, she was even considering forgiving Voyager for abducting her . . . if he apologized nicely enough. He had made excuses for what he had done, but had not actually said he was sorry. As she pulled on the stretchy white jumpsuit and slipped on the sandals she had worn with the peasant costume, she decided he would have to rectify that oversight.

After a few minutes of looking around the facility chamber, she found a drawer of grooming necessities, including a hairbrush with some long, black hairs in it. She only hesitated a second before using it. After all, she figured she'd already slept in the man's bed. How much more intimate could a couple get?

She quickly fluffed her short hair back into its usual simple style and took a look at herself in the full-length mirror on the back of the door. The jumpsuit was very different from the loose-fitting attire she normally wore. She noted that it was just as comfortable, since it fit like a second skin without being constricting, but it failed to leave any portion of her anatomy to the imagination. She always abided by the theory that the less a person revealed, the more curious everyone else became.

The outfit was completely seamless with long sleeves and a rounded neckline that scooped low enough to prove she was a woman, albeit a modestly blessed one—unlike her dearest friend, Aster, whose pregnancy only exaggerated what nature had already bestowed on her.

Cherry remembered the first time she and Aster met. If ever there were two opposites, the two of them fit that description. Aster stood over six feet tall in heels and her body set the standards for the word voluptuous. Where Cherry was outgoing and uninhibited, Aster was shy and retiring. Even their backgrounds were a world apart.

Cherry was born and raised on a dirt farm in Georgia where a low-income bracket would have been a step up. She and her nine brothers and sisters slept in the same room, and none of them ever laughed, or played, or listened to music for fear the devil would possess their souls.

At an early age she learned that *love* was the reason her parents had too many mouths to feed, and *love* was the motivation behind the rigid rules and severe punishments the children received. Their religious fanaticism was even borne of an excess of *love* for God. *Love* was something Cherry was determined to keep out of her life.

From the day she entered first grade and realized she had a name of her own, Cherry wanted more. Up to that time she had answered to "girl" just as her sisters had. There were no individuals; they were all appendages of one unit commonly referred to as "the chiluns."

Her dream of becoming someone special had germinated then, but wishing it aloud had earned her a beating. Her mother swore she would burn in hell for such thoughts, but she couldn't get it out of her head. The first time she saw a motion picture, she knew she wanted to become a star. She would secretly act out her imaginary stories and pretend everyone came to see her, begging for her autograph.

The day after high school graduation, she walked out of that two-room shanty and never looked back. She hitchhiked to California with high hopes and few tangible assets. As luck would have it though, she got a ride to San Francisco instead of Hollywood. Out of money, she found a job in that city as a receptionist for the Mackenzie Foundation, but still intended to follow the stardust trail to L.A. as soon as she could afford it.

The first day of her first real job was when she connected with Aster. It had been Aster's first day, too, but that was the only thing they had in common. Besides their appearances and personalities, there was another major difference between them. Aster was disgustingly rich.

The Mackenzie Foundation had been set up by Aster's grandmother to give away some of the family fortune. Aster had just received her master's degree in economics and had been groomed since childhood to take over the Foundation.

Before long, Cherry had challenged herself to break Aster's mundane lifestyle of working, eating, sleeping, and working again. It had taken months for Cherry to force a good laugh out of her, but it had been worth the effort. Aster turned out to be the best friend Cherry ever had and vice-versa.

Eight years later when her grandmother died, Aster took over as director of the Foundation, and Cherry moved up as her efficient, yet carefree, administrative assistant.

Cherry never made it to Hollywood, nor could she take complete credit for turning Aster's life around. But fate gave each woman her heart's desire in the end.

Aster mated with the man of her dreams and

managed to indirectly make a positive impact on the planet's environment.

Cherry became a star—the only thing she had ever wished for. Achieving that goal in Innerworld had made her happier than she had thought possible . . . for a time. Lately, though, she had become bored with the routine of her work. There was nothing she wanted to do more than act; it simply wasn't a challenge anymore.

The moment she heard about the Noronian Performing Company audition, she had her new challenge. She hadn't even realized how confined she felt in Innerworld until she imagined traveling to other planets.

Freedom. Even a million miles from that dirt farm in Georgia, the word still had the power to make her pulse race. With a smile on her face and the determination to enjoy her first taste of outerspace, she returned to the bridge.

"Oh, my," Mar said appreciatively as Cherry entered, then he immediately turned so that Dot could see what had surprised him with her own eyes.

"Oh, my," Dot repeated in a different, more concerned tone of voice. "You certainly look . . . different."

Cherry laughed. "Geez, I hope so. That peasant maiden get-up is one of the worst." Her gaze moved to Gallant as he started to turn around then paused to adjust his eye patch. She couldn't help but wonder why he had to wear such a thing when any physical defect she knew of could easily be repaired by

Innerworld's medical personnel. *What could it be hiding?*

She waited for the kind of complimentary greeting men usually paid her as Gallant quickly scanned her from head to toe, but he swiveled back around without a word. "Well," she said, when it was obvious he wasn't going to comment on her improved appearance. "What do y'all do around here for fun?" she asked, momentarily slipping back into her southern accent.

Before anyone could answer, she walked to the side of the bridge and touched the glass. "This is really amazing. It's practically invisible. How does it stay so clean?" She pressed both hands against the glass then stepped back. Her prints remained visible for only a few seconds before they vanished. "Self-cleaning, huh?" She turned to see Mar grin at her and she smiled back.

Cherry circled the bridge, looking out from every angle possible. "It's so dark. How can you tell where you're going?" When she received no answer to this question either, she walked up behind Gallant and tried to read what was on the monitor in front of him.

Gallant tensed as he felt her hovering over him. It was bad enough that he had made the mistake of seeing what she looked like out of costume, with her this close he could practically feel the energy radiating from her body. She was making it extremely difficult to think of her as an inanimate object. "Perhaps you would like to read or watch a video.

There's a personal viewer in my room you could use."

"I'd rather take in the view right here. What's this?" she asked pointing to the grid on the screen in front of Mar-Dot.

Dot turned to her with a smile. "That's the sector of space we're in now." She touched an illuminated blue spot on the grid. "There we are."

Cherry bent over to get a closer look at the other spots and configurations on the grid. "Are one of those bigger shapes Earth?"

Dot frowned and glanced at Voyager. "I am sure Captain Voyager would be much more capable of answering all your questions."

With an abrupt twist, Mar faced his captain. "Please excuse us. It is past time for our rest period, and Dot gets quite cranky—"

"I do not get cranky," Dot insisted as she turned her face toward Cherry.

"You do," Mar said, stepping away from the panel, "and we should not subject our guest to one of your moods."

"My moods!"

"You see, you are getting cranky."

Cherry tried not to laugh aloud at the he-she as they left the bridge, arguing back and forth in the same voice. A moment later their voices were cut off by the door to their room and Cherry turned to Voyager. "I guess you're used to that."

He shook his head without looking at her. "I accept it. They're the best navigator in the galaxy."

"So, tell me how all of this works," she said with a wave of her hand over the panel.

"Wouldn't you rather take your rest now?"

"You've got to be kidding. I just rested for twenty-four hours. I'm wide awake." She noticed that he appeared to be totally absorbed in whatever was on his monitor, and she leaned over his shoulder to take another look.

Immediately, he cleared the screen and turned his chair so that she was forced to move aside, while he made some notes on a pad.

Cherry leisurely circled the panel, mainly to see if she could get him to follow her movement. So far, he had managed to avoid meeting her eyes except for the briefest moment, and it was beginning to get on her nerves.

Gallant let out an exasperated sigh. "If you think you could sit still for a few minutes, I'll answer your questions."

Cherry smiled and looked around the Spartan area. "I'd love to. Where would you suggest?"

"Here," he said, and pulled a padded bench out from under the panel where Mar-Dot had been standing. "Mar-Dot doesn't sit often, but when they have the need, they straddle this."

Cherry sat down facing him instead of the unladylike position he suggested. "Okay, shoot." That almost made him look at her . . . but not quite.

"Shoot?"

"A Terran expression for 'go ahead.' Tell me how all of this works."

Gallant turned his screen back on and punched a

few buttons in front of him. His eye stayed on the monitor as he spoke to her. "Very simply, the computer oversees the basic operations and alerts me if anything is not functioning properly. As Dot told you, this ship was built for speed. It's lightweight and powered by a specially customized stardrive."

He went on to explain how the stardrive worked, but Cherry didn't understand enough about engineering to follow, so she let her mind wander. At any rate, for all the attention he was paying her, he could have been speaking to a piece of furniture. With every passing moment, it became more obvious that Voyager was purposely trying to ignore her presence.

There was nothing she relished more than a challenge and with little else to do, she decided to accept the unspoken challenge to make him pay attention to her.

"O-o-oh," Cherry suddenly moaned and covered her right eye with her hand.

"What is it?" Gallant asked in a concerned tone, yet still kept his face averted.

"I got something in my eye." She rubbed it, tugged on the lid, then moaned again. "*Drek.* It's probably just an eyelash, but I can't get it out."

Leaning closer to him, she pleaded, "Can you see anything?" She heard him take a deep breath before facing her, and had to forcibly hold back her smile.

"Move your hand," he ordered. She did. "Open your eye." She tried, but after a little lash fluttering, it was clear she could not keep it open on her own. He hadn't wanted to look at her, let alone touch her, but as her lower lip began to quiver, he gave in.

Steadying his hand on her cheek, he used his thumb and forefinger to gently pry her eye open. Her face muscles strained against his effort for a moment before she relaxed and met his gaze. He didn't find any eyelash or particle, but he did see a definite twinkle of mischief . . . just before she tweaked his nose.

"Gotcha!" she said with a laugh.

He jerked back in his chair and looked at her as if she was unbalanced. "What was that for?"

Cherry shrugged lightly. "I wanted to make you look at me, and I did it. You were being very rude, you know. In fact, speaking of rude, you have yet to apologize."

He slowly swiveled his chair back to its usual position and stared at the monitor. "I told you, the importance of my mission—"

Cherry gripped the arm of his chair and turned it back to her. "Look at me and say I'm sorry or you won't have any peace for the rest of this trip."

Gallant decided she was quite capable of carrying out her threat, and considering how long this trip was actually going to take, he acceded. He looked straight at her pretty face and murmured, "I apologize for stunning you and taking you away without your permission."

Cherry's smile broadened. The expression on his face was one of extreme discomfort. "See? That wasn't so hard. And now that we got that business out of the way, tell me about this grid."

"It's a navigational device."

She smirked at his simple answer. "I gathered that

much. I want to know what all these blips and markings mean. And what are all the red sparkles at the edge? It looks like the tail of a comet or something."

Gallant realized if he didn't answer, she would just keep prodding. "That's an ion trail."

Cherry frowned at the screen. Dot had said the blue spot of light was this ship, and even though the movement across the grid was slow, it looked as though the ship was following the ion trail. The distance between the last red sparkle and the blue spot appeared to be exactly the same as it was earlier. "You said something about an ion trail before. Is there a ship on the other end of that trail?"

Now it was Gallant's turn to frown. He hadn't expected intelligence along with all her other attributes. "Probably. But it's too far away to be picked up on the grid."

She had an inkling that she had just learned something important, but she couldn't put her finger on it. "And where's Earth?"

"Also too far away." He knew she was going to have to be told the truth sooner or later, but he opted for as late as possible. Since it was clear she would not permit him to ignore her, he thought distraction might buy him a little more time.

"Do you play cubit?" he asked as he reached under the control panel and slid out an extension, creating a table between them.

Cherry shook her head. "I don't think I've ever heard of it."

He pulled open a drawer on his side of the table and took out four small cubes which were a different color on each of their six sides: blue, red, yellow, green, orange, and purple. He put them in the center of the table. Then he placed six penny-sized markers bearing the same colors as the cubes in front of Cherry and gave himself another identical set.

"It's fairly easy," Gallant said. "The object of the game is to get four of each color. After an initial toss of the cubes, you have two more tries, during which you can reroll as many cubes as you like to try to get four of one color. If you make a set, or quad, you put aside that color marker. The first one to get rid of all their markers, wins."

"Sounds something like a game I played in Outerworld a long time ago called *yahtzee*."

Gallant raised an eyebrow. "Oh? Perhaps you'll teach me that one next. Does it involve gambling?"

"Not usually."

"Then that's one big difference. Cubit is the most popular gambling game throughout the galaxy. The players and bystanders bet on the outcome, which color quad one will get first, and whether or not either player will roll a quad on an initial try. It's taken very seriously by some players."

Cherry noted the way he made it sound like he didn't take it very seriously himself, but she had a feeling the opposite was probably true. "So, Captain, what are the stakes in this game?"

His answer began with a slow grin. "I wouldn't want to take advantage of your innocence."

Immediately, her guard went up. "Why do I get the feeling I'm being conned here?"

He asked her to explain what she meant by that and then firmly denied he would ever do such a thing. "I'll tell you what, we'll just play for points . . . until *you* decide to make it a bit more interesting."

Cherry's intuition told her she was still being entrapped by a practiced liar, but boredom seemed more lethal than any snare he had planned for her. "Okay. I'll play with you, Captain, but be warned, I'm very good at games."

His only response was another slow grin.

Chapter 3

Inside the Mosque of Omar in Jerusalem, Bessima stood behind a marble column. Shrouded in the concealing garments of an Arab female, she attracted no attention to herself. There were many visitors that day, both the devout and the curious, who had come to see the rock from which Muhammad allegedly had ascended to heaven.

Suddenly a fierce-looking man, in traditional Muslim attire, was standing on the rock, scanning the faces of the people beyond the guardrail. Within seconds, shocked murmurs rippled through the crowd.

"I am the prophet, Muhammad," the man loudly declared in an old Arabic dialect. He waited until several onlookers confirmed that he did indeed look like drawings they had seen.

The prophet continued in a booming voice that echoed off the dome of the mosque. "You must prepare yourselves for Judgment Day. Allah, the one and only God is coming. Those who disobey Allah's words or do not believe will be punished. Behold the face Allah will wear and remember it."

For a few seconds, an image hung in the air above Muhammad, then it and he disappeared.

Bessima sighed with relief as she observed the people around her. This had gone much better than the visitation at Our Lady of Lourdes. The Arabs were properly shaken by the prophet's appearance and appeared to accept his warning. It confirmed her suspicion that she had to avoid the places where large numbers of Americans congregated until the very end of her mission. She had been on Terra long enough to discover how jaded the Americans were.

If the princess had known more about these Terrans before sending off Bessima, her most able warrior, she might not even be there. But the princess had been convinced that Terra was the ideal planet for the relocation of her people and that the natives were a primitive, easily conquered species.

Bessima now knew better, but there was no way to advise the princess of her discoveries. As she had been ordered, Bessima destroyed the ship that had brought her there a year ago. The only thing she could do at this point was head for Asia next, and hope for the best.

The warrior could not help but wonder how the rest of the princess's plan was progressing. From the beginning it had been understood that if the royal plan did not come to fruition, Bessima would be stranded on Terra for the rest of her life. If that were to happen, however, she had already learned of several countries that would suit her needs and accept her leadership.

* * *

Princess Honorbound inspected the platter of cooked morset ribs offered by the servant boy and chose one the size of her forearm. The other four men and five women seated on the floor around the huge stone slab that served as a table waited tensely as she brought the meaty bone to her teeth and ripped off a chunk of meat. A trickle of juice escaped the corner of her mouth and ran down her chin while she tested the flavor and texture. With a wave of the bone, she gave the boy permission to serve the others.

Josep, the princess's elderly chief advisor, selected the smallest piece from the heap of bloody meat. He rarely ate animal flesh anymore, but it would have been an insult to refuse. With the exception of brief visits, such as this one, his duties had kept him away from the princess for most of the last twenty years. During that time he had adopted many of the ways of the more civilized people he dealt with.

Although he still owed his allegiance to Honorbound, he saw her as the barbarian she was. Already taller and larger-boned than the average man, her gold-plated helmet with its morset antlers made her appear even bigger, and she rarely took off the royal helmet.

The animal skin slung around her hips was her only concession to modesty as she was extremely proud of her muscular body with its numerous jagged scars. But barbarian or not, the ornate gold medallion that hung from a leather thong around her neck declared her a member of the royal family of the planet Illusia, and therefore, his superior.

From various civilizations they had conquered, they had gained sophisticated weaponry as well as the ability to travel through space at great speeds, but they preferred to maintain their primitive existence in every other aspect of their life. Besides animal skins comprising most of their attire, fire was still the primary source of light and heat. And their manners and traditions had not altered in a thousand years.

According to custom, no one spoke during the meal; only the sounds of open-mouthed chewing, slurping, and finger-licking echoed through the cavernous chamber.

As Josep glanced at the other eight people who made up the princess's council, he realized how soft he had become in his years away. The animalistic urges that drove these warriors were also present within Josep, but he had learned to control such barbaric tendencies. Now, however, sitting among them, he could almost feel himself regressing to their level once again.

Before leaving his ship, he had removed the flowing red robe he normally wore and donned a fur tunic that failed to completely conceal the deterioration of his aging body. But his status had been determined by his mind, not his strength, so his white hair and sloping shoulders did not alter the respect he was paid by his fellow council members.

As the others did, Josep tossed his unwanted scraps into the center of the table. Before the final course was served, the garbage had grown to a sizable mound of gnawed bones.

Emitting an elongated belch, Princess Honorbound announced the end of a highly satisfying meal. "So, Josep, my friend, do you bring us good news?"

All eyes turned to him in anticipation. "Some, though not as good as you had hoped. When I left Norona several weeks ago, the Consociation representatives were almost evenly divided about what action should be taken with regard to Illusia's dilemma."

With the long curved fingernail of her right index finger, Honorbound picked a piece of meat out of her tooth and flicked it onto the bone pile. "That is not unexpected. What about Gallant Voyager? Where is he?"

Josep noted how unconcerned she tried to look and knew it was for the others' sake. Her anxious thoughts came through to him whether she wished it or not. "The Consociation Regent, Esquinerra, heeded my suggestion to give Voyager the assignment to track down the Weebort trader. At the time I departed, I was informed that Voyager was on his way to Innerworld Earth, where the Weebort was last reported to be."

"And the assassin?" Honorbound asked with a little more interest.

"Frezlo was also headed in the same direction."

"Good," she said, but so much more was going on in her head that only Josep could hear.

He was one of the very few of their people who had been born telepathic. That ability had earned him his position as the princess's chief advisor. On the other hand, her fear of that ability caused her to give him a mission that would keep him far from her side most of the time. It was a mixed blessing at best.

She questioned him on a few other matters before adding her own piece of information. "According to the chronology of our plan, Bessima should be planting her seeds now as well. It is too bad we could not maintain contact with her, but she is most trustworthy. She will complete her assignment in the time frame she was given, then all will be ready for us."

The princess clapped her hands, and a short, plump woman in her middle years appeared seconds later. An abrupt hand signal from her mistress was all the instruction the servant required before she was off again.

"Your timing was excellent, Josep," Honorbound said with a smile. "You may have already guessed by our feast that we had a celebration planned for tonight even before your arrival. Five of our children have reached full maturity and are ready to be integrated."

The plump woman returned then, leading three young men and two young women, all wearing only a piece of white linen wrapped diaper-style, and a white band circling each of their heads. They stood at stiff attention in a straight line as the princess rose and inspected each one from head to toe.

"Not a bad-looking group," Honorbound said to the woman, who immediately beamed at the praise. "You must have fed them better than the last candidates. Let's hope it did not lessen their hunger for more important things."

Josep had not participated in a Maturation Ceremony in a very long time. It was the most important day in the life of an Illusian, but he wondered if he was up to it.

The princess must have caught him frowning, because she laughed and said, "Don't worry my old friend. Your own maturity permits you to sit and observe the first half of the ceremony."

Josep nodded in appreciation, but he had received the unspoken message that his active participation in the second half was mandatory if he did not wish to be shamed in front of the others. His gaze traveled over the maidens and was met by a particularly bold stare from the more well-formed of the two. She clearly intended to receive the high honor of being chosen by the chief advisor. As his body responded to her look of raw sexual hunger, Josep shed his fear that he would not be able to perform as expected.

The princess stepped back from the novitiates and removed the thong and medallion from her neck. With the thong wrapped around her clenched fist, she held the medallion in front of her as she spoke. "This royal medallion has been handed down through my family for nine hundred years. As the current possessor, I have sworn to protect all of Illusia and to regain the power we once held.

"To that end we have struggled to replenish our army with strong bodies and aggressive minds. You five come before the council this evening on the brink of maturity. Are you prepared to shed childhood and accept the responsibility of mature adults?"

"Yes, I am," the five answered in unison.

"And do you welcome this initiation?"

"Yes, I do," they replied.

Honorbound nodded her head and they all knelt. She walked up to the first young man in the line and pressed the medallion to his forehead. "To what do you owe your total allegiance?"

"The honor and glory of Illusia," he responded firmly.

"To whom do you grant the power over your life and death?"

"The possessor of the medallion may take my life if I ever dishonor our people."

"Do you swear to destroy all enemies of Illusia?"

"I do."

"And who are your enemies?"

The young man's face twisted into a savage snarl as he roared his answer. "All Noronians and their allies!"

She repeated the oath-taking with the other four, then turned to her council. "You have witnessed their vows of loyalty. Now witness their bravery and strength. Let the battles begin."

The young people rose and all but the first moved to the edge of the room. The princess's second in command stood and strode to the novitiate. He was taller, heavier, and had the advantage of experience, but the younger man reflected the utmost confidence in his own abilities.

The servant woman brought forward a tray bearing two short-bladed knives and waited until each man had taken up a weapon. The moment she backed away, the experienced warrior and the young hopeful began circling each other.

Honorbound stated the rules of the skirmish. "This is for blood only. Death is not desirable. The fight ceases when the novitiate receives a scarring cut, the badge of his courage. However, I remind you that the longer it takes for the council member to deliver that blow, the greater the honor for the new warrior." She returned to her place, then clapped her hands once. "To blood."

The young man did not disappoint the observers as he demonstrated considerable agility to counter the smallness of his frame. He did not manage to mark the commander, but he avoided being sliced for an impressive length of time.

By the time the first novitiate received his cut, Josep's blood was singing in his veins. He was tempted to change his mind and take on one of the others after all, but another hot look from the girl made him decide to conserve his energy.

A different council member battled each of the young warriors, and every one of them could be proud of his or her show of bravery. After all their wounds were bound in such a way to insure attractive scars, the princess pronounced the end of the first part of the ceremony.

The council briefly rehashed the skirmishes and declared that the two novitiates who had fought the most valiantly and the longest were the second young man and the maiden who had been eyeing Josep. They would be rewarded with the highest honor of all—having their virginities taken by the princess and her chief advisor. The others were partnered by rank and ability in a like manner. In preparation, the stone table was cleared of debris and covered with a white cloth.

Josep completely abandoned his veneer of civility as the princess and the new warrior removed their wraps. From opposite sides, they crawled onto the makeshift stage, growling, clawing, and biting each other like animals. Josep soon found himself urging the young man to greatness as loudly as the others. In practically no time at all, the princess's bellow of pleasure proclaimed the boy to be a man in every way, even before she removed his white headband.

Josep's own performance some minutes later earned so many cheers from his audience that he could hardly wait for the formal ceremony to end and the open celebration to begin. For that night at least, he was once again one of the infamous barbarian warriors of Illusia.

"You're blocking something from me," Aster accused Rom as they finished breakfast. "I feel it as strongly as this baby's kicks. Whatever it is, I'm going to find out sooner or later, so you may as well get it over with."

Rom tried not to appear as guilty as he felt, but she saw through that also. "I just didn't want to upset you. It's nothing serious."

"Then tell me."

With a sigh, Rom ran his fingers through his hair. "Cherry won't be having lunch with you today either."

Aster narrowed her brows at her mate. "Yesterday, you told me she couldn't keep our lunch date because she was tied up. What's today's excuse?"

"I didn't say 'tied up.' I said 'detained,' and that still goes for today."

"Tied up, detained, whatever. It sounds like we're back to variations of the truth game." The Noronian code of honesty forbade anyone from lying outright, but evasiveness was occasionally employed to avoid the whole truth. "Your daughter and I are both getting upset. I want to know what you're hiding."

Rom shook his head in resignation. Actually, he had managed to keep it from her longer than he'd expected, hoping the whole time that Cherry would be back before Aster knew she was gone. It was probably best to get the facts out as simply and quickly as possible. "Cherry witnessed an assassination the night before last and has been temporarily removed from Innerworld for her own protection."

Aster blinked at him. "I beg your pardon? I believe I am still Co-Governor of this colony and, as such, assassinations and Terrans being *removed* from Innerworld would normally be brought to my attention."

"Well, yes," Rom said with a decidedly sheepish expression. "Normally that's true, but under the circumstances . . ." He looked at her swollen abdomen and hoped that would be sufficient explanation for his duplicity. Her annoyed frown told her he'd have to give details.

"The other day, I introduced you to an old friend of mine from the academy, Gallant Voyager."

Aster could not have easily forgotten the dangerous-looking man with the odd name. "Yes, you said you hadn't seen each other for a while and I left you alone to catch up on old times. What did I miss?"

"He was here as part of a highly confidential mission. The only information he would give me was that he was currently in the employ of the Consociation of Planets, and that the future of the entire civilized universe could be at stake."

"You said there was an assassination. Did he—"

"No. He didn't do it, though he is authorized and has been known to use lethal force on occasion."

"Please, Rom, just get to the point. How could there have been an assassination and no one in Innerworld is talking about it?"

"Gallant was on the trail of a man who had come here as a visitor, but the assassin was on the same trail. The man was incinerated in Fantasy World, right in front of Cherry. Gallant was there also, in the guise of an actor, but he was unable to prevent the murder. He convinced everyone that it was a part of the enactment, so that no one would panic. That was why you didn't hear anything about it."

Aster was not at all satisfied with that explanation, but Cherry's situation had to be discussed first. "So, what happened to Cherry?"

Rom shrugged. "Unfortunately, the message I received from Gallant was very vague—only that she was under his protective custody, and that he would return her as soon as it was safe. The one thing I want to know is how he got Cherry out of here without anyone being the wiser. Security has not been able to explain that, but they're still investigating the matter . . . discreetly, of course."

"I don't like any of this, Romulus."

He knew just how upset she was by the way she used his full name, and he sought to reassure her. "There's really nothing to worry about. If Gallant says he's protecting Cherry, you can be certain no harm will come to her. His reputation is mostly hearsay." In spite of his words, he sincerely hoped Aster never got wind of some of that *hearsay*.

She did not care for the sound of that one bit. "Mostly? Even if he's only half as wicked as he looks, Cherry could be in serious trouble."

Rom raised an eyebrow in disbelief. "Our Cherry? More than likely, Gallant's the one in trouble by now."

Aster thought about it for a moment, then decided he might be right. There hadn't been a man born that Cherry couldn't twist around her little finger in no time. Surely Gallant Voyager wasn't that different from the other men Cherry had encountered. But then she recalled her first impression of him—the devil in black leather—and she started worrying all over again.

Chapter 4

"You are in serious trouble, mister!" Cherry marched into the bridge with her fists planted on her hips and an accusing glare in her eyes. She noted how Dot spun away, leaving Mar to witness her anger, but her attention was captured by an incredible sight beyond the bridge.

A giant tortoise suddenly appeared in space, withdrew its head and feet into its shell, then vanished. "What the hell was that?"

After taking a moment to adjust his eye patch, Gallant turned toward her and cocked his head. "Is there a problem?"

"What *was* that?" she demanded again.

"What?"

She pointed at the spot where she had seen the tortoise. "There was a . . . a . . . tortoise, and then, *poof*, there wasn't."

He raised one eyebrow at her in disbelief. "A *tortoise*? Out there?" He clucked his tongue and shook his head slowly back and forth. "Mar, did *you* see a tortoise?"

"No, Captain. Perhaps Cherry is coming down

with space sickness. It is known to cause hallucinations in some species. I don't believe we have any antidote pills on board either."

Cherry didn't know anything about space sickness, but she clearly had hallucinated since there was nothing out there now and no one else had seen what she had. Regardless, she couldn't think about that now. Remembering how furious she had been when she awoke, she took the few steps needed to get into his air space and stared down at him. "How *dare* you do this to me? How *dare* you pretend to be friendly yesterday when you had this planned all the while!"

"It must be the sickness," Gallant said with another concerned head shake. "I don't understand anything you're saying this morning." He moved to rise, but she instantly pressed the palm of her right hand against his chest.

"Oh, no you don't. I have no intention of looking up at you while I'm trying to put you down."

He tried to resist the pressure of her hand, but it was as if he were nailed to the chair. "A robotic arm?"

Cherry eased back a fraction of an inch. "Yes. I don't usually rely on it, but in your case, it looks like I need every advantage I can come up with." She didn't mention the fact that at the moment that arm was acting most peculiarly. If it had been her left arm, which was real, she would have thought it had fallen asleep the way it was tingling.

He looked down at the soft hand rapidly spreading heat through his chest, then let his gaze slide up her arm, over her breasts, and finally to her eyes. "Any other artificial parts I should know about?"

Cherry might have been pleased that he finally seemed to notice that she was a woman, if she hadn't recognized it as another ploy to distract her. "Don't be a smartass. And stop trying to change the subject."

Gallant attempted to look innocent, but he couldn't resist testing her temper. "I didn't realize we even had a subject yet."

"Was my bunk comfortable enough?" Mar asked, abruptly splintering the tension on the bridge.

Cherry looked at the he-she without lifting her hand from Gallant. "Yes, it was quite comfortable. Thank you for letting me use it." When Mar-Dot had awakened last evening, the captain had retired to his room, leaving Cherry to seek her rest in a different place than she had before. "In fact, it was so comfortable, the clock in your room says I slept almost ten hours.

"If my calculation is correct, that means it has been over twenty-four hours since you said we were one day away from Earth. Now, I'm no expert, but there is nothing out there that bears any resemblance to my home, and I don't think that's the way it should be." She watched the captain's mouth twist into a frown, but he said nothing.

Suddenly a light blinked on in Cherry's head and she glanced at the screen in front of Mar-Dot. The blue dot was still following the red sparkles at a distance. "You son-of-a-bitch," she muttered, applying more pressure to his chest in spite of the strange sensation touching him was causing. "We're still tracking that beast aren't we? You never had any intention of turning this ship around, did you?"

His eyes widened with the awareness that she was capable of collapsing one of his lungs with almost no effort at all, and yet his body was responding to her touch as if it were a tender caress. Careful not to make any sudden moves, he said, "I had no choice. My mission—"

"Your mission be damned. You *lied* to me. You're *not* a Noronian, are you?"

"I have no idea."

Dot swiveled toward them. "Captain, if I may make a suggestion. Some explanations on your part might go a long way to relieve Cherry's mind . . . as well as your discomfort."

Gallant smirked at her, then frowned at the dainty hand that hid so much strength. Nothing was going the way he had expected on this mission. Recalling his plan to use Cherry to lure Frezlo out of hiding, he realized he would have to do some fast, believable talking. He wondered if she had any sympathies he could tap into.

Not certain what tidbit Mar-Dot might feel tempted to add to his story, he said, "All right. I'll tell you everything. But let's go to my room so we don't disturb Mar-Dot."

Cherry could see by Dot's crestfallen expression that she did not want to be left out of this discussion, but she simply pursed her lips and turned away.

"Fine," Cherry said and moved away from Gallant.

He took a gulp of air into his lungs as he rose and led the way.

The moment the door closed behind her, Cherry said, "Okay, shoot."

Gallant still thought that was a very odd expression, but he decided he'd better get started testing her sympathetic nature. "I suppose I could begin with my background. I don't know if I'm a Noronian by birth, but I was raised on Norona. I was abandoned as a baby and adopted by a good man and woman. The only thing that was left with me was a note requesting that I be named Gallant Voyager. I possess certain characteristics that are not precisely Noronian, so there is a question of my genetic origins. However, I usually abide by the Noronian codes of behavior I was taught."

"Except when it's not convenient," Cherry added in a sarcastic tone. "If you think I'm going to feel sorry for you because you don't know who your real parents are, you've made a tactical error. You see, I was raised by my biological parents, and always wished I had been orphaned at birth. I figured any foster home had to be better than the one I was in. So forget the poor Gallant angle and try for a truthful explanation of why I'm not back in Innerworld by now."

Gallant realized his plan had backfired. Rather than instill sympathy in her, she stirred it in him. Once again damning the volatile emotions he was forced to live with, he quashed the urge to ask her more about her childhood and sat down on his bunk. Immediately he realized there was nowhere for her to sit but right next to him, which was altogether too close for his comfort. Berating himself for not taking her into the larger, *less intimate* facility chamber instead, he did what any civilized adult would do. He shifted to the foot of the bunk and waved her toward the other end. "Sit. Please. This will take some time, and I don't like looking up while I'm talking any more than you do."

Cherry lowered herself, but her crossed arms and stern expression warned him to make his explanation a very convincing one. It was time for the truth . . . at least enough of it to assure her cooperation. Now he would see if she bore any loyalty to Norona.

"Please understand, the mission I am on is so sensitive, I didn't even reveal details of it to Governor Romulus. He was not personally involved, however, and you are. I see now that you should have been informed of the situation right from the beginning. You must swear that what I am about to tell you will remain confidential. Millions of lives could be at stake."

Cherry clucked her tongue. "You know, you almost had me before that last line. Don't you think millions of lives is a bit much?"

Gallant sighed. "I realize you have reason not to trust me, but I swear by the Noronian code of honesty I was raised with, everything I'm about to tell you is the truth."

"Okay, I promise whatever secrets you reveal will stay inside my head." She proceeded to get into a more comfortable listening position by folding her legs Indian-style on the bunk. "Aster and Rom saved millions of lives ten years ago when an asteroid was heading toward Earth. Is this something like that?"

"I'm afraid it's not that simple. For you to understand, I'll have to go back in history about four hundred years. Within the same solar system as Norona is the planet Illusia. At that time, the Illusians were a barbaric warrior race, kept isolated from the other planets by their own lack of development. It isn't known positively, but it is assumed that a spaceship from a more sophisticated civilization landed or crashed there and, suddenly, the Illusians gained the ability to leave their home planet and make war on one of their neighbors.

"When the first planet was devastated, they moved on. Wherever they went destruction and violence followed. Ultimate power was their only goal. They cared nothing for the people they conquered other than how they could most effectively be used to entertain the Illusian warriors. There are wild animals more civilized than they were."

Cherry wondered at the vehemence of Gallant's speech. He had started out in a matter-of-fact tone, but it quickly altered as he began listing the atrocities accredited to the Illusians. There was no question he was being truthful and that the truth infuriated him. The horrendous cruelties he went on to describe made Cherry's stomach queasy, but she didn't interrupt him until he paused on his own. "But how was it that such primitive people could so easily overcome more sophisticated nations?"

He took a slow breath as he brought his obvious disgust back under control. "The Illusians have the uncanny ability to create perfectly realistic illusions, complete with sound. It was the only mental ability they were known to have, but no other talents were needed. Basically, their victims were either fooled or terrified into submission because of images they saw and believed to be real. The Illusians were able to make a conquering army of one hundred appear to be one million strong. They didn't have to actually possess city-leveling weapons, they only had to make the people think they saw such a weapon aimed at them, then demand their surrender."

Cherry didn't bother to conceal her fascination with his story. "Then how were they stopped?"

"When they attempted to attack Norona, they hadn't taken into account that, unlike the people previously conquered, the Noronians possessed superior mental abilities of their own. A highly perceptive person discovered the deception and put a stop to the Illusians' goal. To determine Illusia's fate and maintain interplanetary peace thereafter, the Consociation of Planets was formed with the Ruling Tribunal of Norona as its leader.

"Due to the treachery of those barbarians, it was decided by the Consociation that they were too dangerous to be given free reign of the solar system, but the Ruling Tribunal was strongly opposed to committing more violence than had already been perpetrated. Instead of destroying Illusia and its people, the warriors were all gathered and returned to their home. Then a barrier shield was created around their planet, which prevented anyone from leaving or going to Illusia. The last message received from them before they were blocked out was a blood oath to one day destroy Norona and all its allies."

Cherry's eyes opened wide. "Innerworld is a Noronian colony. Does that mean the Illusians intended to destroy Earth as well?"

"Exactly," Gallant confirmed with a nod. "But until recently, the threat had been forgotten. Illusia has been visually monitored at a distance by the Consociation ever since. Over the years, they watched the barbarians set aside their warlike ways and develop into a peaceful farming and industrial society."

"I get the feeling you're leading up to the big finish here, but I don't have a clue as to what it might be."

Gallant gave her points for astuteness. Fortunately, he was a master at keeping some things hidden. "The monitors show that a prolonged drought has stricken Illusia and its inhabitants have been relaying visual distress signals from all over the planet."

"Let me guess. The Consociation is trying to decide whether to respond, or let the cretins die off."

For that, he gave her a thumbs-up sign. "The representatives are divided about the wisdom of raising the shield to give assistance, regardless of whether it means the survival of the race. At least half of the reps still recall the stories their ancestors told them about the Illusians. The other half feels the time has come to reanalyze the harsh judgment bestowed on them."

"But you said that was four hundred years ago. It's

totally unfair to assume the Illusians are still the barbaric animals they were then."

Gallant's mouth dropped open in surprise. "Do you really believe that?"

"I wouldn't say it if I didn't believe it. You're the liar, not me. Anyway, I got a taste of that kind of unwarranted prejudice when I first arrived in Innerworld."

"How can you compare the two? Outerworlders had been given their freedom long before that."

"Freedom, yes, with limitations. Equality, no. There were plenty of Innerworlders who believed Terrans were an inferior species capable of terrible violence. Aster and Rom's joining helped change some attitudes, but not all. I still run into a diehard bigot once in a while.

"I realize it's not precisely the same, and you obviously side with those who assume the Illusians are still dangerous, but don't you see how wrong it is to judge them today based on the crimes of their ancestors? Shouldn't someone try to get more facts before a decision is made?"

Gallant never expected her to sympathize with the Illusians. It would have been much easier to remain indifferent to her if she had despised them. "Uncovering the facts is what my mission is about."

"You said you were employed by the Consociation." Cherry inched forward, anxious to find out what all this background was leading up to. "Are you saying your mission has something to do with the decision about Illusia?"

He nodded, relieved that she was making this so

simple for him. "A short time ago, the Weebort trader you saw secretly sold a document to a Con rep. He claimed the document had somehow been smuggled through the Illusian shield and contained information that would help them decide Illusia's fate. The Consociation employed a language and antiquities expert, who confirmed that the document's paper could have come from Illusia, and that it was written fairly recently in a known Illusian dialect."

"Then what's the problem?" Cherry was beginning to lose patience with his long narrative, and it was making her fidget.

"Unfortunately, the expert had barely begun the translation when he was killed and the document disappeared. Two others who had handled the paper were also murdered. The method was incineration, just like the Weebort's assassination, and Frezlo had been spotted in the vicinity at the time of the crimes.

"I had hoped to get to the Weebort first and find out what he knew, but now the only lead I have left is Frezlo. If nothing else, he could tell me who hired him, and that could get me a step closer to the truth."

Cherry frowned. "In other words, if I had heard the Weebort better, your mission might already be over. But the one word that the computer translated was *counterfeit*. Maybe the Weebort was trying to say the document was a fake."

Rubbing his chin, he appeared to be giving her suggestion serious consideration. "That sounds logical, until you consider all the deaths so far. If the document was a fake, it wouldn't matter what it said. No one would have had to steal it or hire an assassin to prevent the Consociation from learning what it said. They could have let it be known that it was worthless much more easily, so I tend to believe the document contained information someone didn't want revealed."

Cherry agreed with his assessment. "Considering their ability to create illusions, is it possible that everything the monitors are picking up is an elaborate hallucination? Maybe counterfeit is a really loose translation."

Gallant's smile was broad enough to show his straight white teeth for the first time. "Good deduction. You have the makings of a tracker, Cherry."

She laughed. "I've been told something like that before. The fact is, I just like figuring out puzzles. So what do you think?"

"The problem with that reasoning is that all we have to go on is what was recorded four hundred years ago. At that time, it was understood that the Illusians' ability involved tricking another being's mind. The monitoring system involves machines."

"Hmmm. What if, instead of a hallucination that's all in the mind, the reason why their illusions seemed so real is that the image actually has, um . . ." She formed shapes with her hands in the air between them.

"Mass?" he filled in for her. "Or at least the perception of mass. That could explain it, even if no one comprehends how it could be done. If you accept that possibility though, then one major problem is still left. If the Illusians have truly changed their ways, there's nothing to fear by raising the shields, and aiding them would be the proper, humane thing to do.

"But what if they haven't changed, and it's all an illusion? How much stronger are they today than they were four hundred years ago? Could we stop them once the shield was removed, or would they have figured out where they went wrong the last time and have corrected the weakness?"

"I get the picture," Cherry said, but her mind was still trying to locate missing pieces.

"I'm glad to hear that, because I need your help."

"My help? You already know everything I know about this business."

He shook his head. "I don't need help with what you know, but what you *do*. I need you to do a little acting."

Cherry laughed. "Now that's an interesting twist. Don't tell me. You kidnapped me to save you and Mar-Dot from terminal space boredom. Well, I'm sorry to disappoint you, but I have an important appointment coming up back in Innerworld, and as long as the Illusians haven't taken it over yet, I intend to be there, not here, entertaining you while you chase bad guys."

"You're not taking this very seriously, Cherry. Don't you believe anything I've told you?"

She shrugged her shoulders and rearranged her legs. "I suppose I believe you, but it's so . . . I don't know, beyond my experience maybe. Remember, I'm only a lowly Terran, and where I come from, the kind of story you just told only happens in the movies. Please try to understand my side of this. I'd help if I could, but since I don't see how, I just want to go home.

"Aster's in the last month of her first pregnancy. I should be there with her right now. And the appointment I mentioned is a once in a lifetime opportunity for an actress. Theodophilus himself will be conducting auditions in Innerworld for the Noronian Performing Company. I *have* to be back in time for that."

"You have an incredibly selfish attitude," Gallant said in a nasty tone.

She looked surprised at the intended insult, then admitted, "Sometimes I am incredibly selfish, but at the moment I'm simply being logical. If the Consociation hired you to straighten this mess out, they must have faith in you. Therefore, I do, too. I see no reason why my life should be turned upside down in the meantime."

"I suppose I should thank you for that vote of confidence, but the fact remains that I do need your help with something. When is this *important* appointment of yours?"

She quickly figured how much time had passed. "Twelve days."

"Then there's no problem. I'll have you back in plenty of time for that. I'm sorry you'll miss some of Aster's pregnancy, but I'm sure Rom is taking good care of her. And you'll be back long before the birth."

Cherry still had a few remnants of anger simmering inside that had to be let out. "First you physically abused me and kidnapped me. Then you lied about taking me home right after I allowed Mar-Dot to touch my mind. Why should I believe you now?"

Gallant had to do a little more chin rubbing before he could come up with an answer for her. "You have a valid point. But I have another. You can't get back without my assistance and the journey will be much more pleasant if you accept what I've said. Also, I could undoubtedly complete my mission without your help, but with it, I should be able to end it much faster. Thus, if you'll cooperate with what I have in mind, I'll be able to return you to Innerworld that much quicker."

Cherry got up and paced the few steps back and forth within the narrow cabin. It didn't sound like she had much choice when he put it that way. "What would I have to do?"

Gallant grinned with what Cherry supposed was a sense of victory. "Just a little acting. There's no reason to go over it until we get where we're headed."

"Which is?"

He got up from the bunk and opened the door for them to return to the bridge. "A fascinating little planet called Zoenid."

Cherry nodded as if she'd heard of it before. She figured if they were following Frezlo there, it must have a civilization of some sort. And civilization meant transportation. If Gallant turned out to be lying again, she might be able to hitch a ride home with someone from there. Meanwhile, she would keep him guessing as to whether or not she intended to cooperate. He deserved to sweat a little for what he had done.

She glanced up at him as she passed through the doorway and gave him her answer. "I'll think about it."

Dot was facing the doorway as they entered the bridge. She was clearly anxious to hear how the explanations went, but neither Gallant nor Cherry satisfied her curiosity aloud. Gallant was brooding again however, and that told the he-she things had not gone as well as hoped.

As Gallant returned to his station, Cherry wondered what she could do to occupy herself for several more days. She wasn't accustomed to so much inactivity. Considering her alternate scheme to hitch a ride home with someone else, one problem came to mind. Gallant had been able to deceive her because she didn't know how to determine where they were in space. As long as she remained ignorant, she would continue to be dependent on him or any other pilot she found.

Strolling around the control panel a few times, she finally decided how to reduce her disadvantage. Putting on her sweetest smile and dripping southern honey, she faced Mar. "Mar, honey, Ah think what y'all do is absolutely intriguin'. It would truly please me to learn more about navigatin' this heah ship." Gallant's groan made it clear she had laid it on a bit thick, but Mar's expression was one of pure male delight.

Glancing at Gallant, he asked, "With the captain's permission?"

Cherry thought she could hear Gallant's teeth gnashing, but after a few seconds he grunted his approval. She bestowed her charming smile on him in thanks, even though he was back to not looking directly at her.

After pulling out Mar-Dot's bench seat, she made herself at home and started asking questions about the panel in front of her.

Gallant kept part of his attention fixed on Mar and Cherry. Her curiosity could be perfectly innocent, he told himself—an antidote to boredom. But he'd already discovered how bright she was, and how determined she was to get back home. He had a feeling her interest in navigation had a deeper basis than simple curiosity.

If he put a stop to her education though, she would probably go back to nervously pacing the bridge, circling the panel again and again, until he was driven to do something drastic, like locking her in his room for the duration.

The problem with that line of thinking was that it made him imagine being locked in there with her, and the last hour had already stretched his control to its limit.

He wanted her to put the peasant costume back on. At least with that he hadn't been forced to notice every feminine curve and swell, or the swaying movement of her slim hips. But he knew the costume alone wouldn't be enough, because it wasn't her appearance that was pushing him to the edge. *That* just made a bad situation worse.

It was the sparkling energy, her zest for life, that

radiated from every cell in her body. He had sensed it the first time he saw her because it called to that part of him he tried so hard to deny. Being near her stirred the sleeping barbarian within him, dared the wild animal to escape its civilized cage, and generally made him want to grab hold of her until all that energy belonged to him.

She frightened the hell out of him.

She was probably the greatest danger he had ever faced.

And he hungered for her more than any female he'd ever encountered. For the first time in his life, he was not free to run away from something that provoked the appetites he was born with.

He had hoped to ignore her completely, pretending she was an inanimate object. That had been a foolish plan from the start. Then he had hoped to gain her sympathy and understanding, perhaps even her friendship, to insure her cooperation. The problem was, she didn't trust him enough to be his friend. The fact that her attitude toward him was his own fault didn't alter the situation.

Before they reached Zoenid, they both needed to be able to trust the other. Not only his mission, but their lives, would depend on it.

His desire for her was prodding him to tie her to him with the one sure method of bonding. But could he do that and not let the wildness out?

He'd already had her in his arms twice: when he dragged her off the Fantasy World set, and when he carried her on board. He had known instantly that touching her put him at risk, but gambling was one of his favorite pastimes, and the higher the stakes, the more exhilarating the game. What higher stakes could there be than his own life?

And revealing exactly what he was could indeed spell the end for him.

No, he told himself firmly, the only bond he could afford to form with Cherry was friendship.

Sitting there, so close to her, he could feel the air vibrating between them. If she was aware of the charged atmosphere, she wasn't giving any more indication of it than he was. Then again, she still had reason to be angry with him, so that might be enough for her to ignore any attraction she might feel toward him. Obviously, he was going to have to find a way past her anger to form any kind of bond with her . . . even friendship.

For a while there, back in his cabin, he had been sure he was making progress. She had been interested in his story and said she believed him, more or less. She had offered intelligent suggestions as if they were actually working together on the problem, and yet, she didn't promise to cooperate when the time came. Perhaps if he had shared a greater confidence, told her why this mission was so important to him personally—

NO. He could never trust her with that knowledge.

Out of the corner of his eye he saw Cherry shift positions on the narrow bench for the umpteenth time. *Drek!* Didn't she ever just sit still? Unable to stop himself from noticing her every movement, he left the bridge with the excuse of getting something to eat.

As soon as he was out of sight, Dot spun around toward Cherry. "Whew! We thought he would never leave."

Cherry raised her eyebrows in surprise. "I had the impression you adored your captain."

"Oh, we do. But he is so tense right now that it is making it extremely difficult for us to think straight."

Cherry again recalled her friend, Falcon, and his ability to absorb others' emotions. "Are you empathic?"

"No, no. It does not require an empath to know what is wrong with the captain . . . only a woman."

Cocking her head, Cherry waited for an elaboration.

"Surely, you have noticed," Dot said in a secretive manner. "Even Mar, a mere, insensitive male, picked up on it." Mar made a snorting sound, and Cherry tried to get a glimpse of Dot's other half. "Do not worry about him. He is the soul of discretion. You can be assured that anything you say will stay between us girls."

Cherry laughed lightly. "What sort of secrets are you expecting me to spill?"

"I thought perhaps you might have some questions regarding our captain." A brief twisting struggle between Mar and Dot ended with Dot maintaining the forward position. "Mar has agreed not to interrupt again, but he does not believe that I should tell you anything more than the captain wants you to know."

"Then why would you?"

"The captain needs you. I do not fully agree with his plan, but he is decided. I can tell that his explanations did not satisfy you."

"His explanations were fine . . . if they were the truth."

Dot frowned. "I see. Since he lied to you before, you do not trust him now. I am afraid that the nature of the captain's business makes it necessary for him to prevaricate on occasion. Our lives have often depended on it. Like any male, he has his flaws, but he is one of the finest men we have ever known."

Cherry's look of utter disbelief surprised Dot. "You do not believe us either? How can that be? We touched your mind. Did you not sense that you could trust us?"

Cherry thought about that for a moment. "Well, I suppose I did."

"Go with your intuition, Cherry. It is quite strong and, I would venture to say, very accurate."

"You'll tell me the truth?"

Dot nodded. "Or nothing at all, but we will not lie to you."

"Are we following a beastly assassin named Frezlo to a planet called Zoenid?"

"That is correct."

"Is Voyager a good guy or a bad guy?"

"Few people can be categorized so simply. Perhaps a satisfactory answer would be that compared to Frezlo, the captain is . . . a good guy."

"Uh-huh." Noting Dot's hesitation, Cherry got up and started wandering around the cockpit again.

"Okay. Will he take me home after we get to Zoenid?"

Dot pursed her lips and seemed to search the blackness beyond the ship for an answer. "We do not know."

"That's what I thought. He lied again."

"Not necessarily. We believe he has every intention of returning you, if at all possible. But since we cannot foresee the future, we do not know what might happen on Zoenid to delay your return."

"All right. How about something easier. Why does he wear that eye patch?"

Dot lowered her eyes for a moment, giving Cherry the distinct impression that she was conferring with Mar. "We are not at liberty to explain. If the captain wants you to know, he will have to tell you. I would like to tell you a story about him, however. It may help you to see him in a different light."

Cherry shrugged, doubting that there was anything the he-she could tell her to change her mind about Voyager's character.

"I told you that we were sold to a traveling circus as a baby. The owner was a horrid creature named Phlylox, whose only concern was profit. We were one of twenty-five strange beings he had bought or captured over the years. We were all featured as oddities of the universe. For most of our life, our home was a cage, smaller than our cabin on this ship. When we were on display, we were kept in chains. It was not uncommon for us to go for days between shows without sufficient food, or to be brutally beaten for any display of insolence."

"How horrible," Cherry said sincerely. "It's a wonder you remained sane."

Dot gave her a sad smile. "Because we had each other, Mar and I were luckier than some. And remember, we never knew any other life. At any rate, about eight years ago, the captain was on an assignment that took him to the remote colony where the circus had stopped. When Phlylox wasn't looking, the captain spoke to us and promised to help if he could. We didn't think much of his promise because we were transported later that day. But he didn't forget us. When he completed the assignment he was on, he tracked down the circus and freed us all. He spent the next several months returning every being to his or her home planet."

"Except you."

"Yes, except us. Since we had no idea where we had come from, and we discovered that we had a natural talent for navigation, the captain agreed to take us on as a member of his crew."

Cherry sat down again. "Gallant said he was an orphan also. He must have felt an affinity for you."

"We believe that is so. The captain understood what it is like to be an oddity."

"An oddity? How so?" Dot said nothing. "Does it have to do with the eye patch he wears?" Again, no answer. Cherry sighed. "I see. So, what happened to the circus owner?"

"The captain killed him." As Cherry's mouth dropped open, Dot quickly amended, "It was justified. The captain wanted to take Phlylox before the Consociation for judgment, but he had other ideas.

They fought. The captain was severely injured, but Phlylox and his evil circus was destroyed."

Cherry felt a slight shiver run through her. It didn't surprise her that Gallant was capable of murder, but that he would risk his life to save a group of abused freaks altered her totally negative opinion of him. She was about to admit that to Dot, when the he-she blurted out the last thing she expected to hear.

"You will be the first female to share the captain's bunk for quite some time."

Chapter 5

Cherry swallowed hard. "I beg your pardon?"

"He insists he does not have a strong sexual appetite, but we believe his desire for privacy has more to do with his avoidance of females than a lack of need. Although, we cannot really be sure. After all, I have offered him the use of my body, but he has never been so inclined."

Cherry's curiosity got the better of her good manners, again. "You mean, you can . . ."

Dot chuckled. "Of course. Mar and I each function normally in that way. In fact, we have the unique ability of enjoying the other's pleasure, which works out very well since we cannot always find a male and female who are both attracted to us at the same time." She lowered her eyes for a second. "Mar agreed not to interrupt, but he wanted you to know that he would be most happy to accommodate if you wish a demonstration."

Cherry had thought she'd heard it all before now, but the he-she managed to surprise her. "I, uh, thank you, but I don't think so."

"Good. Then you will share only the captain's bunk. I believe he might prefer that."

Cherry's smile vanished. "I'll do nothing of the sort."

Dot looked truly confused. "But it is quite obvious that he wants you."

"And what the captain wants, he gets, right? Wrong. On all counts. First off, your captain hasn't shown the slightest interest in me, but even if he had, *I'm* not interested in him. Not only is he a kidnapper and a liar, but I got the impression he didn't particularly care for women even before you told me he avoids them. *When* I choose to bed a man, I prefer him to have a little heat in his blood."

"Hmmph. The heat in the captain's blood is part of his problem."

Before Dot could explain what she meant by that, Mar was facing Cherry. "I believe that's enough girltalk. Let's get back to your navigation lesson."

Cherry gave Mar most of her attention, but a small portion of her continued to mull over all the little hints Dot had given her to the puzzle of the captain. She wouldn't admit it to Dot, but, with each passing hour, she was growing more *interested* in the captain . . . and his secrets.

It was not until much later that day that Cherry and Gallant were alone on the bridge.

By the time she passed in front of him a second time, Gallant was ready to strap her to the seat. "Don't you ever stop moving?" he asked, clearly exasperated.

Cherry grinned. "Occasionally, like when I'm

sleeping. I always seem to have all this energy just busting to get out." Thoughts of sleeping made her recall Dot's assumption that Gallant would soon have her in his bunk.

She forced herself to set aside her annoyance with him and let her intuition take a reading. His brow had raised a fraction when she had mentioned sleeping, then he'd immediately looked away. Yet, now that she considered the possibility, she thought she might have detected a momentary flash of male interest. But since *she* wasn't interested, there was really no reason to pursue it.

Unless it would help her unearth some more of the puzzle.

Cherry strolled around behind the captain's chair and peered over his shoulder, knowing it bothered him when she did that. Purposefully, she exhaled close enough to his neck for him to flinch in reaction. "I'll stop pacing if you'll play with me."

Gallant's hands stilled, and for a moment Cherry thought he may have stopped breathing as well. She eased away and sat on the bench, facing him. "We can even play for credits this time. Of course, if I lose, you'd have to take me home before I could pay you back."

"Cubit," Gallant murmured, then took a breath as he turned toward her. "You're challenging me to a game?"

"Well, there sure isn't much else to do, is there? But if you're too busy, I'll just—"

"*No,*" he interjected before she got up again, and he pulled out the table between them. He couldn't believe his mind had detoured that way. It had been a mistake to even allow certain thoughts to enter his consciousness earlier. It was almost as if just considering sex with Cherry was more than he could handle. What would happen to him if he actually— His body's sudden strong response finished the thought for him and acted as an alarm at the same time.

He quickly began setting up the game. Aside from the infrequent, impersonal encounter, his experience with adult females was pretty much limited to his adoptive mother and Dot, neither of whom would help him analyze Cherry's behavior. But even without extensive knowledge of how her mind worked, he had the distinct impression that Cherry had not only been teasing him, but had guessed his reaction as well. Since he couldn't imagine why she would tease him while she was still angry with him, he decided she must be up to something.

Reminding himself that he needed to gain her trust, he politely asked, "Are you sure you want to play for credits already? Yesterday, you accused me of trying to . . . to . . ."

"*Con* me," Cherry supplied. "Yesterday, I was a novice, but I think I can hold my own today. After all, winning cubit takes more luck than skill, and I'm due for some good luck after the way this week started."

Gallant frowned. "Is that a hint that I'm supposed to apologize again?"

Her eyes twinkled with a life of their own. "If you feel the need, then by all means, get if off your chest." She instantly regretted her choice of words, as she followed his gaze down his partially covered chest. Up to that moment she had been doing her damnedest not to notice what a perfectly splendid body he had. She forced her eyes back to his face again. "Sorry. Another Terran expression. I've never completely abandoned my roots, I guess."

With his plan to befriend her uppermost in his mind, Gallant picked up the colored cubes and rolled two reds and two blues. "Tell me about your roots. I'm familiar with Terra and its people in a general sense, but even when I attended academy in Innerworld, I didn't get to know any Terrans." He rerolled the two blues and got another red and a green, which he immediately rolled again.

Cherry smiled when the last cube came up blue and he had failed to make his quad. As she scooped up the cubes, she asked, "You lived in Innerworld before?"

"Yes. That's how I know Romulus." He watched her make her first roll and try to decide which color to go for since there were no matches. "What was your life like on the surface?"

Cherry left the purple and retossed the other three, but failed to get another purple. "Damn!"

"You should have thrown them all."

She picked up the same three cubes, rolled them between her palms, blew on them, then dropped them on the table. When all three turned up purple, she let out a squeal. "You play your way, and I'll play mine."

As she set aside her purple marker, he snatched up the cubes. "You haven't answered my question."

"What do you want to know?"

"Everything."

She laughed. "You must be more bored than you look. All right, you asked for it. The first eighteen years of my life was spent on a farm in Georgia—that's in the southeastern part of the United States. After that, I hitched my way across the country."

While she told him of that journey, the places she saw, people she met, their game continued. Occasionally he would stop her with a question, then encourage her to continue.

Several hours later, they had each won two games, and Cherry was getting hoarse from talking. She was fairly sure she had touched on every aspect of life in the United States as well as her personal history.

"We have to play one more game to break the tie," Gallant told her. "I think you're ready for a wager."

"*Now* you want to make a bet?"

He grinned at her. "I didn't want to take advantage—"

"Ha! Where have I heard *that* before?"

"Well, we do seem to be evenly matched now."

"Okay. How much?"

"Not credits. I don't take promise payments."

Cherry narrowed her brows at him as she drew her own conclusion about what he was leading up to, but she wanted to hear him say it out loud before she told him off.

Gallant's instincts still told him that sharing confidences was the quickest route to establishing a bond between them. By telling her about his mission, he had already told her more than he should have. Now it was her turn. Unfortunately, she was a very open person. Her childhood had been the only subject she seemed somewhat secretive about, so he honed in on that. "If I win," he said slowly, "you tell me about the first half of your life. I noticed that you carefully avoided talking about those years."

That was far from the forfeit she had expected him to demand. With a shrug she said, "Only because there's nothing interesting to tell." She considered her chances of winning rather than losing. "Okay, and if I win, you explain why you wear that patch over your eye."

He hesitated only a second before nodding his agreement and passing her the cubes. As she made her initial toss, his fingers casually closed over the front edges of his vest and slid downward. A moment later his special set of cubes was in his left palm, ready to be exchanged for the honest ones on the table. She was going to share a confidence with him even if he had to cheat to force it out of her.

Cherry was amazed at how quickly he won the final game. The odds against rolling three quads of different colors on three initial throws had to be astronomical, but Gallant hardly blinked over his unusual good luck.

As agreed, Cherry told him the tale of her dismal youth and described the ramshackle farm she had grown up on. "My parents truly believed that it was God's will that they have ten children and spend their lives struggling to exist. If Pa had put as much effort into that farm as he did trying to beat the devil out of us kids, we might have been fairly well off."

Cherry's voice retained its joking quality in spite of the bitterness her words suggested.

"You were beaten by your own father?" Gallant asked with surprise.

Cherry waved her hand at him. "Oh, it was no big deal. Outerworld Earth is a far cry from Norona and Innerworld, you know. Lots of parents treat their kids worse than mine did. Anyway, I turned out okay." Smiling, she winked at him and added, "As long as I always get to be the center of attention!"

Gallant tried to return her smile, but her light-hearted attitude failed to hide the pain he sensed beneath it. He had known only love and kindness from the Noronian couple who had raised him and experienced only comfort in their home. Cherry's story made him remember how very different his life would have been had someone not tampered with it.

Though it would have been more comfortable to change the subject, his perverse emotions made him ask for more. "Don't you miss your brothers and sisters? Even with so many, there must have been at least one you were close to."

Cherry started to give him another flip answer, but something about the way he was looking at her cut it off. She was always the one who cheered up everyone else, quickly shrugging off any offer of sympathy in return. Why she should act any differently at this moment made no sense.

The feelings his question triggered prompted her to rise and walk to the glass. Staring out into the darkness, she wondered why a look from this stranger had been able to evoke a memory buried so deeply she had consciously forgotten it. A heartbeat later she realized the reason. He was not looking at her with sympathy, but understanding . . . just as Rose had the day Cherry took off for California.

"Rose," Cherry said aloud for the first time in eighteen years, and in her mind's eye she imagined seeing her baby sister's face. "She was ten when I left Georgia; too young to take with me. The day Rose was born, I claimed her as my own. There was a special quality about her that I couldn't resist. Of course, as she grew up, it was obvious what that was—she was just like me. Full of energy and curiosity, and a need to be free that no amount of punishment could wipe away."

An image of the two of them slipping and sliding in a muddy sty while trying to catch a family of piglets made Cherry smile in spite of the sadness the memory caused.

"What happened to her?"

Cherry could tell Gallant had walked up behind her, but she didn't turn around. "I don't know. See, we knew Pa would never let her receive mail from me once I'd left. After all, I was the devil's handmaiden. And it might have even made it worse for her if I had tried to write. So we agreed that I would come back for her on her eighteenth birthday."

She closed her eyes and took a deep breath. "I had it all planned to surprise her. Ten years ago, a group of us were going on a fishing trip out of Fort Lauderdale, and I figured I'd make a detour through Georgia on our way back to California."

Gallant deduced the rest. "And that was when the accident occurred and you ended up in Innerworld."

With a small nod and a sigh, she whispered to the black void before her, "She must have thought I forgot all about her."

Letting his instincts override his common sense, he turned her toward him and wrapped his arms around her.

She stiffened and looked up at him suspiciously, but his hold was gentle and nonsexual, and she gave in to the comfort he offered. Resting her head against his chest, she listened to his steady heartbeat. "For a tough guy, you do a pretty nice hug."

Gallant stroked Cherry's hair and said quietly, "My mother always said that a hug is worth more than ten medical teams."

"Smart lady." She tipped back her head to look up at him. "You're the only person I ever told about Rose. I don't know why I did that, but I'm kind of glad I finally got it out. Thanks. For listening *and* the hug." Placing her hands on his cheeks, she drew his face down to meet hers as she rose on her tiptoes.

She intended the quick peck on his mouth to end the unexpected intimacy that had sprung up between them. Rather than release her, however, he abruptly tightened his hold, and a growl rose from deep in his chest. His body hardened against hers so swiftly that she gasped, only to have her breath taken away again as his hot mouth closed over hers.

Too fast. Too hard.

Yet not nearly enough.

His lips, his tongue, his teeth took all she had and

demanded more. His hands grasped and kneaded, lifting and urging her to join him in wild abandon. She forgot everything except the reckless hunger he incited. Thinking only of her need to feel every inch of the masculine flesh she had previously been trying to ignore, she yanked his vest off his shoulders.

"Oh my," Dot said as the he-she entered the bridge. As if nothing unusual were going on, they approached their station and began running a check on the instruments. "Really, Captain," Mar declared with mock sternness, "if you needed to leave your post, you should have called us. We would have understood."

Gallant and Cherry were each aware of the interruption but their rampaging need kept them clinging to each other for several seconds. Breathing heavily, and knowing any attempt to make a dignified exit was futile, they stepped away from each other and left the bridge without uttering a word. The sound of Mar-Dot's chuckling accompanied them down the passageway.

Gallant stopped in front of his door and opened it, but rather than enter or step aside, he just stood there, blocking the way with his back to Cherry.

Cherry had been embarrassed to have Mar-Dot catch them doing precisely what she had told Dot they wouldn't, but her pulse was still racing with desire. She touched Gallant's arm and was startled when he jerked away from her.

"*Don't,*" he said in a voice that still sounded more like a ferocious animal's growl. "*Mistake.*"

Before Cherry understood what he meant, he was

inside his room and the door had been closed in her face. She blinked at the door several times before she accepted the fact that he had left her hanging there. No man had ever done that to her . . . on purpose. She wasn't counting those that had simply not been able to satisfy her; at least they had tried.

Not only was Gallant guilty of abduction and lying, now he had insulted and humiliated her as well. Why, he was nothing but a tease! She was half tempted to barge in there and—

Her hand was poised over the opener when she realized what she was about to do. She lowered her hand and laughed at herself. Even with a robotic arm, she couldn't force the man to satisfy her. With a shake of her head, she walked to the facility chamber, hoping that the sanitation stall was equipped with a cold air blower.

Gallant leaned back against the closed door and slid to the floor. His hands were shaking so violently he tucked them under his arms so he wouldn't have to look at them.

Minutes. He had been minutes away from paradise . . . or perdition. If only he knew for sure which it would have been! Only once before had he gotten so close to finding out.

He was five years old when his Noronian parents discovered what he really was. Up to that time they had made excuses for his excessive emotional outbursts and occasional acts of violence. Rather than send him away, they carefully schooled him in self-control, constantly reminding him of the consequences should anyone else find out his secret. The eye patch took care of the other deviation.

For the most part, he learned the lesson well enough to have people wonder if he had any emotions at all. But he had not been prepared to battle the hormonal storm that hit him when he reached adolescence. The first time he was alone with a consenting female, his practiced control disintegrated.

He had attended the required classes and read the manuals on sexual behavior, but he had no way of knowing that getting aroused would turn him into a savage. Nor had he known that the aggressive manner that felt so normal to him would terrify the poor young woman. Initially, she had seemed as anxious as he, but minutes later she was crying to be let go and calling him an animal.

Gallant had regained his senses quickly enough to calm her down and convince her not to report him to anyone. By that time, he had already become a proficient liar, out of necessity.

It was not long after that first incident that physical need drove him to discover that he could experience a sexual release without letting go of his control. However, he always felt that it wasn't as good as it could be. The act was pleasurable, yet far from satisfying. Having to use part of his attention to keep the wildness reined in prevented him from thoroughly enjoying what was happening to his body.

As the years went by, his encounters with women became less frequent. A physical release without an emotional one simply wasn't worth the effort.

His breathing had returned to normal and his

hands had stopped shaking, but his thoughts were still in a panic. Had he really growled at Cherry? Yes, he was certain he had, just as he knew he had bitten her lips and earlobe. Like an uncivilized barbarian, he had mindlessly attacked her, and would have used her without a thought to propriety had Mar-Dot not interrupted.

When Cherry had talked of her sister, he had felt somewhat guilty for tricking her into the revelation—guilty enough to try to comfort her, without considering how the proximity of her body would affect him. It was exactly as he had feared. Her vibrant energy struck a chord in his primitive soul, and the result was nothing short of spontaneous combustion.

As his head began to clear, he considered how to repair the damage he had just done. There was no question about his having to be more careful about touching her in the future. The problem was, he might have ruined any chance of getting Cherry to trust him enough to cooperate with his plan to trap Frezlo.

At least she hadn't screamed or cried . . . or used her robotic arm on him. She must have been too stunned by his shocking behavior to fight him off. He knew he had better apologize before the shock wore off.

He heard the door across the hall open and shut and ordered himself to rectify his mistake immediately. Mentally reconstructing his civilized veneer, he left the privacy of his room and knocked on her door. The moment it slid open, he said, "I wish to apologize."

Remaining in the doorway with her arms crossed, Cherry cocked her head at him. "All right. Go ahead."

She was so calm, he assumed she was still in shock. "My behavior was unpardonable, but I hope you'll forgive me anyway. I assure you nothing like that will happen again." She didn't respond one way or the other, so he added, "I'm sorry if I frightened you."

"*Frightened* me? So far, you've infuriated me, humiliated me, and left me frustrated as a bowlegged kid at a greased pig chase, but it would take a hell of a lot more than one aggravating man to frighten me!"

She might have made him squirm a bit longer if he hadn't been apologizing so politely. "Look, I've decided you were right. What happened up there was a mistake, and it was as much my fault as yours. I'm afraid you opened an emotional floodgate and I took advantage of the outlet you offered. I shouldn't have kissed you, even if I was only trying to say thanks. Let's forget it and just be grateful Mar-Dot stopped us before things went too far. This trip is difficult enough without that sort of complication."

Although he nodded his agreement, he hadn't heard anything beyond her pronouncement that he had left her frustrated. He had been so caught up with the fact that he had let himself go that he hadn't allowed himself to notice that *she* might have been doing a fair amount of clawing at *him*. That thought didn't improve his state of discomfort one bit.

Cherry continued to try to ease the tension between them. "Maybe we could try for some middle ground, like friendship. What do you say?"

"Friends. Yes. That's a good idea," he said mechanically, reminding himself that friendship had been his goal to begin with.

"Well then, I guess I'll say good night." She held out her hand.

He didn't want to make physical contact with her again. Not yet. Not until he had a chance to completely rebuild his defenses. Yet he couldn't refuse to return the friendly gesture. As his hand clasped hers, he had to fight the almost involuntary urge to pull her back into his arms. The way her eyes widened with surprise made him wonder if she had felt the same surge of heat or merely guessed at his depraved thoughts.

Cherry withdrew her hand and closed the door. Her robotic arm came equipped with sensors that operated the same way the nerves in her other arm did. She had never noticed that they were more or less sensitive than the real thing. She flexed those fingers now, concerned that the tingling she felt when Gallant's hand had enveloped hers was a warning sign of a malfunction. It still felt a bit strange, as if he had not yet released her hand. She vigorously shook her arm and the sensation faded away, just as it had the other times she had come in contact with him.

She stripped off the jumpsuit and lay down between the clean sheets on Mar-Dot's bunk. She couldn't help but wonder if Gallant would fall right to sleep or if their unexpected moment of passion would replay itself in his head, as it was doing in hers.

She had told him her analysis about why it had happened. Emotional overflow could make a normally sensible person behave strangely. But she hadn't admitted aloud that nothing quite like that had ever happened to her before. It was bad enough that she had been crawling all over him as if she hadn't seen a man in twenty years!

That day set a pattern for those that followed, with Gallant and Cherry sleeping at the same time. Mar-Dot spent time teaching her about navigation and how the ship operated, and Gallant occupied her with endless games of cubit.

They told each other tales of people they knew and places they'd been, but cautiously avoided anything too personal that might trigger an emotional response.

Cherry thought that if it wasn't for the fact that she didn't trust him any further than she could throw him, she and Gallant could have become friends. But that wasn't the only problem. The tension humming between them since the *incident* prevented either one from totally relaxing. She was constantly aware of how careful Gallant was being not to touch her or meet her gaze for more than a second or two and that only made her all the more curious about what had happened and why he had called a halt to it so abruptly.

Gallant was the one who suggested they play cubit for points rather than wagers, but Cherry was quick to agree. So it surprised her when, two days later, he challenged her with another bet.

"A five-game match. If I win," he stated, "you agree to cooperate with anything I ask when we reach Zoenid."

Naturally she was suspicious of why he would change his mind about playing for stakes, but since she had won more games than he had, she figured it was worth a shot. "And I'll claim the same forfeit I did before. If I beat you, you spill the beans about your eye patch." His dismayed look made her laugh. "You should be able to figure that expression out on your own. You know, by the end of this trip, I'm liable to have you speaking American like a native. So? Is it a bet?"

He gave her one of his slow grins that she had already learned to be wary of. "Absolutely."

The similarity of this match to the one that had ended so emotionally was uncanny. They were tied going into the fifth game when Gallant miraculously began rolling quads again. In practically no time, he managed to win the match . . . and her promise to help with his mission in any way he requested.

On her sixth day in space, Cherry awoke before Gallant for the first time. Except for very short periods, she and Mar-Dot had rarely been alone together. As she had once before, Dot wasted no time taking advantage of the opportunity.

"I see you are still determined to share our bunk rather than the captain's."

Cherry held up a warning finger in front of Dot. "Don't start that. This ship is too small for you to pretend you don't know exactly what is going on between Gallant and me. If it wasn't for this mission of his, he'd hand me over to the first passing ship to get me out of his hair."

Dot started to argue, then changed her mind. "At least you are getting along now. Have you agreed to assist him on Zoenid?"

With a sly smile, Cherry confessed. "I was planning to help ever since he explained the situation to me, but I didn't tell him until last night . . . right after he creamed me. *Beat* me," she amended for Dot's sake, but it didn't alter her look of confusion. "At *cubit.*"

"Oh, yes," Dot said with a relieved nod. "I understand you have become quite a formidable player."

"Ha! I thought so also, but the two times we played for more than fun, he's won. I have never seen anybody as lucky as Gallant. It's almost as if he can order those cubes to come up any color he needs. I'm telling you, it's really bizarre."

Dot smirked. "Hmmph. There is nothing uncanny about it. He must be using his—"

Suddenly Mar shifted toward Cherry. "Would you please get us a wake-up beverage? We are unusually fatigued this morning."

Cherry started to go when she realized Mar had rudely interrupted Dot. "You never have refreshments at your station. Turn back around. I want to speak to Dot." The he-she hesitated a moment, then complied. "He cut you off on purpose, didn't he?"

"It was nothing of importance," Dot answered quietly.

Cherry frowned at her. "You promised not to lie to me. What were you about to say about Gallant's luck?" When Dot couldn't seem to find the words to answer, Cherry made a guess. "Is he cheating somehow?" Dot's eyes rolled upward. "Has he got loaded dice? You know, cubes that he can make do what he wants?"

Again Dot's eyes rotated, and Cherry understood that she was abiding by her agreement to be honest or say nothing at all. Since it was clear Mar didn't want Dot revealing whatever this was about, Dot was giving her answers the only way she could. Cherry opened the drawer beneath the table and removed the cubes. "Are these crooked or does he just switch them for another set when he's losing?"

Very slowly, Dot mimicked the way Gallant would rub his chin, then run his hands down the front of his open vest.

How many times in the past few days had she seen him go through those motions? *A lot.* She had thought it was some sort of nervous habit. That son-of-a-bitch! He had been switching cubes with a set he had hidden in his vest.

"What's going on?" Mar demanded, but Dot wouldn't let him turn them around.

Cherry returned the cubes to the drawer, saluted Dot, and marched down the hall to Gallant's room. Without bothering to knock, she pressed the door opener, but Gallant wasn't inside. With her temper building by the second, she headed for the facility chamber.

The moment she stepped inside, she heard the sound of the blower in the sanitation stall. She was tempted to barge right in on him, but the sight of his clothing laid out over a chair gave her a more vengeful idea.

As stealthily as possible, she tiptoed across the carpet and lifted his vest. Within seconds she discovered the concealed cubes and quickly removed them. She suspected if she played with the trick ones for a while, she would surely figure out how they worked. Then she would turn the tables on the rotten cheat. And, of course, she would make sure the wager was something outrageous.

Just as she replaced the vest, Gallant came out of the stall.

Gloriously naked.

Chapter 6

Cherry was caught, and knew she should have been stuttering apologies and excuses for invading his privacy, but the only word that came to mind was *big,* and in a matter of seconds, he was even bigger . . . and bigger. Not staring was out of the question. "Holy stars," she whispered.

Suddenly she was in the midst of a shower of falling stars, but a split second later they disappeared. Another space sickness hallucination?

Except for covering his left eye with his hand, Gallant didn't move or make an attempt to shield any more of himself. To get his clothes he would have to come closer to her. "What are you doing in here?"

Cherry swallowed hard and dragged her wide-eyed gaze up to his face. "I . . . I . . . thought you were still sleeping, and I came in to use—"

"You're lying," he said in a hard, deep voice. "You would have heard the blower when you walked in. I recall your once giving me ten seconds to explain. I'll give you five. If you're not out of here by then, I'll draw my own conclusions. Five."

The temptation to stay was strong enough to make her forget every crummy thing he'd done.

"Four."

God, but he was gorgeous.

"Three."

She simply had to stand still, and all that man would be hers.

"Two."

But then he'd discover what was in her hand. The reminder of why she'd gone in there and how angry she had been kick-started her brain. She wanted revenge.

"One."

She turned on her heel and walked swiftly to the door.

It took several deep breaths before Gallant regained the ability to move. When he could, he went back into the stall to cleanse the film of perspiration from his heated flesh. He was beginning to doubt that he would get through this assignment undamaged.

He couldn't allow himself to dwell on why she had come into the chamber. He supposed she could have been as curious about him as she was about everything else. But the trapped look on her face when he had exited the stall, combined with the fact that she did leave without fully satisfying that curiosity, told him she'd been up to mischief of some sort. He just couldn't imagine what it could be.

If there was any way he could quickly get hold of Frezlo without Cherry's help, he would avoid using her, but no better plan had come to him. Now he had run out of thinking time. They would be docking in an hour. He could only hope that Cherry didn't renege on her promise to help once she heard what she had agreed to.

Cherry sat on Mar-Dot's bunk, closely examining one of the trick cubes. To her eye, it looked exactly the same as an honest one. There didn't seem to be any weight difference either. No shaved edges or rounded corners. She picked all four up and dropped them on the floor. A blue quad came up—the same color set that had won the last game for Gallant. But he had been able to roll greens, reds, and purples at will also, which meant there had to be a way to manipulate the outcome.

She was determined to figure it out if it took the rest of the trip to Zoenid. In the meantime, he would get a surprise the next time he tried to switch cubes on her and discovered nothing but air in the secret pocket of his vest. She could hardly wait to see his reaction!

That thought made her reflect on his *reactions* when he saw her in the chamber. He had covered his eye rather than his body. Although none of the Noronians she knew were overly modest, it still seemed to be an odd response, especially considering just how strongly, and *quickly*, he had responded. The other curious thing was, in the split-second peek she had, his left eye had appeared to be normal . . . which was more than she could say about the rest of his extraordinary body.

All of a sudden she felt pressure build up in her

ears and she automatically yawned to pop them. The sensation of pressure went away a moment later, followed by a drastic change in the sound of the ship.

Quickly, she hid the cubes beneath the mattress and hustled to the bridge to find out what was going on. There, she immediately saw the reason for the change. Looming some distance ahead was a large, rusty brown sphere. Awareness that it was her first glimpse of a planet sent every other thought out of her head. "Is that Zoenid?"

"Yes," Dot answered. "It would be advisable if you were seated somewhere when we dock."

Not wanting to disturb anyone further, but hoping to get the best view possible, she went in front of the control panel and sat down on the glass floor.

Cherry thought she heard Gallant make a groaning sound, but she was too fascinated with the view to be concerned with him at the moment.

The color of the planet didn't improve any as they approached it. She had assumed it would look like satellite photos she had seen of Earth. Instead, the surface was nothing but a never-ending desert. Where were the oceans? Mountains? Forests? Where was the *civilization*? "Do people really live down there?" she asked aloud.

When Gallant didn't answer, Mar did. "Not generally. But there are some small oases in the southwestern quartersphere where some species reside. We will be coming around that side of the planet very shortly."

"*Species?*" She looked backward, but he had returned his attention to the monitor in front of him.

As promised, it was not long before they began a vertical descent toward the section Mar had spoken of, but Cherry wondered how he could have used the word "oasis" in connection with what she was seeing.

At least a hundred boxlike structures, of the same rusty brown shade as the land, encircled a green, bubbling mass that could have been a cross between quicksand and nuclear waste. Had she not been looking closely, the various-sized buildings might have been thoroughly camouflaged. Here and there along the otherwise barren landscape, clusters of tall straight sticks jutted upward, making Cherry think of stands of bamboo trees that had lost all their leaves.

About a quarter mile from the buildings, however, was an even stranger sight: space ships in a variety of shapes were lined up in rows like some futuristic parking lot.

"You've got to be kidding!" Cherry exclaimed to Gallant as they touched down. "I distinctly remember your saying Zoenid was *a fascinating little planet.* What do you call hell—a tropical resort?"

Gallant stood and came around the panel to where she was seated. "Did you notice the bog as we were coming in?"

With a sarcastic laugh, Cherry rose to her feet. "If you mean that sea of slime, I could hardly miss the only spot of color on the whole planet."

"That *slime* is known as the elixir of life around here. Not only does it provide necessary fluid, it has rejuvenative properties. A few glasses of the stuff takes years off a person's life, heals the sick, and mends the wounded."

"If that's true, why hasn't anyone bottled the stuff and marketed it?"

"Because it only works after it's been drawn out through the tube plants, and those plants can't survive anywhere but here. And before you ask, the place isn't overrun by youth-seeking tourists because the residents value their privacy and keep it a secret. There are dozens of oases in the quartersphere, but this is the only one where I'm assured someone will recognize me."

"You *want* to be recognized?"

He shrugged. "It would help. Strangers aren't exactly welcomed with open arms in places like this."

Cherry didn't care for the sound of that. She still wasn't certain Gallant would keep his promise to return her to Earth any time soon. Since she learned he was a cheat as well as a liar, the odds against his keeping that promise had gone up drastically. If the natives were hostile, catching another ride home would be next to impossible. Until she had a better handle on her situation, she decided to play along with him as if she didn't know he had won her promise to cooperate under false pretenses.

"Where are these privacy-loving residents?" Cherry asked when she realized no one had investigated their arrival.

"Inside the shelters, probably just waking up. The sun here is too brutal during the day for anyone to move about. It will be dusk any minute now, and then we'll go have a look around."

"Don't you think it's about time to tell me about this acting gig you want me to do?"

Mar cleared his throat and Gallant threw him a warning look before saying to Cherry, "Yes, it is. If you would come to my room with me, we'll leave Mar-Dot to complete the landing check and secure the ship."

Cherry had been doing a fine job of not thinking about him or his incredible body, but being closeted in that cramped room with nowhere to sit but his bunk had her traitorous pulse picking up speed again. She remained standing with her arms crossed beneath her breasts. "Shoot." Apparently one glance at his bed convinced him to stay rigidly upright as well.

"The first thing you need to know is that just about every being out there has come here to hide from something—usually the law. Some of them would incinerate you just for looking them in the eye. Others might not be murderers, but they're still capable of doing you harm. An attractive, humanoid female has a number of uses in a place like this."

"You're making this planet sound more delightful by the minute," she said with a sneer.

"I only wanted to warn you in case you had the urge to befriend someone out there. You have nothing to worry about . . . as long as you stay with me."

Cherry cocked her head at him. "If everyone's so hostile, how can you be sure they'll put up with you?"

He paused and rubbed his chin. "As I said before, I should be recognized."

"And accepted as one of them?" she asked warily.

"In a manner of speaking."

She had thought he looked dangerous, but she hadn't considered the fact that he might have a criminal background. What had Dot told her? *Compared to Frezlo, the captain was a good guy.* The key words now seemed to be "compared to Frezlo." Cherry's need to pace was building, but there was no place to go.

"You look worried," Gallant noted with concern. "Don't be. I'll protect you."

But who will protect me from you? Cherry was tempted to ask, but held her tongue. "What do I have to do?"

"Nothing . . . except to let yourself be seen with me. Although one of the ships out there looks like Frezlo's, I'm not positive it is. I have no way of knowing if he's at this camp or another. Questions about someone's whereabouts aren't tolerated any more than snooping around the shelters. I need Frezlo to come to me."

"What if he's not here?"

"If I offer the right . . . incentive, he'll hear about it wherever he is."

Cherry's puzzle logic clicked into gear. "Incentive? Like something you have that he might want?" His mouth shifted from side to side and comprehension hit her. *"Me?"*

"It won't—"

"You son-of-a-bitch!" She crossed the room in a flash and delivered a solid punch to his gut. Wincing, he backed up to the door. "You planned to use me as bait all along, didn't you?"

"That's not true."

"You wouldn't know the truth if it walked up and introduced itself to you!"

It looked as though she was preparing to strike him again, so he grasped her wrists and secured them against his chest.

She started to pull away, but a sudden tingling in her robotic hand where it was pressed against him distracted her enough to keep her from moving.

"I did *not* intend to use you . . . until after Mar-Dot touched your mind and came up empty. I couldn't think of anything more effective to lure Frezlo than to let him find out the Weebort had told you something important before he died."

"I don't believe you." She could tell he was getting angry and she didn't care. It was all she could do to ignore the peculiar sensation of warmth creeping up her right arm. "Tell me, were you including beast bait as one of the *uses* a female might have around here? I bet, with a little effort, I could find someone with a use for me that wouldn't put my life at risk."

He inhaled sharply. "You want the truth, Cherry? *This* is the truth." In a heartbeat, his hands moved to brace her head and his mouth came down on hers.

As before, there was no warning, no build-up to the explosion of passion. He was instantly devouring her and she was driven by an urgent hunger of her own.

They dove headlong into an age-old struggle of need and dominance, with neither combatant willing to be the first to surrender, yet both desperate to do just that.

It was wrong and right at the same time. She was furious with him, and she wanted this devastating kiss to go on forever.

But recalling how unsatisfactorily their last bout had ended gave Cherry the willpower to retreat a bit. Perhaps he had been thinking the same thing, because his attempt to draw her back was easily discouraged.

He retained a firm grip on her shoulders to prevent her from moving further away while he caught his breath. After a moment, he spoke in a raspy voice. "I will admit that I intended to use you as bait for the last couple days, but believe this—I'm the *only* one on this godforsaken planet that's going to use you . . . for anything."

With her own breathing barely under control, she simply stared up at him. For once, she had no doubt he had spoken the truth. For better or worse, he had appointed himself her protector, and for the time being, she was dependent upon him.

Slowly, he released her, but another few seconds passed before she moved away and shook the tingling out of her arm. She wasn't sure what happened to her each time they came into physical contact, but she definitely noticed that it was the only time her arm acted up. Whatever *it* was, neither one of them seemed anxious to talk about it, but sooner or later, she was going to discover more about the phenomenal chemistry between them.

Taking another step back from him, she reminded

him of why they were in his room. "You said I needed to do a little acting. What role am I supposed to be playing?"

The question returned Gallant the rest of the way to sanity. He rubbed his chin as he tried to come up with a way to ease into what she had to do. After her offhand threat to seek someone else's protection he really had no choice but to follow through with his original idea . . . for her sake as much as his own. But he knew she wasn't apt to be complacent about it.

He walked over to a storage cabinet in the wall and said, "I've tried to give you a fair picture of the kind of beings that inhabit this area. If there was any way I could draw Frezlo to me without your help—"

"You're repeating yourself, Captain. Get to the point."

He opened the cabinet door and took out her peasant girl costume. "I held on to this. You need to look the way you did when Frezlo saw you last."

"And what if I say I've changed my mind about helping you?"

He raised his eyebrow. "I thought you were in a rush to get back to Innerworld. If you refuse to play along, it could take weeks to ferret out Frezlo. And then there's the little matter of our wager. You lost, remember?"

She opened her mouth to protest that he'd cheated to win that game, then resealed her lips. If she told him that, she'd be giving away her only chance to get back at him later on . . . *if* she was still dependent on him to get home.

Despite Gallant's numerous deceits, Dot had convinced Cherry of the seriousness of his mission and genuine need of her assistance. Besides, she could see the logic involved in using her to speed things up. "Okay. Give me the damn costume."

He waited patiently for her to don the sackcloth gown over her jumpsuit and arrange the braided, blond wig on her head. "Good. Now there's just one more item to add."

She watched him remove something else from the same cabinet, but as he turned around to her, he managed to keep it behind his back.

"Understand, this is the only way I can positively insure your safety."

Cherry groaned. "Spit it out already!"

"First, close your eyes."

"Absolutely not. Whatever you've got planned, I want to see it coming."

He frowned with the knowledge that he hadn't yet earned her trust. "All right, but at least stand still for five seconds."

She gave him three, but it was all he needed to get the collar around her neck and lock it.

"What in the—" Her fingers quickly examined then tugged at the circle of heavy metal links. She had played a slave girl often enough to recognize the collar by feel, but those she'd worn for fantasy reenactments had an escape catch. This one was missing that feature. Before anxiety had a chance to set in completely, Gallant was explaining.

"I swear I'll take it off as soon as I've got you safely back on board."

"Does it ever occur to you to tell the truth to begin with, or do you just naturally have to be underhanded about everything?"

"I beg your pardon?"

"Why don't you try explaining things to me instead of always tricking me into them? I'm an intelligent person. If you ask me to do something, and it makes good sense, I'll do it willingly. Your way only makes me angry, and I'm much more cooperative when I'm not angry."

He let her words sink in before responding. "You have a valid point. My only excuse is that I'm not accustomed to dealing with cooperative people and deception is often the only way I get a job done. From now on, I promise to try to explain things to you first."

She studied him for a moment and decided that a promise to *try* was probably the best concession she would get from him. "Begin by explaining why I have to wear this collar."

Looking somewhat contrite, he said, "It's for your protection. The only way I can be sure you'll remain unmolested out there is if everyone's convinced you're my property."

"Hmmph. You make it sound like all the dangerous characters are so afraid of you that they wouldn't dare mess with what's yours."

"Let's say, I have managed to establish a certain reputation among this element."

She considered asking him to elaborate, but decided she was better off not knowing exactly what he had done to earn that reputation. There were already too many risks involved for her peace of mind. However, her conclusion was that it would all be worth it if it got her home faster. "Okay. I'll pretend I'm your slave. But don't push the master business too far or you'll regret it."

With a loud click, he snapped a chain leash to the back of the collar. On the other end of the leash was a manacle that he clamped over his left wrist. "I'll do my best not to take advantage."

Cherry wondered how he managed to say that with a straight face. Those two white stripes in his hair looked more like devil's horns every day!

As politely as if they were going out on a date, he asked, "Shall we go? I'm sure the sun is down by now."

Lifting a section of chain to take the strain off her neck, Cherry grimaced and gave him a nod of readiness . . . for whatever he was dragging her into.

Mar and Dot both wished them luck, although Dot sounded considerably less enthusiastic.

Gallant opened the hatch and a wave of oppressive heat lapped over Cherry. As she waited for the stairs to telescope their way down to the ground, she noted the red haze on the horizon where the sun had recently set. She couldn't begin to imagine how hot it must be during full sunlight.

"Go down slowly," Gallant instructed her. "I'll be close behind. But after that, be careful to stay a step or two behind me . . . and keep your eyes downcast whatever you do."

She turned and clucked her tongue at him when she reached the ground. "You don't have to tell me how to play a slave girl. I've done it thousands of times. Being lord and master over a helpless woman is apparently a universal male fantasy. *But*"—she wagged her finger at him—"like I told you before, don't get carried away with your role."

Instead of looking threatened, he winked at her. "I promise to whip you only if it becomes absolutely necessary to prove my manhood to the locals."

"Very funny! Can we just get this over with, please?" She readjusted the collar and lifted the chain a little higher. "This rig isn't getting any lighter."

Gallant frowned and gently touched her neck. "Your skin's already rubbed pink. I'm sorry. I didn't think about that. Let's go back and put some kind of padding inside."

He started to go up the stairs again, but she gave the chain a yank. When he almost fell, she laughed out loud. "How about that? This thing works both ways. Forget the padding. A heartless master would hardly think of such a kindness. Anyway, what's a little irritation if I can help save the universe?" The concerned expression on his face was so sincere that she knew she had just gotten another glimpse of the real Gallant Voyager. That confirmation of his secretly sensitive nature went a long way toward relaxing her. "Come on, before someone besides me figures out your wicked reputation is mostly hype."

The rust-colored ground beneath her feet was hard as marble and had cracks large enough to trip in. She was having to be so careful about where she was walking she didn't notice the gruesome display at the edge of the camp until she was right next to it. Staked out on the ground were two skeletons.

"A not-so-subtle warning to unwelcome visitors," Gallant told her. "If an offender is lucky, he'll get put out here in the middle of the day. That way, he only lasts about two or three hours before he's completely dehydrated, and he's not alive to see the ugly little creatures that come crawling around after dark to clean his bones."

Cherry shivered, both from the image his words created and the noticeable change in the temperature. The red haze was gone now, and it was getting darker by the minute. Gallant paused when they reached the inner circle of the windowless buildings, and Cherry cautiously halted a bit behind him, in case anyone was watching.

Picture signs hung above the front doors of several of the nearby structures. While she couldn't identify all the symbols on the signs, a few were generic enough for her to understand, such as the one with the depiction of two animals mating.

Gallant led her to a building with three different-shaped drinking glasses on its sign—obviously the neighborhood tavern.

Inside, it was cool and dimly lit, but Cherry's eyes soon adjusted. With the simple wooden bar and roomful of scarred tables and chairs, it could have been a tavern in any small town in the United States . . . except for the bartender and the four patrons sitting in the far corner.

If she didn't know better, she might have guessed that they were dressed up for Halloween. The bartender made Cherry think of an octopus. Eight tentaclelike appendages extended out in a circle from the upper body, and an oversized head had two bulbous eyes protruding from opposite sides. She thought those characteristics could certainly come in handy for a bartender.

As Gallant sauntered toward the bar with her in tow, Cherry took another peek at the group in the corner. They were more humanoid in structure than the bartender, and seemed vaguely familiar to her. With their skinny, elongated arms and legs, and slanted, black, almond-shaped eyes, they looked like the drawings of aliens that used to be shown on American television programs about UFO's. It was too bad she could never tell anyone they really existed. Then she remembered the stories of abductions and experiments and knew those creatures weren't as harmless as they appeared.

"Stars above, it's Gallant Voyager!" the bartender exclaimed in a very feminine voice.

Cherry wondered if the bartender was truly a female or if the translator she was wearing beneath the slave collar merely interpreted the voice that way. Her curiosity was settled a moment later when a tentacle whipped out, wrapped around Gallant's neck and pulled him close enough for her to plant a loud kiss on his mouth. Cherry had to fight the urge to wipe her own lips after the creature released him.

"It's been a while, Kip," Gallant said with a broad smile.

"I've missed you, handsome. Where have you been?"

"You name it, I've been there."

"And picked yourself up a pet, I see. For some reason, I thought you had an objection to slavery." A tentacle uncurled and tipped up Cherry's chin.

Cherry let herself be inspected without meeting the bartender's gaze.

Gallant smirked. "I won her in a game of cubit and only found out how untrained she was after her former master took off."

"Where did you get her?"

"Innerworld, Earth," Gallant stated in a slightly raised voice.

"She's a Noronian?"

"Terran," Gallant said a bit louder.

Suddenly the murmurs from the back of the room ceased, and Cherry knew without looking that they now had the undivided attention of that group.

Kip gracefully recoiled the tentacle. "If you want to get rid of her, I'm sure the Finites over there would pay you a fair price. You know how they love their Terran specimens."

Gallant nodded. "That's a thought. I'll let you know if I decide to let her go, and you can handle the negotiations. For now, how about setting us both up with refreshers?"

Cherry kept telling herself he was only acting, but the way the four Finites were staring at her made her very uneasy. She inched closer to Gallant.

Kip set two tall glasses of bubbling green sludge on the bar and waved for them to drink up. Gallant picked up one glass, toasted Kip, and handed Cherry the other. She could barely conceal her disgust as he took a long swallow and signaled for her to do the same. She held her breath and took a sip. Though she had never actually tasted nuclear waste, she was certain it was similar to this.

"Drink more than that, woman," Kip ordered. "It's the only thing that will help your body tolerate the lack of moisture on this planet."

Cherry stared into the gurgling slime, then gave Gallant a pleading look.

"Try holding your nose and gulping it all down at once," he said without sympathy.

Even the small amount she had drunk seemed to be eroding her esophagus. When he made a move to hold her nose for her, she pushed his hand aside and forced herself to take three large swallows. Gingerly, she placed the glass back on the bar while she concentrated on not gagging.

"She does tell a good bedtime story though," Gallant declared as if it just occurred to him that she had some value.

"Oh?"

He took another drink that almost emptied his glass. "Yes, indeed. You know Frezlo, don't you?" Kip nodded. "She claims she saw him incinerate a Weebort trader in Innerworld, in front of a dozen witnesses, then casually walk away."

"Frezlo's been known to do that, depending on the urgency of the situation."

Gallant leaned forward as if to confide a vital secret. "*But,* she says the Weebort told her something important right before he died. Now, you and I both know, if that was true, Frezlo would have eliminated her as well."

Cherry knew that was the bait he had come here to dangle, and the way Kip was now eyeing her said the story had captured her attention. She only hoped Kip could get the message to Frezlo quickly . . . before she exploded with nervous energy, or died from that vile drink.

As more customers came in, Kip was kept busy serving and gossiping. A few recognized Gallant and greeted him, but none were as friendly as Kip. Most of them were humanoids, and Cherry tried not to stare at those that weren't, but one patron caught her gaze from across the room and she couldn't make herself look away. Her instincts told her it was a male, and the lizard skin identified him as reptilian even before she saw his yellow, snakelike eyes.

He came toward her in a smooth movement that made him appear to be gliding on air. A peculiar heaviness began seeping into her limbs as he drew closer, and her first thought was that the drink was causing the lethargic sensation. But it was the way she was unable to separate her gaze from the reptile's that worried her enough to nudge Gallant.

A split second later, Gallant slapped her face so hard she staggered backward.

Chapter 7

Without considering the consequences, she raised her robotic arm and swung at him, but he easily dodged the blow. The sound of a roomful of male laughter brought her to her senses before she attacked again.

Quickly shortening the length of chain between them, Gallant whispered, "Get down," then made it look like he was forcing her to her knees at his feet. "I told you to keep your eyes lowered." In a more audible voice, he demanded, "Beg forgiveness, woman."

Her cheek was hot where he had struck it, and she was seething with fury. Until she looked directly at him. He had turned his back on their audience so that they couldn't see the regretful look in his eye, or the way his mouth silently formed the word, *Please.*

She glared at him for another second, sending back her own silent message. If they ever got out of here, she was going to make him pay through the nose. "I forgot. I'm sorry," she mumbled through clenched teeth.

A grumble rippled through the room, and Gallant

jerked the chain up. "I didn't hear you, woman. Louder."

Cherry inhaled sharply, but another nasty grumble stopped her from voicing her real thoughts. "I'm sorry," she said aloud, then added "master," for effect.

"Then you may rise," Gallant said nobly and turned back to the small crowd that had gathered behind him.

The reptile-man glided forward. "You're no fun at all, Voyager. A few seconds more and I would have had her."

"To be precise, you would have stolen my property, and I would have had to kill you. She's mine, Sinbar, and in spite of her lack of manners, I intend to keep her . . . for a while."

Sinbar seemed unaffected by the threat to his life, but it instantly froze everyone else in the tavern. "I'll buy her. Name your price." The last word ended in a prolonged hiss.

"Now why would you possibly want her?" Gallant asked suspiciously.

Sinbar shrugged his narrow shoulders. "She seems . . . amusing."

"How odd. I thought the only thing that amused you was increasing your wealth. What value could a Terran female have to you?"

The snake eyes narrowed to yellow slits. "Do you wish to name a price or not?"

Cherry kept her eyes averted as she followed the haggling back and forth. Several deductions gradually made themselves clear. Sinbar must have heard the rumor Gallant had started about her and figured he could make a profit by buying Cherry and reselling her to Frezlo. Therefore, he probably knew how to contact Frezlo.

Also, based on the reptile's comments, Cherry was certain she hadn't merely imagined that she couldn't pull her gaze from his. It must have been some sort of hypnosis, and Gallant's slap efficiently broke the connection moments before Sinbar "had her." But it was hard to feel grateful to Gallant while her cheek still burned.

After several offers were made and rejected, Sinbar made a series of hissing sounds and slithered out of the tavern. Although the rest of the clientele soon found other means of entertaining themselves, the Finites continued to ogle Cherry until Gallant led her to a table in the opposite corner from them.

She was ready to give him a piece of her mind as soon as they had a measure of privacy, but the moment they sat down, a pleasant-looking man with dark red hair approached them and clapped Gallant on the back.

"Ho, Gallant! I was over at Camp Three when I heard someone mention your name over the transmitter. Had to come see for myself. How the *drek* are you?"

Rather than return the friendly greeting, Gallant's voice was razor-edged. "Alive and well, Dutch. I see some things never change. News travels as fast as ever around here."

"It's still a small sector." He looked around for another chair, but none was available. "Stand up, sweetheart," he said to Cherry with a friendly laugh. "You and I can share that seat and get better acquainted at the same time."

Gallant clearly lacked an appreciation for Dutch's good humor. Sternly, he ordered Cherry, "Come over here."

She rose and moved to his side, but when he tried to guide her onto his lap, she balked.

"Do you need another lesson in good manners?" he asked in a threatening tone.

Sending him another visual promise in retribution, she sat down stiffly across his hard thighs, shifted more to the front, then rearranged her legs in between his so that she was perched on only one of his thighs. When she started to move again he wrapped his arm around her waist and braced her tightly against him.

"Enough!" he growled dangerously.

Even through the cumbersome sackcloth, she could feel the reason he wanted her to stop squirming. It was a shame their safety depended on him having his wits in order, or she could have exacted a fair amount of retribution right then and there. Just to let him know she was thinking about it though, she wiggled her bottom one more time before settling into the possessive hold he had on her.

Chuckling, Dutch sat down in the vacated chair and called out an order to Kip. All the while, he had been openly regarding Cherry, particularly noting the slave collar and leash. "I heard it, but I didn't believe it. Not only does Gallant Voyager have a female slave, but a human one at that. If I'm not mistaken, there's a pretty woman under that get-up. What's your name, sweetheart?"

Because of his friendly tone, Cherry's gaze automatically raised to his. She was about to answer when there was an imperceptible tug on her chin. She didn't know if it was because Dutch presented a danger she didn't sense, or if Gallant just wanted to keep her from making a friend. For the time being, she deferred to Gallant's implied order by shyly lowering her eyes and letting him answer for her.

"Slaves don't have names, Dutch." With sarcasm dripping from his words, he added, "Remember, you're the one who taught me that."

Cherry was curious to hear more, but Dutch only shrugged and switched subjects.

"So, what brings you here, Gallant?"

"Apparently a few things *have* changed since I was here last. Used to be a man's business was his own."

Dutch held up a hand. "Ho, no offense meant. Just making conversation."

But conversation came to an abrupt end throughout the tavern seconds later. Glancing furtively around, Cherry noticed that all eyes had turned to see the imposing figure that had just entered the building.

Frezlo!

Over seven feet of hairy, pig-faced beast surveyed the room before turning his beady eyes on her. With a loud grunt, he lumbered toward their table.

Cherry saw Dutch settle back in his chair with an expectant sparkle in his light blue eyes. Instantly she was certain that he had been aware that Frezlo was on his way and had come to the tavern for the sole reason of observing the fireworks. Some friend he was! In spite of the way Gallant had been treating him like an enemy, she had been starting to consider Dutch as a possible backup ticket home. Apparently, he was even less trustworthy than Gallant.

From the way everyone else was watching them, she also knew Dutch wasn't the only one anticipating a good show.

As soon as Frezlo reached their table, he pointed his metal finger at Cherry and grunted again. Remembering what that finger had done to the Weebort had her burrowing further into Gallant's protective embrace.

Giving her a reassuring squeeze, he said to the beast, "Our translators don't interpret grunt, Frezlo. You know that. Speak words, or go visit someone else."

The nostrils of his snout flared with annoyance, but he complied. "Frezlo . . . want . . . her."

"Really?" Gallant managed to sound surprised. "First the Finites, then Sinbar, and now you. The value of Terran females must have gone up quite a bit since I won this one." He leaned back and scrutinized Cherry's features as if he may have missed something that everyone else saw.

"You . . . won . . . her? How?"

"Hmmm?" Gallant returned his attention to Frezlo. "Oh, yes. It was a friendly game of cubit. I didn't realize I had made out so well."

"Frezlo . . . play . . . Voyager . . . now." He grunted

at Dutch, who gladly relinquished his chair and joined the eager bystanders hovering nearby.

Cherry could feel the tension building in Gallant's body, but none of it was outwardly evident. Taking her cue from his attitude, she forced herself to change her posture from cowering to lounging comfortably against him.

The instant she relaxed, he pretended to be kissing her ear as he whispered, "Good girl. Now play along with me." He lightly ran his fingers up and down her arm, and she didn't need to fake the giggle that escaped her throat.

Frezlo pounded a fist on the table. *"Play!"*

Gallant slid his hand down to Cherry's hip and kneaded it as he spoke. "I don't know, Frezlo. All this sudden interest in my new slave had me thinking about returning to the privacy of my ship."

Cherry put her arms around his neck and whispered against his ear, "I'm probably going to have to kill you when this is all over."

His laughter implied that she had told him something extremely naughty. "All right, Frezlo. It seems the woman enjoys watching the game. And for what she just promised, it will be worth entertaining her a little." Gallant named a reasonable monetary stake to start and Frezlo grunted his agreement.

"Kip!" Gallant called, and the bystanders automatically opened a path between him and the bar. "Three refreshers and the house cubes, please."

Gallant continued to stroke and caress Cherry throughout the first match. Molded into his lap as she was, she alone knew that he wasn't anywhere near as distracted by her as he was pretending to be. If he wasn't driving her so crazy with his seductive touches, she might have congratulated him on his control as well as his superb acting ability.

Somehow, in spite of his limited attention, Gallant won three games in a row for a quick match. In the second match, Frezlo narrowly took one game before Gallant beat him again. When Frezlo stupidly lost the third match also, Cherry decided he was either the worst player in the galaxy or he was throwing the game on purpose. The latter possibility became stronger when he demanded they increase the stakes to make the game more interesting.

"Frezlo . . . want . . . her. What . . . Voyager . . . want?"

Forcing himself to ignore Cherry's wide-eyed panic, Gallant rubbed his chin and glanced around at the interested faces in the room to give himself time to prepare. He knew Frezlo was more cunning than he appeared. The minute Gallant named the forfeit he wanted, Frezlo could figure out that a trap had been set for him. Gallant also knew, however, that Frezlo was a true gambler, and if he did agree to pay a particular forfeit, he would never renege on it any more than Gallant would. The only thing to do was lay the wager on the table and see if it was accepted.

"Seeing as how I've won all three matches so far, I don't suppose there's much chance of my losing tonight." He waved for Dutch to come closer, then asked Frezlo, "Do you accept Dutch as the official witness?" Frezlo grunted. "Fine. One five-game match. If you win, the woman is yours." He had to tighten his grip on Cherry to prevent her from bolting. There was no way to let her know she had nothing to fear. "If I win"—he paused again to make sure he had both Frezlo's and Dutch's full attention—"if I win, you tell me who hired you to eliminate the Weebort trader in Innerworld."

"Client . . . information . . . secret."

Gallant shrugged. "No one will hear your answer but me."

Frezlo snorted. "Why . . . want?"

"Personal reasons. He did me a favor once. Is it a bet or not?"

"Bet," Frezlo declared with a nod and tossed the cubes to begin the first game.

Each quad rolled brought a fresh round of murmurs as side bets were made and renegotiated.

Gallant had hoped to win honestly; a cheat on Zoenid was swiftly rewarded with a special place in the sun, but by the end of the fourth game, he and Frezlo had each won two. He told himself he couldn't afford to lose the opportunity to get information from Frezlo, but in a corner of his mind he admitted that it was Cherry's safety for which he was going to risk cheating.

"Stand up, woman. My leg's gone to sleep." Ever since he agreed to make her a forfeit, she had barely moved a muscle. Like an automaton, she let him guide her to stand behind his right shoulder so that he could keep her in his peripheral vision. As an extra precaution, he placed her hands on that shoulder. Instantly she gripped him so hard, he winced.

"Play!" Frezlo repeated when Gallant took another second to move Cherry's robotic hand back to her side.

Gallant picked up the cubes and threw his initial try of the tiebreaker game with every confidence that he would be relieving Cherry's fears in a matter of minutes. It would have been convenient if he had managed to get a quad, but when his third toss resulted in nothing more than two pairs, he knew what he had to do.

As Frezlo took his turn, Gallant casually ran his hands down the front of his vest. Then, even more slowly, he curled his fingers inside the edges and slid them back up again.

Nothing! There were no hard little bulges in the lining; no special set of cubes to exchange for the honest ones. He felt Cherry's fingers digging into his shoulder, but the shock of the missing cubes kept him from immediately responding to her signal. When he did, the look on her face said it all. Numb fear had been replaced by panic . . . and *guilt*.

A memory of her in the facility chamber, looking like she was up to mischief, flashed in his mind, and he instantly knew what had happened to his cubes. His return look of total exasperation was equally readable. Now he had no choice but to play an honest game and hope his luck held.

He knew he had been hustled as soon as Frezlo's run of foolish mistakes and bad choices came to an abrupt end. Now the beast played a careful game, as if he had miraculously begun to comprehend the odds. With each quad Frezlo accumulated, Cherry's fingernails dug a little further into Gallant's flesh, but he was so tense, he hardly felt it.

The first two games in the match went to Frezlo, and the bystanders were no longer keeping their voices hushed. It sounded as though the betting was fairly even, and Gallant's supporters were growing restless. From what bets he had heard, he knew some of them stood to lose a considerable amount if he didn't win, but he could only worry about one thing at a time.

His luck seemed to have changed in the third game, when he made two of the needed six quads on initial tries. At least the angry threats from the audience quieted back down enough for him to temporarily scratch them off his list of problems. He took the game six to two, which helped restore his confidence, but Cherry's grip on his shoulder didn't ease up in the slightest.

The next game progressed so swiftly and so disastrously, Gallant was certain Frezlo had used cheats. Although he had been watching closely, he hadn't seen the beast make any suspicious moves, so he couldn't prove anything. By the time Frezlo was ahead five to zero by rolling four quads in a row, the observers were also beginning to question his good luck, but no one was willing to come forward to make a formal accusation.

Gallant achieved a quad on his next turn, but it didn't go far to relieve the tension building throughout the room. At least with suspicions aroused about Frezlo's honesty, some of the heat would be taken off Gallant if he lost. That was hardly a consolation though, when any second he could be forced to turn Cherry over to a giant, pig-faced hairball with incineration on his mind.

While Frezlo picked up the cubes for what could be the final round, the room grew silent. Gallant heard Cherry take a deep breath and hold it as the cubes rolled to a stop.

Two greens, an orange, and a yellow.

Frezlo's hand hovered over the orange, then moved to the greens, then back again to the orange. If Gallant's outward show of emotionlessness wasn't so well practiced, he might have been pounding on the table like the beast had. But such a display would be out of character for him, so he forced himself to lean back and fold his hands over his stomach as if he had no particular interest in the outcome of this game.

Finally Frezlo scooped up the orange and yellow and dropped them again.

One blue. One more green.

Gallant could feel Cherry's body vibrating against his back. She was still gripping his shoulder, but now she was using it as a crutch. If only he had gained a little of her trust, she would not have to be so frightened. Then she would know he would never allow Frezlo to harm her, even if it meant having to use his secret.

Considering that, he knew he could not do it here, in front of so many. Not only might it possibly blow his carefully created cover forever, he had no way of knowing if every one of the species in the tavern would be affected in the same way. Before he could think through a solution, Frezlo rerolled the blue.

Cherry sent that little cube the most positive thoughts she could conjure up—orange, red, purple—anything but green. But her message didn't get through. The damn thing came up green. And her heart pounded even harder.

Frezlo's triumphant roar was nothing compared to the overjoyed shouts of the bystanders who had won and the furious shrieks of those who had lost.

If she wasn't absolutely positive Gallant was her only chance of getting out of this in one piece, she'd throttle him where he sat.

"Woman . . . mine," Frezlo declared unnecessarily.

Cherry took a step backward and bumped into a wall of men who had come up behind her. One glance at Dutch confirmed that he was going to make sure Gallant lived up to his part of the bet, with no concern for what it meant to her.

Gallant stood, removed a small hook from the waistband of his pants, and unlatched the manacle on his wrist. "Looks like your luck turned around, Frezlo. Almost unbelievably, I'd say, but the woman's yours now. Kind of a shame. I hadn't quite gotten tired of her yet. Maybe you'd consider leasing her to me for another day or two before I take off."

"*No*! Want . . . her . . . now."

"Fine," Gallant said with a negligent shrug. "I'm sure there's a pleasure female down the way that I can use for tonight." He tossed the manacle and hook to Frezlo. "She's still a little rebellious; I didn't have time to finish training her. Though I don't suppose you intend to keep her long yourself. I would suggest you use her at least once before doing away with her though. I think you'd find her very. . . . What had Sinbar called her? Oh, yes. He said she was *amusing*."

Cherry's sandaled foot connected with Gallant's shin the next instant, but all she accomplished was setting off a round of laughter.

Gallant shook his head as he eased himself out of the reach of any of Cherry's limbs. "As you can see, she's still a bit wild, but she's your problem from here on. As for me, having her hot bottom squirming against my privates the last couple of hours has left me with a problem I think I'll have taken care of right away." He gave Frezlo a farewell salute, turned on his heel and walked out of the tavern without sparing Cherry a glance.

She was furious and terrified, and might have burst into tears if she wasn't certain it would only entertain the heathens that much more. She didn't know precisely what she had expected Gallant to do, but it sure wasn't walking out like that. She had heard the grumbling of the losers and realized if Gallant had hung around much longer, they might have decided to retrieve some of their losses out of his hide. At the moment, she'd be glad to help them do just that!

The sound of the manacle clicking shut drew her attention away from the door. Always a pragmatist, she knew when to face facts. Gallant wasn't going to rescue her, and Frezlo intended to kill her . . . or use her then kill her. Neither alternative was desirable, but at least the latter would give her a bit more time to attempt an escape back to Gallant's ship . . . or prepare for her death.

She stared at Frezlo as he rose from the chair and realized that, based on his overall size, he could probably accomplish using her *and* killing her at the same time. He jerked the chain and she had to follow, or be dragged by the collar, in which case she stood a chance of strangling *before* he incinerated her. Her list of choices were increasing by the minute.

Her robotic arm was powerful, but she didn't like to use it in a situation where violence could be turned against her, and there was no one present with whom she could seek refuge even if she did manage to break away from Frezlo. Just in case an opportunity to escape arose, however, she noted where he had slipped the hook for the manacle.

Encouraging suggestions and wolf-whistles accompanied their departure from the tavern. As she had surmised years ago, males tended to behave like males, regardless of their planet of origin. They passed the building with the mating animals sign, and she couldn't help but wonder what sort of creature was helping Gallant with the problem he claimed she caused.

He had made it clear that he didn't want to use her for sex, but he had also sworn that no one else would use her for anything. There was no reason his breaking another promise should surprise her, except that she had been so sure he wasn't lying when he said he would keep her safe.

Frezlo came to a stop in front of a door and pushed it open. The illuminated symbol above the entranceway meant nothing to Cherry, but the only furnishing inside the small, one-room building was a large bed, and on that, a satchel. This, she deduced, must be the luxury suite of Hotel Zeonid.

If Frezlo had meant to kill her right away, he could have done that outside, where she wouldn't have gotten ashes all over his room. And since she no longer seemed to be in danger of strangling, that only left the *other* alternative.

As he pulled her over toward the satchel, she prepared herself to attempt a karate chop on the back of his thick neck the moment he took his eyes off her. To her disappointment, he reached into the bag without letting her out of his sight. Her curiosity about what he was searching for took precedence over all else. She doubted that it was a weapon, since his death ray seemed to be permanently affixed to his index finger.

Frezlo stood up again and held the object out to her. There was just enough light in the room for her to make out that it was the largest hairbrush she had ever seen. He grunted and she took it from him.

Keeping a grasp on her chain, he then unlocked the manacle on his wrist, removed his tunic, and replaced the manacle.

Her gaze quickly scanned his huge, hairy form. Although he was technically naked, she couldn't see anything that could be construed as a sex organ, but she didn't want to make any snap judgments.

Pointing at the hairbrush, he grunted at her again.

The only thing she could think was that he wanted her to brush her hair, but when she put it to the bangs of her wig, he stopped her.

"No . . . do . . . me . . . first."

Cherry's eyes widened. "You want me to brush you? Is that it?" A softer grunt was her answer. She smiled in spite of the repulsion she felt at the idea of having to touch him. This was far easier to handle than anything else her imagination had been conjuring up. With the brush poised in midair, she tried to decide where to start.

Making a low groaning sound, Frezlo pointed to the brush, then pointed to his feet, his calves, and his thighs. After that he patted each arm, his back, and his chest.

"Oh! I get it. There's a special routine to this, huh? Okay, I can play hairdresser for you. Let's see, are there any problems I should know about? Split ends maybe? I can recommend an excellent conditioner that would get rid of all these nasty tangles at the same time."

"Do!" he ordered and pressed his hand on her head until she sat on the floor.

Brushing Frezlo's hair was much harder than Cherry expected it to be. Not only was it extremely coarse, bits of debris were caught in tangles that the metal bristles of the brush couldn't get through. The first time she separated a tangle by hand and removed a burr, Frezlo actually sighed. Or at least that's what Cherry thought it sounded like.

She couldn't help but think of how much she was going to enjoy telling this story to Aster, and realized she didn't believe for one second that she was about to die.

By the time she finished the two tree trunks he used as legs, she had received quite a few sighs and something she thought might be an appreciative moan, for a beast. It occurred to her that she was grooming him the way monkeys do for each other. She just hoped he didn't expect her to eat any little bugs she might find while she was *doing* him.

She had just moved on to one of his arms when the door burst open. Before he could raise his lethal finger, Cherry clamped her robotic fingers around his wrist and held it down to keep him from incinerating any possible rescuer.

Frezlo's other arm came up to swat her away at the same time as Gallant stepped into the doorway and pointed a small black box at him.

"Hold it right there, Frezlo. I only want to talk, but I'll fire if you lay a hand on her. Woman, you hold on to that arm for a few more seconds while I try to negotiate a deal with your master."

Frezlo snarled at Cherry, but the weapon in Gallant's hand seemed to intimidate him enough to make him stand still. Cherry's attention was drawn to something even more interesting.

Gallant was not wearing his eye patch.

Chapter 8

"Voyager . . . lose," Frezlo said. "No . . . renege."

"Aah, but a gambler's forfeit is reversed if the winner cheated."

Cherry felt the beast's arm twitch and applied a bit more pressure.

"Prove . . . accusation."

Gallant shook his head. "If I figured out how you did it—and I think I would if I examined that tunic of yours—I'd have to turn you over to the crowd in the tavern. And you know how they deal with cheats."

The moment he mentioned the tunic, Frezlo's gaze darted to it, and Cherry had no doubt that Gallant had made an accurate guess.

"Want . . . woman?"

"As I said, I hadn't quite gotten tired of her yet. But I also want what you agreed to give me had I won: the name of the person who hired you for the Weebort kill."

One second Cherry thought Frezlo was going to cooperate, the next, he had pulled her in front of him with his free arm crooked around her throat. In spite of the stranglehold, she held on to his wrist.

"This is a waste of time, Frezlo. She's not *that* important to me. Anyway, in the seconds that it would take you to break her neck and shake loose your arm, I'd get a shot off between your eyes."

Cherry wondered what one called a Mexican standoff if one was a billion miles from Mexico.

"I . . . tell . . . name. Keep . . . woman."

Gallant's eyebrows raised a notch. "That good, huh?"

"Best . . . ever. I . . . keep. No . . . kill." To prove his point, he released Cherry and let her move to his side again.

"That's all well and good, but I've got an even better deal for you." He took a step into the room and moved aside. "You give me the woman and the information, or I let my pet have its annual meal a little early."

He whistled and held out his index finger. A high-pitched buzz filled the room, and a fluorescent blue insect about the size of a large mosquito landed on Gallant's finger. In a flash, Frezlo yanked Cherry in front of him again.

"Now, Frezlo," Gallant said in a tone that implied the beast was a child. "You know she can't protect you from a hungry drillfly. And if you think threatening to kill her or me will keep me from releasing this littler bugger, think again. You make one move, of any kind, and I take my thumb off its leg.

"It's well trained, but being this close to its favorite dish is too much temptation. The moment I let it go, it's going to head right for you. And you know how fast it attacks. Where do you think it will enter? Your ear? Your nose? Your mouth?"

If Cherry didn't actually feel the violent trembling of Frezlo's body, she wouldn't have believed it. That little bug had him absolutely terrified.

"Just so you don't feel left out, Cherry, let me explain why Frezlo suddenly has rubber in his knees. A drillfly is the only natural enemy of Frezlo's species. They've tried for centuries to eradicate them, but they never quite succeed, because only one needs to survive to reproduce.

"You see, the drillfly is born pregnant, carrying thousands of eggs. All it needs to do is fly inside a host's head, where it nibbles on brain tissue until the eggs are ready to hatch. Up to that time, the pain is enough to drive the host insane, but once those babies start their feeding frenzy . . . well, I've heard it's a very unpleasant way to die. But don't worry, it doesn't care for the taste of your brain or mine—only Frezlo's."

With each sentence of Gallant's explanation, Frezlo stumbled further back in the room, and Cherry was forced to follow. But Gallant kept coming closer until Frezlo was pressed into the corner.

Holding the insect a few inches from Frezlo's nose, Gallant's voice sounded like a death knell. "Release her."

Frezlo squeaked and looked at his tunic laying on the bed a few feet away. Raw fear had apparently frozen his vocal chords.

"The hook is in the inside of his tunic," Cherry

quickly offered. "He put it in an inside pocket on the left side." Gallant backed up far enough to fetch the tunic, then came back and handed it to Cherry.

"Oh, look what I found," Cherry said as soon as she examined the inside. Besides the hook, there was a set of cheats, just as Gallant had suspected.

Gallant explained to her how to unlock the manacle with the hook and, within seconds, she was free and standing behind him. "My mother always said cheaters only cheat themselves in the end. Now, give me the information." Frezlo opened his mouth, but only another squeak came out. Gallant stepped a few feet away in hopes that a little breathing room would help Frezlo find his voice. "Try again. Who hired you?"

Frezlo was now shaking so uncontrollably, Cherry was certain she could feel the building vibrating around them.

Gallant raised his finger an inch. "Last chance, Frezlo."

The beast opened his mouth again and this time he managed to make the squeak sound like a word. "Conrep."

Gallant lowered his finger and in a doubtful voice repeated, "A Consociation representative?" Frezlo bobbed his big head up and down. "You'd better be telling me the truth." Between the sheer terror in his eyes and the jerky movements of his head, Gallant decided to believe him. "Which one? And why? Why would a Con rep want to silence the Weebort?"

Another head shake seemed to signify that he had

no idea. "Man . . . masked. Saw . . . emblem. I . . . followed."

Gallant interpreted that to mean that Frezlo followed the man who'd hired him once he figured out his employer was someone of importance. He probably planned to blackmail the Con rep after the assassination. "Where did he go?"

"Lore."

Gallant again repeated the word to make sure he had understood. Lore was an unexplored, uninhabitable planet, shrouded in mist and mystery. "Did he land there?" Frezlo nodded shakily. "Did you?" He knew the answer would be negative. No one who landed on Lord was ever heard from again.

"Nice doing business with you, Frezlo." He nudged Cherry toward the door then backed away himself. "Just to make sure you don't have any thoughts of coming after us, I'm going to leave my pet with you while we take off."

Gallant flicked his wrist and the drillfly took off with a flutter of iridescent wings and a loud buzz. The next instant, Frezlo's enormous body was wracked by a seizure, and he crashed to the floor in a hairy heap.

Cherry stood by in shocked silence as Gallant cautiously approached the body. Keeping his stunner pointed at the beast's head, he nudged its side with the toe of his boot. When there was no movement for another few seconds, he knelt and pressed his ear to Frezlo's back. "He's dead."

Cherry marched over to Gallant and shoved his shoulder so hard he tipped backward. "You *animal*!

How dare you kill him after he told you what you wanted to know?"

That insult coming out of her mouth after he had just risked his life to save her was more than he could stand. He leapt to his feet and stared down his nose at her. "I didn't shoot him! And keep your voice down."

"I don't see any difference between shooting him with that box of yours and letting that insect do it for you."

His nerves were stretched too far to defend himself in a rational manner. "The insect didn't kill him, either."

"How can you say that? I saw you let that thing go and it went right for his head. It flew in his ear and killed him."

Through gritted teeth, Gallant argued, "It didn't go in his ear."

"I saw it—"

"How the *drek* could you see it after I'd already made it disappear?"

They were standing toe to toe, glaring at one another when his words registered in each of their minds at the same time.

Cherry's curiosity temporarily pushed aside her fury. "What did you just say?"

"Never mind. We have to get out of here while it's still dark."

He was out the door before she could get her feet moving, but she swiftly caught up with him outside.

"What—" His hand clamped over her mouth.

"Hush," he whispered. "Do you want to alert that

crowd in the tavern that you're out here with me instead of back there with Frezlo?" He didn't wait for an answer before walking off again at a faster pace.

Cherry's lungs were heaving by the time they reached the ship—both from the exertion of keeping up with him while carrying a length of heavy chain and anger over the multitude of abuses he had heaped on her in the last few hours. She could hardly decide which to scream about first.

As they neared the ship, the door opened and the stairway telescoped down. The moment they stepped inside, the process was reversed and Gallant hurried to his chair. Cherry was right behind him.

"I have a few things to say to you, mister."

"It'll have to wait until we're off-planet," Gallant muttered as he flipped switches and pressed keys in the panel. Mar was busy bringing a grid up on his screen, and when Cherry tried to speak to Dot, the female placed a finger to her lips and closed her eyes.

"Sit!" Gallant barked at her.

She was tempted to try standing throughout take-off just to defy him, but her obstinance didn't go so far as to risk injury. For the next several minutes she remained quiet, outwardly. Inside, she was ranting and raving. At least the enforced delay gave her a chance to rehearse all the rotten names she was going to call him.

Gallant stretched out the take-off procedures as long as possible, hoping for two miracles—that Cherry would calm down and that she would forget what he said about making the drillfly disappear. He may as well have asked for the Supreme Being to make an appearance in the cockpit for all the good hoping did him. The second the ship settled into cruise mode, she was on her feet in front of the panel, ready to tear him to pieces.

Cherry faced him with her fists on her hips, took one deep breath, and fired. "You are the most despicable, vulgar, disgusting, lying, cheating—"

"Excuse us," Mar interrupted.

Simultaneously, Cherry and Gallant turned to him and demanded, *"What!"*

Mar gave them a pleasant smile. "You neglected to inform us of our destination."

"Lore," Gallant said.

"Earth," Cherry countered. "You *swore* you'd take me back if I helped you. Considering what you just put me through I'd say you owe me a hell of a lot more than a ride home. How *dare* you leave me like that? I could have been killed!"

"You weren't in any danger of being killed . . . at least not right away."

"*Aargh!* How can you be so—"

"Excuse us," Dot interrupted. "Do you think you could settle this matter elsewhere while we plot our course? Your . . . *discussion* is somewhat distracting."

"Fine," Gallant said with a huff and rose from his chair.

"That course had better be for Earth," Cherry warned as she followed Gallant into the corridor.

"Lore!" Gallant called over his shoulder. "I'm still the captain on this ship."

"Only as long as I let you live," Cherry said to his back.

His frustration showed as he slammed his fist against the door opener for his room. Not to be outdone, as soon as they were inside, Cherry hit the panel just as hard to close the door again.

Holding the length of chain in front of her, she demanded, "You get this damn thing off me before I use it to beat you with." As soon as she was free of the collar, she resumed her verbal attack. "What you did to me back there was the lowest, most wretched thing anyone—"

"You were never in any serious danger!"

"How would you know? You left me with those . . . those *creatures,* to do who knows what!"

"I wouldn't have had to leave you at all if *you* hadn't taken my cubes out of my vest!"

"I wouldn't have taken them if I hadn't found out *you* were using them to cheat."

"And I wouldn't have had to cheat if you had just been reasonable and agreed to cooperate with me to begin with!"

"Considering how you ended up abandoning me, I was right not to agree."

"I never abandoned you; I was right outside the whole time. Anyway, I knew Frezlo wouldn't allow anyone to touch you once he decided to use you himself."

"And *who* was the brainy bastard who put that idea into his head? He only wanted to kill me before you made it sound like Sinbar had enjoyed me so much he should try me himself!"

Gallant grinned in spite of himself. "That was rather quick of me, wasn't it?"

"Quick? There was nothing quick about how long it took for you to rescue me."

"I told you before. You weren't in any serious danger. The mating ritual of Frezlo's species is extremely long. I was waiting outside his door until I heard the sounds that let me know you had him completely distracted."

"That shows how much you know. All I was doing was brushing his hair . . . not that that wasn't gross enough!"

"Not to him. For Frezlo, a good grooming is the most sensuous foreplay there is. Unlike humanoids, his hair contains nerve cells."

"Are you telling me that while I was untangling knots, I was actually . . . *arousing* him?"

Gallant couldn't resist. "You heard what he said—you were the best ever."

"O-o-oh! I hate you!" Unable to speak another coherent word, she raised her fists, prepared to express her anger physically.

He blocked her attack and ordered, "Stop it. I'm getting sick and tired of you hitting me without reason. The next time you do it, I'm going to hit you back."

"Ha! You already did that, remember? In fact, I think you cracked my jaw." She rubbed the spot he had struck for effect.

"I had to do that to save you from Sinbar! Surely you realized he was drawing you into a trance."

"Of course I did. But you still hurt me." She tried

to hold on to her anger, but suddenly, uncontrollably, tears filled her eyes, and she stammered out the truth. "I've never been so scared in my entire life." His arms opened and the offer of comfort—even from him—was impossible to resist.

"I swore no harm would come to you. You should have trusted me," he said, holding her tightly against him.

She tipped her head back and frowned at him. "How could I trust you? You're a liar and a cheat and—" Before she could utter another insult, he silenced her with his lips.

This kiss was no less of an assault than the other two they'd shared. Only this time, her blood had been boiling beforehand. The strange tingling she had previously experienced in her robotic arm shot through her like a lightning bolt.

Suddenly Cherry felt as though she had been caught in a raging hurricane and the only escape was through the eye of the storm. She relayed her need in the most elemental way. Tangling her fingers into his thick hair to hold him still, she drew his tongue into her mouth, nipped and sucked, then forced her way into his.

She felt him yank off her wig and moaned her frustration when it took him more than a heartbeat to get rid of the gown. His vest hit the floor a moment later, and she pulled her mouth from his to taste the flesh she had uncovered. She ran her tongue down his neck and chest, and when her teeth closed over his nipple, he made that growling sound she found so erotic.

His fingers curled beneath the neckline of her jumpsuit and she stopped stroking his arms and chest to help him eliminate one more obstacle between them. Suddenly his hands closed over hers and prevented her from undressing further. She felt his body go rigid and realized he was trying to rein in his passion once again.

"No! Not this time, Gallant." She pried one hand loose, ran it down his body, and molded her fingers over his hard, pulsing shaft. The realization that her eyes hadn't been mistaken about his size made her take a deep breath of anticipation. "You want me. I want you. Right now, nothing else matters."

Another low growl was his only answer before desire swept away whatever had caused him to hesitate. Only when they tumbled onto his bunk completely naked did he try to speak. With every inch of their bodies pressed together, she felt as much as heard his low, gravelly voice.

"I don't . . . want to . . . hurt you."

"Dear Lord, Gallant, the only way you're going to hurt me now is if you don't come inside right this minute."

His reaction to her words was an entry so hard and fast, it would have been brutal had her body not been so well primed for him. He took her relieved cry into his mouth and groaned his pleasure back to hers.

She met his desperate pace, aware that he not only filled and stretched her beyond anything she had ever known, but he was driving her toward a height she had never before reached.

Within minutes he took her over that height to a climax that had her whole body shuddering with exquisite pleasure.

But he didn't allow her to come down. He turned her, twisted her, left her body and returned to push her over the brink again and again. And when she thought she would surely die of pleasure, he took her with him over one, final, ecstatic peak.

For some time they clung to one another on their sides, unable to work up the strength to separate their bodies. When Cherry finally caught her breath, she realized he was quickly expanding to his formidable size within her once more. With a light laugh, she moved her hips against his and teased, "You must not have found that pleasure female you went looking for when you left me."

"Did you really believe I would do such a thing?"

"I didn't know what to think," she murmured as she traced aimless designs on his chest with her finger.

"You should have. I showed you what you made me feel. Why would I use some other female when it was you I wanted?"

Cherry giggled and licked his collarbone. "Oh, now *that's* precious. You actually sound like you mean it."

"When I lie, you believe me, and when I tell the truth, you don't. You're an extremely exasperating woman."

"Exasperating!" She tried to lift her head, but he pressed it back to his chest.

"Please, I'm not ready to go back to fighting with

you yet." He took a slow deep breath and she settled down again. "You seemed . . . satisfied."

This time she raised her head before he could stop her. "Satisfied doesn't come close to describing the best—" She broke off her intended compliment when she looked at his closed eyelids and remembered that she hadn't yet questioned him about the missing eye patch. "Open your eyes."

"I'm too tired."

She squeezed her vaginal muscles around his hardness. "No you're not. Let me see your eyes." Just when she thought he was going to refuse, he slowly raised his lids and looked at a spot over her head. She stared at his two *perfectly normal*, dark brown eyes. "There's nothing weird about your left eye."

"No."

"Then why the patch?"

"It complements my wicked reputation."

Cherry moved her head from one angle to another, but he managed to keep his gaze averted. "You're lying. You can't look me in the eye and tell me a lie, can you?" He didn't even try to deny it. "Look at me!"

Sighing, he let his eyes meet hers for a split second before he pulled her head down to his. With his lips barely touching hers, he whispered, "I'd rather fight with you again."

The moment his mouth demanded her participation, she gave in with an eating kiss that had him growling in no time. She had thought their first bout had been incomparable, but this second battle replaced desperation with skillful technique.

He found her most sensitive areas and touched her in ways meant to wipe out all thoughts of anything but pleasure.

She caressed and stroked him until he forgot about whatever it was that he didn't want her to know.

This time, the build-up was slower and longer, yet when the finale was upon them, it was no less explosive.

Gallant kept Cherry's warm body curled against his long after she fell asleep. Looking at her like that, it was hard to imagine that beneath such a peaceful exterior lay enough energy to power a star ship. Like a human sacrifice, he had given himself up to that power, and having miraculously survived, was anxious to repeat the experience.

For so long he had feared what would happen to him if he ever let go completely. It had turned out to be neither paradise nor perdition, but an incredible combination of the two, and it wouldn't have been the same with any other woman he had ever met.

Now that he had found someone as emotional and passionate as himself, he wanted to chain her to him forever. He wanted to spend the rest of his days feeding off her sparkling energy, fighting with her, sharing himself with her, and holding her while she slept.

Yet, how could he keep her? She was too curious for him to hide his secret from her indefinitely. It was only a matter of time before she resumed her questioning about Frezlo's death, and it was only by sheer luck that she hadn't seen what was going on in the room around them whenever he opened his eyes. Fortunately when she shared herself with him, she gave it her total attention.

He had been in too much of a rush to don a patch before they landed on the bed and too sated to rise and get it afterward.

What if he simply told her the truth as she kept insisting he should do? Was there any chance that she wouldn't be repulsed? He remembered her sympathetic, unprejudiced comments when he had told her about the Illusians, and wondered if she could possibly find sympathy in her heart for him. If she didn't, however, revealing his secret would be akin to handing her his life on a crystal platter.

Even if she wasn't repelled by the truth, what enticement could he offer to make her want to stay with him? His home was this ship and wherever his next assignment took him; his life itself was one long risk. Like her best friend Aster, Cherry deserved to mate with someone as safe and stable as Romulus.

None of it really mattered in the end. She missed Innerworld, her friends, her career, and once she discovered she wasn't going to get back in time for her *important* appointment with Theodophilus, she would probably refuse to let him come within ten feet of her anyway. Telling her the whole truth at this late date wouldn't change the fact that he couldn't return her to Terra for sometime yet.

Cherry moaned softly in her sleep and snuggled her bottom against his stomach. Gallant hadn't even been aware of the fact that while his mind was analyzing the impossibility of making her his life-mate, his hand had cupped her breast and massaged it to a hard peak. Even in a sound sleep she responded to his touch, and he instantly responded to that knowledge.

He knew without a doubt that if he slipped his fingers between her thighs, she would be wet and ready for him. He wouldn't have to do more than stroke her once or twice and she would awaken for him, willing to charge into their private battle one more time.

But each encounter increased the risk of her discovering the truth, and since he could not expect her to agree to be his life-mate, it was best that she not bear the burden of his secret.

Although he told himself it would be wise to leave her now and never touch her again, his fingers had already crept down to their desired goal. She was neither fully awake nor fully asleep, yet she was fully aroused. Without changing positions, she opened herself to him and he slipped inside.

As their bodies challenged each other to the ultimate duel, he promised himself he would banish her from his mind in an hour . . . or two.

Chapter 9

Aster waddled into her mate's office with as much elegance as her condition permitted, closed his door, and burst into tears. Rom was beside her in an instant, holding and soothing her as she sobbed into his chest. The flash flood was over in a minute.

Though this had happened several times during Aster's pregnancy, he didn't think he'd ever get used to it. He helped lower her into an armchair across his desk, then fetched two tissues—one for her and one for him. "What was it this time, *shalla*?"

Aster blew her nose, not even attempting to be delicate about it. "I can't stand much more of this. I'm sick of being fat and moody and if I don't get a hot fudge sundae in the next five seconds, I'm liable to have a stroke!"

Rom sat on the arm of her chair and stroked her silver hair. "There's less than three weeks to go, but if you really want a sundae, I'm sure Doctor Xerpa—"

"No. If you bother her one more time, she might never agree to let us get pregnant again." Aster sighed and rubbed her enormous stomach. "I'm sorry, darling. A hot fudge sundae isn't going to fix what's bothering me. I miss Cherry. She should be here making fun of me. I can't stop worrying about her. It's been a week, Rom. A week! She should have been home by now. Why haven't we heard anything?"

As he had been doing since Cherry's disappearance, Rom blocked his own concerned thoughts from his mate. Gallant Voyager was going to have a lot to answer for . . . if and when he ever showed up again.

"I told you before," Rom said in his gentlest voice. "If Gallant believes Cherry's life is in danger, he's probably keeping a low profile with her on some quiet planet and doesn't want to risk revealing their location to anyone. The Consociation of Planets will have received my message by now. As soon as Gallant checks in with them, they'll have him contact us."

"You're sure she's safe with him?"

He hugged her tightly, both to console her and ensure that she didn't see how his eyes were about to change color as he lied to her. "Absolutely."

With another sigh, Aster pulled herself back together enough to think of Innerworld business. "Did you see this morning's communication from OMC?"

"Mm-hmm." Rom got up and went around the other side of his desk. The memo was right where he'd left it when she'd come in. He pretended to read it while he considered how best to discuss the matter.

He had asked the department head at Outerworld

Monitor Control to forward all news reports regarding Earth's surface to him alone so that he could decide whether Aster should receive a copy. The situation with Cherry, on top of her pregnancy, had her upset enough for the moment.

He knew he was being devious and underhanded—behavior he had never resorted to in his life—but it was worth a small deception if Aster was spared more stress. Apparently this report had slipped through. He cleared his throat and read it aloud in a voice intended to sound sarcastically doubtful. "Outerworld sensationalist newspapers are reporting strange phenomena."

Aster laughed. "So what else is new? They haven't changed at all in the ten years I've been here."

Rom smiled back and continued. "In the past fourteen days, there have been three supposedly supernatural sightings at religious shrines: an angel at Our Lady of Lourdes in France; the prophet Muhammad at the Mosque of Omar in Jerusalem; and at the Elephanta caves near Bombay, India, a rock sculpture of the Hindu god, Shiva, opened its eyes and spoke to a group of worshipers.

"Emissary P68 was near the third sighting area and reports having picked up a tremendous surge of mental energy during the occurrence, but was unable to identify the source. All three messengers warned of the approach of Judgment Day, at which time the Supreme Being will be arriving on Earth."

The memo went on to say that Emissary P68 was one of Innerworld's most reliable agents in Outerworld, and his efficient record was the only reason such trivial information had been forwarded to the Co-Governors. The emissary was planning to discreetly interview some of the witnesses to the event and see if he could learn more.

Glad to have something to think about besides hot fudge, Astor asked, "What's your analysis?"

"Initial reaction—it's a hoax." Rom wasn't surprised when she rolled her eyes at him.

"Please. You can do better than that. Beginning with the assumption that God is not really on his way, what do you think about the emissary's report?"

Rom shrugged. "It's possible an Outerworlder has perfected mass hypnotism."

"Possible, but not likely. Even in a small group, one or two people would not be taken under with the rest. That memo doesn't give us many details, but it sounds like everyone present saw the same thing."

"The first two sightings could have been created with holographic technology available out there, but I can't see how someone could make a rock move and talk . . . except on film."

Aster shifted positions as the baby did a somersault. "You're talking about special effects, but this wasn't a prerecorded video that could have been touched up. One thing in that memo jarred, and I looked it up before I came over here. Those phenomena involve three different religions. Catholics and Muslims both believe there is one God, and they have histories filled with messengers and prophets.

"Unless something has changed recently, Hindus

worship many deities, so it doesn't make complete sense that one of their gods would warn of the coming of one supreme being. That must have some significance. I mean, if someone could master the technology required to perform such magic, wouldn't they be smarter than to make a mistake like that? We can draw one definite conclusion though. The timing and locations suggest that one person or group moving eastward could have perpetrated all three sightings."

"Exactly. That's why I've sent an alert to the emissaries in China and Japan to maintain a special watch over religious shrines and temples, and immediately report any unusual activity."

"And?"

"That's it for now," Rom said as innocently as possible.

Aster shook her head. "Will you never realize that I can tell when you're blocking something from me? You wouldn't have asked for a special watch if you really thought it was a hoax. By that alone, I can deduce that you believe this is more than it appears to be."

Rom looked directly into her eyes and let her see, as well as sense, his honesty. "It's just a feeling. As if there's something familiar about the circumstances, but I can't put my finger on it. The only thing I am certain of is that it's not good. I've already requested a more detailed report from Emissary P68 as soon as possible."

"Good, because if you hadn't, I would." With some effort, she rose from the chair before Rom could come to her aid. "I have an appointment with the Finance Committee in a few minutes, so I'll see you at lunch." She gave him a tender kiss. "Unless you receive a communication from either that Voyager devil or the emissary, in which case, I expect to see you immediately. Have you got that, Governor?"

Giving her a mock salute, Rom said, "Yes, ma'am." Then pulled her into his arms for a more intimate parting gesture.

Princess Honorbound clapped her hands to get her council members to stop speculating amongst themselves and give her their full attention. They quickly took their appointed positions around the rim of a deep, open pit in which a fire blazed and crackled. Behind them stood several rows of armed warriors.

"There is nothing we can do but wait," she told them firmly. "Josep should be on his way back to us soon with an update. Then we can move ahead. I curse the necessity for this lack of communication, as much as each of you do. I can only assure you that the waiting time decreases daily.

"Soon we will have regained our people's freedom and have a new, challenging world to conquer. In no time, we will have the Noronians on their knees before us, where they belong." Her impassioned speech was not much different from all the others she had made in the years they had been in exile together, but it seemed that the closer things got to the time for action, the less patient her fellow Illusians became with her promises of glory.

"Tonight we offer two sacrifices—one to Ulee, God of War and another to Kan, Mother of all." The boisterous cheers that echoed throughout the cavern signified their readiness to proceed, and she gave the order to the two servants standing behind her.

They hurried off and returned moments later, each bearing one end of a long pole on their shoulders. In the middle of the pole was suspended a wooden cage, the slats of which were spaced only far enough apart to allow the people to see the vicious, snarling mongrel inside.

The council members stood back to allow the servants to position themselves on opposite sides of the pit with the cage hanging above the fire. A flame shot up to lick the cage and the animal howled its terror.

Honorbound stretched her arms upward and called, "Ulee, God of War, witness our respect. We give to you our bravest fighting hound that you should stand among us in the battles soon to come. We are tired of this peace and isolation forced on us. We ask you to end this boredom. Give us *WAR!*"

"WAR! WAR! WAR!" chanted the assemblage as the servants cut the rope that bound the cage to the pole. The shrieks of the burning hound stirred the blood of everyone present, until their cries for war increased to a deafening volume.

The princess signaled for the servants to fetch the second sacrifice before the crowd could no longer be controlled. When the council members saw the little furry creature being handed to the princess, they quieted and motioned for the warriors to do the same.

She held up the rabboset for all to see, as she spoke the sacrificial words. "Hear me, Kan, Mother of All. You have smiled on us many times in the centuries past and our ranks have multiplied a thousandfold. To you, oh generous Mother, we now offer the most fertile animal in the galaxy, that you will also make this, my thirtieth reproductive season, a long and successful one." She paused as the warriors' cheers rose and died down again.

"To this end, we, your faithful servants, must beg another favor. The man who will father the heir to the great Illusian empire has not yet arrived. Bring him to me quickly so that the royal mating can take place before my season ends.

"Bring me *Gallant Voyager*!"

Chapter 10

Gallant managed to break away from Cherry only by sternly reminding himself it was past time to relieve Mar-Dot. Once he did so, a threat to drop them off in midspace was the only thing that cut short their good-natured ribbing.

He could hardly blame them. When two beings shared such close quarters for years on end, there was no privacy or secrets left between them. They knew as well as he how long it had been since he'd last been with a woman, and they probably also knew how very little he had enjoyed himself.

His thoughts flew to Cherry and just how much he had *enjoyed* her. Immediately, he wanted her there, on his lap, or at least at his side, and he was halfway off the bridge when he realized he was out of control.

Right from the beginning he had been aware of how she seemed to call to every one of his primitive instincts, and now, on the brink of leaving the control panel unattended just to have her company, he knew exactly how far she could drive him.

He had spent a lifetime perfecting his cold, hard

shell. By practicing his rigid control in the most difficult of circumstances, he had learned never to let his emotions interfere with his responsibilities. She had to have some hidden power to make him forget something as simple as minding the bridge. If there was one thing his foster parents had drummed into his head, it was that he could *never* forget who and what he was.

He could hardly believe that an hour ago he was thinking of asking her to be his life-mate! Regardless of how fantastic their sharing had been, it couldn't be repeated. He *had* to put all thoughts of it, and her, out of his mind. Taking several deep, meditating breaths, he concentrated on reestablishing the shell he had momentarily allowed to slip away.

Feeling more like his old self, he was able to put his priorities back in order. The first item on the agenda was to follow up on the lead Frezlo had given him.

During Gallant's final year at the academy in Innerworld, Josep, a representative to the Consociation of Planets, had given a talk about choosing a diplomatic career. Gallant remembered how fascinated Romulus had been, while he snuck out a side door halfway through. The mere thought of doing anything so inactive for the rest of his life had him searching for an immediate outlet for his energy.

He also remembered how embarrassed he had been when the representative caught up with him later that day and told him he had seen him leave while he was speaking. The man seemed to understand the problem instantly and told Gallant about another kind of career that would suit his needs much better. He threw out words like secrecy, danger, risks, and adventure, and Gallant couldn't sign up fast enough.

Establishing his reputation as a man with ice in his veins and larceny and murder in his heart began that day. Where he had been a good, respectful student, Gallant was soon balancing on the edge of failure and expulsion, but he always maintained that precarious balance. His mother always said knowledge was a tool, no matter what trade one plied.

He borrowed his standard outfit from a picture he had seen of an Outerworld pirate, exchanged his white cloth bandage for a black leather eye patch, and stopped dying the white streaks to blend in with the rest of his hair.

From the time he was a toddler, his foster parents had done everything possible to make him indistinguishable. For the first time in his life he did things to draw attention to himself instead. The changes he made had been intentional, but he had still been surprised by how swiftly his revamped appearance altered the way others treated him.

Josep ended up being his primary contact at the Consociation, since it was imperative that as few people as possible knew Gallant was a Consociation employee, rather than the free agent for hire he claimed to be. Under that cover, he had to occasionally take on outside jobs, but most of his assignments came directly through Josep.

Some of his missions had been safe and uncomplicated. Others required him to act the part of a criminal to become accepted in places like the tavern on Zoenid. Behavior that men like Romulus would find savage and loathsome, Gallant found exhilarating.

The current situation was both complicated and dangerous—his favorite kind. He sent a coded transmission directly to Josep's private receiver and sat back. To his surprise, Josep's smiling face appeared on his monitor seconds later.

"Gallant! I was just sitting here wondering when you were going to check in. Have you learned anything yet?"

Gallant frowned slightly. Was it possible that Josep was getting so old that he was forgetting procedures? "Assurance, please."

"Oh, gracious, I'm sorry. I was just so relieved to hear from you. Four, five, nine, two, seven."

That series of numbers told Gallant he was indeed speaking to his contact, everything was in order, and their conversation would be completely confidential. "Actually, I've learned something rather unsettling."

He told Josep about the Weebort trader's assassination and his trailing Frezlo to Zoenid, but something told him not to mention Cherry's participation. "Frezlo claimed he was hired by a Consociation representative."

"That's impossible! How could . . ." Josep coughed, cleared his throat, and began again. "I mean, why would he make such an accusation?"

Gallant knew Josep wouldn't want to hear that one of his colleagues might be a spy, but he couldn't hold the truth from him. "Frezlo said it was a man and that he was masked, but apparently something he was wearing had the Consociation emblem on it, so Frezlo followed the man."

"Perhaps Frezlo was lying."

"Not under the circumstances. He was absolutely certain it was a Con rep." Gallant felt sorry for the old man. He had never seen him so upset.

"This is terrible. If it got around, people would panic, they would—"

"It won't get around. Frezlo died right after he told me where the rep headed."

"He's dead? You're certain?"

"Absolutely." He didn't need to say more than that for Josep to understand.

Josep dabbed his forehead and upper lip with a handkerchief. "Did you say he told you where the . . . the representative went?"

"Right. As unbelievable as it sounds, he said the man landed on Lore."

"Yes, that is unbelievable, and, of course I can't order you to go there, but . . ."

Gallant grinned. "But you can gently suggest that I consider it. I already did and I'm on my way there now."

"Now?" Josep grew disturbed again. "What is your current location?" Gallant told him. "I'd like you to make a slight detour to Norona before you go to Lore. There is something I need to discuss with you in person that can't wait."

Gallant couldn't tell him the reason he was in such a hurry to complete this mission, so he had to agree to the one-day delay the trip to Consociation headquarters would cause. "All right. I'll see you in about thirty-six hours."

"Wait a moment. I almost forgot. I've been holding an urgent message for you from Governor Romulus of Innerworld. He requests an immediate answer."

"Oh?" Gallant had a fair idea of what Rom wanted to know, but he waited for Josep to locate the message and read it to him.

"He says, 'Aster is very worried about Cherry. When will you return her?' Do you know what he's referring to?"

Gallant rubbed his chin. "Yes. That's Aster's—" Again he hesitated to reveal Cherry's presence on board. "That's Aster's pet talking bird. She loaned it to me to see if I'd like one of my own to keep me company. If you wouldn't mind, please relay a message back, saying Cherry's fine, and I'll have her home as soon as I've completed my current assignment."

Josep visibly relaxed. "Of course. I'd be glad to send that along, and I'll see you soon."

Gallant signed off, but stared at the blank screen for some time afterward. He couldn't remember ever lying to Josep before—omitting facts, yes, but not out and out lying. Thinking on it, he knew Josep would not be understanding about a Terran female being involved in such a highly confidential mission. If he learned of her, he might insist that Gallant turn her over to the Consociation for the duration.

And therein lay the main reason Gallant had held his tongue. If there was a spy among the Con reps and that spy heard about Cherry, wouldn't he consider her a threat to the secrecy of the mission, and try to eliminate her? Gallant couldn't very well abide by his oath to protect her if he was on a different planet when someone went after her.

He almost regretted making that oath. If he dropped her off on Norona, she'd be out of his system in no time. She might even catch a ride back to Terra from there sooner than he could take her, which he knew would suit her wishes as well.

Might. If no one tried to kill her first.

Besides that, she now knew portions of his secret that he had not yet explained in any satisfactory way. No, even though it seemed to be in his personal best interest to get her off his ship, he couldn't risk having her roaming free either. Which meant he had to figure out a way to keep her secured on board while he met with Josep on Norona. He was contemplating whether there was any way she could be convinced to stay out of sight willingly when Cherry plopped onto his lap.

She caught him so off-guard that he was returning her kiss for several seconds before his voice of reason shouted its warning.

One moment Cherry felt Gallant's heat flooding her body, the next, she was kissing a block of ice. Drawing her head back, she scanned his face and frowned. "Hmmm. I see Captain Voyager's back in charge again, eye patch and all. Care to explain, or should I draw my own conclusions?"

Gallant swiveled his chair to the side then nudged her off his lap. "My rest period ended two hours ago.

If you're in need of more attentive company, I'm sure Mar wouldn't mind being awakened."

Cherry inhaled sharply, but stopped short of slapping him. "That was extremely rude, Captain. In fact, you went a bit too far." She calmly walked behind him to Mar-Dot's station and pulled out their bench. Sitting down, she kept her eyes on Gallant's profile. "All you had to say was, 'Not now, Cherry,' or even 'Don't distract me while I'm on duty, woman.' Instead, you purposely insulted me. Why?"

Gallant studied his monitor as he answered. "We agreed that it would be a mistake to complicate our relationship. We can't go backward, but I can avoid repeating the mistake in the future."

"Look at me and say that again. Tell me to my face that, in spite of how good it was between us last night, you have no desire to spend another eight hours in your bunk with me . . . and I'll accept it and leave you alone."

He turned toward her, met her gaze, and said, "I—"

"Wait," Cherry interrupted, then pulled off his eye patch before he could stop her. "Now, tell me the truth."

He glared at her. He looked away and back. "All right. The truth. I had no intention of sharing my bunk with you, but it happened anyway. It doesn't matter how good it was. I can't afford to do it again."

The pragmatic part of her personality accepted the fact that he regretted having sex with her even though he enjoyed it. Her active curiosity was not so easily satisfied. "Why?" When he hesitated, she prodded further. "What's with the patch? There's no one on board you need to deceive with your dangerous disguise. And as long as you don't intend to evade my questions by kissing me senseless, how about explaining what happened to Frezlo?"

When several seconds passed and she asked no more questions, he asked in a quiet voice, "Do you want to hear lies? That's all I can give you."

Cherry narrowed her eyes at him, but his gaze held steadily to hers. He didn't seem to realize that by warning her rather than automatically lying, he had already given her more than he would have yesterday. For the moment, she decided to settle for that. "Save your lies, Captain. I said I'd leave you alone, and I will. Here." She handed him his eye patch. "I wouldn't want you to feel undressed."

As he replaced the patch, she studied the navigational monitor. "I don't suppose we're heading for Earth."

"No."

"Lore?"

"Not directly."

"No? You may as well tell me. Mar has taught me enough to figure it out on my own."

"We have to make a stop on Norona first. We'll reach there late tomorrow."

"Norona? That's great!" She bounced off the bench and gave him a big hug. "Thank you!" She released him and started circling the control panel. "How many days does it take to get back to Earth from Norona?"

Gallant glanced up at her. "Five, but—"

"Five! Oh my. That'll be cutting it close, but at least I should be back in time for the auditions. I shouldn't have doubted you, Gallant. I'm sorry."

"Cherry—"

"I've got to tell you though, I wish I wasn't in such a hurry to get back. I'd love to tag along and see how this mission works out. Do you think you could send me a note or something later on?"

"Cherry, *sit*!"

She froze in her tracks. "I wish you would stop talking to me like I was your pet dog!"

"Pet bird," he mumbled, then said more clearly, "Please sit down."

Cherry returned to the bench with a sense of wariness. "What is it?"

"I'm glad you're interested in my mission," he began slowly. "I didn't thank you properly for your help back on Zoenid."

He was speaking so formally, she couldn't help but giggle. "I don't know, I thought your *im*proper thank you was just fine."

He started to grin, but attempted to hide it by clearing his throat. "At any rate, I am appreciative."

"I certainly hope so," she countered with a lascivious eyebrow wiggle.

"Cherry, you're making it very hard for me—"

"Again? Why, Cap'n Voyager, y'all are the most remarkable man!"

Gallant gave an exasperated sigh. "Why are you doing this?"

"Because you're acting like an ass. Just give me

whatever bad news you're trying to sugarcoat, and I'll try not to go nuts when I hear it."

Gallant braced himself. "You can't get off on Norona." Before she could react, he hurried on. "You heard Frezlo. It was a Con rep that ordered the Weebort's assassination. He could order yours as easily. I promised to keep you safe, and I can't do that while the spy is free, unless you stay on board."

"That's very *gallant* of you, Captain, but I hereby relieve you of any responsibility for my safety. Just head me toward the ticket counter after we land, then forget you ever set your eyes, er, eye on me."

"I can't do that."

She opened her mouth to continue the debate, but decided to drop it instead. It really didn't matter what he said, she was getting off his ship the minute it landed on Norona. "How about a game of cubit?"

As he pulled out the table and set up the game, he asked, "What's going on in that devious mind of yours?"

Cherry smiled. "As a considerate man recently said to me, do you want to hear lies?"

He muttered something under his breath that Cherry assumed was an obscenity and chose to ignore. "You can toss first. Points only."

Rolling the cubes between his palms, he casually said, "By the way, I'd like my cheats back."

"I'm sure you would, and I'll return them . . . right after you explain what you meant when you said you made the drillfly disappear." The way his cheekbones bronzed told her two things: what he had said was very important, and he was upset that she had remembered it.

With neither of them willing to let the other know what they were thinking, the rest of the day dragged by until Mar-Dot joined them. At Mar-Dot's prompting, Gallant and Cherry filled them in on what had happened on Zoenid, even managing to make some of it sound entertaining.

The mood lightened considerably during those latter hours. However, when Gallant's rest period drew near, Cherry sensed his rising tension and spared them both further embarrassment.

She yawned, stretched, and got up from the bench. "My goodness. How time flies when you're having fun. Good night, y'all." With a smile for Mar and Dot, and an indifferent glance toward Gallant, she headed for the facility chamber, then to Mar-Dot's cabin. When an hour had passed and Gallant hadn't knocked on the door, she knew he had meant what he said about not repeating his earlier mistake.

Wouldn't you know it, she thought with considerable annoyance. She had finally found someone whose passions ran as deeply as her own, and he wanted nothing more to do with her!

It was just as well, she supposed. In about twenty-four hours, she'd be on her way back to Earth, ready to embark on an exciting new phase of her career, and Gallant would be somewhere on the other side of the universe, continuing his own adventure.

Her last thought before she fell asleep was that it really was a shame the audition was scheduled so soon. It might have been a kick to see what other strange places Gallant's mission took him to.

Twenty-four hours later, neither Gallant's sternest order nor his gentlest plea could get Cherry to sit still, let alone take her rest period. She had been keeping track of their progress toward Norona all day, and now that the planet could be seen in the distance, her excitement was boundless.

Unlike Zoenid, Norona looked the way Cherry thought a planet should, and what a magnificent sight it was. There was no cloud cover to mute the brilliant greens of the land and blue of the waters. As the ship got closer, she could also see the radiant glow that marked each city where the sun reflected off the crystal prisms of the buildings.

"Aster described it perfectly," she said, standing as close to the glass as she could get without pressing her nose against it. "I know Innerworld is made up to look exactly like Norona, but it's still exciting to get to see the real thing." She turned to Mar with a bright smile. "Will you be deboarding this time?"

"No," Gallant answered quickly and firmly. "They'll be staying here . . . with you."

Cherry flashed her smile at him, but didn't say a word. Several times during the day he had repeated his reasons for wanting her to stay hidden while he went on his appointment. Sticking with the policy of saying nothing rather than lying, she simply had not made him any promises to abide by his order.

As he had been doing all day, he frowned at her and shook his head. "Take her down, Mar. I'm going to change. Cherry, feel free to use my chair to enjoy the landing."

"Golly gee, what a treat!" she said in a little girl's voice, but took advantage of his offer the moment he left the bridge. "So tell me, Dot, do you ever get to leave this ship?"

With Mar concentrating on their landing, Dot could not fully face Cherry as she spoke. "Of course we do. Sometimes it is our choice to remain behind, however. You remember how you stared at us when you first saw us."

"Oh my, I didn't realize—"

"It was not offensive, I assure you. But there are times and situations that are not quite . . . comfortable. Also, if a hasty departure is required, we stay on board to facilitate same."

"Ah, you're the getaway driver who keeps the motor running in the back alley."

"I beg your pardon?"

Cherry laughed. "Never mind. Why do you need to stay behind here? Norona's civilized and it sounds like the captain has a legitimate business appointment. You probably could use a little stroll around town." She hoped the suggestion sounded enticing.

"The captain—" Dot began.

"The captain said he would not be gone long and requested that we stay on board," Mar finished.

"But surely, you could take a few minutes . . . unless . . . did he order you to stay behind to make sure *I* don't leave?" As the seconds ticked by in silence, she had her answer without them having to speak aloud. "I see. I don't suppose either of you are susceptible to bribes."

"I am sorry, Cherry," Dot said sincerely. "But the captain has explained it is for your own safety."

Mar turned to her with a purposeful leer. "What sort of bribe did you have in mind?"

Dot twisted toward her. "Do not pay heed to his foolishness. We have our orders."

Cherry nodded her understanding, while she tried to figure out how to circumvent those orders. Moments after they touched down, Gallant reappeared on the bridge. Cherry swiveled the chair around and inspected him from head to toe. He was wearing a fitted white jumpsuit, like hers, and had exchanged his black boots and eye patch for white ones also. With his dark hair neatly tied at the base of his neck, he looked extremely dashing, and somewhat respectable, despite the white streaks.

Rising, she complimented him with her best wolf whistle. "Very chic, *mon capitain*. Too bad I can't go with you. We could play the odd couple." Her humor was lost on him, as usual.

"Cherry, I need to speak to Mar-Dot alone for a moment. Would you mind?"

She smiled sweetly, wanting to show him how cooperative she could be. "Of course. Perhaps I should step outside?" Gallant merely smirked at her. "You can't blame a gal for trying. Okay. I needed to freshen up anyway." As she made her way down the corridor past the exit door, she figured the best time to slip away would be immediately after Gallant left. If she timed it right, Mar-Dot might think she was still in the facility chamber and not check on her for a while.

Standing inside the chamber with her ear pressed to the closed door, she listened intently for the sounds that would mark Gallant's departure from the ship. What she heard instead was a soft click very close to her ear. Jumping to the worst possible conclusion, she pressed the door opener, then pushed on the door itself . . . to no avail.

The dirty rat had sealed her in.

Chapter 11

"You son-of-a-bitch!" She pounded her fist against the door. "Let me out of here! I swear I'll make you regret this until the day you die, Voyager." As she stood there waiting for some kind of response to her threat, she heard the unmistakable sound of boot heels walking toward the exit door.

She had underestimated him. Again. Only this time, perhaps he had also underestimated her . . . or at least her acting ability. She gave him ten minutes to be well on his way, during which time she set aside her anger and concentrated on becoming a helpless, near-hysterical woman.

In a high-pitched, frightened voice, she whined, "Gallant? Please don't do this to me. I can't stand it. Please talk to me. Mar? Dot? Somebody? Oh, dear God," she cried a little louder. "Don't tell me they left me alone in here!"

"You're not alone, Cherry," Mar-Dot said close to the door. She couldn't tell which was speaking, but she guessed it would probably be Dot.

"Please, Dot, let me out of here before it's too

late." She wailed pitifully and scraped the door with her fingernails.

"Cherry? Are you all right?"

"It's . . . it's happening already. The walls are moving! They're closing in on me. *No-o-o*!"

"Cherry, are you claustrophobic?"

Wheezing and gasping for air as loudly as she could, she knocked over a chair, then waited silently beside the door.

"Cherry? Are you hurt? Say something!"

Exactly as planned, Cherry heard the click of the seal being removed and the door slid open. The second Mar-Dot appeared, Cherry used her robotic arm to yank them into the room, over her extended foot. As Mar-Dot stumbled to the floor, Cherry snatched the seal, and hopped out the door. Before they could right themselves, she had locked them in.

"I'm sorry," she called through the door. "I hope I didn't hurt you, but I had no choice. Say good-bye to Gallant for me, and . . . and I hope his mission is a success. Well, take care." When she didn't get a response, she had to stop herself from reopening the door to make sure they were all right, but guessed that they were probably only trying to turn her trick around on her.

Seconds later she was outside of the ship, surveying her surroundings. She had observed the landing carefully and knew that they were parked at the edge of a sprawling city beside several other ships of about the same size. A few hundred yards away there was a large building where a number of people were moving about and an air shuttle bus had just floated in. Since there was nothing else nearby, she decided that had to be a terminal or greeting center of some sort, and set off for it.

"Could you help me?" she asked the first woman she encountered inside the building. "I need to arrange some transportation." The woman directed her toward several uniformed people standing behind a long counter. It looked like she had found the ticket counter without much effort at all.

She approached the man with the friendliest face. "Hi. I'm trying to get to Terra. Can you take care of that here?"

"Sorry. This is strictly a local commuter station. The only ships leaving the planet from here are privately owned. Of course, the owners occasionally take on passengers. In fact, someone just landed who said he'd be departing again within an hour or two. You could wait here and check with him. Let's see." He scanned the monitor in front of him. "His name is Captain Voyager."

"Oh, I've already spoken to him," she said, not hiding her disappointment. "He's going in the opposite direction. Where would I be able to catch a regular flight?"

He pointed toward the other end of the building. "The D shuttleway will take you to the main transport center. Someone there should be able to help you."

Cherry thanked him and hurried away. She wanted to be as far away from there as possible before Gallant returned.

She was about halfway to her destination when a

very familiar person walked past her going in the opposite direction. It was so unexpected she continued walking for several more steps before she realized who she had just seen. Whirling around, her gaze immediately latched on to a statuesque woman with a gorgeous mane of silver hair.

"Aster?" she asked herself, then called the name aloud. But the woman didn't turn around. Cherry had heard the saying that everyone has a twin somewhere, but this woman was also pregnant and wearing a dress exactly like one Aster owned. It didn't make any sense, but her eyes told her Aster was here, on Norona. Her transportation problems were solved!

She called Aster's name several times as she tried to catch up, but apparently her voice wasn't carrying far enough. For a pregnant woman, she was walking incredibly fast. In desperation, Cherry broke into a run as Aster exited the building.

Racing toward the parked ships, she never took her eyes off Aster, but all of a sudden the woman was gone—vanished into thin air. Cherry halted in midstride and blinked at the vacant space in front of her, half expecting Aster to reappear again.

"Get back on the ship, Cherry."

She gasped at the sound of Gallant's voice behind her. The shock of his catching her on top of what she had just seen . . . or imagined . . . froze her in place long enough for him to come alongside of her. He had a grip on her neck before she could think to defend herself.

"Don't try it," he warned in a flat voice. "Before

you could use that arm, you'd be unconscious." He gave her a nudge and they started walking toward his ship. "How far did you think you were going to get without a travel visa or proper identification?"

She was so frustrated and angry, she couldn't have answered if she'd been willing. A sideward glance at him let her know he wasn't wearing his eye patch, and he was at least as furious as she was.

"I'll tell you how far. To the first administrator, who would have listened to your story and sent you to his superior. Eventually, you would have ended up in the one place sure to get you in trouble—some Con rep's office. And with my luck lately, it would have been the spy!"

The door to the ship opened and Cherry grimaced at the irate expression on Mar's face as he lowered the stairs to them. When she hesitated, Gallant's fingers tightened on her neck, and she immediately retaliated by stomping on his toes with her heel. "Take your hands off me, and I'll go up by myself. I know when I'm outnumbered."

He released her, but remained close behind as she climbed the stairs.

As soon as the door closed behind them, Gallant said, "I'm getting out of this suit. Mar, take us out of here."

Cherry was about to go after Gallant when Mar turned to go to the cockpit and she saw Dot's face. Her eyes were downcast and a hot pink bruise marred her cheekbone. "Oh no. Did I do that to you?"

"It is nothing," Dot said quietly.

"Nothing?" Mar asked, spinning toward Cherry. "We disobeyed a direct order because we thought you were hurt. For our consideration, we received an injury from you."

Dot faced her with a sad smile. "Mar will get over his anger. I understand why you tricked us. The cage was always more terrible to me than it was to him."

"I really am sorry," Cherry said. "But that man had no right to lock me in." The guilt she was feeling over hurting Dot was instantly obliterated by cold logic. She may have knocked Mar-Dot down, but it was *his* fault. "And somehow he's going to pay for that!"

Marching to the facility chamber, she noticed the seal that had locked her in was nowhere in sight. He probably hid it, suspecting that she might lock him in for revenge, but that would be much too kind. She wanted at least a pound of flesh! She pressed the door opener, but it was sealed from the inside this time. Knocking didn't get her any results either.

"Come on, Voyager," she shouted and gave the door another thump. "Open the door. It doesn't take you this long to change."

His deep voice came to her clearly from the other side. "No, but it takes this long to cool down."

"What do *you* have to cool down from?" she challenged in a voice much louder than necessary. "*I* was the one that got locked in. *I'm* the one whose whole life has been turned upside down. *I'm* the one that missed her one chance to get back home before her whole career goes down the tubes."

"Can't you ever think about anything more important than your career?" he yelled back.

"As a matter of fact, I can think of a lot of things more important than my career . . . when someone explains them to me, calmly and rationally. You just keep throwing me into situations where all I can think to do is fight back! You want me to cooperate with you and care about what you're doing, but half the time, you're lying and the other half you're evading. You've got more secrets than the Sphinx."

"I tried your way, and look how that turned out. I calmly and rationally explained why you had to stay on board. But you never had any intention of obeying my orders."

"*Obeying!* Listen up, Captain. I am *not* your slave. I'm not even your employee. You have no right to give me orders of any kind. So what if you explained one little thing. What about all the rest? Maybe I'd be more agreeable if I had the whole picture. What really happened to Frezlo and the disappearing bug? And speaking of disappearing, did I or did I not see Aster a few minutes ago? Does any of it have to do with your wearing that stupid eye patch? How about telling me how you caught up with me so easily? And then, for a big finish, you can explain why you rejected me like some cheap one-night stand!"

For a long moment Gallant was silent, and when he finally answered, Cherry could tell some of his rage had dissipated. "It wouldn't serve any purpose for you to know everything."

Something vulnerable in his voice cut through her

own anger. "Open the door, Gallant. You're safe now."

Another pause. "What do you mean?"

"You know very well what I mean. Every time one or both of us gets worked up about something, we end up groping each other. For some reason that frightens you. That's why you don't want to argue without this door between us, isn't it?"

She thought she heard him groan, but she couldn't be certain. "You may as well give it up. By dragging me back here, you just consigned the both of us to close quarters for who knows how long. There's no way we're going to make it if you don't start being honest with me. You've got a choice. Either you fill me in . . . on *everything* . . . or I make the rest of this trip a living hell for you. Think about that, Captain, and you know I can do it if I choose to."

Abruptly, the sharp edge returned to his voice. "Then you think about this, woman. You're wrong about one thing. I'm not safe now. And neither are you. In fact, you're the furthest thing from safe. When Mar-Dot signaled me about what you had done, I was so infuriated, I could barely see straight. It took every ounce of my will to control myself when I found you.

"I wanted to punish you, force you to beg for mercy. And more than anything, I wanted to strip you naked and use you over and over again until the fire inside of me died out."

Cherry immediately felt that fire burning right through the door, but in spite of his harsh words, she felt no fear. Instead, much to her shock, desire was getting all mixed up with her anger.

He took a deep, audible breath. "I keep telling myself I am a civilized man, not a barbarian. But when I'm around you, I seem to forget that. I can't open the door, because I still want you so badly that I might hurt you."

She closed her eyes and hugged herself against the onslaught of need his declaration incited. How could this be? How could she want to strangle him and make love to him at the same time? "You know, Voyager, sometimes you can be such an ass. I don't understand where this hang-up you have about hurting me comes from, but you're hardly the first male who thought of using his sex organ to control me. The fact that you realize it and control yourself is what counts. I have bad news for you, mister, regardless of how dangerous you imagine yourself to be, you don't scare me in the slightest.

"If it's any consolation, I'm not real crazy about how confused you make me either. But I do know you're not going to be able to keep a locked door between us indefinitely. Of course, you have a perfectly reasonable solution minutes away. Just tell Mar-Dot to set us back down on Norona where you can personally escort me onto a ship back home."

The door slid open and Gallant murmured, "I can't do that."

Cherry's fingers curled into her palms to keep from reaching out to him. The only thing he had changed was his hair, which looked as though he had been caught in a windstorm. Since he was still wearing the jumpsuit, the proof of his arousal was blatantly evident.

"I warned you," he said in a husky voice.

She dragged her gaze up to his ebony eyes. "Yes. That was very civilized of you."

"You wanted the door open. It's open. Now tell me again how I don't frighten you."

Cherry's eyes raked over him, purposely giving his male anatomy a disdaining look. "There's *nothing* about you that frightens me."

In a flash his hands slipped under her arms, lifted her across the threshold, and brought her up to his height. "I'm a lot stronger than you are." Bringing her body flush against his, he eased her down several inches and up again without letting her toes touch the floor.

"You may be strong, but you're still afraid of me." She wrapped her legs around his waist and pressed herself to him. "Or is it just this?" She moved against him suggestively. "Are you scared that you'll get so distracted by this, you'll spill all your secrets to me?"

"Yes," he whispered as his hands slid down to brace her hips. "*Yes!*" And with a menacing growl, he took her mouth in a kiss that could never be called civilized.

She allowed him to dominate her just long enough to let him think he was in control, then she tore her lips from his. "I'm still furious with you."

"And I still want you to beg for mercy," he said raggedly against her ear as he kneaded her bottom.

"I never beg." She yanked the jumpsuit off his

shoulders. "I demand." Blindly reaching out she closed the door to the chamber. "We can fight later."

He pressed her back against the door and tugged the top of her jumpsuit down. "We can fight now."

She moaned in pleasure as his teeth closed over the tight peak of one breast and then the other. His urgent suckling drove her to a state where she no longer cared what they were fighting about. Inches at a time, the stretchy jumpsuits were lowered to expose more and more heated flesh.

Cherry barely noticed when he separated their bodies in order to shed the suits completely, for in no time she was once more wrapped around him with her back against the wall.

He rubbed his shaft against her sensitive core until she was dizzy with need, but when she tried to bring him into her body, he held himself at her opening.

"Beg," he ordered and nipped her ear.

She trembled and tightened her legs around him. "I'll beg . . . right after you do."

He raised his head as if to say something else, but as their eyes met, their bodies melded together and there was nothing left to say . . . with words.

She made him growl. He made her moan.

Neither begged for mercy. And neither gave it.

Yet when the battle ended, both were supremely satisfied.

Keeping her in his snug embrace, Gallant lowered them to the carpeted floor.

In the back of her mind, Cherry knew they would probably be arguing again soon, but for the moment she only wanted to enjoy the strange gift of peace that seemed to come in the aftermath of their near-violent couplings.

She couldn't remember ever experiencing anything quite like it, but then she couldn't recall any man quite like Gallant Voyager. Certainly no one ever made her as angry, as often, as he. Nor had any man ever given her so much pleasure so effortlessly. She just wished she didn't have to fight with him to get to the good parts. The more she thought about that, the more it bothered her, until the peaceful feeling started to fade.

"Why does it have to be like this?" she asked aloud, without really expecting an answer.

He gently kissed the top of her head. "What's that?"

She sighed. "Do you like this—lying here, holding me?"

"Mmmm. Very much." His fingertips skimmed her spine and made her arch into him.

"As much as last time?"

"Maybe more," he answered with a low-pitched chuckle.

She propped herself up on her elbow, fully intending to get to the root of their problem, but was struck speechless by what she saw. Either she was dreaming or they had been transported outdoors to a sun-drenched meadow filled with yellow and blue flowers. A brightly colored butterfly hovered in front of her face then flitted away before she could catch it.

"How in the world—" Totally bewildered, she

glanced at Gallant and knew from his amused grin he was somehow responsible.

"This is how you make me feel afterward," he said, and stroked her cheek.

Gradually, the meadow misted over, until Cherry thought she had been enveloped by a fog, but she could still see Gallant lying beside her as clearly as before. He blinked his eyes, and instantly they were surrounded by a wall of dancing fire. Before Cherry could voice her terror, it was replaced by the gray fog again.

"And that's how you made me feel before," he said, sitting up beside her. He gave her a soft kiss on her parted lips. "Now, see if you can guess what this is."

In a burst of colors and light, extravagant fireworks silently exploded against a night-darkened sky, then fell to the ground like a million twinkling stars.

Cherry gaped at the last few sparks rekindling for a second before dying out. "That's what I see . . . in my head . . . when we . . . but I thought you said you weren't telepathic."

"I'm not. That's what I see also. But when I see things in my head, the images don't always stay there."

They were back in the meadow again and Cherry was more confused than ever. She ran her fingers over the grass, but what she felt was the carpet. "We're still in the facility chamber, right?"

"Right."

"I haven't been suffering from space sickness, have I?" He gave her a sheepish look. "I have the feeling you've just given me all the answers, but my brain is in shock. What is this?"

"This is my admission of defeat. You win."

Cherry laughed. "Great. What were we playing?"

He gave her a brief smile, then grew serious. "I'm not sure what it's called, but men and women have been at it since the dawn of time. I was under the mistaken impression that if I didn't agree to play, I could avoid the game. It was foolish of me to imagine that I could be near you and not touch you." She narrowed her eyes at him and he drew her back into his arms to lie down again.

With her head resting on his chest and their legs twined together, he began with a question. "Before I distracted you, you asked why it had to be like this. What did you mean?"

She gave a little shrug. "I was thinking about how you only wanted me when we were fighting, but I guess I was really talking about everything that's been going on between us. I was expecting you to say this was another mistake then push me away, like last time, until the next argument."

"No, I won't do that again. It's obvious that particular tactic didn't stop me from wanting you. As you said, it's no longer reasonable for me to try to keep secrets from you. But there's one condition to my complete honesty."

"You'll explain everything? Complete honesty?" He nodded. "What's the condition?"

"Stay here, in my arms until I'm finished, no matter how it makes you feel."

She snuggled against him, her body aroused almost as much as her curiosity. "You've got it. Shoot."

He took a deep breath. "I told you the truth about my mission. What I didn't tell you was that I have a personal stake in its outcome. Under normal circumstances, I would never have involved you, but because of that stake, I was willing to do anything that might speed it along."

Cherry's head shot up. "Are you telling me that you kidnapped me and put my life at risk, and it wasn't even necessary to the security of the universe?" She started to pull away from him, but he held her in place.

"You promised to stay until I'm finished. Perhaps I should ask you not to interrupt as well."

"You can ask, but it won't do you any good. I'm a chronic interrupter." Though she made a face at him first, she settled herself back in his arms. "Okay, I'll *try* not to ask too many questions. Go on."

"I told you that I didn't know what my planet of origin was, but that was not entirely true either."

"Surprise, surprise."

He gave her a squeeze, but went on. "When I was five, my foster parents realized I was different. At first they were only concerned about how uncontrollable I was, but they kept making excuses for my barbaric behavior. My mother tells me I was wild, but I was also a very affectionate child, and that seemed to be all she really cared about. Then they discovered my rather unique talent and had me examined by a trusted physician."

"I assume that talent is the ability to make things appear and disappear."

"Not quite. None of what you see is actually here. It's three-dimensional and appears to be solid, but it's still only an illusion. As a young boy, I didn't know how to control the ability. Whatever image came to mind was instantly in front of me. If I was angry at someone, ferocious monsters filled the room. If I was happy, it might have been balloons. I still have a problem controlling the images if I'm highly emotional, unless I'm wearing the eye patch. The doctor figured out I needed both eyes to create, either on purpose or accidentally."

"Ah-hah. Now we're getting somewhere. That's why you took it off on Zoenid; you *created* the drillfly that frightened Frezlo, didn't you?"

"Right. I just had no idea he could be literally frightened to death by it."

"But I heard it buzzing."

"Sound can be part of the illusion."

"And Aster? When you caught up with me you weren't wearing the patch then either."

"Yes. I knew that was one person you would follow. I only saw her once so I wasn't sure I could duplicate her face or voice well enough to fool you."

"Hmmph. So that's why she didn't turn around. I know I'm taking this a little off the track, but how *did* you catch me so easily?"

He shook his head. "I almost didn't. Mar-Dot signaled me just as I was boarding the shuttle to take me to the Consociation headquarters. Fortunately, you weren't aware that their telepathic abilities are strong enough to send messages."

"I should have guessed. I've met plenty of people with extrasensory powers, and some of them have that ability. I've never known anyone that can do what you do, though. You said a doctor examined you. What did he come up with?"

"The physical examination proved beyond a shadow of a doubt that I was humanoid, but not Noronian, or from any other advanced civilization. Physiologically and psychologically, I was a primitive, except for my power to create illusions. After weighing all the facts, he came up with the only solution possible."

When he hesitated to continue, she rapidly reviewed all the hints he had given her to date and came up with a shocking conclusion. Her head bobbed up again. "You're an *Illusian*?"

"It would seem so." He didn't force her to lie down again, but neither did he meet her gaze. The meadow faded, leaving the facility chamber looking as it normally did.

"But how? You said Illusia had a barrier around it that no one could penetrate."

"That's what everyone thinks. But if I am of Illusian descent and I was found on Norona, how did I get there? Am I a throwback from a mating that occurred four centuries ago, or did someone manage to remove me from Illusia when I was a baby? And why only me? Considering my mission, my presence on Norona could be a vital clue. If I *was* smuggled out, then the document could have been also, meaning it is legitimate and important. Unfortunately, I can't share my knowledge with anyone."

"I don't understand."

"My foster parents and the doctor agreed that if anyone found out about my existence, I would be exiled without being given a chance to prove that I could behave in a civilized manner. The patch prevented me from accidentally revealing my secret ability. My parents dyed the white streaks in my hair and trained me to control my emotions in public. But I could never forget what I was hiding. The hatred and fear of Illusians is very widespread. I could still be exiled today simply because of my genetic makeup. Mar-Dot, and now you, are the only others who know the truth."

"Holy stars. That's why you're so worried about hurting me. You actually believe all those things you were told about the Illusians are true about yourself."

He turned his unsmiling face to hers. "I believe it because all those things are true." His voice was charged with hostility. "You have no idea what I'm capable of. I am *constantly* at war with this primitive nature of mine. But I had been doing a formidable job of keeping my secret . . . until I ran up against you."

"What's that supposed to mean?"

"It means that, in spite of all my training and good intentions, you make me act like a barbarian. For whatever reason, you bring out the worst in me."

Not able to lie still another second, she pulled

them both up into sitting positions and held his hands tightly as she spoke. "Isn't it possible that I bring out the *best* in you instead? Holding in all your emotions is unhealthy. Maybe you were fated to meet me before you burst at the seams. Tell me this. Have you held yourself back in any way when we've had sex?"

"No, but—"

"No buts. I realize there are women who prefer lukewarm men, just like there are people who prefer vanilla ice cream. Maybe that's the only kind of woman you've encountered, but I've never been with a man who excited me more or satisfied me better than you do. You have definitely not *hurt* me. And I don't believe for one second that you really could, not physically anyway. Of course, there's always the possibility that I'm a barbarian, too. That might explain a lot of things."

Gallant laughed out loud. "I've said it before and I'll probably say it again. You are the most exasperating female I have ever known. I've been agonizing over your figuring out what I am for days. Then here I was, fully prepared for you to be repulsed by my confession, and what do you do? You compliment me on my performance as a barbarian."

"It's called being truthful. Are you convinced that I'm not disgusted by your genetic heritage, or afraid of you—either in or out of bed?"

His slow grin said it all.

"Good. Please note how well being honest worked on you, and use the method often in the future . . .

at least with me. I assure you we'll do a lot less fighting that way."

He pulled her back down to the floor and rolled her beneath him. "Well, there's fighting, and there's *fighting.*"

She stopped him just before their lips met. "Wait a minute. I just remembered something. What happened to your appointment?"

He lifted himself partially away from her and frowned. "That was very odd. Before I went looking for you, I made a quick call to Josep, my contact at the Consociation, to tell him I'd be delayed, and I was told he had left Norona this morning on an emergency. I can't figure out why he didn't send me a message in time to save me the trip."

"Maybe the emergency was such that he forgot about your appointment."

"Maybe. The last few times I've spoken to him, he's forgotten something."

"How old is he?"

"I don't know. He looks ancient. Why?"

"When Terrans age, they sometimes lose their memories."

"That can't be it. Josep is from the planet Gilliad. They are a gentle people known for the fact that their intelligence increases throughout their lives, which might be as long as a thousand years. In fact, there are Gilliad representatives to the Consociation who personally recall the Illusian invasion. Josep is the only one among them that wants to see a change in the current policy. From what I've heard though, he's slowly bringing them around to his way of thinking."

"Good for him."

"You really mean that, don't you?"

"Yep. I told you before that I thought it was totally unfair to judge the Illusians purely on past history. Now that I know one personally, I'm even more convinced that their reputations are probably much worse than they are for real."

He gave her a quick kiss. "I'm beginning to think you're a hopeless optimist."

"An optimist—yes. Hopeless—never. In fact, I'm hoping something right now."

His hand clamped onto her hip and pulled her to him. "I think I can accommodate."

"Close, but no cigar." She laughed at his dumbfounded expression. "Although I admit my body was hoping for a rematch, my mind was actually hoping something along a different line."

"Oh?" he asked with a raised eyebrow.

"Now that we've worked out your problem, I was hoping we could work out mine." His expression grew ominous, but she ignored the warning. "I accept the fact that you can't afford the time it would take to return me to Earth, but at least take me back to Norona."

Chapter 12

Gallant tensed. His confession may not have repulsed her as he had expected it would, but she was still anxious to get away from him. As before, while he held her quietly in his arms, his imagination had run straight to thoughts of forever. Those thoughts had started to crystallize when she seemed to understand. But her request to be returned swiftly brought everything back into a realistic perspective.

"Gallant? Are you afraid I'd tell someone about you? I swear I wouldn't."

He rolled away from her and sat up. "There are those who could discover what you know without your telling them. Besides, you're still in need of my protection, whether you want it or not."

Cherry slowly rose to her knees. "Protection? Or captivity? You said the condition to my getting an honest explanation was that I stay in your arms. You didn't warn me that hearing that explanation would strip me of my freedom."

"It's only temporary," he said with a frown. "Until I can discover the truth about the Illusians."

"And what if you never do?" Her voice rose a few decibels. "You can't keep me chained to you forever."

The truth of her words forced him to turn away from her.

"I see." Cherry reached for her jumpsuit and pulled it on. "How silly of me to think we'd made some progress. You just can't deal honestly no matter what."

One glance at her face let him know that endless days of gnawing tension and unsatisfied desires loomed ahead. He watched her walk to the door before he knew what he had to say. "Wait. Please." She turned to him and crossed her arms. "At least hear me out before you condemn me."

She walked over to the chair where his black outfit lay in a heap. Tossing his clothes to him, she sat down and said, "Put these on and I'll listen."

The awareness that his body could disturb her, in spite of her annoyance with him, made him feel somewhat better about his own mixed feelings.

As soon as he was dressed, she motioned for him to take the other chair. "Shoot."

"It wouldn't do any good to take you back to Norona. I couldn't get you on a ship without the proper authority, and I know if I try to explain the situation to anyone to get that authority, you stand a good chance of being incarcerated there. At least as long as I keep you with me, I know you're safe. No matter what you think of me, I will not ignore the fact that I am responsible for your safety."

"For the rest of my life?"

He almost said yes before his common sense

kicked in. "Of course not. I'll return you to Terra as soon as I can."

"But not in time for me to audition for Theodophilus, and maybe not even in time to be with Aster for her daughter's birth."

He shook his head. "I'm sorry."

"Just not sorry enough to do anything about it."

"That's not true." Rubbing his chin, an idea occurred to him. "I can't change the child's birth date, but I should be able to do something to make up for your missing the audition."

Cherry's eyes widened and she leaned forward. "Go on."

"Certain privileges come with my employment. I'm sure it would be possible to convince Theodophilus to hold a private audition for you after my assignment is completed. Wherever in the galaxy he is at the time, I give you my word, I'll take you there."

She cocked her head at him. "You're not just saying that to make life with me more peaceful?"

Leaning back and stretching his long legs out in front of him, he gave her a dismayed look. "I'm trying to play by your rules, but I don't see the point in being honest if you're going to question everything I say."

Cherry bounced up from the chair and walked the width of the chamber several times before coming back to stand over him. "Okay, let me get this straight. You're going to be truthful with me from now on, and whenever this mission of yours is over, you'll help me get an audition with Theodophilus."

He nodded. "What about the fact that I know your secret?"

He shrugged. "Taking risks is part of my life. If I give you what you want though, you won't have any reason to betray me. Besides, if I can prove the Illusians have changed, it will no longer be necessary for me to hide what I am."

"I almost hate to admit it, but you're making sense."

"Truce?"

She started to offer her hand, then withdrew it. "I have one more condition before I agree to peaceful coexistence."

He didn't think it would be very diplomatic of him to remind her that she was in no position to negotiate, so he simply raised an eyebrow at her.

"I can't just sit around on this ship, twiddling my thumbs, while you go off in search of the truth. Let me work with you, like on Zoenid—only better informed."

"Cherry—"

"Don't say no. I need to keep busy, but I also *want* to be involved. Please?"

He shook his head with a sigh. "I have no idea what kind of situation we're heading into. Lore is supposed to be uninhabited because of the poisonous mist that surrounds it. But from what Frezlo said, something must be there. I had a good reason for taking you with me to Zoenid, and I had believed I could adequately protect you then. Of course," he added with a grin, "I had no idea *someone* was going to take my cheats out of my vest."

Cherry sat on the edge of the low table in front of him. "I promise I won't do anything like that again. In fact, I'll even give them back to you right now." She paused a moment before making her final offer. "I'll let you put the collar back on me, and I'll behave however you want me to . . . in front of others." He rolled his eyes in disbelief.

"Well? Can I go?"

"We'll see."

She accepted that as a positive answer. "When do we get there?"

"About three days."

Cherry smiled as she glided from the table onto his lap. "That should be long enough."

Although he looked at her suspiciously, his hands and body welcomed her back. "Are you trying to influence my decision with sexual favors?"

Nuzzling his neck, she said, "Why, Captain, that would make me as devious as you are. But, just for the record, would it work?"

Uttering a low-pitched growl, his hand cupped her breast and gave it a gentle squeeze. "I'll let you know in three days."

Rom interrupted his telecommunication with the chief of Outerworld Monitor Control, and called Aster to join him in their living room. "OMC is going to transmit a film of an American newscast that was televised a short while ago. She suggested we view it immediately." He turned on the monitor and sat on the sofa next to his mate as the program began.

"Good evening, ladies and gentlemen. This is

Betsy Arnett with news from around the world. The top story today has everyone trying to remember when the last time was that they said their prayers. There has been another supernatural sighting at a religious shrine—this time, however, someone had a video camera on hand and was able to tape the final portion of the sighting. For the story, here's our man in Japan, Ray Valez."

The picture switched to a balding man holding a microphone. "At twelve noon in Kamakura, Japan, approximately five hundred people were milling around this huge bronze statue of the Great Buddha." The camera panned to the statue, then showed the stunned faces of various people in the crowd behind the reporter.

"I was told by several eyewitnesses that four bolts of lightning suddenly streaked out of the sky and hit the statue, all at the same time, accompanied by crashing thunder. With the last bolt, a man appeared, looking very much like the statue behind me. He stood on the Great Buddha's thumbs and spoke to the crowd in Japanese, in a voice almost as loud as the thunder. He greeted them as, quote, my children, unquote, and warned them that Judgment Day is coming. A tourist managed to turn on his video camera in time to catch the tail end of the appearance."

The grainy quality of the film identified the beginning of the amateur's tape. The messenger did indeed look like the statue, and his words were being translated into English across the bottom of the screen.

"The Supreme Being of all the universe is coming to Earth. As the wicked nonbelievers and the greedy will be punished, so shall the obedient believers and the generous be rewarded. Prepare yourselves to meet your Maker and obey Him in all things. Now look upon His image and remember it."

Over the face of the Great Buddha statue another face was superimposed for a few seconds, but the cameraman's hand was unsteady and the features were blurred. Then with another flashy display of lightning and thunder, both the Buddha look-alike and the image vanished.

The program was turned back over to the anchorwoman, who went on to review the other sightings that had recently occurred around the world. "Our most recent poll shows that in the United States eighteen percent of the people believe the sightings are true messages from God, thirty-three percent are convinced they are hoaxes, and forty-nine percent are still undecided.

"It is interesting to note that in the countries where the sightings occurred, the percentage of believers is considerably higher. Perhaps, we Americans are just waiting for a more personal message."

The film ended a moment later and the serious face of the OMC chief reappeared. "As you requested, we had assigned several emissaries to keep watch at all religious shrines in the northeastern quartersphere on the surface. Coincidentally, P68, who had been near the sighting in India, was at the statue referred to in this newscast. His report has just come in.

"Again he states that he picked up a surge of mental energy, only at close range it was much stronger than what he had sensed before. However, the surge did not last long enough for him to narrow down its origin. He reports that a one-thousand-meter square around the statue has already been searched, and no evidence of electronic or photographic equipment has been found. The search area is now being expanded, but based on what he sensed, he doubts that anything physical will be found."

Rom asked the chief to stand by for a minute while he and Aster discussed what they had seen.

Aster rubbed her abdomen in an attempt to calm her daughter. "Interesting."

Rom smiled. "Still don't believe it?"

"I suppose we should allow for the remote possibility that the sightings are legitimate warnings. Some of the governments of Outerworld have made strides toward peace and improved living conditions since I was out there, but not enough to make any vast difference in the future of the planet. Perhaps the fear of a global Judgment Day is just what is needed to put individuals on the right track, then the governments would naturally follow. God *could* be behind this."

"Or someone bent on total world power," Rom countered. "In which case, we can't afford to let that person get away with it. I think it's important that the messages all contain the warning that nonbelievers will be punished and the obedient will be rewarded."

Recalling the near disaster they helped Earth

avoid ten years ago, Aster angled her head at him. "You think we might have to interfere again?"

"At least we have to be prepared for the worst. The face that Buddha showed is the only clue we have, but I could barely see it." He asked the chief to replay that segment and have the computer enhance the image.

The blurred face was frozen on the monitor, then in a matter of seconds, it was clarified.

Aster gasped and reached for Rom's hand. "Dear Lord. Is that who I think it is?"

The man staring out from the screen was not wearing an eye patch, but the two white streaks in his long black hair helped identify him positively for Rom. "Unless he has an identical twin, it looks like the forthcoming Supreme Being is Gallant Voyager."

Bessima smiled at the three young men she had lured to her table in the San Francisco hotel's cocktail lounge. It didn't matter that they thought she was their favorite entertainer. She was in violent need and would use any illusionary trick it took to drive these males into a frenzy of animal lust. She had already discovered that Terrans did not normally get aroused to the point of oblivion as Illusian males did. They had to be teased into it, and she could see her efforts were beginning to pay off with her present companions.

When she had first arrived on Terra, her illusionary talent had yet to be tested in a practical situation. As she successfully accomplished larger and more complex illusions, her confidence grew. It took very little to convince a Terran that the paper in their hand was currency or tickets for transportation, or that the little booklet was the required passport for travel between countries.

The princess had equipped Bessima with a translating device that Chief Advisor Josep had given her, claiming that many Noronians wore them to aid communication. It allowed her to speak and understand thousands of Terran languages, but until she saw with her own eyes that the people were deceived, she hadn't believed it would work.

During her years of training for this mission, she had practiced creating sounds as much as images, but she had never even tried to produce an illusion as magnificent as the lightning and thunder at the Buddha statue. She decided that would have to become a regular part of her demonstration.

As confidence in her abilities mounted, she dwelled more and more on her options should the princess and her army fail to show up. She had come to the conclusion that one of the newly merged Middle Eastern countries, like Iranraq would be the best place to set up her kingdom. They held power, yet were less advanced than most other countries, and the people had strong religious beliefs. All she had to do was have an illusion of the Supreme Being proclaim herself His personal messenger to them.

For a while she had given consideration to some of the South American countries, but their proximity to the United States was a definite drawback. Although she was in America now, she was concerned about whether or not she would be able to deceive them. She had heard their skeptical news reports and was prepared to create an even more elaborate "miracle" than she had in Japan to try to impress them.

Returning her attention to the present, she noted that the young man sitting next to her had inched his way closer until their knees were touching. While the other two continued to gush over her music and glamorous appearance, she ran her hand up the inside of the male thigh closest to her. When he got over his initial shock, he relaxed and spread his legs to let her explore his pride at will. She decided he would do nicely, and slipped off one of her shoes to let her bare foot investigate what the two across the table had to offer.

Once there was no doubt she had them hooked, she suggested, "Why don't all three of you come to my cabin, and we can continue getting to know each other . . . in private?" They practically knocked over the chairs in their rush to cooperate.

Her triumph in Japan had stirred up a hunger that she doubted these three could satisfy, although she intended to force them to do their best. What she required to release the pent-up excitement was a blood fight, but she wasn't so distracted by her need that she would take such a risk. As she ogled the young flesh that would soon be exposed for her pleasure, she thought perhaps she could get away with drawing just a little blood. After all, she had learned that celebrities are usually excused for their eccentric behavior.

Chapter 13

"You have been a student long enough, Cherry," Mar said, standing beside her. "It is time for a test."

She looked up at him from the bench seat and laughed. "Yeah, right. Why don't you just turn the controls over to me and see where I take us?"

"Go ahead," he said with a perfectly serious face.

"You are kidding, aren't you? Dot, you tell me."

Dot turned to her. "It is not a joke. We have intentionally taken the ship off course for this exercise. You may show us that we have not wasted our time with you by plotting a new course, then calibrating the time it will take to get there."

Cherry glanced at Gallant, who was leaning back in his chair, absently rubbing his chin as he observed them. "Is this okay with you?"

He shrugged. "Mar-Dot *has* given you a lot of attention. I think it's only fair that you prove yourself."

She wondered exactly what he meant by that. Did it cross his mind—as it had hers—that if given the chance she would plot a course back to Earth? Was this a test of her newly acquired navigational skills, or a test of her loyalty? With a nod of acceptance, she turned back to the panel and monitor, determined to show off for all of them.

The last two and a half days had been the most fun she'd had in ages. Her truce with Gallant had brought about several positive changes. The constant tension between them had vanished, and the atmosphere on the bridge lightened tremendously, much to Mar-Dot's relief, and everyone's entertainment.

Without the fear of accidentally revealing his ability, Gallant quit wearing the eye patch, and found that, in spite of the emotional state Cherry kept him in, he was able to control his talent . . . except when they coupled. Then Cherry never knew what to expect. Anything from balloons and flowers to tidal waves and volcanoes might suddenly appear in the room around them.

What she did know was that she was happy . . . and extremely relaxed. She had lost count of the number of times he had given her a release, and after each encounter she was certain she wouldn't find the energy for another round. Until he touched her again, and the energy flooded back tenfold.

The only criticism, and it was a weak one at that, was that they had yet to go slowly. Oh, they may have thought about it, but every time their lips met, they were suddenly desperate to couple. Before this journey was over, Cherry was determined that they would enjoy each other like two people, instead of a pair of wild animals in heat.

She completed the task Mar set for her in about fifteen minutes, but took an extra quarter hour to recheck her work before letting him "grade" her. It only took him fifteen seconds to confirm that she had passed.

To Gallant, Mar said, "We are back on course to Lore, Captain."

Gallant bit his cheek to keep from smiling. "And what does our apprentice navigator predict will be our time of arrival?"

Cherry straightened her shoulders as if standing at attention. "At our present speed, we should dock on Lore in eight hours, forty-five minutes, Captain, sir."

"Well done, apprentice," he replied, and held out his hand to congratulate her. As soon as she gave him her hand, he stood up and pulled her along with him. "Now let's see how well you can navigate your way out of here. Our rest period should have begun an hour ago."

"Mar," Dot said with a smile. "Do you remember the captain ever before requiring so much rest? Perhaps he is ill."

"Or getting on in age," Mar offered helpfully. "He should probably have this constant state of fatigue checked by a physician."

Cherry giggled at the half-hearted glare Gallant gave the both of them before they left the bridge. The moment they were out of Mar-Dot's sight, he pulled her into his embrace. Remembering her decision to try to slow them down, instead of kissing his mouth, she pressed her lips to his chest, and got a surprise. "What's this?" she asked, brushing her fingertips over the spot she had just kissed. "It feels like stubble."

He made a groaning sound and captured her

hand. "I'll take care of it. You go on in the room. I'll only be a few minutes."

"Gallant Voyager! You know better than to say something that cryptic to me. Explain."

With a shake of his head, he said, "Will you allow me no secrets from you at all?"

"What do you think?" she asked with a sly smile.

"I think that if I don't explain, we'll be standing in this corridor for our entire rest period. All right, you win again." He took a breath and made his confession. "I have an excessive amount of hair on my chest."

She wrinkled her nose at him. "So?"

"So, I was too . . . self-conscious, to have it permanently removed like my beard. I have to do it myself."

"Why?"

He took another deep breath before answering. "Because it makes me look like the primitive being that I am."

"Oh phooey! That has to be the single most assinine statement you've ever made. *I* happen to be crazy about chest hair on a man."

Gallant couldn't help but grin. "Yes, my pet, but we've already come to the conclusion that you're a barbarian at heart, so your opinion doesn't count."

"Hmmph. Flattery won't get you anywhere. Well, if you insist on removing it, let me do it for you."

"I might if I used a depilatory, but I haven't found one that doesn't irritate my skin. I have to shave, the old-fashioned way . . . with a razor."

Her eyes lit up and she wiggled her eyebrows at

him. "Ooh. What a wonderful way to show how much you trust me." She ignored the look of horror on his face as she pulled him into the facility chamber and over to the sink. "Okay, where do you keep your stuff? I've been in and out of the storage drawers a hundred times and I've never seen a razor.

The worried look seemed to be frozen on his face, but he opened a cabinet beneath the sink and withdrew a small cedar box from behind the supply of linens. Opening it, he revealed a brass, double-edged razor, shaving mug, soap, brush, and a supply of razors. "It was a gift from my mother—an antique actually. I was able to find someone who could make the razors. Are you sure you want to do this?"

She took the box from him and set it on the counter beside the sink. "Absolutely. I think it will be very erotic. And I'll do my best not to draw blood."

He rolled his eyes, but removed his vest for her.

"You have got the most beautiful body," Cherry told him, not able to resist stroking his skin. She smiled when his nipples instantly tightened for her. Her fingers followed a line of stubble down to his waist. "You'll have to take the pants off so I can get this, too." He groaned and she added, "Don't worry, I know where to stop."

As he shed his boots and slacks, she got out two fluffy white towels and a hand cloth and covered the counter with one of the towels. "You sit on this, and I'll cover your *essentials* with the other." When he turned around and she saw the condition he was already in, her smile broadened. This was going to be great fun!

First, she filled the sink with hot water and dropped in the hand cloth. Then, after adding a few drops of water to the soap in the mug, she used the brush to work up a lather. Her actions apparently convinced him she had some idea of what she was doing, because he sat down as instructed.

She stepped in between his knees and draped the towel over his lap, as if she didn't notice the obvious protrusion. To prepare his skin, she partially wrung out the heated cloth and wet the areas she would be shaving. With the mug in one hand and the brush in her other, she began lathering up his chest. "Does this tickle?"

"Yes," he hissed.

"Then why aren't you giggling?"

"I don't giggle."

"No, you growl." She teased his nipple with the brush and he couldn't hold back the grin any longer.

"If you don't get on with it, you're going to get more than growling," he threatened, but couldn't quite erase that grin.

She worked the lather down the center of his abdomen and laughed again when those muscles automatically contracted. "Now, be nice. There's something I wanted to talk to you about." She exchanged the brush and mug for the razor. "You know I like having sex with you."

His chest rose with the deep breath her words made him take.

"Don't do that. You have to stay very still." With a

smooth stroke, she scraped the razor down the center of his broad chest, lightly ran it back up the same line using the other side of the blade, then dipped it in the sink to rinse off the lather. As she repeated the procedure on another strip, she got back to the subject she wanted to discuss. "Anyway, I want you to know that I'm not really complaining, but I have noticed a decided lack of foreplay in our relationship."

Only the fact that the razor was skimming the edge of his nipple kept him from proving her wrong immediately. Each stroke of the blade reminded him not to move while it teased him to do just that. "Cherry, don't you think this particular subject could be discussed *after* you put down the razor."

She noted the twitching movement beneath the towel on his lap. "No. This is the perfect time to discuss it. Sit up straight so I can get your stomach." He did as he was told and she added a little more lather. The feathery swipes of the brush caused him to suck in his muscles even more than he already had. Careful not to touch that part of him that was making a tent of the lap towel, she ran the razor over his navel.

"You see, this is a perfect example of what I'm trying to say. I know how much you want me right now, and that's very exciting. In fact, I'm so hot, I could get off just by rubbing against your leg a few times, but I won't. Fighting the temptation to do something can be more erotic than the act itself. That's why I covered you. I like to look at you, but when I do, I have to touch and taste." Her gaze caressed him, and she was rewarded with the sight of dampness on the peak of his mountain.

His hands balled into fists, yet he kept them at his sides.

"There," she said, rinsing the razor for the last time. "First part's done. Don't move yet, though." She drained the sink and wet the cloth again. As she wiped away the remains of the soap, she taunted, "Are you counting the seconds, Gallant? Are you sitting here imagining yourself plunging into me? Are you thinking about how tight and slick I'm going to be around you?"

His only answer was a low growl as he devoured her with his eyes.

She set aside the cloth and got a bottle of moisturizing oil out of the drawer. "Imagining and thinking are good. I just want to postpone the inevitable a little longer." Holding one end of the lap towel, she dragged it slowly away from him, causing him to inhale with an audible gasp. "Everything is better when you have to wait for it."

Pouring some oil into her palm, she prepared to add more fuel to the fire. The moment she placed her oiled hands on his chest, she knew her case for waiting would soon be lost. His flesh sizzled beneath her touch, and the crazy tingling burst up her robotic arm. Through sheer willpower, she forced herself to massage every inch of his chest and stomach before giving in to the ultimate temptation. Adding a little more oil, she brought her hands closer and closer to the heart of his fire, until finally, as slowly as she could, she wrapped her fingers around it.

His eyes closed and his jaw clenched as she slid her hand along his length, drawing his foreskin upward, then back again. Regardless of her manipulations, he kept his hands at his sides, proving to them both that he could indeed control his primitive urges as well as, if not better than, any civilized man.

Until her tongue teased his lips and he tasted the essence that was Cherry's alone. With a growl that rose from deep within his chest, he came off the counter and pulled her to him. In a heartbeat he assaulted her mouth with savage intent, and she willingly met him on their private field of battle.

Suddenly he broke the kiss and twisted her around so that she was facing the mirror over the sink and he was behind her. His hands grasped her hips and moved upward to capture her breasts. Dipping his head, he nipped her ear and murmured in a voice heavy with urgent need.

"You want foreplay?" His hands roamed over her jumpsuit, from her breasts to her hips, massaged her stomach, and eased between her thighs. "I thought that was what we were doing every time we looked at each other. Every word out of your mouth, every breath you take, arouses me. It doesn't have to be planned or discussed.

"You're the one who insists on the truth. Be honest with me now, Cherry. When we're on the bridge, talking with Mar-Dot or playing cubit, when you're eating a meal, or washing your face, aren't you really thinking about how long it will be until I'm inside of you again?"

She watched his fingers find her nerve center and

press and rotate until the only reason she was still standing was because he was holding her so tightly. "Yes," she whispered, barely able to breathe let alone talk. "All the time. I can't stop thinking about you and your body. No matter what you give me, I want more."

"And I want to give it to you, whenever and wherever you want it. You seem to be under the mistaken impression that I'm a sheep in wolf's clothing. I'm not. The clothes I wear suit me perfectly. And like the wolf, when I'm cornered, I bite." Remaining behind her, he stripped her naked and, in seconds, recommenced his stroking and kneading, all the while making her feel him, hard and swollen against her back.

Clinging to his thighs, she rode the waves of desire higher and faster until she crashed to the shore, and still he would not release her.

Wordlessly, he placed her hands on the counter's edge in front of her and urged her to lean forward. As his fingers quickly returned her to a state of desperate hunger, she parted her legs to ease his way.

He wasn't slow or gentle, and she didn't want him to be. She saw the truth in the mirror and accepted it.

They *were* a pair of wild animals in heat, equally driven, equally matched.

Sometime later, Cherry lay nestled with Gallant on his bunk, watching a crackling campfire beneath a clear, starry sky. "This is nice. Too bad we didn't bring any marshmallows." She had to explain what she meant by that before he could grant her wish.

Once she described the image for him, a stick appeared in his hand with a plump white marshmallow on the end. "Would you like the honors?"

She sat up with a giggle and pretended to take the imaginary stick into her hand and hold it close to the fire. When the treat was just the right shade of toasty brown she brought it to her mouth and blew on it. "You have to be very careful not to burn the roof of your mouth, you know." She pulled the invisible marshmallow off the stick with her teeth and made a show of savoring the sweetness. "Mmmm. Wonderful. You ought to try one."

"No thanks. I never eat my own creations." He pulled her back down beside him. "I used to do things like this all the time when I was a boy. I forgot how much fun it could be to play pretend."

Cherry kissed his chin. "Well, I must say, your little talent certainly adds a new dimension to the game. You'd be very helpful as a teacher in a mime class." She trickled her fingers over his chest and stomach. "Smooth as a baby. But I'd still like you to let it grow." She felt him chuckle silently. "I'm curious. Why weren't there any images in the chamber before?"

"Probably because I never took my eyes off you and that razor."

"Scared ya, huh?"

"Cherry, I—"

She clapped her hand over his mouth and propped herself up on her elbow. "Let the image go and look at me." She waited for him to bring up the room's lighting enough to see him. "I just want to warn you that if you are thinking of apologizing, or asking if you hurt me, or frightened me, I will be forced to give you a demonstration of precisely how well I can defend myself with this arm of mine. If you ever do anything I don't like, I am capable of stopping you, the same way I stopped Frezlo from shooting you on Zoenid." She took her hand away and gave him a peck on the mouth to make up for silencing him.

Giving her a smirk, he said, "All I was going to say was that I would never be able to look at my mother's gift to me in the same way again."

"Oh. Good. Then there's only one more thing to discuss before going to sleep." The sudden tension in his body suggested that he knew exactly what she was going to ask. "Will you take me along with you tomorrow?" He closed his eyes, and she could almost see his mind sorting through excuses to deny her.

"My job is not a game or an illusion, Cherry. The risks are real."

"I know that as well as you—I was with you on Zoenid, remember?"

"I had a specific reason for taking you then, and besides, I knew what the risks would be there, and I was prepared for them. I have no idea what might be waiting for me on Lore. There are reports that no one landing on Lore has ever been heard from again. They simply disappear, ship and all, into the mist, which, by the way, has been tested and found to be lethal to humanoid life forms as well as most others."

"Well, the way it sounds, you're already risking my life just by taking the ship down there. It was your decision not to put me off when you had the chance on Norona."

"Cherry . . ." he murmured in a warning tone.

"Okay. I won't start on that again, but the fact is I *am* on board, I *want* to be involved, and I might be of help. Two heads are usually better, you know." His frustrated sigh let her know he didn't have an argument for any of her points. "What are you going to do about the mist?"

"Wear a protective suit, although if the reports are true, it might not be sufficient."

Cherry studied his features for a moment. "But you don't believe the reports. You're thinking about a certain Con rep that landed there and obviously returned to Norona because all of the reps are now accounted for, right?"

He gave her a small nod. "Right. If he went down there and left safely, I can, too. The fact that he went there at all is what's important. As far as I know, no one has bothered to investigate the planet in decades, so anything might be going on there without being noticed. Someone or something must be on Lore, or the Con rep wouldn't have run to it directly from hiring Frezlo. Thus, that something must have a bearing on the Weebort's assassination."

"And your mission."

"Exactly."

"I agree completely. Now *you* agree that if you

leave the ship to go exploring, you'll be making me Mar-Dot's responsibility. Won't you be worried about what I might do without your *protective custody*? While you're hunting down clues, part of your brain will be preoccupied with that concern."

"You wouldn't"—his expression filled with the worry her suggestion prompted—"Would you?"

She gave him an enigmatic smile. "What do you think?"

"I think I've been conned." He rubbed his chin a few times. "Listen, the deadliness of the mist is not its only factor. It's also too thick to see through. *If* I took you along, and we got separated, I might never find you. Are you still willing to wear the collar?"

She grimaced. "If that's the only way you'll take me. But if it turns out not to be necessary, it comes right off, okay?" When he didn't answer right away, she tickled his side. "*Okay?*"

He grabbed her hand and brought it to his mouth for a kiss, then held on to it as he asked, "Will you promise to behave like a slave, do everything I tell you to, and trust me to know what I'm doing, even if it looks like I'm abandoning you, as it did on Zoenid?"

She got to her knees and bowed to him. "Yes, master. Whatever you say, master. Is there some special service I can do now that will prove my loyal obedience?"

His thumb brushed across her taut breast. "I'm sure I could come up with one if I give it some thought." He coaxed her to stretch out on top of his body. "As I recall, you did imply you were going to use sexual favors to influence my decision." With a squirming motion, she cradled him between her legs. "I admit I have been influenced by your efforts." She licked one of his nipples, then the other. "Hmmm. I think one more favor ought to do it."

She slithered up his body and nipped his lower lip. "You're an insatiable barbarian."

Before they fell asleep, he lived up to her description . . . and agreed to take her exploring with him on Lore.

The next morning, Gallant was already out of bed when Cherry awoke. Her first thought was that he had tricked her again, leaving her behind in spite of his promise, but the sound of boot heels in the corridor outside reassured her that he had not. The door opened and he came in carrying a tray.

She smiled, and with a luxurious stretch sat up with her feet beneath her thighs and the sheet tucked under her armpits. "I thought I was supposed to be the slave."

He set the tray on the bed in front of her knees, then gave her a kiss before sitting down on the other end of the bunk. "There are times when the slave is so good she earns a few special privileges. I hope toast and a scrambler will do."

"Only if they're real," she answered with a laugh as she picked up one of the mugs of wake-up. "Your marshmallows didn't fill my stomach very well."

He clucked his tongue at her. "I give you my best efforts and all I get is sarcasm." With a smile, he stuck a fork into the yellow protein mixture and fed it to her.

Her taste buds assured her it was real, and hadn't improved any since yesterday, or the day before that. "What I wouldn't give for Belgian waffles smothered in blueberries and heaped with whipped cream." In a flash, the boring plate of food looked like a gourmand's delight. "Perfect! Now if you only had the power to improve the flavor, I'd be in heaven."

Swallowing a bite of toast, he shook his head. "Never satisfied, are you?"

She wiggled her eyebrows at him. "You should know the answer to that."

Instantly, her appetizing breakfast burst into a flambé. Without thinking, she jerked away from the flames and bumped her head on the wall.

The fire vanished, leaving her plate in its original state. She rubbed the back of her head, but her chuckle let him know she was unhurt.

"That's what you get for teasing a barbarian," he said with a sexy grin. "I fully intended to keep my mind on my mission this morning."

Her eyes widened. "Oh! I almost forgot. Where are we?"

"Circling Lore. Mar-Dot is scanning for life forms. Take your time. They haven't found anything down there yet."

Nonetheless, they joined Mar-Dot on the bridge a short while later.

"Anything yet?" Gallant asked hopefully.

Dot smiled a greeting at Cherry before answering. "We have scanned the entire planet, and there is not one sign of life, either animal or plant. It appears to be as uninhabited as we had heard. As you suggested, we used the vacuum technique to take samples of the mist from several locations and had the computer analyze it."

Gallant sat down in his chair and Cherry perched on its arm beside him. "Results?"

The he-she turned their body so that Dot could continue facing the captain with Mar still able to see his monitor. "It is made up of a poisonous gas compound, but there is nothing in it that would damage the structure of the ship."

"Will standard suits protect us?"

"Us?" Dot's eyes widened with apprehension.

"Not you," he assured her quickly. "Cherry and I. Never mind how she talked me into it."

Dot's smile said she didn't need to be told. "The suits should be more than adequate. Of course, ours will need some alterations if she is to use it."

"This is most interesting," Mar said, turning toward Gallant. "Once we were certain the mist would not affect the ship, we moved in closer for additional testing. The gravitational pull is quite strong, but not enough to cause a ship to crash. Also, the outside temperature is a fraction above freezing—not low enough to create any problem with the drive unit. At first, I could not see any reason for a ship to enter the mist and never come out. However, the computer just completed the tests on the surface samples."

"Must you always go into a long dissertation before getting to the point?" Dot asked with obvious annoyance.

"Yes," Mar replied indignantly, "whenever the situation requires one. As I was about to say before I was so rudely interrupted, the surface is slush, at least a mile deep."

Cherry leaned forward. "Slush, as in sloppy snow, sleet, and not quite ice?"

Mar nodded. "I believe that description fits. Between the soft surface and the strong gravity, a ship attempting to land on the planet would be sucked beneath tons of the matter before the crew had a chance to reverse its position."

Gallant rubbed his chin. "And yet Frezlo saw a ship go down there that had to have come back out."

Cherry put her mind to the puzzle. "Maybe that ship just circled the planet within the mist like we're doing."

Frowning, he shook his head. "I don't think so. Frezlo made it sound like the ship headed directly in without stopping. Only someone who knew in advance that the mist wouldn't damage the ship—or someone bent on suicide—would go ahead without running tests first. No, there has to be something we're missing."

Cherry got up and strolled around the panel. "Mar, you said the slush goes about a kilometer deep. Then what?"

"It appears to be solid rock below the slush."

Cherry circled the bridge again. "Could there be a civilization inside that planet, like Innerworld is in the center of Earth? If the Noronians built tunnels into a planet ten thousand years ago, why couldn't some other people have done it here as well?"

Gallant caught her hand as she made a pass by

him and pulled her onto his knee. "Sit still, woman, you're making me dizzy. She's got a valid idea, Mar. Look for any magnetic fields similar to—"

"Already started, Captain," Dot said, without turning toward him. "We'll have the results in a few minutes."

Gallant pulled Cherry close enough to whisper in her ear. "Do me a favor and get me an eye patch before I embarrass you with an image of what you make me want to do."

She burst out laughing, but when she leaned back she saw that his hand was shielding his left eye.

"What can I tell you," he murmured, "I love the way your brain works, too." He gave her a nudge and she got off his knee.

As she headed back to his room, she replayed his last sentence in her head. He had used the word "too," but as far as she could recall, he had never said he "loved" anything about her.

Love was one word that usually sent her fleeing from any man who spoke it to her. Other words that gave her the shivers were *commitment, faithful,* and *forever.* All of them conjured up visions of two-room shacks and ten whining brats . . . prison bars and leg irons. They were all antonyms of *FREEDOM* and thereby stricken from her vocabulary.

She found one of Gallant's eye patches and stopped in Mar-Dot's room to get the set of cheats she had never returned to him. By the time she returned to the bridge, she convinced herself that he hadn't consciously used that *word* on purpose.

"You did it, Cherry," Gallant said with a broad

smile, as he adjusted the eye patch, then slipped the cheats into his vest. "Mar-Dot found twelve magnetic fields around the planet, almost in the exact positions as Terra's. In each of those spots, the slush is much more shallow than the random locations first tested."

"Captain," Mar interrupted. "I think we have something of importance at one of the fields. There is a large rocky plateau jutting above the slush. The readings also indicate that there are a number of inanimate objects constructed primarily of a metallic substance on that shelf."

"Try to get a configuration on the screen." A few seconds later several outlines took shape on both their monitors. "I'll be *drekked*! They're ships!"

"And that makes the plateau someone's private parking lot," Cherry concluded. "Hurry up guys. What's below the plateau?"

Mar turned his face slightly toward her. "Based on the computer's density analysis, there appears to be a network of caves beneath the solid shelf."

"Bingo!" Cherry exclaimed with a snap of her fingers.

Gallant gave her a thumbs-up sign as he rose from his seat. "Take her down, Mar, but keep the security shields activated just in case. Cherry, come with me to get the suits."

With each passing second, Cherry's anxious fidgeting increased until Gallant had to threaten to leave her behind if she didn't stand still. He explained how the headpieces were equipped with communicators so that they could speak to each other and Mar-Dot. After making several adjustments to Mar-Dot's protective suit, Cherry could move about somewhat normally.

He waited until they were ready to exit before closing the collar around Cherry's neck and fastening the manacle to his left wrist.

She immediately noted how he kept his right hand free to handle the weapon clipped to his belt. "There's one thing I want to know. This chain will keep me close to you, but if the mist is that thick, how will we find our way back to the ship?"

"Right outside the door is a lead line. I'll attach it to my belt before we go anywhere. But even if something happens to the line, Mar-Dot could guide me back in mentally."

"Okay then. Let's rock."

Gallant didn't bother to ask what that expression meant as he gave Mar the signal to seal off the corridor so they could open the ship's door. Any mist that drifted inside would be detoxified after they left and the same procedure would be followed in reverse upon their return.

The moment the door closed behind them, Cherry felt as if someone had dropped an icy, white sheet over her head. There was some light, but no visibility whatsoever. She groped for Gallant's hand, and the contact reassured her a little.

It only took a few seconds for the protective suit to adjust its temperature to keep her from feeling the outside chill, but it was long enough to know that if the mist wasn't lethal, the cold air would still make it impossible to get around without a suit. She couldn't help but wonder which would be worse, dying from asphyxiation or exposure?

Though Gallant had to release her hand long enough to attach the lead line, he came back to her immediately. "Have you got a fix on us, Mar?" he asked aloud.

"Yes, Captain. If you would begin walking, I will direct you toward the location that appears to have a tunnel between the surface and the underground network of caves."

"Visibility is absolute zero, so try to warn us about any high or low spots on the ground also."

The words were barely out of his mouth when the mist suddenly parted before them like a curtain. Cherry screamed as a huge four-legged beast with two long curved tusks came charging toward them.

Chapter 14

Gallant yanked Cherry toward him and leapt aside in the nick of time. What appeared to be a prehistoric mastadon thundered by, heading straight for the ship.

"Mar-Dot! Brace yourself," Gallant exclaimed.

"What is happening?"

"You're about to be—" He cut himself off as he realized the animal should have already collided with the ship, yet he had heard no crash. "Did you pick up anything unusual on the monitor just before I yelled?"

"Negative. I was scanning the surface elevations as you suggested."

"Check for life forms again. Something that seemed very much alive just about trampled us to death, then got swallowed up by the mist somewhere between us and the ship."

"Gallant," Cherry said with a tug on his hand. "How is it that we could see that animal as clear as day, yet we can't see each other?"

"Good question."

"Captain, we are showing life forms besides yours now."

"Anything four-legged?"

"Negative. The readings are indicating that five humanoids are about fifty meters to your right."

Gallant turned Cherry in that direction and started walking again. "This way?"

"A few centimeters back to your left and you should bump right into them."

Cherry's stomach clenched with a combination of fear and anticipation, but she reminded herself that coming along had been her idea and she ordered her feet to keep moving. Not being able to see was causing her to be more frightened than she normally would be.

"Captain," Mar-Dot said in an urgent tone. "We are picking up a powerful surge of energy emanating from those life forms."

As suddenly as before, the mist lifted, and a throng of painted savages came running toward them, brandishing spears and howling like banshees. Cherry could see them perfectly as they closed in on her, but she still couldn't see Gallant right beside her.

A short, high-pitched buzz alerted her that Gallant had used his little black box, and yet she was unable to see the beam of light that she knew would accompany the shot he had fired. Again and again she heard that buzz, but none of the savages fell.

When they were almost upon them, Cherry tried to pull him away. "Gallant! We've got to get back to the ship!"

"Stand still," he said much too calmly for her peace of mind. One of the savages balanced his spear high in the air and thrust it toward Cherry with terrifying force. As Gallant held her in place, she screamed again, certain it would be the last sound she ever made.

But nothing happened. The spear never hit her. It simply vanished, and a second later, so did the savages.

"What in the world—"

Gallant squeezed her hand. "Mar-Dot, what've you got?"

"The energy surge has dissipated."

"And the five life forms?"

"In the same position."

"All right. Guide us to them."

Cherry's heart was racing as they followed Mar-Dot's directions. "I don't get it. What's going on?"

Gallant's tightly controled voice made her imagine how wary his expression probably was. "Remember your breakfast?"

Cherry gasped. "You think these are illusions?"

"It would seem so. Did the savages look solid to you?"

"Absolutely. Why?"

"The animal charged by too fast to notice, but the savages looked almost translucent to me. I was immediately certain they weren't real."

Without warning something dropped over Cherry's head and body. She put up her hands a fraction too late to stop what felt like a net from tightening around her and Gallant.

Mar-Dot confirmed the obvious. "The life forms are now in a circle around you, Captain."

Gallant snorted. "Very timely, Mar-Dot. I believe they're about to escort us below, so just keep the channel open. Usual orders stand."

Cherry felt a nudge from behind and took a step forward at the same time as Gallant did. They were definitely being prodded along to somewhere.

"Are you all right?" Gallant asked.

"I'd be doing a hell of a lot better if I could see, but I'm okay. What are Mar-Dot's usual orders?"

"If our suits are taken away, we won't be able to communicate with them, so they'll contact me mentally every other hour. I can't return any messages, but they'll be able to ascertain whether I'm still alive. As long as I'm breathing, they won't leave the planet without me. In the meantime, the security shield should protect them and the ship from harm. Mar-Dot, someone just removed my weapon and the lead line from my belt. We'll be relying completely on you to guide us back when we're done here."

"Understood, Captain."

Their escorts brought them to a stop. Cherry could hear a long scraping sound, like rock against rock, and guessed that they had come to the entrance of the tunnel that Mar-Dot had mentioned. They were pushed forward another few feet and halted again.

Slowly, the rock beneath Cherry's feet began to vibrate with a humming sound similar to that of an elevator motor, and it took her a moment to realize that they were indeed descending. Clinging to Gallant's arm, she whispered, "Aren't we being a little passive about all this?"

"If they wanted to kill us, we'd already be dead. There is no logical reason to put up a fight . . . yet."

As soon as the rock elevator touched bottom, they were moved off it, and the humming sound indicated that it was rising again. In the next instant, a great gust of wind practically knocked Cherry off her feet. She could hear and feel it whirling around her and upward. The blowing stopped at the same moment the humming sound did, taking with it enough of the mist to allow her to note that a bluish, phosphorescent light emanated from the walls of the cave. Cherry immediately took advantage of the improved visibility to check out their guides.

As Mar-Dot had reported, there were five life forms moving around them, but it was impossible to tell what they looked like as they were completely shrouded from the tops of their heads to the ground like ghosts, but in reflective silver material instead of white sheets. The only indication that they had faces was the two circles of convex black glass that made Cherry think of bug-eyes. Since it was obvious that they had been able to see her and Gallant in spite of the mist, she assumed those eyes had something to do with that ability.

While one of them removed the net that bound her and Gallant together, another shoved a large flat rock a few feet across the cave floor, revealing a narrower opening than the one above them. Then that being and another figure lowered themselves into the abyss.

The one who had removed the net pointed at Cherry and Gallant, then to the hole. Once she and Gallant stepped to the edge, she could see there were steps leading down.

"Hold it," Gallant told her. "Let me go first. That way, if you slip, I can catch you instead of strangling you with this chain."

"My, my. Even in trying times you live up to your name. Well, go on then. I'm right behind you. Or rather, above you."

Once they were all within the second cavern, one of the guides pulled down a lever protruding from the wall. Automatically, another gust of wind swirled around them, carrying more remnants of the mist upward through the opening. Before the last figure descended the ladder, he slid the rock back over the hole. This entire procedure was repeated two more times without their guides uttering a word.

Cherry estimated that they were now about a hundred feet below the surface and there didn't seem to be any traces of the mist left. However, it wasn't until the figures began removing their shrouds that she assumed the air was safe.

The five beings turned out to be one female and four male humanoids, wearing animal furs over most of their bodies. It may have been an effect of the bluish light, but Cherry thought their facial skin was so pale it had an opalescent quality to it.

Using a series of hand signals, one of the men directed Gallant to remove the slave collar from Cherry's neck and get out of their protective suits. Gallant quickly took off the collar and chain and handed it to the man, but he was much slower about his suit.

Following his lead, Cherry unfastened the headpiece, took a shallow breath, and waited to see how the air affected her before pulling it off completely. Gallant gave her a nod, and they helped each other out of their suits. The female took possession of those items and the slave collar.

The man who had given them their instructions signaled to another, who then wrapped his hands around a rock protruding from the wall and turned it. His efforts produced a loud grinding noise, followed by the appearance of a crease in the cavern wall. Countless turns later a portion of the rock opened outward like a hinged door.

Cherry and Gallant were motioned ahead of the others through the opening and into an enormous cavern at least two hundred feet square. The bluish light was brightened and modified by the presence of thousands of stalactites hanging like iridescent icicles from the ceiling thirty or so feet above. At the far end of the cavern was a low oval-shaped table carved from the same glowing stone as the walls. Around the base of the table, a number of mats were scattered, implying that this was either a dining or meeting area, with "primitive" being the key word for decorating.

The escorts stopped Cherry and Gallant when they reached the center of the room, and all the males departed through a corridor on the left. Still carrying their suits, the female marched straight ahead in military fashion, rounded the table and went into another corridor behind it.

Cherry waved her hand in front of her nose. "The air down here may not kill us, but it smells like rotten eggs and boiling cabbage mixed together."

Gallant grimaced. "Mostly sulphur, I think. With just a hint of unwashed bodies."

"Maybe if we asked real nice, they'd let us put the protective suits back on. Any idea what happens next?"

"From the looks of it, I'd say we're in a receiving—"

A cacaphonous blasting of horns made them both return their attention to the end of the room where the table was. Two male children, carrying ivory tusks nearly as big as they were, marched stiffly out of the corridor. Wearing only white cloths wrapped around their lower bodies diaper-style and a white band around their heads, they each took a position against opposite walls and blasted the horns again.

Cherry and Gallant spared one curious glance at each other before the parade continued. Out came eight of the biggest, brawniest, *ugliest* people Cherry had ever seen. The three men and five women, one of whom was the female from the escort party, wore short, sleeveless jumpers made of a variety of animal hides and furs.

The simple covering made it possible to see that they all had a pearly quality to their pale skin, just as the first group had. On the other hand, the multitude of scars marring the flesh suggested that the skin tone did not denote weakness, only a lack of sunlight.

Without making eye contact with either Cherry or Gallant, they lined up in front of the table. Another ear-splitting screech of the horns caused them all to raise their chins a notch and stand at stiff attention.

Cherry couldn't help but gape at the next person who entered the hall and strode purposefully toward them. Though the almost nude, scarred body was as muscular as any man's, the ample breasts proved that it was a female.

She stood over six feet tall in her bare feet, but on top of her head was a gold-plated helmet with a set of antlers that increased her height by at least two more feet. Several furry animal tails were tied to the center of a gold chain around her hips, covering the other proof of her gender, and a large gold medallion hung from a leather thong around her neck.

"Holy stars!" Cherry muttered without thinking. The next moment she felt the back of the woman's hand striking her cheek. Before she could defend herself, Gallant stepped between them.

"The female belongs to me," Gallant declared. "If she requires punishment, I'll dole it out."

The amazon met his unblinking gaze. "I was informed that she wore a slave collar when she arrived. We do not find the device necessary, since there is nowhere that a slave can go from here. The first rule she will have to learn is that slaves are not permitted to use verbal language. If I decide to let her live, she will have to learn the signs like the others. But we shall discuss her disposition later. I wish to hear your name."

Cherry's cheek smarted, but she was relieved that her translator was interpreting whatever language the woman was speaking into Americanized English.

Gallant prevented her from stepping forward again as he answered, "My name is Gallant Voyager . . . from the planet Norona."

"I think not. Kneel, Gallant Voyager, and bow your head." He did as she requested, and using the long curved fingernail of her right index finger, she parted his hair along the white streaks on each side of his head and examined the roots. "How is it that your hair is striped in this fashion?"

"I was born this way," he answered cautiously.

"Did you inherit the trait from your parents?"

"I wouldn't know. I was adopted," he answered, clearly unsure where this interrogation was leading.

"And on what date were you adopted?" He told her and she stepped back from him. "Rise then, Gallant Voyager and meet your destiny." As soon as he rose to his feet, she removed the helmet from her head and shook her long black hair free.

From the center of her widow's peak to the ends of the hair down her back was a thick white stripe. "I am Princess Honorbound, daughter of the late sovereign and ruler of the planet Illusia." She motioned for one of the boys to come and take the helmet from her.

"According to the edict passed on to me by my father, you have been tested. You found your way to us in spite of the obstacles thrown in your path. You have been trained without being told of the purpose, and the time has finally come for you to assume the position you were born to."

She removed the medallion from her neck and held it in front of her. "I have kept this medallion in trust for the heir apparent to my father's throne. You, Gallant Voyager, the son of the brother of the late sovereign, are my cousin. But it was you and not I that was born with the royal mark of the double stripes. I have sworn to abide by the nine-hundred-year tradition in our noble family. Therefore, I pass the medallion to you, the new sovereign of Illusia." She placed the leather thong around his neck and knelt before him.

The men and women behind her shouted, "Hail to the new sovereign, Gallant of Illusia." Then they knelt as she did.

Cherry tugged on Gallant's vest from behind, but he ignored her, so she inched her way around to his side. She was desperate to see his face and confirm that the ridiculous pronouncement was as much of a shock to him as it was to her, but his next words stunned her even more.

"I have known what I am for some time," he stated in a perfectly level voice. "But I'll require further proof of what you're saying before I'm willing to take on the responsibility of a dying planet."

From the tight expression on the princess's face, Cherry was positive that subservience did not come naturally to the woman.

"With your permission," the princess said, and waited for him to wave his hand before she rose.

The others remained on their knees until he gave them his permission as well. "You will have your proof and the answers to all your questions in a moment.

"First I must give you a warning. As I know you are aware, the mist above is deadly and blinding, but the air within these lower caverns is perfectly safe. Taking the precautions you witnessed is the only way to keep the two atmospheres separated. We have been told that mixing them for any length of time could result in a destructive explosion, and we have no interest in testing that theory. Therefore, the exit tunnel is always well guarded . . . to make certain no one *accidentally* opens the series of doors improperly.

"Also, your protective covering has been stored and will be returned to you when it is necessary. Be assured, you would not survive on the surface without it."

Cherry easily read between the lines and deduced that Gallant may be an honored guest, but not yet a trusted one. Sovereign or not, he was only going to be allowed to leave alive if the princess approved it.

"Now let me introduce you to your council. They are impatient to meet you after so much time." She stepped to his side and faced the others. "Jaro, your second in command."

A giant of a man, with very short blond hair and a beard, he seemed to have a few less scars on his face and arms than the others. He came forward, looked directly into Gallant's eyes, bowed his head, and returned to his place. Each person was introduced in a like manner.

"There are two more members to your council. Bessima, your first in command, is on a mission elsewhere. We will explain the details later. And you have already met your chief advisor." She clapped her hands and a stoop-shouldered man with snow white hair shuffled into the room.

"Josep?" Gallant asked, failing to hide his surprise. "*You're* the Con rep spy?"

The princess laughed. "It is good to see that growing up among the Noronian fiends did not entirely strip you of your emotions. Let us sit down and fill in the years for you." She crooked a finger at the boy holding the helmet. "You. Take this girl to the slave quarters and have the officer there assign her to a duty . . . though she does not look strong enough to be of much use."

Jaro stopped the boy with his hand and approached Cherry. Only the fact that he was several inches taller and broader than Gallant made her stand still for his inspection. Light gray eyes seemed to strip the jumpsuit from her body as his lips curled back to show gritted yellow teeth. The low growling sound he made gave her chills. "She is built more like a boy than a girl. I might find it interesting to have such a bed-slave."

His hand was within an inch of her breast when Gallant grasped his wrist. "You must not have heard me before. This woman belongs to me, and until I tire of her, my bed is the only one she'll be warming."

Jaro backed away with a nod. "Of course, my lord. Forgive me."

The boy took another step toward Cherry, but this time Gallant stopped him. "She stays."

The princess pursed her lips, but said nothing. After shooing the two boys out of the room, she guided Gallant to a floor mat at one end of the oval table. She sat to his right, Josep to his left, and the others took the remaining places.

With a brief movement of his eye, Gallant told Cherry to sit behind his right shoulder. She had made him a lot of promises concerning her behavior and she trusted him to know what he was doing, but when she had made those promises, she certainly hadn't expected him to be named head honcho of a bunch of savages, nor would she have expected him to be so complacent about it.

Josep held up his hand and the others immediately quieted. He began with a deep breath and a sigh. "Gallant, there is a lot you need to know that had to be kept from you until now. Since the late sovereign made me responsible for you when you were born, this tale must logically start with the events leading up to that time.

"After the Consociation created the barrier around Illusia, the people were prevented from warring with their neighbors. Thus, they returned to the pattern of warring amongst themselves. For almost three hundred years, they battled over possession of the smallest property, ultimately destroying much of the planet along with the population. The subsequent pollution of the air, water, and soil became as much of a problem as protecting oneself from enemies.

"Illusia was dying slowly but surely. The people needed the challenge of war, but they also needed a new world to inhabit. Your ancestors maintained supreme control of the planet by sheer force over many centuries, but your grandfather came up with a way to unite the Illusian people toward a common goal, which would satisfy both of their primary needs. He formulated a hundred-year plan and had all of the underlords sign their agreement to it. When he was assassinated by a traitor, your uncle became sovereign, and he and your father continued with the plan. The traitor was caught and executed by the way." He had to take another deep breath before he could go on.

"A team of the most talented illusionists was selected from among all the noble families to create a continuous image for the benefit of the Consociation monitors. The war-ravaged planet gradually took on the appearance of a peaceful, productive land in order to convince outsiders that the Illusians were no longer a threat to anyone."

"Excuse me for interrupting, Josep," Gallant said. "But I never had the opportunity to do much experimenting with my ability to create illusions. I understand how easy it is to deceive other people, but how are they able to fool the computers?"

Josep smiled. "Illusians have never been interested in exploring the deeper mysteries of life. We know only that our creations seem to take on a solid appearance, even to machines."

"And yet, the savages on the surface didn't look solid to me."

"Correct. The power is of no use against another Illusian."

Cherry's mind was formulating questions a lot faster than Josep was talking, but Gallant was apparently on the same wavelength as she.

He rubbed his chin as he drew his first conclusion. "That had to be what the Weebort trader was referring to when he used the word 'counterfeit.' The document he had seen must have explained the deception being perpetrated."

Josep nodded. "Actually, the document was a copy of the one-hundred-year plan smuggled off Illusia. But you're getting ahead of the story. Convincing the Consociation they were no longer dangerous was absolutely necessary to get them to lower the barrier. The scheme, as you must now realize, was to first appear passive, then helpless against a drought. They had no doubt that the gentler people of the Consociation would want to offer assistance to the poor, desperate victims, and thus raise the barrier.

"But the more important part of the strategy was to be ready to take advantage of their would-be saviors when the time came. They had to replenish the armies and improve the weaponry to a level where they would be able to deliver a lethal offense and defend themselves against those who were not taken in by illusions."

"Like the Noronians," Gallant inserted.

"Right. They were also aware that a direct attack on Norona, even with sufficiently armed troops, would not insure victory. What they needed was a way to get at them through a vulnerable point. By taking control of something vitally important to the Noronians, they would not need to fight them at all." He paused to catch his breath, but he also seemed to be waiting for Gallant to come up with the solution on his own.

"Innerworld," Gallant murmured.

"Earth?" Cherry blurted out.

Princess Honorbound glared at her, then at Gallant, as if ordering him to deliver the blow the slave deserved. "Perhaps," she said slowly, "we will have to cut out the girl's tongue if she is too stupid to learn the rules. That method has worked well with others like her."

"Have you dealt with many other Terran slaves?" Gallant sounded as if he had no idea of the magnitude of the information he had just revealed to the princess . . . and she reacted exactly as Cherry expected.

Bolting upward, Honorbound stepped toward Cherry. "She is from Terra? The planet that holds Norona's prize jewel?" Grabbing a fistful of Cherry's short hair, Honorbound pulled her to her feet.

Cherry clenched her jaws to keep from crying out, but she could do nothing to stop the tears that filled her eyes. The next second, the princess shoved her back down to the ground. "Ha! As puny and weak as we were told. We will have no trouble taking over their planet." She returned to her mat with a satisfied grin. "I will question her further at a later time."

Gallant leaned over and brought his mouth close

to Honorbound's ear. Cherry had to strain to hear his words as he murmured, "I will not remind you politely again. This woman is my property. *I* will decide whether she is to be questioned." The princess's answer was a stiff nod.

Josep's brow wrinkled with concern as he said, "You didn't mention this woman in your report."

"No," Gallant responded shortly. "I had no idea she was of any importance to my mission."

Josep did not look convinced, but he let the matter drop. "Let us get back to the explanations. During the time when Illusia was successfully conquering other worlds, they took captives along with the technology they stole. For the most part, the captives and their descendants were kept as slaves, but occasionally some would rise to a higher position. It was these captives who helped develop the weaponry and solved another problem for the royal family.

"Your grandfather's was not the only assassination that took place. In spite of the underlords signing the agreement to work together, there was still an unending struggle for superiority. It was just more discreet than it had been before. The hundred-year plan would work for whoever was in power, not only your family. Thus, if you were all wiped out, another would become sovereign."

"I was the firstborn," Honorbound declared haughtily. "It was imperative that I be protected at all costs so that even if both our fathers were eliminated, I could still lead our people to glory when the appointed day arrived. That turned out to be a very wise decision. Not only are both of our fathers now gone, but every other relative we had as well. You and I are the only ones left to carry on.

"From the days of the Great War, records had been salvaged regarding Lore and an early civilization that went underground to survive an ice age. They eventually died off, but the shelter remained. There was nowhere in the galaxy as well hidden or easily guarded as this place.

"Shortly after my birth, I was brought here with a hundred of our family's loyal followers and some slaves. Over the fifty years since then, three more ships came from Illusia with people, supplies, and reports. The last was a little over a year ago, announcing the deaths of our fathers, which triggered the final stage in the royal plan."

Gallant held up his index finger and turned to Josep. "You said the document was smuggled off Illusia. Honorbound and others were brought here. I have to assume I was taken off-planet as well. How did ships travel through the barrier without anyone being the wiser?"

"I understand your impatience for answers," Josep responded. "And you will have them all before we are through. But it is time for the evening meal to be served, and custom dictates that there be no discussion to distract from the pleasure of eating."

Chapter 15

Gallant would have preferred to postpone the meal until he had a few more answers, but his alleged position of authority did not seem secure enough yet to demand a change in these barbarians' customs.

The princess clapped her hands twice and three young women entered balancing enormous platters of food on their heads. The rough woven material of the sleeveless sacks they wore seemed to identify them as slaves, and the way they kept their eyes downcast confirmed their status. They had to squeeze in between the council members to set the heavy trays on the stone table, and Gallant copied the behavior of the others by not assisting or even moving aside to make their job any easier.

As he was seated at the head of the table, however, there was more room on both of his sides than the others had. Therefore it was definitely not necessary for one of the girls to press her body against his arm to offer him a selection of the meats and vegetables. Nor was there insufficient room for her to walk behind him without brushing against his back.

When the girls left and returned carrying tankards filled with a foamy liquid, the same one again made blatant physical contact with him. He then noted one of the other girls behaving the same way with Jaro. Apparently, the custom of no distractions during a meal did not extend to sexual matters.

Whatever doubt he may have had as to the girl's intentions was wiped away when a small chunk of meat fell from the rib he was chewing on. It barely had time to hit his lap when she reached for it, and before she brought it back up to his mouth, she took a moment to *search* for anything else that might be in the vicinity.

Not knowing what sort of behavior was expected of him, he chose to ignore her advances and, instead, motioned for her to offer some food to Cherry. He was somewhat surprised when he turned toward her and saw the dangerous gleam in her eyes as she glared at the forward serving girl. But what the servant did surprised him even more.

In one quick movement, she picked up one of the ribs and hurled it at Cherry, hitting her squarely in the chest. Meat juices smeared the front of Cherry's white jumpsuit before she could grab hold of it. Gallant held his breath, as he fully expected Cherry to throw the rib right back at the girl, but instead, she picked the rib up off her lap and took a dainty bite.

He relaxed a second too soon. As the serving girl walked behind him, she suddenly let out a cry and stumbled to the floor on her face. One glance at Cherry's extended leg told him how the girl had tripped.

Clearly enraged, the girl made a series of hand movements at Cherry as she leapt to her feet. But a loud clap from the princess put a stop to whatever she was trying to say.

Your concern for the woman is showing. It is considered a sign of weakness here. Be careful.

Gallant heard the voice in his head, but instinctively knew it was not Mar-Dot thinking to him. Casually, he let his gaze touch on each of the faces around the table, but they were all intent on their food. *Who are you?* he thought.

When nothing else came to him he hoped that it was because whoever it was could not read his mind any better than Mar-Dot could without touching him. He was slightly shaken by the awareness that these people—or at least one of them—was telepathic. Since he had no such ability and no records indicated otherwise, he had been under the impression that Illusians could not communicate mentally.

One thing these Illusians *did* do was appreciate their food. Several more platters were brought to the table before one after another tossed their last scrap into the center and belched their satisfaction.

Cherry watched the council members pick their teeth and wipe their hands on their clothing and immediately understood what caused the sour smell that surrounded them. She had been hungry enough to clean the tasty meat off the rib she was tossed, but the table manners of the Illusians killed her appetite for any more.

At the princess's signal, the serving girls cleared the table and hauled away the remains. As they were leaving the room, Honorbound gave a separate signal to the girl Cherry had tripped, then spoke to Gallant.

"Though Josep managed to arrive before you, we had no way of knowing precisely when you would get here, so we planned no festivities for your first evening with us. However, it appears that you have brought our entertainment with you." Her eyes shifted to the left and narrowed on Cherry. "Your slave attacked one of mine. For that I have the right to punish her . . . without your approval. But I will waive that right if she accepts my slave's challenge to fight her."

Cherry's eyes grew wide as Gallant turned to her. He had to know she didn't know the first thing about fighting! Besides, that girl looked at least twenty years younger and fifty pounds heavier than she was. On the other hand, she really didn't want to know what the princess considered fair punishment for a slave.

"How's your arm, woman?" he asked, pointedly nodding at her robotic limb.

As the light bulb came on in her head, she almost spoke aloud, but caught herself just in time. Instead she gave him a thumbs-up and a nod of comprehension. Even though she had never been forced to use her arm to defend herself, she knew she could do it if she had to.

Her confidence faltered when the girl came back in the room wearing nothing but a white diaper and headband like the horn blowers had worn. Cherry stood up as the girl approached the princess, knelt before her, then rapidly moved her hands and fingers. Cherry could guess half of what she was saying simply by watching. But when she turned to Gallant and practically stuck her heavy breasts in his face, the other half became pretty clear as well.

Honorbound interpreted the sign language for Gallant. "This girl's name is Vella. Though she was born a slave, she has earned the privilege of training with the novitiate warriors. If she proves herself worthy, she will eventually be permitted to change her status. You see, we are always anxious to increase the number of our soldiers.

"As much of an honor as that would be for her, she is willing to forego it for another honor. A novitiate must remain virginal until he or she completes the required training. But Vella would relinquish the opportunity to advance for the privilege of becoming bed-slave to our new sovereign."

Much to Cherry's dismay, Gallant paused to look over the goods being offered. "I'm unfamiliar with your customs," he told Honorbound. "If I accept her sacrifice, but she doesn't please me, what then?"

The princess shrugged. "As sovereign you may keep as many slaves as you wish and reward or punish them as you see fit. Once you have used her, you may dispose of her. She understands that and would strive to please you all the more because of it."

Gallant rubbed his chin and motioned for Vella to turn slowly around for him to inspect the rest of her. "She might be entertaining," he said after some consideration. "But I'd like to see what passion she possesses. The way she fights will tell me a lot."

Honorbound gave a husky laugh. "Well decided, my lord." She rose and tapped Vella's shoulder. "Take your place." Turning toward Cherry, she sneered down at her. "Slaves are not permitted weapons. You will have only your body and your mind. We would appreciate it if you would make an attempt to defend yourself, but even if you do not, Vella will not spare you. The fight begins when I clap and continues until one of you is unconscious . . . or dead."

Dead? Cherry stared at Gallant's profile, but he only had eyes for Vella. All she needed was a brief glance from him, anything to let her know that he wouldn't allow the girl to actually kill her. How far was "trusting him to know what he's doing" supposed to go?

As the seconds ticked by and he continued to ignore her and ogle Vella, anger oozed into her mind. It didn't matter that she had asked to come here with him. He could have stopped her if he'd really cared about her safety. Hell! He could have left her in Innerworld to begin with and saved them both a lot of trouble.

Straightening her shoulders and lifting her chin, she walked out to the open area to meet her opponent. What she really wanted to do was fight with Gallant, but Vella would do as a substitute. She met the girl's narrow-eyed glare with one of her own and tried to remember any boxing or wrestling matches she had ever seen.

The only thing that came to mind was an old Mohammad Ali quote, "Float like a butterfly, sting like a bee." The expression seemed to be appropriate advice considering her smaller stature, but how she was supposed to render the girl unconscious with a bee sting was beyond her. Cherry shook the tension out of her arms and legs, discreetly testing her robotic reflexes. She supposed she was as ready as she would ever be.

The instant the princess clapped her hands, Vella lunged forward with her hands aimed at Cherry's throat. A quick duck and a sidestep left Vella off-balance and grasping for air as Cherry lifted her foot into the girl's path. Again Vella landed facedown on the stone floor and came up spitting mad.

Like a matador with a frustrated bull, Cherry waved Vella to try again. This time, as the girl attacked, Cherry spun out of her way at the last second and gave her a poke in the back as she passed. Her robotic strength was barely needed to cause Vella to tumble once more.

Bounding to her feet, the girl was determined to avenge herself. Cherry thought Vella looked more like a cow than a bull with her big udders jiggling around as she bent at the waist to deliver a running head-butt. Just to change the routine, Cherry stood still as Vella charged, then raised her right arm at the last possible moment. A light shove against the girl's forehead sent her sprawling backward.

The palm of Cherry's hand tingled a bit after contacting Vella's skin, and she hoped her robotic arm wasn't going to start acting up now.

At first, the council members were mumbling among themselves, but Vella's clumsiness soon had them laughing out loud and urging both females on.

Cherry made the mistake of glancing Gallant's way and instantly paid for it.

Vella brought her to the floor in a bone-jarring tackle around her legs. She tried to kick free, but Vella's weight and strength were a definite advantage in a close encounter.

They rolled across the floor, one over the other, as Cherry tried to escape and Vella strained to hold on. The battle escalated when Vella bit Cherry's left thigh so hard, severe pain shot through her hip. It immobilized Cherry long enough for Vella to straddle her waist and go for her throat.

Bucking and squirming, Cherry's thin fingers clawed at the girl's meaty ones. Although her robotic arm was able to drag one hand away from her throat, Vella was strong enough to maintain the choking hold with the other.

While the tingling in her arm was increasing with the continued contact, Cherry felt her strength ebbing. She knew unconsciousness might soon follow, but the look on Vella's face said she would not be satisfied with anything short of Cherry's death.

Anger took a back seat to desperation as Cherry realized she was truly fighting for her life. Without another thought, she released Vella's hand, pulled back her fist and slammed it into the girl's jaw.

Vella's teeth clacked together as her head snapped to the side. Cherry barely had time to gasp for air, however, before Vella tried to return the punch. Cherry's arm flew up to block the strike, then reversed itself to deliver a backhanded swing against Vella's other jaw. This blow had sufficient power behind it to throw Vella off and send her sliding across the floor.

Lungs heaving and throat burning, Cherry struggled to her knees and prayed the girl would not get up.

Her prayer went unheard. Vella lifted herself on an elbow, shook her head, then climbed drunkenly to her feet. As she staggered forward with bloodlust in her eyes, Cherry forced herself to rise as well. Swaying on her feet, she wondered how much more it would take to end this insanity.

The answer came to her with her next strained heartbeat. It was going to take everything she had.

In preparation, she sucked in as big of a breath as she could hold. The second Vella was within reach, Cherry drew back her fist and aimed for the girl's diaphragm. The punch lifted Vella off the ground and threw her several feet in the air before she crashed down again.

The hoots from the onlookers might have been satisfying if Cherry hadn't been so sickened by the cracking sound she heard when the girl hit the ground. In spite of the knowledge that she had had no choice in this, she feared she might have killed the girl.

The princess's clap signified the official end of the match. Cherry stood by anxiously as a plump, middle-aged woman bustled out of the corridor and over to Vella. Two girls of Vella's age followed closely behind. The woman felt for a pulse, raised Vella's eyelids, then skimmed her hands over the girl's unconscious form. A cursory exam of Vella's skull caused her to groan.

"She will be able to report back to work tomorrow," the woman declared, then walked out of the room.

Each of the girls who had followed her in grabbed one of Vella's wrists and proceeded to drag her away.

Cherry breathed a sigh of relief that Vella was not seriously hurt. The moment she relaxed, however, exhaustion threatened to buckle her knees, but she was afraid that if she collapsed, someone would come and haul her off, too.

"Your little Terran has more strength than one would imagine," Honorbound said to Gallant. "My curiosity is aroused. Perhaps you will permit us to question her now."

Gallant cocked an eyebrow at her. "I believe there is the matter of *my* curiosity to be satisfied first. Besides, I'm disappointed with her at the moment and would prefer to have her out of my sight. She didn't even give her opponent a decent nosebleed."

Cherry's gasp was covered by the laughter that echoed through the room.

Honorbound was still smiling as she called for the woman who had examined Vella and instructed her to take Cherry away.

"Is there a private area I can claim for my rest period?" Gallant asked.

"Of course," the princess answered quickly. "It has been prepared for some time awaiting your arrival."

"Good. Take the woman there." He caught Cherry's eye for a brief moment. "Don't go to sleep. I'll expect you to make up for your lack of fighting passion when I join you."

The others around the table clearly approved of his disgusting attitude, but if Cherry's mouth wasn't so dry, she would have spit at him. Before she even left the room, he was back in deep discussion with Josep.

The woman led her down the side corridor and made several turns. She finally stopped in front of an animal hide that hung on the rock wall from about Cherry's thigh level to the ground. Lifting a bottom corner, the woman motioned Cherry through an opening barely large enough for her to crawl through.

As small as she was, it was no problem, but she knew Gallant would have a difficult time squeezing in. She also realized that meant several of the barbarians would not make it through at all, which seemed to be a positive factor under the circumstances.

Before Cherry knelt down, she pantomimed to the woman that she needed something to drink.

"That is good," she responded. "You are not only a decent fighter; you learn quickly. There is a container of refreshment inside. Be sure to leave most of it for your master."

As soon as Cherry crawled through the opening, the hide flap was lowered behind her. She was relieved to discover the floor had been padded with plush furs. The dim blue light emanating from the walls allowed her to see that the niche was about the size of Gallant's room on his ship, though not high enough to stand in. More furs were folded in a pile against one wall, and a ledge on another wall bore a quart-size ceramic pitcher and a small bowl.

A peek inside the pitcher told her it was filled with liquid, undoubtedly the refreshment the woman had spoken of, and her nose said it didn't smell any worse than the cavern itself. Her thirst demanded she take at least one sip. She poured a bowlful and finished it all. It was neither good nor bad, and it was close enough to water to quench her dry mouth. She figured one more bowlful would do the trick.

She wished she knew what to think. Gallant had promised to be honest with her, and had made her promise to trust him.

But Gallant had lied before.

He had seemed disgusted by his heritage when he had told her about it.

He also seemed to have become one of them without the least difficulty.

Which was the actor, and which was the real man?

He had told the princess he had known what he was for some time. Had he been referring to his planet of origin, or the fact that he was heir to a kingdom of warriors?

She took several more swallows of the liquid straight out of the pitcher. When a few drops dribbled down her chin and onto her chest, she was reminded of what a mess she was. There was nothing she could do about her stained, dirty jumpsuit, except to get out of it, so she did.

The woman had warned her to save the refreshment for her master, and one glance inside the pitcher let her know there was less than one bowlful left. *Her master!* That'd be the day any man was her master.

She poured the remaining liquid into the bowl. Searching through the pile of furs, she found a linen sheet and dipped a corner of it into the liquid. A long soak in a hot bubble bath would have been her first preference, but wiping the wet cloth over her skin was better than nothing. Strangely, the moisture evaporated almost as fast as she applied it. With each stroke she felt increasingly refreshed. In fact, she could feel herself smiling despite the lack of cleanliness, despite the brutal fight . . . even despite Gallant!

All of a sudden a wave of dizziness assailed her and she tossed aside the cloth to hold on to her head. It occurred to her that she might have been injured in the fight and not realized it at the time. Or she hadn't had enough to eat for how many calories she had burned. At least she was certain she had consumed enough liquid.

The moment she thought about the liquid, a possible reason for her dizziness *and* the smile came to mind. It had been ten years since she had consumed an alcoholic beverage, but the memory of how her system responded to alcohol stayed with her. And the way the liquid had evaporated when it touched her skin certainly acted like alcohol as well.

She was drunk! And damned if it didn't feel great. Tomorrow morning she might feel like one giant headache, but for a short while, the pains and bruises were numbed. She looked down at the thigh Vella had chomped on and saw the teeth marks clearly, but the niche's blue cast prevented her from seeing if it was already discolored.

Why in the world had Gallant allowed that fight? Could he have really been as entertained by the raw violence as he had appeared? And why did he insist she be taken away afterward like a naughty child? Considering what she had just gone through, he could have at least allowed her to sit quietly in a corner and listen to the rest of Josep's story. Perhaps he knew what was coming and didn't want her to hear it.

Of course, she realized that she was somewhat to blame. There would have been no excuse to fight if she hadn't tripped Vella. But the girl had—

What had she done? She had tossed her a rib, in the same manner the others were doing with each other. No one at the table seemed to be aware that trays could be politely passed around any more than they would know what to do with plates or silverware. If she had simply caught the thrown rib, maybe nothing would have happened.

A little voice laughed at her rationale.

"It wasn't that." Cherry glanced around the area before realizing she was the one who had spoken.

You were jealous, the voice teased.

"That's stupid. I've never been jealous in my life."

You were.

With a disgusted frown, she decided to ignore the voice and make up a bed with the extra furs. Since he had ordered her to stay awake, she wanted to be certain she appeared to be sound asleep when he got there. Then she could pretend to wake up to deliver a tongue-lashing he'd never forget. As soon as she lay down, however, her eyelids drifted shut.

"I wasn't jealous," she mumbled to herself. Everyone knows you have to really care about someone to be jealous.

You care.

Cherry turned onto her uninjured side and, nestling into the furs, let the effects of the refreshment send her to a place where she couldn't hear the irritating little voice.

Gallant crawled through the small opening prepared to immediately hush Cherry until his escort was out of hearing range. The sight that awaited him swept away all such practical concerns.

By *drek*, she was a beauty. Stretched out naked on her back, her fair skin gleamed against the dark furs beneath and scattered around her. Her small breasts moved with each shallow breath and one knee was bent just enough to give him a full view of the place that fitted him so perfectly.

When Vella had offered herself to him, he had purposely taken his time looking her over. She was young, voluptuous, and would encourage him to be as forceful as his primitive nature demanded. Yet all he had found himself doing was comparing her attributes to Cherry's.

He was a bit surprised that she hadn't stayed awake, if for no other reason than to argue with him.

The look on her face as she left the main room had promised swift retribution. He was certain his explanations would have calmed her . . . if he could have gotten her to listen at all. In a way, though, her falling asleep was the best thing that could have happened. He needed a few hours to digest all the information he had been given in the past hours and decide what he was going to do about it.

As he stripped off his clothes, he noticed the pitcher lying on its side and grinned. He had had one tankard of the brew served with dinner and his faculties had been dulled. Cherry would have had no way of knowing what she was drinking, until it was too late. If nothing else, she was guaranteed a sound night's sleep.

He lay down beside her, intending to leave her in peace. And he would have, if she hadn't immediately turned toward him . . . or if she hadn't instinctively reached for him. His arms enveloped her and pulled her close. As usual, when he came in contact with her, he was instantly aroused. Yet when her fingers skimmed that part of him, he gently moved her hand to a less sensitive area.

Their couplings were always desperate and unbelievably satisfying, even when they were both half-asleep. But for tonight, the only thing he truly wanted was to hold her close.

Thinking that he could have lost her made his chest tighten, as it had several times since they landed on Lore. Though he knew he would have to give her up eventually, at least it wasn't going to happen tonight.

* * *

Cherry felt Gallant's leg and arm weighing her down before she was fully awake, but she could also tell he wasn't the only thing holding her down. There wasn't an inch of her body that wasn't aching. She parted her dry lips to tell him to get off her, but all that came out was a cross between a groan and a croak.

"Lie still," he told her, moving away. He was back beside her in a moment, helping her to sit up and bracing her with his arm.

She felt him press something against her lips and she raised one eyelid to see what it was. The sight of a bowl filled with liquid only made her groan and reclose her eye.

Gallant chuckled. "It's only water, with some restorative herbs in it. Drink up."

Figuring she couldn't possibly feel any worse, she took one swallow then another, until the bowl was drained. But her voice still cracked when she tried to speak. "I hate you."

"Hush, woman," he said in a low whisper. "We can't let anyone hear you speaking to me. Anyway, between the drink and that wrestling match, you're in no condition to fight with me yet. I'll make you a deal. You let me talk while I take care of you, then when you feel better, you can call me any names you want . . . as long as you whisper them into my ear."

Her answer was another groan. Taking that as her assent, he insisted she drink another two bowlfuls of water. She could almost feel her dehydrated body tissues plumping back to normal as he lowered her to the furs again.

"I had a servant bring me a few items before you woke up. The water was one. This was another."

She couldn't see what he was referring to, but when his fingers lightly rubbed something warm and slick onto her bruised thigh, she guessed it was a salve, and hoped it had some magical restorative powers as well. She let out a sharp gasp as he pressed a bit too hard on one spot.

"So, it feels as bad as it looks, huh? This stuff should help. Anywhere else?"

"*Everywhere* else," she whispered back, not even trying to be stoical about it.

"In that case, I'll just start at the bottom and work my way up."

As his hands smoothed the salve over one of her feet and his fingers massaged each toe, she decided she would let him do this service for her. Even though she was angry with him about the fight and didn't know whether to trust him or not, he owed her this much. "I can't believe I once said Illusians should be given a chance to prove they've changed. The Consociation should forget the barrier and just send them all to hell."

"Ho, would you kindly remember that you're including me in that condemnation?"

"I couldn't very well forget, *Your Majesty.*"

He cleared his throat nervously. "I *am* sorry you had to fight."

"Hmmph."

"Anything I might have done to stop it could have

put us both in serious jeopardy. You must realize that. And please note how I'm not blaming a certain injured party for causing the problem to begin with."

She opened one eye to glare at him, but his fingers worked their way into her calf muscles, and it felt too good to voice her annoyance.

"Someone at the table was communicating with me telepathically off and on the whole time, advising me how to behave to win the council's approval. In fact, it was that person's suggestion that I send you off the way I did."

Cherry opened both eyes and lifted her head to look at him. "Are you serious?"

"Sh-sh," he sounded, touching his index finger to his lips. "No talking, remember?"

She lowered her head, but didn't close her eyes again. With the pounding in her head subsiding, plus the fact that he wasn't wearing the patch, she was able to note his expression as he spoke.

"I don't know which one it was, but I was warned not to show any concern for your welfare and ordered to let you fight your own battle, or else the council would consider me a weakling. You might have picked up on the fact that they don't tolerate weakness very well." His hands moved to her other foot to work on that leg next. "I don't think I've ever had to do anything quite so difficult."

He looked and sounded completely sincere, but she reminded herself of how believable he had looked and sounded last night as well.

He winked at her. "But you did better than I ever

expected. I'm thinking of exchanging one of my arms for one like yours."

This time she remembered to whisper her question. "If you weren't really ashamed of how I fought, why did you want them to take me away?"

"I suppose I could have let you fall on your face, which is what you were about to do. I only wanted to give you a chance to rest without embarrassing either one of us."

"Oh. But I would have liked to have heard more of Josep's explanations."

"I know, and I meant to repeat every fascinating detail when I crawled in here last night."

She couldn't help but wonder if he honestly meant *every* detail or just those bits of information he wanted her to know about. "Then tell me now. The last thing I heard was how the poor, abused Illusians hid away the lovely Princess Honorbound in this ivory tower for safekeeping."

Chapter 16

Gallant chuckled and moved up to massage her left arm. "I did learn how that was accomplished. The people that were working on weapons also found a vulnerable spot in the barrier and discovered a way to poke a small hole through it. The special team that kept the Consociation believing things had changed on Illusia also became responsible for keeping the hole disguised."

"Why didn't they blast the whole barrier away and be done with it?"

"Remember what Josep said. They knew they couldn't win a head-on war against Norona, and that's what they would have gotten if they had blown away the barrier all at once. The plan to use Innerworld as a bargaining tool was much more practical, even though it was also more complicated and would take a lot longer to set up.

"At any rate, they've had this opening for some time, but in order to assure secrecy, they have only used it a few times to send ships out. No ship has ever returned in case they might be followed."

"That explains why there are ships parked outside of the tunnel."

"Yes, but I figure that also means no one on Illusia has proof that Honorbound or I are still alive and continuing with this part of the plan. Since our fathers' deaths last year, there has been no further communication from Illusia. I can't help but wonder if Honorbound really has the backup power she's expecting. Either way, though, now that we know what they're up to, we've got to put a stop to it."

"And I'm dying to hear how *we're* going to do that, but first, where do *you* fit into that royal plan of theirs? And how does Josep get away with everyone thinking he's a Con rep? And—"

"Give me a chance, woman. Why don't you roll over so I can get your back? I assume your robotic arm doesn't need a massage."

"Funny you should mention that. Do me a favor and hold that hand." He looked at her curiously, but did as she requested. "How odd. It's doing it again."

"What?"

"Whenever I touch you with that hand, it tingles, and if I hold on to you long enough, the whole arm gets warm. It never did that before and I was beginning to think there was something wrong with it."

"I don't suppose I should just take that as a compliment."

Cherry laughed. "It's not that kind of tingling. Anyway, it happened again when I touched Vella's skin. But after the workout I gave it last night, I'm positive there's nothing wrong with the mechanical parts."

"Since it's stronger than a human arm, couldn't it also be more sensitive?"

"What do you mean?"

"I told you the doctor who examined me when I was a child noted certain differences that helped him evaluate my genetic background. One of the differences was in my body's chemistry. Could it be possible that the robotic nerves are oversensitive to that chemistry?"

"I suppose. But I'd have to touch a few more Illusians to test out that theory and drawing their attention isn't very high on my list of priorities at the moment." She rolled over onto her stomach. "Now get back to the explanations."

He dotted her shoulders with salve and kneaded the muscles there as he spoke. "Did you realize your whole back is scraped up?"

"Gee, Doctor, thanks for the news flash. I wonder if being dragged across a rock floor had anything to do with that. Go on."

"All right. Josep said I'm fifteen years younger than Honorbound. From what I understand, being born with the second stripe in my hair was a royal big deal. It changed everything. Because I was the sovereign's nephew instead of his direct descendant, it was decided that, in order for me to take precedence over Honorbound, I would have to overcome a trial to prove myself worthy.

"Josep and my father came up with a test that everyone agreed with. To tell you the truth, it sounded so convoluted that I don't think anyone really wanted me to pass. But, for whatever reason, Josep practically led me through the maze by the nose."

"Didn't he say your father made him responsible for you?"

"Correct. The first step was to plant me as an infant on Norona, where I would be brought up among the Illusians' worst enemies. The logic was that I would gain a true insight into the Noronian mind and culture. A trained spy could never ascertain the same type of knowledge because he would never be able to completely let go of his own background. Apparently, I was given the name Gallant Voyager as both an honor and a sort of tag to help someone find me later.

"In the meantime, Josep infiltrated the peace-loving population on Gilliad. I think I told you he was from there. It was the only place where some of the inhabitants had been alive during the Great War, and part of his job was to prevent their memories from negatively influencing other members of the Consociation. He worked his way up politically until he became a representative."

Gallant went on to explain how Josep guided him into his present career and became his sole contact.

"Ouch!" Cherry complained as Gallant touched a sore rib. "Then he was the one who put you on to the Weebort."

"Right. According to the trial I was to undergo, Josep couldn't simply come out and tell me who and what I was, then send me to Lore. Not only would that have been too easy, they weren't sure they could trust me. After all, I'd been raised by the Noronian devils. I might have developed a loyalty to them stronger than my ties to Illusia."

"So," Cherry concluded, "they set you up on a wild-goose chase to get you here without your questioning it. Then if you proved yourself unsuitable as their new sovereign, they could just toss you in the slush outside and be done with you."

He pinched her waist. "Don't sound so pleased about it. If they decide to do away with me, you'll be chained to my wrist. Anyway, it wasn't a fabricated mission. A copy of the hundred-year plan really was smuggled off Illusia and passed to the Consociation through the Weebort. But it was Josep's decision to take advantage of the emergency to lure me here. He used Frezlo as bait."

"And didn't care who got killed along the way," Cherry added.

"You've got the idea. Unfortunately, it gets more complicated."

"You're kidding. I already feel like I'm in a house of mirrors."

"A what?" He pressed the heels of his palms into her buttock muscles and rubbed the stiffness out.

"Ooh, that's good. A house of mirrors is like a maze, only trickier. Just when you think you see the exit, you walk into a wall of glass, keeping you in."

"Well then, here's the tricky part," he murmured in a sarcastic tone as his fingers eased down the back of her left thigh. "When Honorbound was introducing me to my council, she mentioned that Bessima, my first in command, was on a mission elsewhere. Do you want to guess where?"

Cherry pieced the facts together and came up with the most logical answer. "Holy stars. She's on Earth, isn't she?"

"I believe your expression would be *bingo*. I wasn't given the details yet, but apparently, she's preparing the Terran population for a peaceful takeover."

"But that's not possible. Romulus's people keep tabs on everything that goes on in Outerworld. They'd put a stop to anything that would place the planet at risk."

"True. If they see it coming." He moved to her other leg. "I purposely let Honorbound know you're a Terran, in hopes that she would consider you worth keeping intact for a while. There's no question I'll have to let her interrogate you. But whatever she asks you, keep your answers general and make it sound like your people are passive and defenseless. If she learns the truth, she could decide to change the plan to a full-scale military attack. And under no circumstances reveal that you know anything about Innerworld."

"Okay, but there's a big hole in this plot, and Josep's in the center of it as far as I can tell."

Gallant finished the massage and stretched out beside her. "I'm afraid my head is so full right now, you're going to have to spell it out for me."

She shifted to her side and propped her head up. "Josep is the only one who has had the freedom to come and go from here, right?"

"Right. And I was told his visits have been very rare to keep suspicion at bay."

"But he *has* visited. And as a representative to the

Consociation living on Norona, wouldn't he know as much about Earth as you do? Or even me, for that matter?" Gallant nodded slowly. "Wouldn't he know how Innerworld monitors Outerworld? And wouldn't he have access to information about the strength of Terran defenses and their affinity to war rather than submission? What would lead Honorbound to believe that they could pull off a peaceful takeover of Earth?"

"As I said, they didn't give me any details yet, but I think you've got a good point about Josep. Someone at that table was feeding me advice that gave me a chance to be accepted quickly. It would make some sense if it was Josep. Maybe he's not as supportive of the princess and her plan as he seems to be. Considering how difficult it's going to be to get out of here in one piece, we could really use someone on our side."

"Then again, maybe it's another trick to test your worthiness. You know, let you believe you have a friend to whom you can confide your true feelings about everything you're being told."

Gallant smirked at her. "I knew I could count on you to add to my confusion. Have I mentioned how I love the way your mind works?" He leaned forward and placed a light kiss on her lips.

That *word* kept her from kissing him back.

"What's wrong? Still uncomfortable?"

She could have lied, but that would have made her as bad as he was. Raising herself up to a sitting position, she looked around the niche, then started sifting through the furs. "Did you see my jumpsuit anywhere?"

"I had the servant take it away. She's going to bring you one of those diaper things to wear in honor of your fighting ability."

She stopped her search and glowered at him. "You'd better be kidding."

Surprised by her hostility, he sat up and took hold of her shoulders. "Yes, I'm kidding. What's your problem?"

She remained rigid for a moment then relaxed. "Nothing. I just wanted to get dressed."

"Why? Are you afraid I'm going to take the massage to its logical conclusion?"

She clucked her tongue. "Don't be ridiculous. I'm not afraid of you."

"You're afraid of something, Cherry, and you've got to tell me what it is. We're partners in a very dangerous situation, and for our mutual safety, we should each know what to expect from the other one."

Her eyes lit up. "We're *partners*?"

"Against my better judgment, if you'll recall. Now I want to know what's going on in that head of yours." His eyes narrowed. "Do you think I'm lying to you again? Is that it?" Her hesitation annoyed him. "You promised to trust me. Remember? And I promised to be honest with you. I took my promise seriously. What about you?"

She sighed. "You are very convincing as a barbaric sovereign."

"And you're very convincing as a helpless, hysterical female. But I know better. Being convincing is what makes you a successful actress and what keeps me alive. I need to know you trust me enough to follow any order I give you while we're here. Our survival could depend on your not doubting me."

She knew he was right and her intuition also told her he had relayed all the facts he'd been given. "I trust you. You're not dumb enough to think you could make war on a whole planet of people like me."

With a silent laugh, he hugged her close. "I'll be *drekked* but I do love arguing with you."

Her body tensed for a heartbeat before she could prevent it.

"What?"

"Nothing."

He held her away from him and studied her face. "Who's lying now?"

"It's personal."

"*Personal?* From the woman who won't permit me a single secret? As you have previously said to me, spit it out, now."

"It's really no big deal," she insisted with a shake of her head. "I have a little problem with a certain word, and I . . . I'd rather you didn't use it."

He rubbed his chin as he tried to recall exactly what he'd said. "I give up."

"I know you didn't *mean* to use that word—"

"*Cherry* . . ."

"Love. I'd rather you didn't say you *loved* anything about me."

"I don't understand."

"Of course, you don't. How could you? You were

raised by affectionate, *loving* parents. You couldn't possibly know what it was like to be told you were being belt-whipped because your parents *loved* you. My mother was a virtual slave to my father because they *loved* each other so much." She took a deep breath. "I'm sorry. I shouldn't have said that."

"Wrong. You should have said it sooner. Here I was worried about physically hurting you when all the while one four-letter word could lay you low. My mother always said the three most powerful words in any language are—"

Cherry pressed her fingers to his lips. "Please. Leave it alone, okay?"

"Why? What do you think would happen if I told you I love you?" She looked away from him. "Do you think I'd put the collar back on you and throw away the key? Do you honestly believe I'd treat you any differently than I have so far? What—"

"Stop!" Cherry exclaimed, then grew alarmed thinking she may have been heard.

"Don't worry, anyone who heard that will imagine that I'm forcing you to have sex with me."

"Fine. Then have sex with me and forget this stupid conversation."

"No."

Cherry's eyes widened. *"No?"*

"You heard me. I didn't realize until now that you have never used the phrase 'make love.' You always say 'have sex,' or 'couple,' or some other euphemism for the act. Well, my dear, we are going to make love now. And I intend to prove that it won't hurt a bit."

With his last words, he pressed her back down to the furs.

"Gallant, you're scaring me."

"Impossible," he hissed into her ear and laid a trail of kisses down her neck. "You're not afraid of me. Remember?" His kisses continued on down to her breast.

"That's right, I'm not. But you're making me very uncomfortable." She moaned as he drew one puckering nipple into his mouth then released it.

He raised his head to meet her bewildered gaze. "And I absolutely guarantee that you'll be a lot more uncomfortable before I'm finished with you."

"Is that a threat?"

That earned her a sly grin. "I believe *you* were the one who complained of a lack of foreplay in our relationship. Just let me know when you've had enough." With a restrained gentleness that he had never before shown her, his lips met hers and coaxed a like response. "All you have to do to hurry things along is tell me you love something about me."

"Hmmph. You'll die of old age first."

"We'll see." He teased her eyes, nose, and ears with velvety caresses. He made slow love to her mouth until she almost forgot why she was resisting. When her body moved against his, he left her face to pay homage to her breasts.

As he worked his way downward, she stroked his hair and ran her hands over his shoulders and arms, telling him without words how good he made her feel. And when he went lower still, her damp heat was as revealing as her hushed moan of pleasure.

He took her to the very edge and kept her dangling there for endless minutes. Or was it hours?

"Enough," she whispered, and he slid his body up along hers. She felt him, hard and pulsing, yet barely touching that part of her that needed more attention.

"Say it," he murmured against her lips. "Say the magic word."

"Please," she said, rearranging her spread legs to entwine with his.

"Wrong word. Try again." He returned to seducing her mouth as he rubbed the tip of his shaft over her aroused flesh.

She sucked in her breath as a spear of desire tore through her, but she couldn't say what he wanted. The taste of herself on his tongue made her dizzy with the need for more. His kiss intensified, promising a faster pace as he lured her deeper into the well of passion. Yet when she was certain he would give in, he pulled away to renew his exquisite torture of her body.

Her mind was too drugged to understand why he was holding back, or even how he was accomplishing it. Was this the same wild, impatient animal that had never been able to resist entering her for more than a minute or two after kissing her?

Again he brought her to the brink of climax and stopped. This time she couldn't prevent a frustrated cry. And again he returned to her mouth with his body stretched out over hers.

"You know what you have to say to end it."

Instead, she used her robotic arm to push him

onto his back. "We'll see," she said, repeating his warning to her. It was one thing for him to tease her and restrain himself, but she was certain he wouldn't hold out under the same treatment.

She used her teeth, tongue, hands, and body to excite every nerve in his body, but each touch also aroused her more than she already was. He couldn't hide the fact that he wanted her as badly, yet he continued to control the urge to take what he needed.

When she crawled up his body and attempted to straddle him, he sat up with her on his lap and grasped her hips to keep her from lifting. "Say it." He growled and nipped her neck.

She shook her head to refuse, but he pulled her tightly against him, enticing her in the most elemental way to give up the fight. "I . . ." Another ripple of pleasure caused her to gasp before she could go on. "I love . . . um . . . your hair." She tried to take him into her, but he held her still.

"You can do better than that." A slight adjustment of both their hips encouraged her to comply. Quickly.

"I love . . . your body."

"More," he ordered with another seductive stroke.

"I love solving puzzles with you. I love sleeping next to you. I . . . I love how you make me feel even when we're arguing. Okay?"

He raised her high enough to bring them together, but prevented her from sliding down more than an inch. "Now, say, I love you, Gallant."

Leaning back far enough to glare at him, she muttered, "Don't press your luck, mister."

And with a low growl, he accepted the slight advantage he had gained and ended the battle.

Some time later, she was fully aware of the concessions he had won from her, but she was too sated to resent it. "How is it that you could never do that before?"

His fingers made lazy circles up her spine. "Do what?"

She gave his shoulder a nudge. "You know very well what. You held out against some of my best efforts."

"Perhaps," he said slowly, skimming his hands over her bottom, "I didn't have a strong enough motivation before. However, if I were you, *love*, I wouldn't count on such restraint again for a while."

She muffled her laughter as he rolled her onto her back and immediately proceeded to demonstrate his usual lack of patience.

Aster braced herself in the doorway of Rom's office. "I swear I'm going to hang that man by his ankles and use a cat-o'-nine tails on him!"

Rom raised an eyebrow at his normally nonviolent mate. "Anyone I know?"

"Cute. After what I just learned, I should string you up next to him." She made her way over to the straight-back armchair Rom had moved into his office for her use. "Would you care to explain why I never received a copy of yesterday's report from Outerworld Monitor Control?"

Rom flinched. "I don't suppose denial would work." Instantly, he received a mental image of himself hanging upside down, naked, from a high tree limb. "I see." He pulled the report out of his desk drawer and set it in front of him. "Obviously, my influence over at OMC is not what it used to be."

"Oh, you still have influence. I just have more. Women on the verge of giving birth are very sympathetic figures, you know. And the way I've expanded this last week, everyone holds their breath when I walk into their office. I heard they're running a pool on where I'll be when my water breaks!"

"You could relieve everyone's minds by—"

"Don't you dare suggest I stay home. All I would do is worry about Cherry. At least here, I can get distracted for a few minutes at a time."

Rom shook his head as he picked up the report and scanned the update. Whoever or whatever was behind the supernatural sightings had escalated their efforts. Yesterday, a magnificent display of thunder and lightning tied up rush-hour traffic on the Golden Gate Bridge in San Francisco. The light and sound show stopped as suddenly as it started and was replaced by a heavenly rendition of "The Hallelujah Chorus," sung by a choir of about a hundred white-robed specters standing atop the arches of the bridge.

When the song ended, the face of the alleged Supreme Being appeared in the sky. He announced that He was on his way and would soon be making a personal appearance on the White House lawn. Press was welcome.

Aster got tired of waiting for him to speak. "Apparently, he's building momentum, although the special effects would have been more appropriate in Hollywood."

"I know you want to think the worst of him, but I can't believe Gallant Voyager has anything to do with this. He's too intelligent to try to pull off such an elaborate hoax right under our noses. I tend to think it's being done by someone who doesn't know of our existence here. I also think it's important that there's never any mention of when 'soon' is."

With a sigh, Aster reluctantly agreed. "I know you're right about him. Not knowing if Cherry is safe compounded with this blind waiting for the next event is driving me over the edge. I understand we didn't have anyone near this sighting, but at least we can be prepared for the one that's supposed to take place in Washington."

"I've already assigned a team of trackers, all of whom should be able to pick up any strong surge of mental energy and follow it to its source."

"Have you contacted Falcon?"

"Yes. By sheer coincidence, he and Steve were out of the San Francisco area yesterday, or they might have picked up the wave. They're standing ready if we want them to head for Washington, but I don't see the point in pulling them away from home when we have so many others in place."

"But none of them are Falcon. Send him, Rom. He should be there, too."

Knowing how Aster felt about their friend, Rom didn't bother to discuss it further. He would recontact Falcon and have him head for Washington, D.C. He recalled a time when Falcon had a problem dealing with the noise and emotional intensity of Outerworld. The crowd that would undoubtedly be descending on the White House would be worse than anything he had experienced before, but Rom knew Falcon was still the best tracker they had, and if Aster wanted him there, that was reason enough to send him.

"I may agree with your logic about Voyager, but there's no question in my mind that he is involved in this somehow. All I can say is he'd better be taking good care of Cherry no matter what else he's up to."

"I'm sure he is," Rom said as he walked around the desk and helped Aster to her feet. "And knowing Cherry, I'm sure she'll make sure he gets her back here before the baby comes."

Aster narrowed her brows at him. "You may as well know, I've already decided I am *not* going into labor without Cherry."

Smiling, Rom gave her a hug. "It would be interesting to see how you manage that, but we still have about two weeks left. She'll be here."

"She'd better be, or I promise you, Gallant Voyager will pay dearly."

Aster blocked Rom from reading the true source of her anxiety. He would probably be hurt if he realized just how important it was that Cherry be with her when their child was born. Rom was a part of her, but he was still a Noronian, someone who belonged there. No matter what else happened, she would always be a stranger.

In the latter months of her pregnancy, she had become dependent on the knowledge that Cherry—one of her own kind—would be there to stand by her and the baby. Cherry's absence would create a void that no one, not even Rom, could fill.

Bessima listened to the evening news in her motel room as she dressed to go out. Las Vegas was the perfect reward to herself after her spectacular performance in San Francisco. She had heard of this place, but only visiting it could make it real to her.

There was so much she wanted to see and do in the United States—such an erotic mixture of advanced civilization and primitive violence. She had been avoiding the country for fear of being caught, but now she was beginning to believe that this was the place she belonged. Her choices for power and entertainment were unlimited, and her chances of discovery were much slimmer than she had imagined.

Of course, she was not fool enough to abandon her mission or the timetable; the princess could be on her way this very minute. Yet the independence she had experienced this last year, combined with the heady sensation of ultimate power, had her hoping that the plan had fallen apart.

According to the schedule, Gallant Voyager should have gotten to Lore by now and the princess and her council would be in the process of judging his fitness as their new leader. Assuming he accepted his responsibilities once they were explained to him, a messenger then would be sent to Illusia letting them know the invasion of Terra would move ahead as planned.

The princess should be arriving with the new sovereign and her troops in Washington, D.C., in fifteen days, and the main Illusian force should be no more than a few days behind them. Bessima intended to be at the rendezvous point as agreed, but she was going to take her time getting there.

Chapter 17

Cherry's fighting skills earned her the privilege of tagging along behind Gallant rather than being assigned to a more useful task in the lower caverns. The princess had readily accepted his explanation that one of his personal slave's duties was to guard his back. The rough-woven sack she was given to wear, however, announced her menial position to anyone observing their passage.

As they were given a tour of the underground village, Cherry had to keep reassuring herself that Gallant was only acting out a part, and that if she ever wanted to get back to Earth, she would have to trust him and behave like an obedient slave.

One enormous cavern was used as the training field for the soldiers, and an impromptu demonstration was put on for their new sovereign. For several hours, men fought men, women fought women, and women fought men. They battled with and without lethal weapons. Cherry watched in awe until the first gush of blood poured from a knife wound. After that, she kept her eyes downcast and tried not to think about what each grunt and cry signified.

"How many trained soldiers are here on Lore?" Gallant asked after the winners were duly congratulated and dismissed.

The princess seemed to grow an inch as she answered, "We are almost one thousand strong. Our men and women have taken their responsibility to reproduce as seriously as they have trained to fight."

"I don't wish to minimize your efforts, Cousin, but how do you plan on conquering Terra with a mere handful of followers? An illusion of strength will only last so long."

With a laugh, she said, "Let us return to the main hall as we talk. The council will be gathering now to eat, and we have something very special planned for afterward." As they started walking, she explained how they intended to take over Cherry's home planet without having to raise a single weapon—although they would be ready to do so if necessary.

Cherry was glad she wasn't permitted to speak because she was rendered speechless by the explanation. Gallant managed to hide his shock under a thick blanket of skepticism. "And exactly when am I supposed to be making this grand appearance as the Supreme Being to whom all Terrans will automatically bow down?"

"By this time, Bessima will have warned the inhabitants all over the planet to expect you soon. The precise moment is flexible according to when our fleet arrives, but now that you are here, there is no reason to put off our departure. Preparations will begin tomorrow. There is one small adjustment you will need to make though."

"An adjustment?"

"The eye patch you wear. Josep said it is not concealing any flaw and instructed Bessima to project an image of you without it to make you appear less . . . evil. I hope you can manage without it."

He shrugged, not willing to let her know the reason he wore it. She might interpret his occasional inability to control his illusions as a weakness. "If I must. But I'm still not clear on the rest of the plan after the Terrans accept my supremacy."

"It is quite simple. We know where the twelve doorways in and out of Innerworld are. As soon as we arrive, we will install explosive devices at each location, set to detonate if anyone attempts to open one of the doors. The tunnel beneath would be destroyed in seconds. In other words, we would have the power to seal the colony off from the rest of the universe. Simultaneous to our arrival there, a message will be delivered to the Ruling Tribunal on Norona and the Consociation, informing them that Terra is under our control and we are holding Innerworld hostage."

It was immediately clear to Cherry that Honorbound was seriously underinformed if she truly thought it would be that simple. Why hadn't Josep filled her in better?

Gallant nodded and stroked his chin. "So far, so good. What demands will we be making?"

"We will allow limited trade—controlled and taxed by us, of course—between Norona and Innerworld, if they agree not to interfere with our rule on Terra;

they will remove the barrier around Illusia; and they will turn over control of the Consociation to us."

They reached the main hall before Gallant had a chance to form another question. Most of the members were already at the table and the princess motioned for Gallant to take the place he had had last night. Cherry didn't wait to be told to sit down behind him since she wanted to remain as inconspicuous as possible.

The princess went on to give Gallant more specific details of how the fleet of ships from Lore and Illusia would set up a protective guard around Terra and how they expected to maintain control once it was handed to them.

Cherry was under the impression they had forgotten her presence until Honorbound suddenly snapped her fingers at her.

"Girl! Come here."

Cherry rose and took a few steps forward, but stayed well out of her reach.

"Your master has given us permission to question you, and since you do not know the hand language of the slaves, I will allow you to speak. Josep has told us much about your people, but he never mentioned that they have great strength. Is your fighting ability typical?"

No!

Cherry blinked in surprise. Someone had sent her a thought without physically touching her. As tempting as it was to glance around the table to see if she could figure out who it was, she carefully kept her gaze lowered and spoke in a humble tone. "No. I'm

. . . very unusual. My aggressive nature was one of the reasons I was sold into slavery to begin with."

"In that case, would you describe Terrans as a passive race?"

Yes!

Again Cherry sensed rather than heard the words. "Usually, that is true." Based on what she'd listened to so far, she added, "They're a very spiritual people. Religion is very important to them."

Honorbound's face was a picture of satisfaction. "Excellent." She asked Cherry a series of questions about Terra's defenses, which Cherry swore she knew nothing of, being such a lowly slave as she was. With regard to any extrasensory talents of her people or their ability to travel through space, Cherry was able to answer with complete honesty.

"Which country on Terra has the most influence?" the princess asked.

Cherry hesitated, hoping to be told the correct answer, but her mentor must have decided she was doing fine on her own. "The United States of America—where I'm from."

"Are you then familiar with the White House?"

"Of course. There's where the President lives," Cherry answered in a childlike voice.

"And if this President believes something, will the other countries believe it also?"

"I would think so, yes."

The princess turned toward Josep, nodded, then smiled at Gallant. "Your slave has answered honestly and confirmed what I had already been told."

Cherry purposely did not glance at Josep, but now

she was almost positive that he had to be the one feeding her and Gallant advice. *Why?* And if he could send thoughts so easily without touching her, would he also be able to read hers, or, as with Mar-Dot, was it only one way? She needed more information before she could puzzle this one out, but with a loud clap, the princess ordered the food and drink to be served, and that was the end of her interrogation as well as all other discussion.

This time she was prepared when a servant tossed her some food that looked like a turkey wing and a purple banana. Although she had witnessed the barbarians' behavior the evening before, she still wondered if talking through the meal would really be worse than all the vile noises they made while they were eating. She almost laughed out loud when Gallant belched in midchew. No one had better table manners than he did. Undoubtedly that was more of his mother's influence, but he was doing a fine job of keeping it hidden at the moment.

She tried to imagine what was going on in Gallant's head and was surprised to realize that as long as she let go of any doubt about his loyalty she knew the way his mind worked very well.

He never used force if subterfuge was a viable option.

He could slip in and out of different roles with ease and was a master at instantaneous improvisation, going along with any situation until a solution made itself known.

He would cheat rather than lose.

And he would protect her life with his own.

Damned if she wasn't crazy about that man! A warm memory of his teasing game from the morning flooded into her system. Crazy, yes. But *love*? No way. *That* crazy, she wasn't. She asked herself the question she always posed when a man interested her for more than one evening.

Would she miss him if she never saw him again?

Her stomach did an upsetting somersault, and she frowned at the greasy bird wing in her hand. Heaven only knew what she was eating, but it must not agree with her. With effort, she mentally switched channels to return to the topic of how Gallant intended to get them out of here.

Knowing they would soon be headed toward Earth with no plans for an offensive attack was the key to everything. Escaping from this underground vault was next to impossible. And after all the trouble the Illusians had taken to lure Gallant here, it was unlikely they would simply allow him to leave in his own ship with a promise to return.

The princess put on the pretense of respecting Gallant's position, but Cherry suspected she highly resented his superiority. As for the rest of the council, they had been loyal to her for a lifetime, where Gallant was the new kid on the block as well as an unknown factor.

Conclusion?

Cherry flinched at the intrusion. The mysterious mentor *was* reading her thoughts. She took a moment to recall the steps in her analysis thus far, then spelled out her conclusion. The safest, most logical course of action would seem to be to go along with the princess and head for Earth with her army. At least it would get them out of this hellhole. *Right?* She waited a moment, but received no response. *At least tell me who you are.*

Her question fell into an empty void.

An enthusiastic round of rude bodily noises announced the end of the meal, and Cherry recalled the princess's promise of "something very special" for afterward. She only prayed the evening's entertainment didn't require her participation this time.

The servants cleared away the scraps, then covered the table with a white cloth. After refilling the tankards around the table, they slipped silently out of the hall.

"A salute!" Honorbound exclaimed, rising from the floor. They all lifted their drinks toward her. "Our gods have smiled on us at every stage of the royal plan. May we hope that their blessings continue."

"*Salute!*" the council members shouted in unison. Every one gulped down the entire contents of their tankards, then slammed the metal vessel down on the stone table.

Honorbound turned to Gallant and held out both her hands. "My lord, will you rise and stand beside me, face our friends with joy, meet our enemies without fear, and lead our people to glory?"

Gallant placed his hands in hers, but wobbled a bit as he stood up. Cherry wondered if the potent brew was getting to him. As far as she could tell he hadn't had any more than he had the night before.

The princess's toothy smile was feral as her eyes raked hungrily over him. "As I mentioned before, there is no reason to put off embarking on our journey any longer, and so, tonight we will fulfill the next stage in the plan. In order to continue our royal family line, it has been decreed that you, Sovereign Gallant, and I, Princess Honorbound, daughter of the late sovereign, will become life-mates and produce the heir to the sovereignty. As fate has ordained, I am at the height of my fertile season, and thus ripe for the royal mating."

Gallant's only reaction to the shocking proclamation was a slight swaying movement. Cherry couldn't believe he was so drunk that he failed to come up with one lousy word of protest. What was wrong with him?

Drugged. Be careful.

The words had barely registered when Honorbound climbed onto the cloth-covered table and tugged Gallant up beside her. Still holding both his hands, she shifted so that they were both facing Josep. "We are ready for you to say the words."

He narrowed his brows and stared at her in such a way that Cherry was certain he was speaking to the princess telepathically.

"No!" Honorbound shouted at Joseph, and Gallant swayed away from her voice. "It *must* be tonight." As abruptly as she had switched from pleasant to angry, she calmed herself. "You will say the words now, Josep."

Clearly disapproving, Josep struggled to his feet. "Sovereign Gallant, Princess Honorbound, although you have walked separately since your births, you are about to step onto a brave new life path together."

My God, Cherry thought, they're actually getting married! She listened to Josep's words, heard Honorbound speak vows, and watched Gallant's head bob in a semblance of agreement to everything that was being said, and yet she couldn't believe it was happening. Her mentor's firm warning was the only thing that kept her silent before such a farce.

Finally, Josep said, "The words have been said. Let the consummation begin. Sovereign Gallant, see your life-mate as the Gods formed her." Honorbound unhooked the gold chain at her waist and tossed aside her only covering.

Cherry had the most awful premonition of what was coming next, but until she watched Honorbound removing Gallant's vest and boots, she didn't quite believe it. The princess flashed Cherry a superior look as she undid Gallant's trousers and pulled them off him.

The applause and cheers of the council members were disgusting, but the sight of Gallant's engorged manhood jutting out from his body was an obscenity. How could he possibly be aroused at a time like this? Surely he didn't desire the grotesque princess!

Drugged.

Drugged? Cherry thought he looked drunk, but that wouldn't explain the state he was in. Unless . . . Without further assistance from her mentor, she reasoned that the drug could be an aphrodisiac. *This isn't right! She's going to rape him.* She pleaded, not knowing if she was being understood. *He has tremendous control. Help him use it!*

The princess ran her hand up Gallant's arms and

over his abdomen. With lusty appreciation she grasped his swollen sex organ and alternately stroked and squeezed him, all the while growling and showing her teeth like some ferocious beast.

Suddenly, she released him and took a swipe down her own chest with her one long fingernail. As blood seeped from the diagonal line she had drawn, she sliced Gallant in the same manner, then pressed their bodies tightly together.

Cherry cringed back against the wall, fully expecting Gallant to react violently, but he simply stood there. When the princess stepped back however, Cherry—and everyone else—could see that Gallant *had* reacted after all.

He had gone limp as a cooked noodle. The council members found it both funny and disappointing, and loudly voiced their encouragement. Whether it was his own doing, the princess's bloodthirsty tactics, or help from their mentor, Cherry didn't care. Gallant was back in control. Somewhat. He still looked like a zombie, but at least the princess couldn't rape him in his current condition.

Honorbound's nostrils flared indignantly, but she wasn't ready to give up. When her hands failed to bring him to more than a semihard state, she knelt down and took him into her mouth.

Cherry closed her eyes, but the loud sucking sounds created an image as vivid as if she were watching. Honorbound's husky laugh caused Cherry to reopen her eyes in spite of her revulsion.

Gallant was once again erect and the princess had turned away from him on all fours, and was gyrating her buttocks at him. With a low groan, he dropped to his knees behind her, savagely grasped her hips . . . and froze.

He appeared to be in excruciating pain as he held himself stiffly in place. Then slowly, unbelievably, he went soft again.

This time, the princess did not hide her fury as she spun around and slapped his face. In an inhuman voice, she growled at Josep. "What is his problem?" she demanded.

Josep shrugged. "He is not accustomed to performing in front of an audience, at least not one with other males. You must keep in mind that, regardless of his heritage, he was raised in a different culture than ours. Perhaps you should take him to your private warren . . . with the required two witnesses, of course. I would recommend young, unscarred females, similar to his slave." His suggestion implied that Gallant's lust would be amplified by the added efforts of such witnesses.

As Honorbound called for two novitiates, Cherry wondered if she had been wrong about Josep being her mentor, but she didn't have time to find out. Honorbound's next order was to have Cherry taken away and safely secured. Cherry tried to get Gallant to look at her as she was being led away, but he seemed to be drawn completely inside himself.

The last thing she heard Honorbound say was, "Bring along another special brew for my shy mate."

Holy stars, Cherry thought, as she realized Gallant would be forced to ingest more of the aphrodisiac. He didn't stand a chance of resisting after that, and there was nothing she could do to help him. At least he wouldn't have to be further humiliated by her watching his abuse.

Go, her mentor demanded. Bowing her head, she complied, only to become more anxious when she realized the two giants that had been assigned to escort her weren't heading toward the niche where she had spent the previous night. In fact, they were going into an area that had not been included in their tour of the village.

When she balked and tried to turn back, they each grabbed one of her elbows and moved her along. Even if she used her robotic arm on one of them, she had no doubt the other man would break her real arm in the next instant, and that wouldn't accomplish anything in the long run. They walked for several minutes and had to climb down two ladders to get to their destination. Cherry didn't need to be told this didn't bode well for her immediate future.

She supposed she should be grateful that her guards either had no interest in her or no desire to mess with the property of the new sovereign. It was difficult to be thankful, however, when they lowered her into a narrow pit, considerably deeper than she was tall, and covered it with a metal grate.

"Please don't do this, guys. I'm claustrophobic. I'll . . . I'll scream all night and no one will get any sleep. Come on! What will it take for you to forget your orders? Hey! Don't go away!"

The moment she heard their footsteps fade in the distance, she pressed her back against the damp rock wall and used her feet and hands to scale her way up to the top. She wasn't surprised to discover the grate was locked tightly in place.

Unlike the upper caverns, the only light was coming from a burning torch on the wall above the pit. She couldn't help but wonder how long it would be before she was in the dark as well as trapped.

Would anyone ever come back for her, or would they tell Gallant she simply disappeared? Surely, he wouldn't believe that. But what would he be able to do about it without risking his own life and his mission? What if they all left the planet tomorrow without freeing her? Exactly how long did it take to die of starvation?

That line of thinking caused a terrifying wave of helplessness to wash over her, and she ordered herself to think of something positive. If she was still here in a day or two, then she could consider the negatives. Positively speaking, she was alive and more or less unhurt. Also, she and Gallant seemed to have an ally on the council. What else? When nothing came to her quickly, fear started creeping into her mind.

Okay then, happy thoughts. Flashes of memories fluttered by like colorful butterflies. She and Aster on vacation together, tipping over a canoe in an ice-cold lake. Her baby sister Rose playing in the mud with the newborn piglets.

But thoughts of Rose always made her feel sad. If only there had been some way to let her know she hadn't abandoned her all those years ago.

Happy thoughts!

Her amazing discoveries in Innerworld. The first time she was given a starring role. *Men.*

She tried to focus on her favorite males from all her years as a mature woman, but there were only a few whose faces and names were memorable. And those, she realized, she remembered only because they were friends rather than lovers, like Falcon and Thor; or lovers that remained friends after the initial case of lust waned, like her beautiful Apollo.

Gallant's face loomed in her mind's eye—with and without the patch—frowning, laughing, teasing, *loving.* Was he so different from all the others, or did the prolonged togetherness he had forced upon her only make it seem that way? How could she know for sure, when she had never spent this much time with one man? To be perfectly honest, she couldn't think of another man that she could have tolerated for this long without a break, regardless of the circumstances.

Accepting that as a fact, she decided Gallant Voyager could be placed on her list of Grade A happy thoughts. When she put some concentration into it, she was able to come up with about ten more Grade A experiences before she started on those that she considered Grade B. Despite her best, most optimistic efforts, however, every minute that passed felt like an hour.

Where are you?

Her mentor was back! "I'm in a hole—"

Hush. The guard will hear you. Think of the route you took, and I will come to you.

She imagined herself being led from the main

hall, through the maze of corridors and down the two ladders. A few minutes later, a shadow partially blocked the torchlight from above. She looked up through the grate to see Josep's face peering down at her. "It *was* you!"

"Yes, and I will explain everything, but we must free you first. Princess Honorbound intends to kill Gallant as soon as she receives his seed."

"Dear God! Get me out of here." As soon as Cherry heard him unlatch the grate, she began inching her way to the top.

"I have placed a strong suggestion in his mind that should keep him semiconscious and impotent in spite of the drug she gave him. It should last for the time I need to explain a few things to you."

Once again, her robotic arm came in handy as she used it to heft herself out of the pit. He replaced the grate to make it look like she was still in the pit.

"You said there was a guard."

"Yes, on the level above, but I put him to sleep. Fortunately, my mental powers have not lessened with my maturity. Come, I'll talk as we go."

Cherry sped up the first ladder and saw the peacefully napping guard, then had to wait for Josep to slowly climb high enough for her to help pull him the rest of the way up. She was shocked by how fragile he felt, but said nothing.

"It is only old age, little one. The mind may still be strong, but the body is failing. Your concern is heartwarming, however."

"Do you butt in on everybody's thoughts without

permission?" she asked in an annoyed whisper as he paused to recover his strength.

"Whenever it suits me. I have walked a double path for so long that my special abilities have become my primary means of self-preservation. However, not even the princess is aware of the extent of my power. Had she known, I doubt I would have survived till now." He motioned her to head toward the second ladder. "Before we rescue our friend, I must tell you some things that you will relay to him for me when he is clearheaded.

"My allegiance to Illusia prompted me to heed the directions outlined in the hundred-year plan, but my oath to Gallant's father, who was my closest friend, has been my greater motivation. Some time ago, I began to worry that the two loyalties would one day conflict."

When they reached the foot of the next ladder, Josep hesitated again. "There was no mention in the royal plan of Honorbound and Gallant mating to secure their family line. She lied this evening, but I could not afford to confront her before the council. There are those who doubt my loyalty because of where I spend most of my time. They would have sided with Honorbound and neither I nor Gallant were in any condition to defend ourselves.

"At the time the plan was written, no one suspected that the entire family would be eliminated. Honorbound has always been jealous of Gallant's existence, but had continued to harbor the hope that he would either not show up as planned, or would not accept the responsibilities of sovereign. In the latter case, she had the right to execute him immediately. No one on the council is aware of her personal ambitions, and, until today, I did not perceive her true intentions.

"Once she is impregnated with Gallant's child and arranges Gallant's timely death, she becomes guardian of the heir or heiress, and ruler in that one's stead until he or she comes of age."

But what about that business of Gallant's image being projected to the people on Earth?"

"She assumes that a few illusionary tricks will establish her in his place when the time comes. For the sake of the council, she had to at least appear to be following the stages of the royal plan. Because of my promise to protect Gallant and his right to inherit, and knowing how strong her jealousy was, I never kept her fully advised of all the facts, as you quickly noticed.

"I have known for a very long time that the royal plan would never work as it was first written, but to reveal that knowledge too soon might have resulted in her ordering a more aggressive war, which would have spelled catastrophe for several civilizations, including ours."

He held up a hand to indicate that he needed a moment to catch his breath before going on. "I have fluctuated between two worlds for too long. The time has come for me to make a choice. I have lived among the Noronians and know they are not the devils Illusians have built them up to be. Yet I am first and always an Illusian at heart. I cannot change that, but I have the power to stop my people from taking an action that I am now positive would ultimately cause the extinction of the entire race.

"I could not stop it, however, until Gallant was brought to Princess Honorbound and told of his inheritance. Although I did not believe he would accept the role of sovereign, I could not make that decision for him. By leading Gallant here, I fulfilled my part of the royal plan as promised, but I must now fulfill my vow to his father to protect his life at all costs."

He urged her to climb the ladder to the upper level, where she saw another sleeping guard. "I'm confused about the copy of the plan that was smuggled off Illusia and ended up at the Consociation." She pulled Josep up beside her. He seemed to take even longer this time before he could speak.

"No copy was smuggled out. It was the one given to me by Gallant's father. The princess had begun to listen to the grumblings of those council members who would have preferred to eliminate me as her chief advisor. You see, I am the only one among them with telepathic abilities, thus I represent a danger they cannot fight with brute strength.

"I needed to give her a fictitious person to focus her suspicions on, instead of me. I also needed to come up with a convincing lure that Gallant couldn't resist following to the ends of the galaxy. By passing the document on to the Consociation and letting her know about it, I accomplished the first goal. By having it stolen before anyone could do more than verify its authenticity, I provided the irresistible incentive for Gallant."

"Incredible. I would be impressed with the complex logic of it, if it wasn't for the fact that several people and a beast ended up dead because of your lure."

Josep shrugged. "Casualties of war. It could have been millions had I chosen a different course. At any rate, I am not looking for your approval, only your comprehension." From inside his tunic, he removed a brown parchment that had been folded down to palm-size. "This is the document that could convince the Consociation that the barrier around Illusia must be reinforced immediately. Give it to Gallant. It will be his decision what to do with it, but I believe he will do what is just."

As he pressed the small square into her right palm, he enclosed her hand between both of his. Instantly, the usual tingling started again, though it was much milder than when she touched Gallant.

"Shall we go rescue your man?"

"He's not my—"

"Tch-tch. Remember, I know your thoughts. Remain behind me. If anyone stops us, I will say the princess ordered you to come assist your master in doing his duty."

Chapter 18

"Get out of here, you useless girls!"

Cherry could hear the rage in Honorbound's voice and quickly cowered behind Josep's bent frame as the novitiates scurried from the princess's warren. She hoped her fury signified that Josep's mental suggestion had kept Gallant in an uncooperative condition, yet still alive.

Stay here until I call you, Josep thought to Cherry.

"Princess?" he called softly. "I saw the girls leaving. Is everything in order?"

"No!" she replied as she pulled aside the animal hide hanging over the opening.

Cherry held her breath, but Josep entered before Honorbound could step outside.

"This is impossible, Josep! There must be something you can—"

The princess's sentence was completed with the sound of a muffled thud.

Come in now.

In spite of his invitation, Cherry's entrance was cautious. The princess lay in an awkward sprawl just inside the opening, and, in the center of the room, on a deep pile of furs, Gallant looked like a naked corpse. "You *can* bring him out of it, can't you?" she asked in a worried, yet hushed voice.

"It would be better if I didn't have to, but there's no way you and I would be able to carry him out of here."

"Why would it be better?"

"When I withdraw my suggestion, the drug will take over again. With the extra portion the princess gave him, his sexual need will be uncontrollable. It will be next to impossible to reason with him."

Cherry made a face. "I suppose I could—"

"No, no. You don't understand. One quick release won't even begin to relieve him. It could take hours of continual . . . *activity*, and we don't have hours to delay."

"Oh, I see. How long before the suggestion wears off on its own?"

"About an hour, but the need will be the same either way," Josep said with a frown.

"Well then, there's only one solution that I can think of." She knelt down, completely wrapped Gallant up in the large fur beneath him, and hefted him with her robotic arm around his middle. "Lead the way."

Josep stole into her mind for the explanation and smiled. "And a very good solution it is."

Only once on the way from the princess's warren did someone see them, and Josep put that person to sleep with little more than the blink of his eyes. He did the same to the two council members who had remained in the main hall and the guard on duty at the tunnel entrance. But Cherry didn't begin to relax until they were inside the first enclosed cavern of the tunnel.

Josep pried open a concealed vault in one wall and removed a pile of silver material. "I couldn't take the time to get the protective suits you arrived in. You'll have to use two of our personal shields. They're a bit cumbersome to move around in, so I'll carry them until we reach the top. The air will be safe until we open the final door."

Cherry had a bit of difficulty hauling Gallant up the ladders, though Josep helped as much as he could. She noted that with the exception of the first door he was leaving all the rest open along the way, and she assumed the safety procedure was different working backward. By the time they reached the elevator shaft to the surface, they were both exhausted.

"Shield him, then yourself. With the goggles over your eyes, you should be able to see his ship once you're on the surface. Move as quickly as possible. You will have no more than five minutes to get off-planet."

"Come with us, Josep. You can help Gallant deal with the Consociation."

He shook his head with a sad smile. "My time is done, as is my duty. The responsibility is now his . . . and yours. You have the document, but there are two final messages for Gallant. When he contacts the Consociation, he should give his report to no one but the Regent Esquinerra herself. She is the only person besides me who knows his true status and the mission he was on.

"The princess had not yet arranged for anyone to deliver a message to Illusia letting them know they were ready to act, so there should be sufficient time for the Consociation to reinforce the barrier before any more ships attempt to leave that planet.

"Once he has made his report, Gallant must go to Terra. Bessima's instructions are this: commencing twelve days from today, she is to be at the front gate of the White House every afternoon from three to four, until the princess shows up for the rendezvous. Gallant will have to eliminate Bessima. She is power-hungry and vicious, and mustn't be permitted to remain free. There is no telling what she could do with her abilities in a nontelepathic society and no one to control her."

Cherry finished sealing the protective shield around Gallant, then, with Josep's assistance, put one on herself. There were built-in boots to make walking possible without tripping over the bottom hem, but other than those and the goggles over her face, it was just one huge, shapeless piece of heavy material. Josep helped her get a hold on Gallant in spite of the lack of separated arm extensions, but it was going to be quite a feat getting back to the ship.

"Don't you need to be wearing one also?" she asked Josep as she dragged Gallant onto the lift. Without answering, Josep grasped one of two levers sticking out from the rock wall and pushed it up. The hatch at the top of the elevator far above them began to open, and Josep took hold of the second lever.

"Josep!" Cherry cried. "The mist is coming in! You're not protected." He raised his hand to her in a farewell gesture and shifted the lever. As the lift took her and Gallant to the top, realization of what Josep was doing set in, and there was nothing she could do about it. He wasn't only ending his own life. By leaving the tunnel doors open, the mist would blend with the oxygenated air inside. The princess's warning came back to her with the clarity of a fire alarm.

Mixing the two atmospheres for any length of time could result in a destructive explosion.

Josep had said she had no more than five minutes to get Gallant aboard his ship and take off. Good God! He must believe the whole planet was going to blow. As she neared the surface, she lost sight of Josep, but she knew he could not survive long with the deadly mist swirling into the cavern. She forced herself not to think about how he might suffer and sent up a prayer of thanks that he had chosen to make his final act a heroic one.

A moment later her thankful prayer became a plea for help. The goggles functioned well enough for her to make out the shapes of a number of spacecraft in the distance. But they weren't individually distinguishable, and they were spread out over a large area.

Which one was Gallant's? Which direction had she and Gallant come from? Without being able to see, she hadn't had any way of getting her bearings or noting the markings on the ground that were visible with the goggles.

Panic began setting in as she imagined hearing the seconds ticking loudly by. If she headed for the wrong ship, she could waste the entire five minutes. She stared at the markings again, comprehending that they were directional arrows pointing toward the tunnel from one of the craft, but that was of no help to her now.

Cherry? It is Mar-Dot. Please excuse my unauthorized intrusion.

Thank you, God!

I cannot read your thoughts, but I am sensing a strong disturbance around the captain and have the distinct impression he cannot hear me.

Cherry's frustration mounted with each of Mar-Dot's words. They had no way of knowing how precious each second was, and she couldn't tell them the problem.

I assume vision is still limited out there, but I'm mentally fixed on Gallant, and as long as he is with you, I should be able to bring you both in using my built-in navigational ability. Turn ninety degrees to your right. Take a few steps. Good. Angle slightly to your left. Too much. Excellent. Keep walking straight now.

Cherry picked up her pace as much as she could and practically tripped over the lead line that had been hooked to Gallant's belt. Grabbing the end of it, she gave it a jerk and felt it tug her along like the retractable cord to an old Outerworld vacuum cleaner.

A few steps short of the ship's door, it opened and the stairway came down to meet her. With a renewed burst of energy, she leapt up the stairs and hauled Gallant inside. The narrow corridor was sealed off from the bridge and cabins as it had been for their deboarding.

You will have to remain in there for two minutes for complete detoxification.

Cherry lowered Gallant to the floor and banged on the door blocking her from the bridge. "We don't have two minutes!" she shouted. "Take off now!"

She wasn't certain she was heard until she felt the merest vibration in her feet. It rapidly built to a low hum and she knew they were lifting off-planet. Suddenly a tremendous explosion sounded and the ship listed violently to one side then the other. Cherry slammed into a wall and was thrown to the floor on top of Gallant.

A powerful gravitational pull paralyzed her in place and the ship seemed to be spinning in circles. Just when she was certain they would crash, the pull ended and the ship stabilized.

The detox light overhead burned a bright red, then orange, paled to yellow, and faded off. Another minute passed before the doors on both sides of the corridor slid back into the wall and Cherry rolled off Gallant. Getting to her feet was not so easy.

"Dot," she called toward the bridge. "I could use some help whenever you can leave the controls." Though she only had to wait a short while before the he-she came to her, she managed to get hopelessly twisted in the voluminous shield in the meantime.

"Oh my," Dot said gaping at a silver-shrouded Cherry and the cocoon on the floor. "What happened?"

"You name it! Help get me out of this contraption. I've got to get Gallant to his bunk before he comes to." While Dot helped free her and Gallant, and they carried him to his room, Cherry gave them a condensed version of everything that had happened since they'd left the ship yesterday, concluding with an explanation of the explosion. From the magnitude of the subsequent fireball Dot described, the tunnel itself would definitely be gone and, more than likely, the caverns below would have collapsed as well.

Dot was unflustered by the fact that Gallant was nude beneath the shield or that he was semi-erect. She was familiar with the type of drug he had been given and even helped Cherry fix a few trays of food to take into the captain's cabin in preparation for a long, exhausting stay.

After Mar-Dot was up to date, Cherry said, "I remember it took three days between Norona and Lore, but between Earth and Norona we detoured to Zoenid. How many days does a straight shot take?"

"With the stardrive, we can make it from Norona to Earth in five days," Mar replied proudly. "However, Norona is out of the way from here. Earth is also a five-day journey from Lore in a different direction. I do not believe the captain will be in any shape to make a decision for some time. I suggest we head straight to Earth and the captain can contact the Consociation Regent by interstellar communication on the way."

"Nonsense," argued Dot. "Anyone could be listening in. There are still twelve days left until the rendezvous, and even if the captain got tied up on Norona, Josep told Cherry that Bessima will go to the appointed spot every day until the princess shows up. We should plot a course for Norona."

"And what if we encounter some unforeseen problem?" Mar countered. "Or Bessima decides not to show up again after the first day? We should not take any chances—"

"Whoa, guys!" Cherry said with a laugh. "I don't think I'll ever get over the fact that you two could be sharing the same brain and never agree on anything."

"We agree on many things," Mar said.

"Hardly ever," Dot retorted.

"Enough already!" Cherry exclaimed. "Head for Norona. When Gallant comes out of it, I'll take the responsibility." A low moan caught her attention. "Speaking of which . . ."

Dot grinned and said, "Do not hesitate to call for me if you find you need a break."

Cherry smiled back and winked. "Thanks, hon, but I think I can handle it." She entered Gallant's cabin and closed the door behind her. At least part of Josep's suggestion had worn off. Gallant was no longer lying on his bunk like a corpse; he was moaning and thrashing from side to side. When he kicked the sheet away from his body, she could also see that his lust was no longer being subdued either.

Without hesitation, she pulled off the rough sack she'd been wearing. As she lay down and embraced him, his skin felt feverish against hers. The physical contact ripped away the last of the suggestion. His eyes popped open and he frantically took in his surroundings.

He made a sound like a wounded animal, and Cherry hugged him as hard as she could. "It's okay, love. You're safe. We're on your ship heading home, and I'm here for you."

Again he attempted to speak, but the sound he made against her neck could only be described as mournful. As if she heard his thoughts she answered him. "You won't hurt me."

Countless hours passed before his passion was finally spent and they were both able to rest.

As they settled into what had become their regular sleeping position, he whispered, "You called me *love.*"

"Did not," she murmured back.

"Did. I heard you. And you know what?"

"Hmmm?"

"I love you, too."

She knew she should contradict him, but she was too tired, and besides, it was probably only some leftover effect of the drug making him talk crazy.

Gallant was pulled out of the last shreds of sleep by the awareness that he was alone . . . and it was not a comfortable feeling.

His muscles complained as he stretched out the tightness, but he didn't feel all that bad, considering what he'd been through. Sitting up, he spotted a glass of water that Cherry must have left for him and quickly quenched his thirst. He needed to get cleaned up. He needed food. He needed Cherry.

He knew it was selfish to have wanted her there when he awoke after she had given so unselfishly during the long night. His need for her at the moment, however, had nothing to do with lust and everything to do with love.

Despite all his mother's sayings and pretty words on the subject, he hadn't been prepared for how it would really feel.

Between the drug and Josep's suggestion, he had been immobilized, but he had still been able to hear and comprehend parts of what had gone on around him.

She had saved his life. He owed her everything, yet the only thing she wanted from him was a lift home to see Aster, then a ride to wherever Theodophilus was for an audition. He had already agreed to that much, and he wouldn't renege, even though it was in direct opposition to his own wishes. He had to come up with something else—a way to thank her and say good-bye at the same time—something she wasn't expecting. An idea started to percolate as he headed for the facility chamber, and by the time he felt presentable again, he knew how he would surprise her.

He was the one to get a surprise though, when he entered the bridge and saw Cherry alone at the navigator's station. "Where the *drek* is Mar-Dot?"

Cherry turned around and smiled sweetly. "What a lovely greeting. Are we a bit hung over or just the usual grumpy?"

He gave her a sheepish grin as he bent down to give her a soft kiss. "Sorry, love. Good morning." He kissed her again. "Or rather, good evening." With a blink of his eyes he made an enormous bouquet of red and white flowers in a crystal vase appear on the panel in front of Cherry. "I would give you the real thing if I could." Taking her hand, he sat down in his chair and pulled her onto his lap for the kind of greeting he had meant to give her. "Thank you."

With a twinkle in her eye, she said, "It was my pleasure, sir."

"That's nice of you to say, but—"

She briefly pressed her lips to his. "If I say it was a pleasure, it was. Now tell me how you feel."

"I'm fine. Better than fine actually. And I am extremely appreciative of everything you did, but I would like to know why you're at the controls."

"Mar-Dot was dead on their feet. I may be an amateur, but I'm at least alert, and I know enough to call for help if something happens. Anyway, I've only been alone here for a couple of hours. We're heading for Norona, by the way." She explained the reason for her decision, which he agreed with, then they reviewed everything that had occurred while he was incapacitated.

"You should get a commendation, love. You may be an amateur, but you performed like a real professional. Probably saved millions of lives besides mine."

"Really?" Cherry beamed with pride. "Wait till I tell Aster she's no longer the only Terran heroine in Innerworld. I wonder how she's doing. That baby is due in another week or so."

He gave her a squeeze. "From everything you've

told me about your friendship, she wouldn't dare go into labor without you being there. I promised to have you back in time and I will, you'll see. There's only one thing I'm concerned about."

She sat up and cocked her head at him.

"I have no idea what Bessima looks like. I realize she would recognize me by my hair, if nothing else. But if she has been projecting my image to the Terrans, everyone else might recognize me, too. I figure I'll have to disguise myself to prevent panic, in which case Bessima would have no reason to introduce herself to me. How am I going to locate her?"

"I suppose you could go back to the rendezvous point several days in a row and look for a big, ugly, scarred woman who showed up every day."

"Your assumption about her appearance is reasonable, but not necessarily accurate. At any rate, we don't know for certain how many days she'll keep going back before she gives up. And what if there's a big crowd?"

"Hmmm. A crowd in front of the White House is a definite possibility. *Shoot!* What am I thinking of? There's no problem. I forgot to tell you. Josep made my hand tingle when he touched it. Now I'm positive you were right about the Illusian chemistry business. All I'd have to do is walk around and touch anyone who might be Bessima, then point her out to you."

"Wait one minute. Who said you were going with me?"

"Of course I'm going with you. By your own admission, I'm your *partner* on this assignment. That means I get to see it through to the end. I've already figured it all out. We make the report to the Consociation Regent, then we check in with Rom and Aster in Innerworld. They'll help us with everything we need to get along in Washington while searching for Bessima. We should have several days' leeway. I could even show you around the Capitol!"

"We'll see," was his only answer, but when they landed on Norona two days later, he was convinced that she should accompany him to give his report and turn the document over to the Consociation.

With both of them dressed in their white jumpsuits, Cherry thought they looked quite official as they were brought before Regent Esquinerra. After all they'd been through together, Gallant hadn't thought to warn Cherry about the Regent.

Although the Ruling Tribunal of Norona made up the strongest element of the Consociation, Esquinerra was not Noronian . . . nor was she anything close to humanoid.

Sitting on a wheeled pedestal in the Regent's chambers was a big, squishy lump of pink clay about the size of a beach ball, with a single black marble in the front. As Cherry and Gallant approached, the clay moved on its own, reshaping itself into a tall, straight column. The black marble seemed to be staring down at them.

"Madame Regent," Gallant said to the clay with a gentlemanly bow, "it is good to see you again. May I present Cherry Cochran, a special friend and my partner on this last mission.

A bit stunned, Cherry did the only thing that came to mind. She curtsied.

A sound similar to glass wind chimes whispered around her and the Regent relaxed back into a lump. Blended in with the pleasant tinkling had been the word "Welcome."

Gallant proceeded to give Esquinerra a concise account of his mission, revealing both Josep's duplicity and his final act of heroism. The truth of his own origins remained a secret, however. He had Cherry personally relate Josep's final messages. After the Regent was briefed, Gallant held out the copy of the Illusian hundred-year plan and a portion of the clay formed an extended arm to take it from him.

"You have done well, as usual, Gallant Voyager," the Regent tinkled. "And your friend has earned our gratitude. Is there any service you desire?"

"Yes, madame. Due to Cherry's involvement in this assignment, she was unable to keep a very important appointment with Theodophilus, the director of the Noronian Performing Company. I would personally appreciate it if you would use your influence to acquire another appointment for her with him in the near future. The location is irrelevant as I've promised to provide her transport."

"It is done. The old maestro owes me a favor or two from his early days."

The Regent and Gallant discussed his course of action regarding Bessima, and she assured him she would attend to the matter of securing Illusia's barrier immediately.

Outwardly, Cherry appeared to be paying attention; inwardly, she was working on a personal puzzle. She thought she should be overjoyed to hear the Regent's implication that an appointment with Theodophilus was a simple matter to arrange. It was what she wanted more than anything in the universe. *Right?*

Half of her mind shouted, *absolutely*! But it was the other, silent half that had her worried.

Chapter 19

"Good Heavens, Rom, what is it?" Aster paused to catch her breath after the hurried trip from her office to his. He had sent her a mental message to come quickly without elaborating why.

Rom's eyes sparkled the bright green they always did when he was happy or up to mischief. "I didn't say you had to run, but I'm glad you did. There's something in the adjoining suite I want you to see."

He opened the side door of his office and waved for Aster to precede him.

Cherry's delighted squeal was probably heard throughout the building as she caught sight of Aster.

Aster started crying immediately and only a very long, clinging hug calmed her. "Thank God you're all right! I've been so worried." As soon as she recovered from the welcome shock of seeing Cherry, she turned on Gallant. "You, I am not happy to see. Your execution is scheduled for dawn. Be there!"

Cherry burst out laughing at the look on Gallant's face as his gaze darted between the three of them trying to tell whether Aster was serious. She gave her best friend another hug. "It's good to be home, kid. I missed you. I'd rather you cancel the firing squad, though. The man looks like the devil, but he has proven to have a number of angelic qualities."

Cherry could see neither Aster nor Rom was entirely convinced, and it was up to her to break the tension. She held out her hand to Gallant and he grasped it like a lifeline. "Let's sit down so we can fill you in."

Throughout the telling of their story, Cherry held Gallant's hand and occasionally touched his cheek or his hair. It was her way of reassuring everyone—including him—that he was forgiven for kidnapping her as far as she was concerned.

When the conversation switched to talk of babies and false labor, Rom suggested the two women remain in the suite and visit while he and Gallant attended to the arrangements for his trip to Outerworld.

"Cherry Cochran!" Aster exclaimed as soon as the door closed behind the men. "I don't believe you finally got bitten, and I wasn't even around to witness the phenomenon."

"What are you talking about?"

"Don't play innocent with me. I know you too well. You look at that man like . . . well, like I look at Rom. How dare you fall in love without my written approval?"

"Love?" Cherry practically choked on the word. "Don't be ridiculous. The baby must be affecting your memory. I'm immune to that particular disease and you know it."

"Oh, I see. We're still in the denial stage. Fine.

I've waited this long to see it happen to you; I don't mind waiting a little longer."

"Listen, kid. Don't waste your time fantasizing about me and Gallant living happily ever after. As soon as I finish helping him tie up this assignment, he's taking me to audition for Theodophilus's company, then he'll be leaving on another mission, probably in the opposite direction from anything remotely similar to civilization. It's been fun, but it's almost over. So, let's talk about what you're going to name our little girl."

"I don't get it, Gallant," Cherry said the next morning as she daubed the black dye into his white streaks. "You told me you didn't want to do any sightseeing, so why would we go to Outerworld today? Bessima isn't supposed to show until the day after tomorrow."

"I just want to be ready ahead of time. This is not the way my mother used to tint my hair. Are you sure it will come out?"

"After a couple of washings . . . with shampoo and water, that is. Your ship's sanitizing beam won't have any effect on it. Which reminds me, you really ought to figure out some way to put a real shower on board."

"We'll see."

Cherry smiled at his usual response. "You might consider wearing a hat and tucking your hair up in it even though the streaks are hidden. Also, you definitely need to wear sunglasses, whether you have the patch on or not, and a less conspicuous outfit is a must. From what Rom and Aster said last night, Bessima has really managed to create a major disturbance with her illusions. It doesn't sound like there's a person on the whole planet who hasn't seen your face."

Gallant frowned. "She accomplished exactly what the princess expected her to by this time. It's quite amazing actually. I wouldn't have thought Terrans were so gullible."

"Just because they're all talking about God's arrival doesn't mean they believe it will really happen. If you showed up in front of the horde that has collected around the White House, the chances of you being stoned to death are probably equal to your being worshiped. In fact, some newspaper undoubtedly did a poll on that issue already."

"I could always have a little surgical rearrangement of my features—"

"Don't you dare!" Cherry said, meeting his gaze in the mirror. "I like your face just the way it is."

He grinned at her. "You could make me feel really good and say you *love* my face."

"I could. But I won't. You're too cocky as it is. Someone has to keep you humble, and at the moment, I'm the only one volunteering for the job. I see you got one of those special rings from Rom."

He held up his left hand and moved it back and forth so that the ornate gold ring with its fire opal setting picked up glints of light. A portable extension of Innerworld's central computer, the ring had innumerable capabilities. "Rom gave me enough instruction that I should have no problem using it to transport us from place to place and back into Innerworld when the time comes. Using it as a communication device would take a lot more practice than I have time for though."

"Why would we need to go from place to place?"

Gallant raised his eyebrows and shrugged his shoulders. "We don't. Are you about finished with my hair?"

She made a face to let him know she suspected he was evading, but she let it go for the moment. "Leave the dye on for five more minutes, then go rinse it off in the shower. I'm going to start packing some clothes and toiletries for each of us. They don't have computerized supply stations and recyclable clothing out there, you know. Thank the stars it's summer, otherwise we'd have to take a whole wardrobe along with us."

By midday they were in the transmigrator cell, dressed in typical American jeans and shirts, with Gallant carrying one satchel for the two of them. They were about to be dispatched to Outerworld, and Cherry's feeling that he was hiding something was stronger than ever.

Her suspicions were justified the moment they materialized on the corner of a busy city intersection bearing street signs with the names Broadway and 47th Street. A quick scan of the neighborhood confirmed that they were in New York City, not Washington, D.C. "Either the transmigrator technician got the signals seriously crossed, or this is part of the secret you've been pretending not to have."

"Who, me? Have a secret from you?" He gave her

a kiss on the nose. "I refuse to reveal any information one second before it's absolutely necessary." Placing his arm around her shoulders, he urged her to walk with him. "It should be right down here."

"*What* should? Come on, you're driving me crazy." His sexy grin didn't help her bewilderment at all.

"Here we are."

He had brought her to the ticket window of a theater. While he picked up matinee tickets that had miraculously been reserved for him, Cherry glanced at the advertising poster for the show.

"Dear God," she whispered as her eyes focused on one line: STARRING ROSE COCHRAN. Words escaped her as she gaped at the poster then at Gallant.

With his index finger under her chin, he closed her mouth and gave her a light kiss. "She's expecting special, *nameless* guests backstage after the performance and no one else will be with her. But the decision is yours."

Her eyes filled with moisture as she threw her arms around his neck. "You dear, sweet man! I can't believe you tracked her down, and . . . and . . ." Again she was rendered mute by emotion and settled for hugging him as hard as she could.

"I gather you like my surprise," Gallant said with a satisfied smile. "Let's go see if she's as good as you."

Cherry knew that Innerworld had Noronian emissaries that lived quietly in Outerworld, keeping their eyes and ears open for problems. These men and women were placed in strategic locations and careers so that they might be able to accomplish a variety of things without any Terran being aware of alien interference. But reserving center front seats for a big Broadway show on a moment's notice and arranging a private appointment with its leading lady were not the sort of things Cherry imagined they usually did.

The play may or may not have been wonderful. Cherry had no idea. She only had eyes for her baby sister, Rose. The physical likeness to herself was incredible, but she felt the younger woman's stage presence completely outshone her own, and it made her proud enough to burst. As the curtain closed for the final time, Cherry's hands started shaking. What if Rose never forgave her for abandoning her? What if she didn't even remember her? What if—

"Ready?" Gallant asked gently, squeezing her hand.

She took a deep breath and stood up. "It's good you didn't warn me ahead of time. I'd have been a basket case before we got here."

A stagehand escorted them to Rose's dressing room, knocked, and announced the arrival of her guests. Rose opened the door with a bright smile . . . then turned ghostly pale.

The stagehand was about to press the panic button, but she quickly assured him that everything was fine and stepped back for her guests to enter. When she closed the door behind her, she slumped against it, saying, "I don't believe my eyes. You're going to have to convince me that I'm not hallucinating."

Cherry was paralyzed with the fear that she would not be welcome or that she would say the wrong thing, until Gallant gave her a nudge toward Rose. "When's the last time y'all played in the mud with a passel of piglets, baby girl?"

Rose's eyes widened and tears made them sparkle. "It's really you? My big sister?"

Cherry nodded as tears of her own ran down her face. "Would you object to a hug from a virtual stranger?"

Rose opened her arms and they met each other halfway.

Gallant smiled as the women's first minutes together were filled with nonsensical noises and unfinished sentences. He could see they were happy to see each other, but he himself had never felt so good about something that had nothing to do with him personally. Instantly he corrected that thought. Anything involving Cherry personally affected him as well.

Eventually, the explanations began and Gallant was amazed at Rose's automatic acceptance. She believed every word she heard simply because Cherry had uttered it.

"I have always known something freaky had to have happened to you," Rose said. "Otherwise you would have come back or at least written for me."

Cherry's expression revealed her relief. "You honestly never thought I forgot about you all these years?"

"Hell, no. I can't explain it, but I just held on to the thought that you weren't dead, only detoured somewhere in your life. All the time my career was progressing, I kept thinking that wherever you were, you'd hear about me, and if at all possible, you'd come see me, since I didn't know how to find you."

"Thank you, baby, for not giving up on me, and especially for making such a success of your life. You couldn't have turned out any better if I had been there every step of the way."

"But, Cherry, you *were* with me every step, in my heart. How else would I have made it this far?"

Gallant swallowed down the lump in his throat as he watched the two women break into tears and hugs again.

They went out to dinner and spent the night in Rose's apartment in Greenwich Village. Though Cherry was determined not to ask, Rose insisted on talking about the rest of their family.

"Tully's wife writes me a card every Christmas, but the rest of our kin has abided by Pa's declaration that I was cut out of the family the day I left Georgia. Like with you, he told them the devil had possessed my soul and it would be fatal to make contact with me."

"I'm sorry to hear that," Cherry said.

"Don't be. All that hate and Bible-thumping was damn depressing, but apparently you and I were the only ones who thought that way. The rest of them have little rug-rats of their own to dominate now and, from what I've read between the few lines I've received, Tully's the only one of our brothers who hasn't followed precisely in Pa's tyrannical footsteps."

Cherry would have enjoyed hearing a fairy tale about how everyone had ended up living happily ever after, but she knew real life didn't usually work that way. Besides, if Rose had said they'd all changed, she might have been tempted to go back and visit them, too. This way, she didn't need to feel the least bit guilty about not seeing them.

When Gallant awoke the next morning, the ladies were still talking, but at least the tears had been replaced by sporadic fits of giggles. Rose insisted on playing tour guide for the remainder of the day, letting her stand-in cover for the matinee and evening performances of her show.

Despite the endless hours of talking, however, they were still catching up when it was time for Gallant to get back to work the following day.

"You can stay if you'd like," he offered, making it clear that he meant either for another day or forever.

Cherry was terribly torn, but she knew she couldn't give up her career, Innerworld, or her friends there, nor would she break her promise to Rom and Aster to return as soon as the mission was over. She understood the reasoning behind the law that prohibited transplanted Terrans from returning to the surface. There was always the risk of discovery. Although she had broken the law by telling Rose everything, she was certain it would go no further.

"Thank you, Captain, but I think that would constitute shirking my responsibility as your partner." She held up her robotic hand. "This mechanical wonder still has an important job to do, and where it goes, I go."

"Will you ever be back?" Rose asked, the waterworks threatening to start all over again.

Cherry wanted to make her a promise, but it took

her eighteen years to fulfill the last one. She glanced at Gallant for help with her answer.

"We'll see," he muttered.

Cherry's face lit up into a smile as she told Rose, "He always says that when he doesn't want to say yes but he knows I'll get my way sooner or later. I can't say when, but I'll be back someday."

It took a while longer to say all the things they wanted each other to remember. Then Gallant programmed his Innerworld ring for a location a few blocks away from the White House in Washington, D.C., and he and Cherry were off.

Where their arrival in Manhattan had been smooth and completely unnoticed, this migration landed them in the center of a shoving match, which their abruptly added presence escalated.

"Watch it, bud!"

"Where the hell do you think you're goin'?"

"Gimme a break! I've been standing in this same spot since yesterday."

"Excuse us," Gallant said, and used his larger frame and the satchel to make a wedge through the crowd with Cherry in tow.

"Holy stars!" Cherry exclaimed as they headed away from the White House and toward the edge of the throng. "There must be ten thousand people gathered here. When I said a crowd was a possibility, I had no idea what we were going to encounter."

"Apparently everyone is hoping to be a witness to the greatest event in the history of this planet."

"Or to the greatest hoax. Finding Bessima is going to be like hunting the proverbial needle in a haystack. Your robotic hand's sensitivity to her Illusian body chemistry isn't going to do us any good if you can't move around to search for her. Listen, it's only noon now. There's plenty of time to go to the room Rom arranged for us, drop off that bag, and get some lunch before we have to fight our way to the front gates."

As she waved down a taxi, a positive thought occurred to her. "One thing for sure, with that crowd, nobody will think anything of my touching them. I was a little concerned about someone thinking I was trying to get fresh." On their way to the hotel, she explained what she meant by that, promptly adding to Gallant's concern for her safety.

Two hours later they returned to discover that the afternoon sun had sent a portion of the bystanders away to seek air-conditioned shelter. Because the crowd had thinned, Cherry and Gallant were able to quickly discern another problem.

A two-block area in front of the White House had been cordoned off with a yellow-and-black-striped plastic ribbon, and an army of helmeted, baton-bearing police were very seriously obeying the order not to let anyone but members of the press pass the line. Within the secured area was a sea of people, cameras, cables, and lights. Umbrellas provided shade for many of those who couldn't squeeze beneath one of the trees along the sidewalk.

"Any ideas?" Cherry asked Gallant.

"Bessima has followed her instructions up to this point. I think it's safe to assume that she will do whatever she must to be as close to those front gates as possible at three o'clock."

"Yes, but how?"

Gallant's greater height gave him a definite advantage as he studied the area. Suddenly he grasped her waist and lifted her so that she could see from his perspective. "Look. An officer just let that man in the yellow shirt go through. He doesn't look so different from me. Perhaps you just have to ask the right authority." He set her back down on the pavement.

"No way. He probably showed him a press pass." She explained what that was. "I don't suppose Rom thought of giving you one of those."

"No, but if you point one out to me, I can duplicate one for each of us. That's probably what Bessima would do, too."

Cherry frowned in confusion for a moment before she understood that he meant he could create an *illusion* of a pass. Now she knew why he had chosen not to wear the eye patch beneath his sunglasses. "See the rectangular cards attached to those people's shirts or hanging from a string around their necks? And there . . ." She pointed to a case sitting on the street a few feet away, with a pass tied to its handle.

"All right. I've got it. Just hold your hand out in front of you as if you're holding a pass. Since I don't know how to make two separated images at the same time, you'll have to keep your hand right next to mine."

Within a few minutes, they were inside the restricted area and picking their way through equipment and reporters in an effort to get near the front gates. Cherry laid her hand on every person she passed and was again glad that the summer heat had people wearing as little clothing as necessary.

Gallant had suggested she not eliminate anyone as possible suspects. If Bessima looked anything like the female Illusians they had already encountered, she might be able to pass for a male. He also figured she was probably good at assuming a variety of disguises, since she had obviously blended in with so many different groups around the world without drawing attention to herself.

Unfortunately, the simple act of walking around in an area where everyone else tended to be stationary, was attracting attention to Cherry and Gallant, and they weren't able to check out as many people as they would have liked. It became apparent that Gallant was too big to go unnoticed and he agreed to stand still and let her stumble around without his escort. But he watched her every second, prepared to move at her signal.

By four o'clock, they estimated that Cherry had touched at least a hundred individuals without any of them causing the slightest tingle. They would have to return tomorrow and try again.

Disappointed, but not completely surprised, they headed back to the hotel for air conditioning, showers, and room service.

"I suppose she could have been delayed," Cherry offered while they ate dinner at the small table in their room. "After all, she did have to cross the continent from her last extravaganza, and from what

Josep told me she would have to use normal transport to get around."

Gallant buttered the last roll in the basket and gave Cherry half of it. "I lean more toward the possibility that she was there; we just didn't find her. I was thinking, we spent the whole hour close to the gates and people started noticing us. Maybe Bessima was hovering less conspicuously at the fringes, waiting for the princess to show up before coming forward."

"It's worth a try tomorrow. I got the distinct impression all those media people had staked out their own piece of the street and would remain in the same spot where I touched them today."

"Right." He drained the last drop in his glass. "What did you call this drink?"

"Dr. Pepper."

"Remind me to take a can back to have it analyzed. I'd like to have it added to my ship's supply station menu."

Cherry giggled. "That station of yours needs a lot more than a new drink selection. It should be completely overhauled."

"Fine. Before we take off again, you have it reprogrammed the way you'd like. Neither Mar-Dot nor I have cared enough to take the time to have it done."

"I don't know how you can say that when I've watched you eat every meal since we've been here as if it were your last. And let's not forget your enthusiastic appreciation of the princess's food. You may as well admit it. You were afraid if you enjoyed the pleasure of eating too much, you'd be acting like a barbarian."

He caught her hand and pulled her out of the chair. "Is it absolutely necessary to strip me of every secret I have?"

Her eyes sparkled as her fingers undid the top button of his shirt. "Let's just say I find it necessary to strip you, period."

His hand stopped hers from proceeding, and with a look of sheer deviltry, he asked, "How about a game? I brought my cubes."

Cherry narrowed her eyes at him. "Which ones?"

He managed to look indignant. "The honest ones, of course."

"And what might the stakes be in this game you're suggesting, Captain?" She slipped her hand out of his and ran it down his chest and over his flat stomach, but once more he stopped her from going further.

"If you want to strip something off me, you'll have to get a quad, and I get to do the same to you. One quad, one piece of clothing forfeited."

"Mmmm. Sounds interesting, but counting both my shoes, I only have six pieces to lose, and I know you have even less. What does the winner get if all the clothing is already lost?"

A low growl accompanied his slow grin. "In this game, love, the winner gets anything he wants."

"*He?* Don't count on it, mister. Let's play."

Using the room service tray, he set the game up in the middle of the king-size bed.

Cherry got the first quad, and knowing he wasn't

wearing underwear, considerately removed one of his boots first. She tickled the arch of his bare foot and said, "One down, Captain. Only three pieces to go."

However, he got the next set of four and went right for her blouse. He took his time undoing each button and peeling the silky red material down her arms. His brow raised admiringly as he saw how a red lacy demi-bra lifted her breasts.

His leering expression caused her to sharply inhale and her aroused nipples peeked out over the top edge. Unable to hide his pleased grin, he said, "So, this is why you dressed in the bathroom this morning. When you have my supply station reprogrammed, you can do something about the clothing selection, too."

Using only his index finger, he skimmed her bare flesh and she playfully slapped his hand. "No touching. You haven't won yet."

He managed to get another quad on his next roll, and though he was clearly anxious to see whether what was hidden beneath her blue jeans was as seductive as the brassiere, he had no choice but to remove her shoes first, one at a time.

Cherry could see he was growing increasingly uncomfortable in his tailored slacks, and wickedly left them for last. His luck ran better than hers in the following innings, and soon he was discovering the sexy panties that matched the bra.

His darkening eyes revealed just how hungry she was making him. "And to think all this time I was glad my station couldn't provide you with underwear."

As he sat there trapped in the tight trousers, he began to wonder if she was purposely losing. Before long, he had the pleasure of removing both the flimsy pieces of enticement . . . very, *very*, slowly. As his fingers barely caressed her flesh, her breath quickened, and he knew she wouldn't want to play much longer, at least not with cubes.

On her next turn, she threw a quad and demonstrated a definite lack of patience as she stripped off his slacks to bare his lower body.

Despite both their desire to change the game, neither was willing to be the one to forefit. It was necessary for each of them to take several more turns before Gallant was able to conclude the match by tossing a green quad.

By that time, Cherry was ready to pay whatever penalty the winner demanded. But in the end, she was the one doing the demanding and, as usual, one explosive release wasn't nearly enough.

Later, when their pulses finally slowed and urgent need became affectionate cuddling, Cherry said, "I just remembered. There are a few more things besides your supply station that need replacing. Your protective suits had to be left behind on Lore, and so was the slave collar and chain."

"The suits I can take care of in Innerworld. The collar is just as well gone."

"Oh? It seemed to be a fairly useful prop for you."

He grimaced. "If I didn't have it, I'd have come up with another idea. I should never have kept it once I got it off."

Cherry raised her head to look in his eyes. "I beg

your pardon?" With his hand at the back of her neck he pulled her head down for a kiss, but she resisted. "What did you mean by that? On Zoenid you said something cryptic to Dutch about being a slave also." His hand fell away from her neck and he let out a sigh. "No secrets, Gallant. Spit it out."

He shook his head as if he didn't believe she could do this to him so easily, but he told his tale anyway. "It was an assignment. I was given the job of tracking down a report that a slaver was illegally working within the Consociation borders, primarily abducting adolescent children from the more passive cultures and selling them to a breeder farm. Making contact with the slavers and infiltrating their tribe was a rather routine matter for me.

"Stomaching the abusive way the children were treated, however, was more than I could quietly handle. I objected one too many times and ended up with that collar around my own neck before I could get out of there to make my report. Dutch was the man who won the privilege of teaching me precisely what rights a slave has."

Cherry held herself very still as his eyelids lowered, temporarily shutting her out. She could sense him replaying a nightmare in his mind and forced herself not to ask him to say more than he wanted to.

"The only reason I let him live to throw it back in my face was because he and that collar ended up saving my life. One night, a rival tribe of slavers attacked the camp where we were staying. I'm sure if I had been chained to a post, I'd have been massacred along with everyone else. But Dutch had been having some fun with me, so he was using his wrist manacle. When the bloodbath started, he couldn't find the key fast enough and took off with me still chained to him."

He paused a moment before continuing. "When the princess drugged me, and I was helpless, it was like being back in that slave camp again." This time, when he pulled her closer for a kiss, she gave it willingly. "I will never forget what you did for me back there, love."

She gave him another long, sweet kiss. "And I'll never forget you, Gallant Voyager."

Before falling asleep, with her head tucked beneath his chin, Cherry murmured, "Have I told you how much I loved your taking me to see Rose?"

He briefly tightened his embrace. "As a matter of fact, you've thanked me at least a thousand times, but I don't believe you ever said it exactly that way. Did it hurt much?"

As exhaustion carried her toward the land of dreams, she smiled to herself and whispered, "Hardly at all, love. Hardly at all."

Shortly before three the following afternoon, they were back in front of the White House. As planned, Cherry worked the crowd furthest from the gates, yet still within the restricted zone. Four o'clock passed with no better luck than the day before.

On the third day of their vigil, a continuous downpour chased away all but a handful of diehard reporters. Gallant and Cherry agreed that she had tested every one of them already, which was a good thing because most of them, like themselves, were wearing hooded plastic ponchos that were being sold by an enterprising man on the street. They hesitated to leave the area before four o'clock though, despite the fact that it appeared to be a waste of time.

At about three-thirty, Gallant saw a figure of medium height hurrying toward the police line not far from where they were standing. The person was wearing a tan raincoat, dark slacks, and sneakers, and carrying a large umbrella, none of which was remarkable. But when he or she attempted to duck under the plastic ribbon right past the police officers, Gallant nudged Cherry.

She looked in the direction he nodded in time to see two of the officers drag the person back behind the line by the arms. Cherry couldn't make out what was being said, but the hand motions indicated that the person did not have authorization to enter the area and was frustrated as hell about it.

Cherry and Gallant watched the person back off when one officer started slapping his nightstick into his palm. The figure started walking away, but halted a few feet from Gallant and Cherry to take another look at the White House.

The umbrella tipped back, revealing an extraordinarily unattractive woman with a thick scar across the bridge of her nose and another along her jaw. Cherry's memory flashed an image of Honorbound. Without waiting for Gallant's approval, she acted. "Excuse me? Ma'am? Maybe we could help you."

Gallant squeezed Cherry's upper arm twice, letting her know he was going along with her.

The woman took a step closer, her narrow-eyed gaze darting suspiciously from one to the other.

"Hi," Cherry said, extending her right arm for a handshake. "I'm Jane Doe of Channel 6 News."

The woman hesitantly raised her hand, but a split second before their fingertips met, she caught sight of the thin gold choker around Cherry's neck that housed the universal translator. The woman's hand instantly withdrew to touch her identical neckpiece, and her eyes widened with recognition of the enemy. Dropping the umbrella, she took off at a run.

"Wait!" Cherry shouted as Gallant leapt over the plastic ribbon. She bolted under it right behind him, but his longer legs outdistanced her in no time. She simply kept running after them, knowing he couldn't spare the seconds it would take for her to catch up.

"Would you care for some assistance?" a gravelly, accented voice called from behind her.

She kept running as a tall man in a hooded, nylon rain parka and aviator sunglasses caught up with her and placed his hand on her lower back. The voice had sounded familiar so she refrained from reacting violently, and when the man lowered his sunglasses to reveal luminous, gold topaz eyes, she was certain of his identity.

"Falcon! I had no idea you were here." His hand on her back somehow helped her pick up speed and they began closing the distance to Gallant.

"You were not supposed to know, but I have been

keeping an eye on you . . . and him. Aster was worried."

"She's okay now." Cherry couldn't get over how fast she was running without losing her breath, though she knew Falcon well enough not to be surprised at anything he was capable of. "Where's Steve?" Falcon's wife was one of those few women Cherry had felt an instant connection with.

"She and the children are visiting her brother today. You may recall he works for the Treasury Department here. I did not think she needed to be out in such inclement weather."

The rain slick sidewalk ended the chase when the woman attempted to make a sharp turn into a park and lost her footing. The moment her body hit the pavement, Gallant dove on top of her and held her down with her arm twisted up her back.

"Who are you?" he demanded as she struggled to free herself.

"Jane Doe, and I'll have you arrested for assault, you bastard! Get off of me!"

"I think not." He looked up to see Cherry and a stranger hovering over them.

"This is Falcon," Cherry said quickly. "He's one of ours."

Gallant nodded at the man, but immediately returned his attention to Cherry. "All right, love. She's all yours. But be careful. I heard Illusian females bite."

With that reminder, Cherry avoided touching the woman's face, and grasped her hand instead. A second later, she recoiled as violently as if she had contacted a live electrical wire. "Wow! Is she ever!"

"Let me introduce myself, Commander Bessima. My name is Gallant Voyager."

"Impossible!" she cried. "The princess would be with you, not that . . . that demon child of Norona. I know the real Gallant Voyager bears the two white stripes of royalty in his hair." She twisted against his restraining hold in spite of the pain such movement had to cause.

"Actually, Commander, it doesn't much matter what you do or don't know. Honorbound and her troops won't be joining you and the Illusian barrier has been refortified."

"*Liar!*" she shouted.

"I'm afraid not," he continued, not sounding the least bit sorry. "You're the only one left free now. And you have an appointment on an operating table in Innerworld. Cherry, I could use that hand of yours, if you can stand to hold on to her for a few seconds."

Prepared for the contact, she controlled Bessima while Gallant pressed several of the little gold nodules on his ring.

Seeing that everything was under control, Falcon said, "I will advise the other emissaries that they may return to their homes now." He gave them a mock salute and walked away.

Putting one arm around Cherry while gripping Bessima as well, Gallant turned the ring's opal one complete rotation.

In the blink of an eye, they were gone.

Chapter 20

"Hold on, Rom," Dr. Xerpa warned anxiously. "Here comes another strong one." Delivering a baby was not in her normal realm of medical services, but Aster had refused to allow any other doctor near her throughout her pregnancy.

Propped up next to Aster on the double-wide, slanted obstetrical bed, Rom squeezed his mate's hand as he personally felt the same wave that contracted her abdomen. He didn't even attempt to block it out. When it passed, he asked if she was all right as if he wasn't experiencing every feeling along with her.

"Will you both please calm down," Aster said with a laugh. "I swear, I feel terrific. Before I came to Innerworld and was treated for it, I had regular menstrual cramps, worse than these little twinges."

Innerworld's medical technology hadn't been able to spare her nine months of pregnancy, but the labor itself was about as strenuous as a jog around the administration building. She had had the option of the totally painless method of surgically removing the infant, followed by an hour of treatment under the healing beam. That would have to have been done before labor began, however, and she was determined to wait for Cherry as long as possible.

"You are now fully dilated, Aster," Xerpa said. "It should only be a little longer."

"No! Not yet. Not until Cherry gets here. What's taking her so long?"

It was Rom's turn to laugh. "She and Gallant only arrived from the surface a half hour ago with their prisoner. You know she has to go through sanitizing before coming in here."

"Can't they turn up the damn beam or something? What good is all your damn technology if you can't even get my best friend here when I need her. Damn it! I promised her I'd wait."

Dr. Xerpa patted Aster's bent knees. "I'm sure she'll understand. Get ready. You're going to have to start pushing, and I'm afraid *this* is going to be a lot worse than a twinge."

Aster didn't want to disappoint Cherry, but the urge to push was too strong to hold back. Simultaneously, she and Rom groaned and clutched the handrails as their daughter began making her way down the birth canal.

Cherry burst into the delivery room and screeched to a halt. "Holy stars, if that ain't a sight! I hadn't realized Rom would be in labor, too."

"Your humor is not appreciated at the moment, Cherry," Rom grumbled through gritted teeth.

"Don't listen to him," Aster countered in a strained voice. "Doctor, you can deliver our daughter now."

And with another long push, a big, beautiful baby girl slipped peacefully into the doctor's waiting hands.

Rom, Aster, and Cherry shared hugs and kisses while Dr. Xerpa finished her job with mother and baby. As quickly as possible, she had the infant cleaned, wrapped, and snug in Aster's loving embrace.

"What did you finally decide to call her?" Cherry asked, unable to take her eyes off the little dark-haired angel.

Aster and Rom glanced at each other and smiled before giving their joint answer. "Shara."

"Well, how do you do, Miss Shara. I'm your Aunt Cherry." With a feathery stroke on the baby's soft cheek, she promised, "You're going to have a wonderful life, kid. I'm personally going to see to it."

Aster smiled at her obviously smitten friend. For the moment, she forced aside her worries about Shara's future as the first child born from the joining of a Noronian and a Terran. There would be time enough to worry in the years ahead.

Chapter 21

As soon as Romulus was able, he made arrangements for Bessima's mind to be fully reprogrammed and her appearance surgically altered. An adjustment to the retina in one of her eyes prevented her from ever accidentally creating images, even though she would have no memory of being an Illusian. She was then shipped off to another planet to begin a new, productive life.

The day after Shara's birth, giving Romulus a fabricated excuse, Gallant and Cherry returned to Washington, D.C. to perform the final act in Bessima's play. Mother Nature, or possibly the real Supreme Being, decided to help them along. The rain stopped shortly after sunrise and an incredible double rainbow stretched over the White House for over an hour. Taking that as a promise of miracles, the largest crowd yet turned out that morning.

All of the Innerworld emissaries and trackers had been recalled, so Gallant had no fear of one of them picking up the energy wave he was about to create. He knew Rom and Aster would be suspicious after they heard about the incident, but Gallant and

Cherry had agreed that it was best if their friends not be burdened with the truth.

At eleven o'clock in the morning, the spectators in front of the White House watched a spot of white light, similar to a star, separate itself from the sun. The spot moved across the sky then grew larger and larger until people began to realize it was coming closer.

Before panic could set in, a huge ball of sparkling light was hovering directly above them, and a deep man's voice reverberated clearly over the noise of the crowd.

"Fear not, my children. I come in peace."

Within seconds, the only sounds on the street were the clicking and whirring of cameras.

"The images you have seen regarding the coming of the Supreme Being were false, created by someone whose only god was power. That person has been dealt with and will not be able to deceive again.

"I will leave you now with the same messages you have been told before. Love one another. Treat others as you wish to be treated yourself. And remember that every day of your lives is Judgment Day. I am watching."

With that warning, the ball of light soared back to the sun. Long minutes passed before the people began to talk and move again.

When they did, Gallant and Cherry returned to Innerworld.

The following day, Cherry went back to work in Fantasy World at the Indulgence Center. Not having an immediate assignment elsewhere, Gallant rationalized that he should remain in Innerworld until Regent Esquinerra contacted him regarding Cherry's appointment with Theodophilus. Cherry had invited Mar-Dot to stay in the extra bedroom of her apartment, but the he-she preferred to reside on the ship. Gallant didn't need an invitation to share her home while he was there.

Compared to the last month of practically being glued to one another, their time alone together was drastically reduced. While she performed, he kept busy doing repairs and making modifications on his ship. Another chunk of each day was spent fussing over Shara with Rom and Aster. But during the times they were alone, the passion that had sparked aboard Gallant's ship flared anew and carried them over until their next private hours.

Cherry stopped questioning why she hadn't grown bored with Gallant, and simply enjoyed having him around. What she *was* questioning was why she wasn't more anxious to hear from the Regent about Theodophilus. She knew she still wanted the audition; she just wasn't all that concerned anymore about how long it took to arrange.

A week later, Gallant caught up with her in between reenactments. He was smiling as he handed her a piece of paper, but Cherry's personal antennae picked up an underlying tension.

Referring to what she was sensing rather than the paper, she asked, "What is it?"

"Read it," he answered with forced enthusiasm.

Cherry skimmed over the message quickly, then reread it more slowly to be sure she hadn't imagined it. "He's coming here! Oh, Gallant, do you believe this? Theodophilus is coming back to Innerworld just to audition me!"

He laughed as she jumped up into his arms and almost knocked him over. "I don't know why you sound so shocked. I'm sure he is well aware of what a coup it would be to add you to his company."

She released her stranglehold on him and started pacing. "He'll be here the day after tomorrow. Holy stars! What'll I wear? Which piece should I perform? Should I invite him to my apartment for dinner or would he think that was too personal?"

Gallant grabbed her hand as she passed and brought it to his lips for a kiss. "I'm sure whatever you had planned to wear and perform the first time around were the right choices."

"Of course they were. How silly of me. Listen, I have a reenactment in about five minutes and I still have to change. Do you want to hang around and we can do something to celebrate after I'm finished?"

He leaned over and whispered in her ear. "I'd rather celebrate someplace less public. Just come home when you're through. I'll be there."

But the celebration didn't have quite the tone Cherry expected. Gallant set the mood with soft background music and softer lighting. He touched her throughout their meal as he often did, but the contact was not the seductive stroking she was accustomed to from him. Instead, each touch, every look was an affectionate caress that silently spoke volumes about how he felt about her.

How he *loved* her.

They didn't talk. There didn't seem to be anything left to say between them. That night, when he took her into his arms, she denied him nothing. And began saying good-bye the only way she possibly could.

With her body, her mind, and her very soul, Cherry Cochran made love to Gallant Voyager.

The morning before Theodophilus was scheduled to arrive, Mar-Dot joined Gallant and Cherry for breakfast in her apartment. One glance at Dot's face made Cherry think that this was more than a simple social call and Gallant's somber mood throughout the meal confirmed it. When the plates were cleared away and less than a dozen words had been exchanged during the past hour, she demanded, "All right, what's going on?"

Gallant cleared his throat, took a sip of coffee, and coughed lightly.

Cherry smirked at him. "It can't be *that* bad. Just spit it out."

Wiping his hands and mouth on a napkin, he stalled for another few seconds before confessing. "We're leaving this morning. I told Mar-Dot you probably wouldn't forgive them if they didn't say good-bye properly."

A chill swept over Cherry as his words registered. "You're leaving? This morning?"

"We have a new assignment," he said quietly, not meeting her gaze.

"But can't you leave tomorrow? Or at least wait until after my audition this evening." Cherry could hear herself whining, but her disappointment was too great. She had been mentally preparing herself for them to go their separate ways in a few days, maybe a week. Not in five minutes, with no warning whatsoever.

"I stayed too long as it is."

Cherry pouted and crossed her arms. "I don't understand. In fact, I don't understand anything about you."

Gallant raised his brow in disbelief. "Come now. There isn't a person in the galaxy who knows as much about me as you do . . . including Mar-Dot."

The he-she rose at the mention of their name. Dot faced Cherry first. "I believe there are things the two of you should discuss without company, but not until we get our farewell hugs." She held her arms out and Cherry stepped into them with a sad smile.

"What can I say, Dot? I'm going to miss you. I'll never forget you."

"And we will never forget you, Cherry." Dot released her and turned around.

Mar placed his hands on Cherry's cheeks, tipped her head back and kissed her passionately before she had a chance to either brace herself or protest. When he ended the kiss, he said, "I've been wanting to do that since we met, but if I had, you would never have given the captain a second look, and it was past time for him to bring someone like you into his life."

Cherry laughed at him, then smiled at Gallant. "The captain is lucky to have the *both* of you."

It took several more rounds of flattery and teasing before Mar-Dot left Gallant and Cherry alone. The moment they were, Cherry let her frustration rule her tongue. "I can't believe you didn't tell me you were leaving ahead of time."

"I almost didn't tell you at all," he murmured.

She was shocked that he would even consider such a cowardly route. "Why?"

Gallant almost smiled. "I love you."

She let out an exasperated breath and paced a few steps before asking, "Then how can you leave like this? How can you say you love me and not want to stay with me until the last possible minute?"

Placing his arm around her shoulders, he led her to a chair and sat her down on his lap. "I promised to be truthful with you. The truth is, I love you, but every hour we've been together since we heard from the Regent has been filled with farewells. I'm not a masochist, Cherry. I can't stick around to watch you go."

She fought down the emotion that his words caused and asked again, "Then how can you leave at all? If you really loved me—"

He quieted her with a kiss. "I once told you that my saying I love you wouldn't mean I wanted to enslave you. I respect the fact that you need your independence and that nothing and no one is as important to you as your acting career. But my understanding that doesn't stop me from caring deeply about you. My mother always said that true love is demonstrated best by giving the one you love their freedom. She proved that the day she let me go. I'd like to think I'm as good a person as she is."

Cherry hugged him close. "My sweet Gallant. If I was ever going to allow myself to fall in love with any man, it would be you."

He held her away from him and shook his head. "You still don't get it, do you? Love isn't something you give yourself permission to feel. You either love someone, or you don't. And, unfortunately, you don't."

She was tempted to ask him to make love to her one more time before he left, but she was no more of a masochist than he was.

After he was gone, she ordered herself to concentrate on her upcoming audition. In spite of Gallant's assurance that Theodophilus would be lucky to have her, and her own self-confidence in her talent, she knew better than to assume it was in the bag. No matter what trick she tried to get her mind on track though, it kept sliding off.

She kept promising herself that she could think about Gallant and how confused she was later, after the audition was over, but his words kept bouncing around in her head.

He had told her he loved her and asked nothing in return. Why? Better question—how? Love was possession, dominance, captivity. It was *not* the freedom to leave. If he really loved her, he would have insisted—

She cut off her own thought by recalling his mother's attitude about love. She'd said it before.

That woman was one smart lady. Obviously, a hell of a lot smarter than she was.

She had just let the only man she'd ever loved get away.

Trooper that she was, Cherry gave a spectacular performance for Theodophilus that evening and managed to look happily stunned when he offered her a lead position in the Noronian Performing Company.

The only problem was his returning to Innerworld for her had cost them valuable time. They were committed to a six-month tour throughout the Consociation of Planets, commencing with Norona in two weeks. She could study her roles en route, but it was absolutely necessary that she be prepared to depart Innerworld in two days.

The time should have sped by in a frenzy of activity. Anything would have been preferable to wondering if she had made a terrible mistake about Gallant. Unfortunately for her state of mind, she had very little that needed attending before she could leave, and she could only spend so many hours with Aster and a sleeping baby.

It was uncomfortable knowing that she would miss six whole months of Shara's infancy, but Aster promised to maintain a detailed visual record of every important moment and repeatedly assured Cherry that she had to take advantage of this opportunity.

Eventually, the minutes became hours and the sleepless nights passed one after the other, until it was time to board Theodophilus's ship. She couldn't stop herself from glancing into the docking bay where Gallant's ship had been, even though she knew it wouldn't be there.

He was gone. In another hour, she would be also. And the odds against her running into him while they were on tour were at least a zillion to one.

Forget him, Cherry, she scolded herself. *There's a whole universe of men out there, just waiting to adore you!* With that thought in mind, she pasted on a smile and walked on board.

Theodophilus greeted her briefly, then turned her over to one of the crew members for a tour of the ship she would be living on for the next six months. As the fawning young man escorted her from one level to another, she kept wondering how something this enormous could ever get off the ground. Why, Gallant's whole ship would fit—

Damn! There he was again, insinuating himself into her every thought. Since this was a mental handicap she had never experienced before, she fretted over how long it would be till she was rehabilitated.

When they reached her quarters, she thanked her guide and promised to have dinner with him some evening. She had been very pleased to hear that she had a two-room suite with a private bath and supply station. Automatically, she thought of Gallant's miniscule cabin and knew before she saw the suite which one she would have preferred walking into at this moment.

The living room was an ultramodern masterpiece

of design, and she supposed she would get used to it . . . sooner or later. Hoping the bedroom had a little more warmth to it, she opened that door.

And gasped.

The room was a picture of femininity in pink-and-white chintz, with a ruffled canopy over a four-poster bed, and a decorative dressing screen in the corner. Only one thing was wrong with the picture.

There was a man in it. A very big, dangerous-looking man to be precise, stretched out in the middle of the bed, with his back propped up by a stack of frilly pillows.

Cherry's bewildered gaze traveled from his bare feet, up over tight black leather pants, to a matching vest with no shirt. Two silvery gray streaks ran through his long black hair, and a black patch covered one eye. Even without the piratical costume, the look on his face was enough to frighten any sensible woman.

But then, no one ever accused Cherry of being sensible.

She took two steps into the room and abruptly stopped again. Around his neck was a black leather collar with a row of short silver spikes sticking out of it and a chain that ran from the collar to a manacle clamped around one bedpost.

Her heart was pounding in her chest. That mindless organ didn't care in the least why he was here, just so he didn't go away again. Ever. Seeing him once more was all she needed to confirm how foolish she had been to think she could forget about him. But her mind needed something more before giving in and admitting her weakness aloud. "Explain, please," she said without getting any closer.

"Isn't it obvious?" Gallant said casually. "I'm giving myself to you. To do whatever you want with me. I was a day off of Terra when I realized you were absolutely right the whole time. Love does make a slave of you. My mother always said that it was best to accept the inevitable. So, here I am."

"You're crazy," Cherry murmured.

"I'm in love."

"But you despised being a slave."

"Being your slave would be better than living without you. And this way, you don't ever have to worry about my making a slave out of you. *You* are the master, er, mistress, and I'm here to submit to you."

As Cherry's gaze took a second, slower, tour over his muscular body, her eyes twinkled with the possibilities his declaration suggested. She recovered from her shock sufficiently to take a step closer to the bed. "Just so I don't jump to any false conclusions here, exactly how long is this term of slavery?"

"Aah, that is one of the conditions to my subservience. The term is forever."

"I see. But what if I get bored with you?"

His uncovered eye narrowed with warning. "One of my duties as your slave is to make sure you *never* get bored."

She angled her head and tapped her chin thoughtfully. "I don't know. I tend to think a slave who did everything I ordered, and agreed with everything I said, would become rather tiresome."

"I think it would be safe for you to assume that I

would occasionally refuse to do your bidding and frequently argue the clothes right off you."

She couldn't hold back the grin or the eyebrow wiggle. "Promise?"

"Guaranteed," he said with an answering smile.

"You said there were conditions, *plural,* to your being my salve. What else besides the term?"

"Because of certain arrangements I've made, you'll have to allow me to go without the collar outside of your bedroom."

"What arrangements?"

"I'm still working secretly for the Consociation, but it was decided that I needed to change my operating cover. Being a free agent for hire carries too many risks, and it makes it difficult for the Regent to contact me when she wants to. After some consideration, I came up with the perfect solution."

"Are you going to get to the punch line, or do I have to beat it out of you, *slave*?"

"If you keep interrupting me, we're never going to get to the good part. Now, where was I? Oh, yes. The solution. As you may have noticed, my previous cover required a fair amount of acting ability. I auditioned for Theodophilus this morning, and he admitted that I'm adequate—which is a compliment from that old crank. I've been hired on as a regular member of the Noronian Performing Company."

"What?" She was too stunned to fully comprehend.

"With a few special privileges that only Theodophilus, and you of course, will know about. After our first stop on Norona, you and I will travel in my ship instead of with the company. Mar-Dot is already flying there ahead of us. In between appearances, we may be asked to handle a problem or two for the Consociation, and it would be best if we had independent transportation."

"Did you say *we*?"

He managed to keep a perfectly straight face as he said, "Didn't I tell you? The Regent officially approved you as my partner."

"Holy stars," she whispered, then repeated the exclamation several decibels louder. A rush of adrenalin urged her to pace back and forth as she absorbed what he was saying. "This is incredible! Never in my wildest dreams could I have come up with this." She started toward him, but halted again. "Is that everything?"

He shook his head. "Now we get to the good part." He paused just long enough to make her anxious. "The good part is where you agree to all of the above. Then we make up for lost time."

"Well, let's see. I agree with the part about you working with the Company, and I definitely agree with me being your partner on secret missions. Did you renovate your supply station?"

He chuckled. "You can have waffles for breakfast and toasted marshmallows at night. You'll also have your choice of the latest fashions, and by reducing the cargo area, we were able to have a larger water recycler installed. You'll be able to take short, but genuine, showers."

"Okay, then I also agree with traveling on your ship instead of this monster. But that collar," she said, pointing to it, "I don't agree with." His smile faded so quickly, she realized he misunderstood. She hurried to his side, but when her fingers reached out to stroke his cheek, they encountered nothing solid.

The man on the bed was only an illusion! The imaginary Gallant vanished and the real one stepped out from behind the dressing screen . . . without his eye patch. In the next second, the blatantly feminine decor also disappeared, leaving modern furnishings similar to the outer room.

Gallant answered her unspoken question. "I thought if you were going to reject me, it might be easier to take if I didn't have to experience it first-hand. I was wrong."

Cherry went to him and took his hands in hers. "Oh, love, I'm not rejecting you. All I meant was, I don't want you as my slave, any more than I want to be yours. If we stay together, it should be because we make each other happy. I want you to tell me you love me again and again, yet feel free to leave if you ever stop feeling that way."

She had repeatedly demanded honesty from him and now it was time she faced the truth herself. "Because of you, I learned how wrong I was about love. The right kind of love doesn't enslave you, it sets you free—the way I feel when I'm with you. I should have said this before you left, but I guess it took your walking away for me to fully understand what you'd been trying to show me.

"I love you, Gallant. I don't want us to be slave and master *or* mistress. I want us to be life-mates."

He pulled her into his embrace. "Say it again."

She took a breath and met his heated gaze. "I love you, and I want to be your mate."

With a low-pitched growl, he carried her to the bed and made love to her with all the passion of several days of abstinence compounded by a much-needed release of nervous tension.

When Cherry was able to speak again, she said, "I take it that means you accept my proposal?"

He kissed the tip of her nose. "Without a single condition. I shouldn't have been so surprised by your change of attitude. My mother always said a good man eventually gets what he wants if he's patient enough."

"Hmmm. Am I ever going to meet this paragon of parables?"

"You and my mother, in the same room, at the same time?" Gallant had to think about that for a moment. "We'll see."

DANGEREOUS DESIRE

- ☐ **FALLING STARS by Anita Mills.** In a game of danger and desire where the stakes are shockingly high, the key cards are hidden, and love holds the final startling trump, Kate Winstead must choose between a husband she does not trust and a libertine lord who makes her doubt herself. (403657—$4.99)
- ☐ **MOONLIGHT AND MEMORIES by Patricia Rice.** A lovely young widow and a handsome, wanton womanizer make a bargain that can only be broken—as this man who scorns love and this woman who fears passion come together in a whirlpool of desire that they both cannot resist. (404114—$4.99)
- ☐ **TO CATCH THE WIND by Jasmine Cresswell.** Between two worlds, and across time, a beautiful woman struggles to find a love that could only mean danger. (403991—$4.99)

Prices slightly higher in Canada

Buy them at your local bookstore or use this convenient coupon for ordering.

PENGUIN USA
P.O. Box 999 – Dept. #17109
Bergenfield, New Jersey 07621

Please send me the books I have checked above.
I am enclosing $__________ (please add $2.00 to cover postage and handling). Send check or money order (no cash or C.O.D.'s) or charge by Mastercard or VISA (with a $15.00 minimum). Prices and numbers are subject to change without notice.

Card #________________ Exp. Date ________
Signature________________
Name________________
Address________________
City ________ State ________ Zip Code ________

For faster service when ordering by credit card call **1-800-253-6476**

Allow a minimum of 4-6 weeks for delivery. This offer is subject to change without notice.